Solitude

Sovereign Citizen:
Solitude

A Novel by

B.F. Galligan

Paperback Edition ISBN: 979-8-9889517-0-4
Hardback Edition ISBN: 979-8-9889517-1-1

Comments, criticisms, and accolades welcome:
bfgalligan@protonmail.com
@bfgalligan

Grief

I
Vapor

Date night rarely came around. The exhaustion and excuses compounded so that time flattened with repetition interspersed with periodic new additions. Somehow, everything coincided tonight and gave them a
chance at some bit of marriage. It was a slide. It
was an uneventful alignment that had the nature of being an incidental bump in the flattened disc that time
had become. It was a sushi dinner that was more expensive than delicious, but quiet was the main feature. The couple were able to start out awkwardly,
unsure of how to actually be a couple. Ordering took
longer than normal as they discovered the full breadth
of the menu options now available to them; would they
route through a deluge of entrées then try to jam in
some dessert, or would they be more discrete, so they
wouldn't feel like weighted balloons as they walked
out? These were crucial questions. They did some
version of the middle ground, still feeling balloony
but still capable of walking out the door with a ker-
nel of sexual arousal.

They walked holding hands. This too started awkwardly, perhaps a bit forced, but once the familiar
feeling took over, it was as love and comfort again as
it had always been over thirteen years. The arousal
stirred a bit more at the sensation of flesh, albeit
small. They walked. The realization that hit dinner
was the extent of their plans, they had no particular
agenda left and no direction as they walked. Somehow
they each felt this was a missed opportunity, and they
failed the other by not making suggestions earlier.
They walked, since it stalled for time and distracted
from their failings.

She noticed the small venue first. The thump of muffled music inside was the hallmark of a neighborhood's
launchpad for small and hungry bands, and it was an
enticing departure from their middle-aged lives. She
didn't have to mouth the invitation; he was just as
eager and they went inside. Settled at the edge of
the pit, they enjoyed songs they'd never hear again as
she shifted her hips and he stood still. When it was
over, they left in full satisfaction and with loins
quite abuzz.

He drove them home and they planned it all out: she
would start the shower and take off her makeup while
he checked the house and looked in on their six-year-
old son, who would be asleep as he was not one to exploit a babysitter's lack of authority. True to form,
he was sleeping. The babysitter was paid and discarded, after which time he went upstairs and slipped
into the tub behind her. He washed her back, and they
took small chances at erotic caresses without deviat-
ing too far from the basic utility of the bath experience. It only took ten minutes before she was done,
and he stayed in to take advantage of the free space
and plunge into the water to clean his still dry face.
She was waiting for him in the bed. Inspired by
events, the awkwardness was less severe as they laid
down to cuddle and air dry. After some time, the awkwardness returned as he bungled his way into position
above her. They kissed again and again until the raw
feelings came to life and let everything move on as
planned. When he arrived at the correct place and began to ease in carefully, her face transformed and
took on the distance that a woman does when the inside
of her body is no longer her own. His easing stopped
and the rhythms took over. As he was ready to increase the pace, he was suddenly alone. She was gone.

His confusion was profound as his brain shifted from
the distant plane where he always went, to the now
empty room with sheets that had damp traces where her
body, still wet from the bath, had laid. There was
nothing, not even light. He whispered her name and
patted around the bed, then called for her name before

standing up. He backed up from the bed while the confusion climbed, then plunged into a swirl of frustration and fear. The lights now confirmed that he was
alone, but his disbelief wondered if he lost some moment somewhere when they agreed to stop for her to get
out of bed. That belief was powerful and irrational
in the face of the obviousness that it was untrue. He
searched the bathroom, then the closet. He dressed
and walked around downstairs in the dark whispering
her name. Nothing.

The disbelief subsided and confusion returned, which
was overtaken by panic as he rushed upstairs to his
son's door to opened it and see a rumpled blanket in
the dim nightlight. His eyes tried to focus on how
large that lump was, still acting as if the child was
asleep and a touch would wake him unnecessarily. His
focused eyes saw that the blanket was flat, elevated
by nothing. He turned on the light and the strike of
pain forestalled the chance to absorb the entirety of
the room, but only for a flashing second after which
he powered through the tension to take in the full
sight. His son was also gone.

He went from room to room throughout the house, systematically turning on lights and closing doors. His
was a not a family of jokers. They respected one another and would not go to lengths to fuck with his
mind, so he understood the emergency when he had finished his room sweep and found nothing. As he did so,
his mind went through the rote registry of items out
of place that is normal for a lived in home. Here,
the babysitter's plate on the counter, washed but left
to dry. There, a box of legos on the floor as a half-
built city frozen within the stage of a child's scenario cut short to begin the process of bedtime. The
dreadful ordinariness of everything terrified him because there was no sign of emergency. Everything was
so normal he couldn't help but feel that he fell into
his mind; he was actually surrounded by his family
walking through the house with him in a desperate effort to wake him from his dream and recognize that all
was fine. He was afraid that he was who disappeared

from the house. The possibility of an inverted reality made him panic in need for confirmation one way or the other.

He ran upstairs to his phone to call 911. It rang. Then it rang some more. No one answered. Dumbfounded, his confusion roared in to paralyze him. He had checked the boxes and came up empty. The centralized number that had been drilled so deep into his mind that it was a function of muscle memory had failed, and he felt untethered. What next? Where does one go when all lifelines are all unreachable?

Over the years at this new house, he had occasionally seen his neighbors but could not reasonably say they were friends. Neither would he even put them down as acquaintances. They were somewhat lesser entities that somehow required a familiarity and were thus called neighbors. Theirs were doors that certainly would never be approached, especially at night. They were entities where you hold onto whatever message you want to deliver meets with a chance to utter it if the listener happened to come within earshot. Nevertheless, he was there at, not one, but four doors to knock then, by the fourth, bang. From the outside, everything was typical: lights were on, the pale glow of televisions behind curtains were on, dogs barked, cats licked their balls and watched from a safe distance. Nothing seemed unordinary except that no one answered. What box remains in this situation?

He went back to his house and sat down outside to gaze back and forth from one end of the street to the other. The dissonance between the image and the outcome of his experiment couldn't be fully reconciled, and he lacked the emotional ability to do anything other than chuckle worriedly. He took out his phone and began to call his contacts, starting with close friends then on the circle to work friends and family before dialing random others in his contact list, some of which he'd forgotten to whom they were linked. There were some two or so dozen options that weren't international numbers and his panic had not yet mounted to the point where he risked the inflated charges for calling those. Instead, he sent out a battery of "hi" messages through his chat apps. Many still had online statuses and with these he was hopeful, but as the minutes had worn on these dropped from active to "last seen" minutes ago. This alone wasn't that unusual though, as his contact list here were scattered all over the planet. He turned on the TV in search of late night local news. This had been a difficult challenge as he never figured out the complexity of modern television with their countless remotes full of Byzantine operations. Once this was overcome, though, he couldn't find any news except national shows that were on repeat from earlier in the day. He had a vague recollection that late night television used to be recorded live, if only he could pull the right channel from among the myriad of network doppelgängers in the channel menu. It took some work, but he found local iterations of the outdated network channels. Two were running commercials for what seemed like too long and the other was an image of the host's empty desk without explanation. As these images displayed, he was on his phone scrolling through his news feed to look for updates, but the same pattern emerged after an hour with no new posts.

The distraction overtook him for some while as he doom-scrolled through the news of the former president's arrest after he failed to show up to court for the day the first of his four his criminal verdicts were to be read. He was found guilty on all counts and sentencing was postponed until he was apprehended. There was wide speculation that he either fled the country to Belarus after loyalists liquidated his PAC, or even that he killed himself. Either was an equally plausible end to a years long comedy that whipsawed the nation from crisis to crisis, stitched together by scandal. Everyone but his most ardent supporters were exhausted and would be glad to see him gone without the chance of return. But none of the comments had been more recent than much earlier in the evening after bylines closed, although some obvious bot accounts continued to post, as did the accounts of more than a few of the most popular influencers, which gave him both hope and pause. Satisfied with dissatisfaction, he shut the TV off and went back upstairs, shutting off lights as he passed.

On the bed next to the now dry imprint of his wife's back, he lacked the vision for how to proceed except that the overwhelming fatigue from all the confusion and fear flooded around him, and he laid back to stare up at the emptiness of the dark ceiling. His paralysis was marked only by a deep concentration on the sounds of the house and the strain to hear any sign of cars outside. The hum of the refrigerator mixed with the high-pitched hiss of the cable box downstairs and eventually gave him the impression that a soft radio station played a muffled and distorted song he could not identify. This was not unusual, though. Bouts of insomnia were normal, and he'd learned that these auditory hallucinations were his signals that he crossed beyond the degree of normal sleepiness to an encasement of ash. His eyes bulged under pressure and his hands vibrated with subtle tremors as he listened to the ambient sounds of the house undisturbed by anyone else. In this otherworldly mind, he wondered if he was mistaken. His ability to overpower his own observations was not new, and it eventually led to a dangerous form of hope that lingered intangibly on his mind throughout the remaining hours of the night, marking an endpoint from where all thoughts departed and returned.

Shortly before dawn, he slept. Briefly. Then his habitual time to wake up forced him to repeat the same checklist he'd followed in the night, but fatigue kept him numb from a renewal of panic while he replayed the same discoveries as before: the plate, the city, the abandoned scenario, all featured as placards against a hazy backdrop. With the house still empty and 911 still unreachable, he checked the neighborhood again. All the same windows seemed to have the same blue glow of a TV and dogs seemed more desperately calling out. He peaked around the back gate to one of his more friendly neighbors, an elderly man who retired from the State Department after thirty years, and saw his dog's nose push through the gap in the fence and snort heavily at him. This dog knew his smell, but he was not confident enough to open the gate and test its reception. He left.

As he walked back, sprinklers were turning on for their scheduled dowsing of the summer grass. If he squinted, not much looked out of place for a Saturday morning. Except that in the light, he was able to make out a car at the far end of the block that had its door ajar. He went over to investigate, and the scene chilled him. He saw a pair of women's shoes neatly on the pavement as if she simply stepped out of them from where she sat, sideways in the front seat. In front of them was a man's outfit rumpled over his shoes, as if he stood outside the car facing her. Her dress was half in the car and half falling out; it was clear what the scene was.

Feeling taught inside, he turned back to his own house and decided to continue his search, but then expanded it with a drive. Once out of the quietude of the residential streets, he saw roads that were equally quiet but showed signs of distress. There was moderate chaos where some cars had crashed to into one another after what looked like idling off the line at a red light. There was little damage, just as if their breaks had been simply disengaged. At some intersections, there were terrific wrecks when cross traffic plowed through and T-boned others. Mostly, however, the streets were empty and these scenes were clustered near night spots or busy intersections. He saw empty parking lots everywhere and most stores were closed except for ones that boasted 24-hour availability or had otherwise been open at around midnight the night before.

He decided to drive to the area where he and his wife had date night and went to the sushi restaurant. Out of habit, he made sure his parking was neat and legal. The door was still open and the lights on. There were around half a dozen tables full of dishes, including

the one where they sat. It was not their food. This
looked like a younger group that had ordered sake and
beer to wash down their rolls. Again, their clothes
were all still in the chairs, and he vacantly reached
down to look in a purse looped to the back of one. He
found the items a young woman might take on a night
out and not much more. He saw her phone on the table
and tested it knowing it would be locked. He put everything back down and went down the street to the
venue he visited and found that it was also open. Inside looked like a laundry room with clothing scattered about the floor near glasses of various shapes,
sizes, and fill. Instruments on stage were still set
up, and the guitar hummed loudly as he tested it with
his foot.

"What the actual fuck is going on?" he said, quietly
at first then yelled into the mic several more times.
"Are there fucking zombies coming next? What the fuck
is this fucking cliché apocalypse bullshit?" he asked
but no one answered.

He didn't want anyone to answer. These were the words
of a man convinced in his disbelief. He left and
checked several other businesses on the street and
found scenes so equally disturbing that they already
became unremarkable in their horror. But his words
did begin to echo, and he began to seriously wonder if
some mutated humans were on the way for him, that he
should be prepared to fight or take his own life. He
drove across the bridge to Virginia and found his way
to a gun store, where he decided to risk breaking the
window and climb in. If anyone came to complain,
they'd be a welcome sight.

Once inside, he had a hard time choosing what weapons
would be best. He hadn't shot anything since he was
handed an M16 by a guerrilla who invited him to play
with it. He fired at a leaf in the jungle and was
satisfied with missing. He knew from childhood,
though, that he didn't like handguns and preferred rifles. The shop had a garish selection of AR-15s, but
he wondered whether they would have stopping power.

They were clearly quite effective at slaughtering children and their teachers, but would one keep the same efficacy if it confronted their zombie forms? Out of shear expediency, he took one with a shortened stock and a strap, then reluctantly grabbed a 9 mm pistol. He left a note on the register:

Can't figure out where the fuck everyone went and can't rule out a zombie apocalypse, so I broke into your store and took a few things. If you read this, please call me…especially if you know what the fuck is going on! I'll pay you for what I took, and maybe we should meet up and keep each other safe from whatever the fuck is out there. Good luck.

— Chris (301) 832-3214

His first transition to post apocalyptic warlord looked like an uncomfortable suburban man fumbling with how to load an extended clip without shooting himself inside his new tiny EV car, which had already begun to run low on power. He did all this while docked at a recharge station in Arlington.

He called his wife endlessly throughout the morning and by then left some ninety-seven calls and forty texts; he decided it was no use. He thought that he needed to get a sense of the region in case there really was a zombie apocalypse brewing, and he needed to know his routes. He continued into Virginia away from the district and made his way to Tyson's corner, using Route 7 all the way to Leesburg. Everything was the same, though with variations on how clustered the cars were. On the highways, he saw scatterings of tractor rigs that ran off the road and crashed into concrete pillars under bridges or were saved from sheering off building fronts by flimsy guardrails that were just enough to redirect the trucks as they ripped the metal out like ribbons. Other than this, the roads were clear. When he was hungry, he stopped at a gas station near Ashburn and grazed on food that was out on display and hopped over the counter to check if the milkshake machine was left on or had it been cleaned and shut down overnight. When he went in, he felt a combination of caution and self consciousness for carrying the AR-15, so he only went inside with the 9 mm holstered under his shirt. This was Virginia, after all. He wanted to find a good balance between feeling safe and nonthreatening to anyone who might be inside, though he figured it would be a wild stretch of imagination that anyone would hide there by choice, especially since the emergency outside was not apparent and others might be like him just wandering around.

Nevertheless, he kept this decorum as he raided the refrigerators because the night crew shut the kitchen down before they left for the night. Their names were Alejandro and Safi. He knew this by checking the schedule posted near the washing station. Their shifts ended at 10:30 and he assumed they left pretty quickly, it having been a Friday night. The cashier's name was Robert and Robert was still piled on the floor in front of his register—or behind his register, depending on your perspective. Robert was thirty-two and lived out in Chantilly. He had a medicaid and single bank card in his wallet, but also had around eighteen dollars stuffed in. His shoes were heavily worn on the bottom, but he had kept the tops in fairly good condition. Black. Robert's belt was huge and scuffed with plastered sweat stains on the back. As he examined all this, he felt both remorse and respect that he seemed to be the only one left to mourn Robert.

He went outside and noticed two cars parked in the back near the dumpster and decided to take a look. The cans of tall boys resting on the trunk with a bee circling the mouth and the uniforms piled on the ground told him all he needed to know, so he didn't bother to sift through the night shift's clothes. He looked in the bag where unopened cans had been waiting and saw the receipt, this told him everyone was still alive at 10:53. He himself had stopped noticing the time since the drive home after the concert and had no idea what time the event took place. He knew offhandedly that the babysitter was booked until 11:00 and that his phone log showed his frantic calls to 911 began at 11:46. The nearly empty cans he saw now told him that Alejandro and Safi had taken their time. The way their clothes fell, under but close to the trunk, meant they had been talking. Now they were gone.

The absurdity of everything was better rooted in his mind, more so than the distress he felt before. What was the point of vaporizing everyone at the same instance? If everyone was taken, then he should be gone too, so if he were to stay behind there must be a point, but no point would be reasonable. Every possibility he came up with just seemed as bland and stupid as the last. This was the makings for poorly framed science fiction, endlessly rehashed over and over again each generation that pretends the idea is something new and not at all overdone. It's not. It's dumb, and he was in the middle of it trying to superimpose some meaning or else completely lose his moorings. He was angry, but there was nowhere to direct his anger. Should he kick something? Shoot it? There was no point in that either, so he choked it down and went back to his car but sat at the wheel for what felt like a half hour but was actually four grueling minutes of white knuckles over claws in his forearms, while his breathing labored under the pressure of his silent screams. By the time he started the engine again, those breaths had transitioned to be hefty and slow as would occasion someone's struggle to maintain balance.

A few miles more and he approached Dulles to check whether it was in fact accurate to say that the skies were unusually empty for the nation's capital on the weekend ahead of the 4th of July. It was. There were no lines of taxis shuffling in and out of the departure loading zone to block him. Nor were there officers or airport staff nearby to warn him about leaving a car unattended. He knew what he'd find inside and hesitated before pressing through the doors. Much like other places he visited, he found laundry scattered around, mostly beneath heavy luggage that top-

pled over when their support was removed. In a daring
act he crossed the security lines unticketed and
walked towards the shuttle terminals completely unmolested by what should have been a wall of TSA agents
and the squat gray buckets that were their primary
stopping force. He casually walked through the most
secure barriers that most Americans would ever encounter, and his only thought was that there didn't
seem like a lot of laundry lined up.

As he walked out the doors, he felt his phone vibrate
from within his pocket and he nearly jumped. It was
now almost 18:00, meaning he had been frantically
alone for nearly a full day of searching for signs of
another person and the moment finally came. His fingers seemed to stop working as the clumsily pulled his
phone out and he answered without the instinctive
glance at the caller ID. Had he done as he would have
at every other moment in his life since cell phones
became ubiquitous, he would have been disappointed
with the call some five seconds prior to when he actually was. The caller ID would have reminded him that
he knew nobody out of North Carolina, let alone someone who would call on a Saturday afternoon. He had to
reach this conclusion after waiting for the unhealthy
silence that a bot needs after the call connects in
order to commence its tedious recitation. He hung up.
Not to be outdone, the bot called back. Again. And
again. In rapid sequence, he received no fewer than
six calls, each of which was a painful reminder of
what it was that he was, in truth, most hopeful to
hear out of all possible sounds. Each vibration res-
onated in his viscera and he begged it to stop as he
declined to answer before finally he beat the interlude and was able to block the number before the
screen lit up again to hide the function. This ended
the experience.

Extremely shaken, he got back in his car to find that
the panic attack was waiting for him to close the
door. That silent scream that was as full throated as
it was breathless and fractured his skull with the repeated plea of "I won't hit myself" over and over un-

til he felt his right fist pound in rapid fire on his forehead above his left eye. When this reflex had passed, the scream grew in strength, and he felt his nails bite deep into his shoulders and drag across down to his elbows. A third and final wave found that his watch was deeply agitating and needed to be wrenched from his wrist and the disfigured strap was flung to the passenger floorboard. The familiar calm absorbed him as the throbbing on his forehead wore off and left behind a dull soreness. In a state of emotional numbness, he started the car and decided to drive home.

Driving was easy. His movements were more deliberate and more agile after his explosion. He had long since found himself falling into the trap of letting his frustration boil up and be turned inward. He had countless scars, large and small, hidden under his shirt and each represented an innocuous event or thought that somehow became the most pressing bit of blight in need of eradication. Mostly it centered around his insomnia and the torture of watching a finite night disappear. Not always, though. Occasionally it was something other than sleep, but he and he alone was always the sole object of derision. In a fucked form of post-hoc rationalization, he believed that he had no right to inflict violence on another person, but he was free to do as he liked to himself. He did not like this. This was a reflex born from the chaos of panic. In the best of times he could intervene on his own behalf and change his violence to simple fists on resilient muscles that could heal without scarring; it was a left of launch intervention. In the worst of times he failed and his efforts to stop the reflex meant that he was unprepared to stop his fists from sending concussive waves to the front of his brain. These waves always left him hollow in the aftermath so that, with a pause in his internal narrative, he was hyper aware of the movement of his body until the shock wore off and he returned to normal, which in this case happened as he drove through Tyson's Corner.

By the time he drove into Georgetown and pulled up to
his house, it was almost 19:30, meaning the sky was
still bright, and the air was muggy in the July heat.
This made it as still as the emptiness of the entirety
of the DMV area as he saw the landscape from his window, making record time without the congestion of cars
except in a few areas where he needed to cautiously
hop the curb to navigate around particularly messy
crashes. All along the way through Virginia, he saw
pop up fireworks stands offering two for one sales
that encouraged untrained people to cart away dangerous explosives almost certainly to heavily populated
areas where police would either tolerate the hours of
destruction scattered throughout, rather than make a
passable effort at enforcement of safety laws. The
4th was on Tuesday, meaning the days of destruction
would begin tonight by the most eager of patriots.
This thought was thin on his mind as he drove across
the empty towns with his trunk full with the sort of
fireworks that would reach high and loud enough to
draw anyone in the vicinity to him. He was eager for
nightfall and moved the first tranche out to the entrance of a park a bit down the road.

Walking back through his neighborhood, he heard the
muffled sounds of barks from behind curtained windows
and shut doors. This was an eerily normal experience,
so it took some blocks for him to realize the significance of the barking: while he was a prisoner to confusion and free to roam around outside to cosplay his
own millenarian nightmare, countless pets were trapped
as real prisoners inside home that were designed to
keep them from escape or from accessing food that almost certainly was just beyond their reach. As a good
urbanite does, he pushed the suffering outside his
mind but struggled to do nothing when he reached his
neighbor's house where he saw the same nose push out
between the same gate as before. This dog was one of
his own and in need, so he resolved to do the unthinkable and shit in his own backyard by breaking through
the side door to his neighbor's house.

Out of a sense of neighborly decorum, he wanted to use a method least likely to pulverize the door frame so that it could be repaired easily, in case all the events of the last day turned out to be a hoax. Broken glass was the smoothest, but he was scared to think what might happen if he severed an artery without any doctors available. The sheer madness of the joke was too much. He would have survived the apocalypse only to die in the most stupid way within twenty-four hours, just to feed a dog that was probably only moderately dehydrated and hungry. No. This was not the way. He found in his garage a chisel and heavy hammer with which he could rip out the handle and deadbolt and later patch the hole. Instantly he realized the absurdity of this as he banged away at the door which only roused the fury of the animal he hoped to rescue. He gave up and decided to toss some food over the fence. But once he started on this road, the pull of guilt dragged his mind down the streets to force him to acknowledge the hypocrisy of ignoring the rest of the animals. It nagged at him as he went back inside his own home, dividing his attention from the extreme discomfort of a still empty home and the stirrings across so many other homes. Not even the light imprint on the left side of his bed had shifted since he last observed it from the gray glow of the early morning. She had been there. She existed once. Something changed and she only existed in memories. Behind were left no signs to mark the trauma of an event on which her departure could be blamed. The severity of the emptiness already pulled like a vacuum on the strength of her memories in those first hours after she disappeared. This differed from his son, who seemed less distant, less of distinct from himself that he somehow still remained an active personality in his mind, with whom he still talked and his son's voice still echoed in response. The echo now said that he should go outside and let the dogs loose, so they could at least run and play.

At the first house, it was obvious that he'd underdressed and would be welcomed by a gnash of teeth once inside. He returned with several layers of thick pants, boots and a heavy coat, gloves, and a bike helmet with some ridiculously fashioned face guard, all of which made him exactly the sort of this that would invite a dog to attack almost immediately once he broke in. He took it all off after he kicked in one door and found that the dogs were more terrified than ready to attack. It was a home with two smaller and easily fielded fluffy dogs that had rushed past him out the door never to return. The next house had larger shepherds that stood their ground until the backed up and stood it again, all the way through the kitchen and then disappeared to the bedrooms where he could hear their intimidating croons muffled by the layers of wall as he searched for their food. They came back, quite curious of him, when they heard their familiar and welcome sounds. They dashed back and forth behind furniture, staring deeply at their now full bowls. He left the door open behind him. This repeated in various ways across a dozen or so houses up and down the blocks and there was now a scattering of barks heard several streets away as they made new friends with one another.

By now it was dark when he exited the last home and a chill hit him as he surveyed the neighborhood with its growing pack of dogs. He estimated that there were probably thirty or more by now, most of which had formed a small group, likely friends from dog parks or from distant calls. The echo of his son had quieted down in favor of the cold logic that so many dogs on the street would be hungry quite often and they would begin the process of finding their own food. He multiplied this across the city, state and nation, wherever he might go as some twisted Johnny Appleseed releasing dogs into the wild, he would be creating a new wild species. That was the last house for the night and he himself had grown hungry, but was a bit far from his own. At any rate, he had little interest in returning to darkness and loneliness so he decided to look around a stranger's emptiness rather than his own.

In the kitchen, he found a well stocked setup and a proper gas range. He found vegetables and pork loin to fry together and eat with rice, just as he would have at home. As the rice cooked, he passed the time opening drawers, a process that began organically as him trying to locate whatnots for his meal. He found himself migrating further afield to look through the sundries drawer at utility bills, receipts and countless smaller objects that must be part of a larger item that he could not identify. He ate as he walked through the ground floor inspecting family photos on the fireplace and tucked in bookshelves. They were a middle aged couple like he and his wife, but they had three children and the oldest looked to be around 11. They took vacations in South Carolina and Florida and had all the stock visual proofs of this planted at strategic locations in the living room, which was neither quite tidy nor messy. There were remnants of children's games from what looked like a Friday night movie night that was shut down as the crew moved onward to bed. Between chews, he could hear a TV on in a room down a narrow hallway beyond the stairwell.

As expected for upper middle class Washington, the TV revealed that someone had been worked in the home office instead of participating fully in the household. He recognized the network on the screen, which was still running shows. He flipped the channels and saw that most still had programs but many only had dead air. The laptop was on standby and he could not access it, as expected. More interested by now, he pulled open the drawer to see what he could find, but was disappointed to see a collection of pens and other office supplies. One drawer, however was more than interesting since it was locked, but it didn't take long to find the key sitting on a shelf just out of reach of the most ambitious child. Inside were the boring documents a family keeps safe from children but not safe from invaders. He glanced at the mother's diplomatic passport and saw that she was a well-healed traveler to Brussels. Her diploma and certificates on the wall confirmed his estimation that she worked at the Department of State and probably was assigned to the NATO desk. He pulled back those frames to search for a wall safe and found one behind a bookshelf, which is quite an inconvenient location for quick access. It seemed like it had simple security and he tried a few codes like wedding and birth dates from the documents he found in the desk. The expiration date of her passport worked and he found inside several hard drives and several Trezor wallets, along with some bullion and a few file folders. None of this seemed particularly valuable if his circumstances continued, so he ignored the contents and took his bowl to the kitchen with the safe still open.

Up the stairs seemed the logical next place for any invader and, without the erstwhile barking of a home defender, he was free to climb up without incident. This was a fairly typical three bedroom home where two children appeared to share one room and the one on their own in the other. He know from the photos downstairs, that the older one was a girl and the younger ones were a boy and a girl who looked like identical twins. Since the rooms were gendered, he assumed the two girls slept in one and the boy enjoyed the freedom of space in the other, or was excluded from the closeness of the shared room, depending on one's perspective. Both showed signs of extended play that slipped outside into the hallway. There was a mashup of blankets with dinosaurs and princess toys that clearly were left uncollected by exhausted parents who no doubt proclaimed it Friday night as a desperate means to send everyone to bed without the excruciating ritual of cleaning up beforehand. Friday nights have always been for suspended instructions and the waste of early morning structure. In the large girl's bed, he saw three sets of pajamas under the covers and turned off the light again, careful to shut the door behind him.

Their parent's room was the confused scene of a stage set to await a mother to finish whatever work she completed downstairs. The TV was on but stuck in its screensaver. A touch of the remote returned it to the streaming app's binge prevention message that asked no

one if they were still watching some Korean series he
didn't recognize. There were women's pajamas on top
of the covers and her phone was on the floor. He
smelled stale bath salts from the bathroom and saw a
full tub, now cold with coagulated oil on the surface.
It reminded him that he had not himself bathed that
day and debated about climbing in, but he wondered
whether it had been empty when everyone left or if
somewhere in the water he could find traces of someone
if only he looked. If not, then this idea still felt
too foreign and he decided to check the cabinets before walking back to the bed and opened a side drawer
that had a protruding key. Inside he saw a small collection of massagers and other adult toys and assumed
the women also planned their own form of date night
once whatever urgent work that had come up was over.
The closet was less eventful, with the expected range
of clothes on hooks and shoes in boxes on the ground.
All in all, its blandness was disquieting as he felt
the tremors of household echoes still swimming through
its walls. This was the power that kept him from his
own home that day and into the night, which was approaching the one day mark since the final utterance
of its inhabitants sent out their echoes to fade. The
fatigue was oppressive as he shuffled through the hall
and down the stairs, as fingertips slid across it all
as he passed. Standing at the entryway, he saw the
destruction he brought to the door frame, which he
hadn't the skills to repair but knew enough to see
that soon the house would be overtaken by wind and animals as a result. He closed it with a heavy chair as
reinforcement, then left through the side door that
could be shut properly and made his way out into the
bark of night and back home.

He was not far from his street, but far enough that
walking back took some time. He missed the evening
hours to set of the first tranche of fireworks and decided that a late start now, as a sort of twenty-four
hour memorial seemed more fitting, if for no other
reason than that it would scatter the dogs from his
area and postpone his day of reckoning with their new
society forming. As he went, he was aware that some

watched him, conflicted about approaching the man who destroyed their homes but unlocked the food they desperately wanted. Still pets, they had not yet discovered the fear of humans that kept other wild animals far away, so it was the most docile of the groups who now tailed him out of habit. At the park entrance, he made out what looked like four dogs of various sizes in the distance, with another three close enough for him to pet. He knew this would change as soon as the first of the explosions burst overhead, so he paused long enough to give one of them a hug and advise it not to worry about the sound. It did. It ran away faster than all the others and cowered so completely that it ran into the edges of brick walls as it slipped on the concrete in a frantic motion of escape. It got away with only a deep gash on its leg. He watched it hold one leg up as it ran out of sight when the last of his eight bursts had dwindled into overhead crackles.

Thus is was quiet again. He strained his ears for what felt like a long time hoping to hear some stir of reciprocation in any direction. None. Maybe it was too soon, so he shuffled back home and heard his neighbor's dog whine, but from inside the house. He peaked over the fence to see how this could be, since it was stuck outside. A large pane glass window had been shattered, with fragments of wood covered in fur and blood. When he went to investigate he saw that the animal had crashed inside, unaware that its people were not there since it had been stuck outside since they disappeared. It was destroyed. A large shear of glass had severed its forehead down to its heckles. A pool of blood was filling the kitchen floor. On any other day, he would have rushed to its side and whisked it away to a pet hospital. Today, he shot it just above the gash and left for his own door not bothering to clean up the carcass that enjoyed its full belly for a time.

The echoes were waiting again, but the shock of the slow burn trauma had already erected the beginnings of a barrier which left him feel more distant as if he returned to someone else's home, but muscle memory took over and led him from door to door to check locks. His basement in particular felt otherworldly and caused him to feel with absolute certainty that something was down there in the dimness and he slipped on one step as he rushed upstairs to lock the door as he exited. But there was simple nothingness that chased and it waited upstairs too, though with less of a paranormal feel. The redundancy of it frustrated him as he repeatedly encountered the same thought over and over without reprieve: nothing, nothing, nothing. But of course everything was left in its place and the volume of material only served to highlight the absence of a composite that had dispersed itself widely across the planet. All else was nothing. Two specific items were everything. The glasses were there and so was the orange juice container, though it was a quarter down from the top. The caked glaze of the babysitter's meal on her unwashed bowl was there and he felt no point in thinking to himself that she should have at least rinsed off the curry so it wouldn't crust over. The faucet was still there, with its predictable rush of water available in a selected range of temperatures for a wide variety of purposes, like washing the day old caked and hardened glaze of food from a dish. All these materials still existed in the kitchen under the soothing natural light he installed when they moved in two years before, after a decade overseas, frequently living without electricity or heat where his job was to ensure the palliative existence of humans in some of the worst environments possible. The irony was not lost on him.

Upstairs, he sat on the edge of the tub and listened to the sound of the water rush down and felt the steam slowly rise and accumulate in the air. It had to be hot as shit to wash out the weariness deep in his pores. So hot that he still managed to keep the habit of shiver as he eased in and struggled to breath until his body acclimated, then he just laid there in the wet darkness just as he'd done countless times before. So familiar was it that he managed to disappear himself and let his mind wander the breadth of his memories until it pulled from its catalog the image of being locked away alone under COVID restrictions when he was unable to travel out of country to meet his wife and son. He bathed profusely then, even though the climate was hot and tropical with his air conditioner regularly an empty shell of plastic and wires without power. He bathed and sweated in the heat and stood in the crosswind of open windows naked at night when no one in the conservative society could see him. Now, back in Washington, in one of the richest neighborhoods in the country, he remained the same. When he stepped out of the heat, he entered a casing of chilled air from the air conditioner that actually worked. Throughout his years of work and even prior, he had moved and changed homes so often that at times he would awaken in the blackness and not be sure where exactly he slept that night. Tonight, he felt uneasy about sleeping next to the empty shadow of his wife in their bed and he chose to sleep in his son's room, as he would on nights when sleep failed to come.

The boy was gifted and focused his energies on elaborate stages for lego people to go about their lives. They had installed a special table for him with a cutout center so he could choreograph a world replete with mountains and special platforms towering above, now frozen in time with unknowable scripts as yet rehearsed. He sat within that central opening and scanned the scenes, taking care not to touch anything or disrupt the perfection that his son had reached. He knew some of the characters and their main story lines, but not all. Most of the buildings were constructed according to the original plans, with minor modifications that evolved through game play but never fundamentally changed their structure. His son's pride was a castle that they built together by combining pieces from three separate castle sets to make a mega castle, which also served as a railroad station. This was the beating heart from which all scenarios had sprung over the last seven months since Christmas. His son was spoiled, but in a way that doting parents do for a mild tempered child with a deep capacity for empathy. He was the child of trust and love, and this came out in all his scenarios. As he scanned the table and all its personalities, he could see with clear understanding what his son played. It was from this vantage that the echoes were loudest and it became the most precious something he felt was left.

He moved away so as to not bump or move any piece and went across the room to the bed. He shut out the light and rolled into the soft and cool mattress and only slowly came awareness of his mounting paranoia about the possibility that something was coming to him in the night or that in the morning he'd find that his hallucination was over and the destruction he exacted would invite consequences. The tension from this struggle had made him uncomfortably hold the 9 mm, with which he had already taken a life. What if, in his hallucination, he fires on a mutated being that his blindness could not recognize as his family? The prospect invited confirmation in the ambient shapes he saw in the darkness as the blanket of sleep began to fall but was violently snatched away at the deafening sound of a metallic pop of a surprise nocturnal discharge and he vaguely heard, from outside the stinging ring, the sound of small pieces of plastic flung across the room.

II
Search

The bullet grazed the mega castle and caused significant damage but not destruction, before it continued
onward into the next room. From there, it ricocheted
off a support beam on the far wall and danced around
before falling behind the toilet. For all of Sunday,
he stayed in bed. When hunger stirred, he got up and
ate handfuls of mixed nuts as he absently looked in
the fridge for something else to eat. Afraid to do
more damage to his son's room, he returned to his own
but changed the sheets, with the old ones carefully
set aside and folded.

By Monday morning, pure habit urged him to visit his
office in a discrete portion of a downtown building
where he worked at one of Washington's fungible foreign policy think tanks advising a disinterested audience on humanitarian policy in East Asia. This uncontrollable urge was driven by the odd effect of sunlight as it changes depending on the day of the week.
His weekend sunrises welcomed his repose, but the
crispness of the weekday light pounded his eyes and
told him that the hours of forthcoming productivity
demanded his attention. So he obliged, but without
the sense of urgency as would be typical. He dressed
and ate the same set of eggs and bread, made the same
green smoothie and packed his courier bag as he'd done
every day in the past and in several continents before
stepping outside into a completely new planet.

He could hear a scuttle from the kitchen of his neighbor on the way out and his stomach churned, knowing
that this was the sound of decayed flesh as it was re-
cycled by curious visitors. He had little interest in
discovering which of the possible scavenger animals
might be at work that morning, so he mounted his bicy-

cle and careened down the street towards downtown past the occasional group of dogs already acclimated to their new freedom. Other animals also appeared quite satisfied by the empty streets. More birds would congregate on the road than usual and he hadn't recalled so many squirrels or rabbits since the pandemic, but this faded as he crept into the urban density of the city that was sterile except for the chime of birds whose chatter carried through the concrete corridors from the periodic parks that dotted the city.

His building was open to the mezzanine and he reached the elevators but hesitated, balking at the idea of the metal cube that would be a trap without anyone outside who might rescue him should something go wrong. The doors opened and clapped shut again as he walked towards the stairwell to climb the dozen flights up to his office. He left his bicycle in the lobby rather than carry his folded bike up with him or deal with an uncomfortable elevator ride with other passengers to mutely curse him for the unnecessary bulk. No one would steal it. Up he trudged, straining under the exertion and temptation to check in on other floors with the sort of curiosity one has in the doings of others. He found his office shut down for the weekend and not brought back online despite the late start for his day. At 10:30, lights were still off, but the vacuums of the night cleaners were still on, though their handles had fallen to the floor. He switched them off because the din was grating on his ears and brought a sense of dark absurdity to what should otherwise be a solemn moment. Seated at his desk, he checked emails and found only that his spam folder had grown in size, but he still decided to send an all-hands email just in case. It fired off and he heard some distant pings from charging phones that were rightly left behind over the weekend where their notifications could disturb no one. He looked around his office and saw how little he'd customized it since his first day some months back. It had never felt inviting. Nor was it particularly inviting in that moment either. He had spent nearly all his time there watching for the appropriate time to leave, as would the others. Much of their office chatter had the feel of decoration to distract from an ambivalence they all shared towards one another. The rest was genuine comradeship and gallows humor, though this was by far the minority of minutes expended.

On the next morning, with its still-crisp and aggressive light, he got up with the memory that it was July 4th and there should be an orgy of violently exploding flowers above Capitol Hill. The plan had been to spend the morning in front of the TV with his son before they headed out to the carnival events around town, then make their way over to the mall by late afternoon to wedge themselves somewhere comfortable and watch the show. Obviously this could not happen. Still, he went downstairs and sat on the couch to try and sit through as many of the original Star Trek as he could without his son there to marvel at how strange 1960s television was. Together, they'd laugh at William Shatner's love for wrestling and how high his waist was. But despite the ridicule, they both loved this show and it would be the second round of watching it together. He couldn't even make it through the pilot, shutting it down after Spock's only smile of the entire franchise. Instead, he finished a show that he and his wife had begun and dozed during the credits until it was 14:40 and he felt agitated in the house again.

As before, he took his bike outside and heard the shuffle from next door, except that it sounded more dispersed and out in the yard. Steeled by an adaptive personality he peeked over the gate and saw what one would expect when a large deposit of raw meat was left open for scavengers to reach. The main carcass was still inside, but trimmings were scattered all over the doorstep and various birds had made their way down and were looking about with faces full of boredom in the afternoon heat. He mounted his bike and made the habitual check for cars as he left the drive.

A pass through Georgetown showed none of the fanfare from the year before, nor did he see the crush of crowds near the Lincoln Memorial as he hopped up to the pedestrian path under the row of trees lining the reflection pool. The entire length was the same until he reached below the final section of the pool where dozens of ducks had congregated in the hope of securing a good spot from which to watch the show in a few hours. Seated on the bank, he watched them and remembered calling out to his son to draw his attention to one or another as they did something comical. This had always been a cherished spot where they could rest after the hours long trek through museums before the bussing back nearer to their home. He still laughed and tried to catch the attention of the echo to see a duck ass wiggle in the air as it dove to eat some slime below the surface. He continued his tour and saw none of the preparations that should have been made. Not even the ramparts of law enforcement vehicles to demarcate the realm of the public from the realm of the badge, which was a constant fixture in downtown Washington but rarely so pronounced as during the 4th of July.

He circled Capitol Hill and rode over through Chinatown before heading back down Pennsylvania Avenue's wide course. All the way, traffic lights continued to announce their directives, and he still glanced to both sides as he crossed an intersection in contrast to them. Curiosity made him turn down to Metro Center, but hesitation made him gaze deep into the void all the more intimidating by the long escalators. Cautiously he descended and listened after each step that was made as lightly and silently as he could achieve. Lore had warned him that this would be the bastion of ogres and zombies. His mouth dried from the hours of riding in the summer heat now felt sticky and thick. He strained to avoid clearing his throat. At the bottom, he was yet more terrified to discover the huge cage had not yet been drawn for the night and nothing separated him from the vastness of the underground world. The yellowed light within shrieked with danger as he pressed on only as far as the first of the stairwells that led down to the platform below. He left as carefully as he arrived, allowing himself

to fully turn and rush as he reached the top third of
the escalator and grabbed his bicycle with a heart
thumping. As he rode off the curb in a rush, he mis-
calculated its height and nearly lost his grip of the
handles but managed to correct and head back down towards the White House.

He decided that he'd stay in for the rest of the week
and not bother to venture out and check on the city,
as this proved painful and exhausting. He also decided that home stay was an exercise in perpetuating a
disappointment that had the added value of increasing
the risk that he'd disturb the shrine of his family's
final activities. The slow rot of the carcass next
door contributed to the suggestion and he relocated
back to a house down the street that he'd entered over
the weekend. It had no signs of children, only an
overly tidy white couple who had expended significant
energy in removing all personality from their interior
and made the space feel as impersonal and inviting as
a magazine exposé. Fortunately, the era of telework
made for a mobile personality and he could take with
him all his entertainment and resources packed in a
small bag, so there was little change if one were to
squint carefully. It was the right place for him to
mourn without also bearing the additional cross of
tragedy from the previous owners. They no doubt left
their mark on the world in other ways, but this he
could not discern from their home. It was perfection,
except that he had to nail the door shut in light of
the destruction he could not repair otherwise. From
the well-positioned couch, he spent the next week and
a half in online research to find any trace of what
happened that night, with dark evenings in their bed
flipping through family photos from his wife's phone.
He ate from the fridge and sat at the kitchen table to
read through articles that he'd only gleaned in the
era of incessant new articles posted each day. Now,
without those new ones to come in and revamp the prior
day's information, he was able to go through them at a
more considered pace.

He had ceased the frantic page refreshes that he did in the early days, as he now began to accept the facts if not yet the reality that no new updates to the news feed would come. But there were new posts. Constantly. Bots carried on with vigorous efficiency the flood of traffic until all trending hashtags were for new NFT projects or vitamin supplements. They had done so well that the comment sections to new posts would devolve into bot communication that were indecipherable code. His mind wondered if they would carry on and evolve some day, but nothing of interest surfaced. Algorithms still pushed the same posts and autoplay still cycled through from children's cartoons to the racist right-wing conspiracy theorists, many of whom still seemed to post new videos; none of these contained information hinting at a global conspiracy that led to the evaporation of humanity. They were still stuck on Hunter Biden or George Soros, so he guessed that they were automatically uploaded on a preset schedule. At best, these were trite irritants on modern society but now, with an audience of one, they felt depressingly like missed opportunities to alleviate human suffering in civilization's final hours. And here they were, still uploaded afresh with a newness already obsolete.

In between these sessions, he would sit outside and let a few of the dogs that roam about to come to him and reclaim their place as a human companion, if for a short while at least. By his count, he'd entered some twenty-eight homes to release dogs, some with more than one, but exactly how many he could not recall as that was impossible in the chaos of breaking them out. He was certain that at least ten houses had more than one, so at least thirty-eight family pets, less one, should have been circulating throughout the area and, since there were no cars to grind them down; all thirty-seven should still be out there. At first, some five would tail him when he'd go out to walk around the neighborhood, though none came close to him. At least not until food appeared outside on the sidewalk. His method was the same that humans perfected over centuries and dogs knew to trust: he used

a repetitive sound at feeding times, in this case a
click of his tongue that he learned to use as a signal
for his approach through familiar streets full of
semi-feral dogs in cities of Southeast Asia and, once
learned, he was able to safely cross through without
being attacked as so many others had. For those who
appeared aggressive, a simple posture and short but
urgent charge usually worked to have them retreat a
bit in the primal game of chicken. These dogs,
though, were house pets and they craved people. They
were as confused and lonely as he was, so the simpleness of food worked to have them congregate near his
new house and fulfill their ancient role as coopera-
tive guards to the perimeter of the human world. They
were an eclectic pack of all sizes and breeds. By
Friday morning, there were nine permanent ones who
stayed close by him as he walked, though there were
two who always disappeared and reappeared presumably
scouted ahead. He felt like these were his enforcers,
his lieutenants, to assist as he commanded the rest of
the pack. Each walk would pick up a new one who, if
it stayed with the group long enough to reach the
food, would stay on as a new permanent addition. They
roamed as far as eight blocks away in each direction,
but he was careful to avoid walking in front of his
own home.

The one time he accidentally did this, he felt the
quiver of recognition that felt like ice melting behind his eyes as he fought the urge to go inside,
which itself was driven by an instinct of habit that
had not yet learned the horror show of memories that
waited. He stood outside his front door and replayed
the sequence of movements that effected the dialing of
the most important contacts on his phone, with his
wife's being called over and over again though he knew
that her phone was charging blocks away in the new
house. It was the narcotic comfort to listen to the
long learned anticipation in the sound of a ringtone
that held him there for longer than it took for him to
know it was a waste of time, if time even existed in
such form as it could be wasted. Still, these walks
helped so long as he stayed clear of his block. This

was easy enough, as his new home was far enough away to lend itself to a wide berth from there.

By Sunday night, he had exhausted all the food in his new home, which had included food he brought from his old home. His family had a habit of stocking large quantities of eggs, so this supply had carried him through most of the week when coupled with the sack of rice and frozen items. The tidy home was rather well stocked with frozen meats and conveniently portioned frozen leftovers that he found quite delicious. Altogether, he was well-fed, but this was nearing the end.

With all the empty houses and full freezers so close by, there was little cause to hold back except for the unpleasantness of entry to face new echos desperate to be noticed. He let his dogs guide him when the walked up to houses into which he'd already broken and observe if any from among his group showed signs of a homecoming. It took several attempts before a corgi took the prize and ran inside with a stumpy wag that vigorously hoped to find what nothing left behind. It was a pitiful episode to watch this new friend disappear and reappear sniffing the air and change its demeanor from one of friendship to one of distrust now that he had crossed into forbidden territory. He sorted through the freezer and cabinets quickly without a tour through the house as he'd done before. Clearly it was the wrong approach, and he doubled back to the homes where no one seemed to recall the inhabitants. These were less unpleasant as he felt more like an intruder than before, with him totally free to pass the time as he liked. He somehow felt crass to walk directly into the kitchens, so he made an obligatory stop in the family rooms to view photos on display and, after the second house, dared to walk through the private living areas as well. This was a ritual of vicarious mourning effected through the safety of strangers, not a fetishism enjoyed without restraint. Each detail discovered was a sadness unforgotten. In the corgi's house, there was already a living memory and his attention was unneeded. He was mistaken in his initial belief that shared suffering

would somehow heal them both so he left it to its
grief as he continued his first survival expedition
into the homes of his community.

A total of four homes was all he could stomach. The
crowd of echos in his head competed for relevance and
had begun to drown out one another and this was what
sickened him most. The emergence of adaptation and
disregard was too much too soon, just as the pain of
witness to too much human misery in his past allowed
him to disconnect and concentrate on various compartments of work focused on alleviating that suffering.
But unlike then, there was no solution available for
which pieces could be separated and reassembled
through a technical program. It was the literal absence of suffering that was most unsolvable and he
couldn't stand that his toolkit was outmoded so
rapidly. With a full cart of new supplies carefully
loaded and placed in a mishmash of Mylar lined bags,
he made his way back to the tidy home a few blocks
away.

The echos remained as he unpacked and loaded the
freezer. Even his hunger and keenness over eating
some bits of food was muted by the flashes of faces in
the photos connected to their frozen microwavable
snacks. For a brief moment, he laughed at the truth
that this or that box summed the total of their
legacy. All their life experiences and hopes towards
which they'd worked in preparation to actualize were
discarded and replaced by a package of frozen plant-
based hamburger patties or a package of pork gyoza.
Decade up on decade of effort and this was how he remembered them. He laughed aloud and punched the
freezer door shut, even relishing the sting on the
back of his hand for its realness. When the moment
was over, he felt transformed in some way yet unclear,
but he was certain of the importance of it inflection.
It was a moment where he realized that he did this an-
thropomorphization to his own home as well, with even
his own son being captured in the plastic pieces of
his lego city and his wife locked inside the very
walls of the house they bought together not two years

before using a crypto windfall that was sheer dumb luck, which he described as calculated skill. The suffering was real and existed inside him so it must have a solution if he could break it apart and re-build.

This significance was not yet within his reach. For the life of the contents of the freezer, he continued on as he had before, with the daily walks and doom-scrolling through the internet and his family photos. When not in pursuit of food or self-destructive grief, he displaced boredom by watching movies and series that he either had pirated from the past or streamed online. He discovered that nearly all of the stations that had active broadcasts before were now offline, with a very rare success rate on the cable roster when he scanned through the channels. This took a little under two weeks, since he shared as much of his food as he could with his pack even though he still had a mountain of dog food stationed in a house across the street. When the time came to resupply, he reflected back on the experience before and decided to instead visit commercial freezers in restaurants nearby. As with all cities, the choices were plenty and he tried to game out which ones would have the least perishable menu in their walk-ins, so that he could stave off the need to tap the freezers. As it turned out, none had much beyond cheeses and sauces that had survived the three weeks since their army of staff rotated stocks. Freezers it was. And since there was always a fully stocked kitchen nearby, he took to cooking on site rather than create a mess in the tidy home. It was still no simple matter to make the proper selection. He would have to choose between the destruction of doors to gain entry to those shops that had already closed before the event occurred or enter those that were still open, to navigate around the small piles of laundry. In some way, he found, the actual remains of people seemed far less personal than the intimacy of their homes, making it a little thing to brush aside the shoes and trousers and make way for him to reach the burners, of which many were still on despite the best efforts of overhead sprinklers that could only forestall the eventual carbonization of whatever ensemble was in the pans. In some, the flames had spread to walls, thanks to laundry heaped up on the surface, but he saw surprisingly few structurally damaged buildings.

Despite the smokey air, he ate quite well each day as he ventured further from home in order to check certain restaurants he'd known for especially good food, but was often disappointed to learn how few frozen ingredients were available. One such outing brought him as far down as Falls Church to investigate the longevity of pho at one shop he frequented. Not that one. The other one. He had little hope for a bowl because, even if anything survived, he lacked the skill to prepare them at the same level as he'd known. He did have some skills in terms of noodle soups, but pho was a dish better left to others. His real objective was to visit the large pan-Asian grocery in the same center because this had been the longest stint of exclusively western food he'd had in over a decade. The rear doors to the grocery were still open to let the late shift clean and restock. Inside he found that most of the fish had decayed in bins and there were only a few survivors in the tanks to feed off the carcasses of those who left first. It was not unlike wet markets he'd seen before so he was able to disregard all this and enter the main area of the store to begin his shopping.

Shelves and stacks of dried goods were left entirely unmolested as they always would. Not even a bit of dust had begun to coat the plastics and he felt the oddness of comfort at going through such an ordinary practice of item selection that only just made apparent to him the newness of the situation when he realized he would not pay for anything, so there was no reason to check the prices. He heaped into two baskets a full supply of curry and season packets, dried noodles, sauces, pulses and rice before looking across the expanse to the side with vegetables and cold storage. By contrast, this was a repulsive experience to navigate the aisles of rotten produce so dusted with

mold that he pulled the front of his shirt over his
nose to keep the spores out. But not all was rotten.
Many of the more durable fruits and vegetables, particularly onions and roots, were doing quite will and
even began to start a new life there in the sea of
fertilizer. But row after row of what he craved was
irretrievably gone. All the lovely greens and herbs.
Most of the chilies were soft and brown. The tofu was
slimy but the kimchi and the lemongrass were worth
taking. He checked expiration dates on almond milks
and juices. Packaged fresh noodles and dumpling
skins. He dusted off what he could and filled another
couple of baskets before shifting over to the freezers, where everything was all in order but the first
real experience of the transitory nature of food left
its mark and he decided that he'd need to be vigilant
and restock his supply with a fury.

Rather than return home, he decided to stop first at a
restaurant close by and load the freezer, since its
size lent itself for his hoard. He took a more modest
store back with him to his new house with the fresh
realization over the sever limitations his own small
car presented for such excursions. Surely to do a repeat would be more efficient with a utility car, such
as the rarest of items in Washington, the pickup
truck. The challenge was less in reaching the truck
that was a few doors down, but rather to identify to
which house it belonged for him to locate the key, as
this was a street where curbside parking was the norm
over driveways. This was the most vile of practices
over which he had so often fumed. Very little indication could be seen from the interior, except a kayak
window decal and a gas station drink cup in the center
console. Imagining himself some kind of sleuth, he
walked up to the nearest door and peaked through to
the living room but saw nothing of relevance. He
tried both doors on either side and came away with the
same. Still disinclined to break into three homes and
search them through and through for a key fob, he decided to instead revisit the already opened homes and
hope to find a large vehicle nearby. This, in all
likelihood, was more work and took longer, but that

was no matter. The first house that matched this turned up two fobs, both of which were small sedans. The second, third, and fourth were the same. By the fifth, he found an Outback with a rack and cleared all its contents to the curb, but carefully placed the stroller and car seat back in the foyer. The drive in an unfamiliar vehicle was never a welcome experience for him, particularly in the confined space of urban roads. Doing so now taught him that the source of his dislike was rooted in a fear of traffic police, which when gone, made him feel at ease during the transition into this new machine.

As usual for an American with an interest in bulk groceries, he drove out towards the closest warehouse store where he had a general sense of what they'd offer. He was met with aggressively reinforced doors in both the front and back, which made it impossible for him to luck into simply pulling one open as done in the grocery a few miles away. While he had an innate sense for how to break a residential door, with a flimsy latch embedded in wooden frames, he had no idea how to bypass an industrial door that had a metal frame and robust mechanisms. A further complication was the difference between opening directions between home doors and business doors, which had to comply with fire codes that demanded external swings and made for a difficult time to breach them with force. This dilemma subsided when he spotted a construction site nearby with a forklift outside the office module. Surely there would be a key either already in that machine or in the office, with a much simpler door. So, he went over to investigate. Luck matched aspiration and he found the keys hung in a shallow cabinet behind a desk, but the next problem was how exactly to drive this equipment over and ram its teeth under the rolled metal door of the front entry. However, once the initial jolt of learning was over, he reached the smoothness of asphalt. The actual process of girding the teeth under the lip of the door was less straightforward than he'd imagined, but the entry was open in short order.

The warehouse was dark but for the sparse glow from skylights far above. He knew this space well and the dimness was only an inconvenience while he looked for the main switches that he imagined would be near the administrative office that faced the row of registers. Good enough. A few lights were on now and he made his way deep to the rear. He'd not yet thought hard about the needs of a survivalist, but as he passed the hardware aisles his eye was drawn to the large portable solar battery and propane generators, realizing that these might soon be valuable. He took one solar unit down and placed it at the aisle head to move on and shop for more, intending to return here for a more consolidated pickup at the end for such a heavy item. The pungent smell of rotten food was here as well but the grandness of the space made it seem less unsettling. He saw little of the meat that was trustworthy, but eyed many of the baked goods. Interspersed among the fresh produce were boxes of dates and perfectly ripe avocados, if not somewhat soft. He discovered the main source of the sweet pungent smell from the watermelons that had over ripened at the bottom of the bin and were now crushed under the weight of those above and, since July had been peak season, the bins themselves were spread across the produce alleys. It pained him to see so much food rotting at once in such a small area. But it was the rows of wine that injured him most, with the electric pulse it had always signaled now untempered by moral weights. It struck him hard as he circumnavigated the central bins full of fluid that had proved so nearly impossible to excise from his daily routine. The nausea and quivering nerves echoed to remind him that it was not morality that kept him safe, but instead was founded on the sickness of addiction overcome. He moved further through to the freezer section and out from the gaze of those bottles in repose.

Once in the back, he saw a new mountain of dog food and he did a mental estimate for how much food he'd need to keep his pack dependent and loyal. The figure was staggering, but he opted for a smaller store and would resolve the problem another day when he had more transport than the now nearly full small space of the outback. As he wheeled his third cart of supplies to the front, he looked at just how much he'd taken, which was at the margins of just too much for the car and enough to justify an upgrade. Back at the construction site he found a delivery truck that suggested to him that he should stash far more than he already had pulled from the shelves, so he returned to the aisles to more liberally collect from them anything that might be of use. His pack would approve of his new selections. He also took two freezers, a larger TV and some video game consoles he'd avoided in the past. Fully loaded, he drove his new machine back to the narrow streets of Georgetown unconcerned by the dearth of parking spots that awaited.

By mid-August, he'd managed to settle into his new paradigm with a modicum of grace in lawlessness. He kept reality away by drowning time immersed in several sandbox games where he either lived in a fantasy post-apocalyptic world of nuclear fallout, where he traveled around to shoot monstrosities or a desolate and uninhabited planet where a once mighty ancient civilization mysteriously disappeared. These breaks from reality gave him some sense of perspective for when he rode his bike around the emptiness of the city.

In passing the White House on one ride, he stared intently at the unsupervised gates. Here he was loitering outside one of the most secure properties on the planet with an AR-15 slung about his shoulder and not a soul came to tell him to fuck off or at least ask him to state his business. A reluctant mischievous hand raised up and held the bars to test whether the gate was locked. A few moments of thrill ended flatly so he let go and examined the rest of the grounds with no gate security and no Secret Service. Nothing. He wondered whether it would be prohibited for him to enter, whether it was an issue of law, morals or self-preservation that kept him out in the face of all empirical evidence that no one was there to stop him. All but the last would be intangibles comprised out the imagined community of Americanism, which has al-

ways been an opportunistic community that could rationalize a circumvention of both laws and morals on a
transactional basis, rooted in contextual needs but
usually boiled down to the immediate gratification of
a violation unsanctioned. He thought back on the
throngs of insurrectionists who not so long before
crowded this city and discarded the notion of lawful
transition of executive authority on the basis of a
perceived unlawfulness in the selection process. So
it was easy to drop the thin anchor of stability once
a foundation of excuse had replaced it. And yet he
still felt the pang of regret at the simple act of
imagining a trespass that itself might no longer be as
such. Surely the laws still existed, but laws unen-
forced starve into nothingness and his violation could
be no more than a pitiful step over a corpse unless
the moral ghost of the law still carried a proscrip-
tive effect that compelled him to carefully walk
around in reverence. This agitated him more to recall
the grossness of the pretend soldiers aligned in the
ellipse ready to rewrite the moral strictures of the
nation. He himself stood where they stood, dressed as
they dressed, and considered the right to the same and
whether it ought not be done, even now when he knew he
stood alone with no one else with whom to form a democratic consensus. It was a tiresome exercise he'd
witnessed in other societies, but those too now had
authorities that were presumed to collapsed into him
as he stood on the edge of the power center of the nation. In traditional thought, this consolidation of
the power of violence into a single human unit was the
essence of statehood. But monopoly suggests the existence of an oppressed other, so it almost couldn't be
that a single human could suddenly possess the monopoly when they hadn't anyone on whom to exact that
power even as he didn't lack for control over physical
territory. Even this moral clarity had begun to fade
over the preceding month as he began to view all quarters of the city as his own but his statehood was as
incomplete as it was irrelevant.

This idea of power and violence swirled in his mind
without the restraint he might have otherwise imposed

on his thoughts when he had the presence of others to consider. It now took him to the brink to explore the gravitational centers of state violence as he made stops around local police precincts in the hope to claim their accouterments. What he encountered was the legacy power of security glass and magnetized locks on reinforced doors. One by one he discovered the same barriers at each but, with only a moderate impress of ambition to make his way beyond, he spent a limited effort to breach the security zones. Mostly, he sat in the intake lobby and tried to imagine what sort of misery had also sat their not long before. He played out in his mind a number of hypothetical scenarios where fretting spouses sat for news from the doors just beyond or drunk and angry friends thrashing about to let it be known the injustices being carried out. All of this seemed equally plausible. It had been more than fifteen years since he worked the criminal justice system in America to see the interior of a facility, but he knew them from elsewhere and already the lobby felt more comfortable and ready to accommodate these scenarios than what he'd seen before with their entryways little more than portals for cattle and hostile corrupt bureaucrats standing watch over them. Anyone interested enough to approach came with dignity discarded, else risk an enhancement to the suffering within. It all had a disorienting effect as he sat there and the anger built to meet the scene.

He began to inspect in earnest the tensile strength of the glass and wondered what machinery he could use to break inside. He guessed that there existed consumer-grade equipment that he could easily find that could do the trick, assuming the real issue would be time needed, which was something the security precautions no doubt excluded. It would be unimaginable that someone would be free to walk up to the doors and casually destroy the doors over time without a deluge of officers to disrupt them. Unthinkable yet now a current reality. He had no idea and no training on this whatsoever. Once, when he was younger, he learned how to use an acetylene torch, but he lost all that knowledge on how to set one up. He was out of his depth with ambitious overreach. But he wanted to give it a go so the best idea he could come up with was to visit a hardware store and wander the racks to see what destructive tools were available, but this would require more hauling power than a bicycle. He routed back home and changed to his delivery truck, just in case he felt like an expanded trip. At the store, entry was an issue as always but he was less inclined towards care here as he expected no harm would come if the inside was overrun by animals. This freed his hand to use votive bricks from out front to break the glass and clear the larger shards so they wouldn't sever his neck as he crossed into the already familiar spookiness of a once known space fallen dark.

A quick online search had discouraged him from an attempt to breach the ballistic glass as he'd originally planned. Based on his review, he estimated that he would become exhausted and bored long before he actually entered the facility. The second option was to cut through the metal doors using a saw, at least enough to disable the magnetic lock and cut out the standard latch. This made far better sense and a far better use of his bottomless time. He found his way directly to the right aisle and was frustrated to recall that such equipment was locked within a cage below the displays. This brought him to search for a bolt cutter to cut the mesh, and along the way he found various safety goggles and ear protection that he felt obliged to use. He took his time. Shopping here was an exercise in imagination. So large was the skills gap between the options and reality that he mostly had to blow past aisles full of equipment he never hoped to understand. But he managed to decipher the selection of blades and match them to the right tool, choosing both a battery and plug versions, so he wouldn't have to return again. He also packed other tools like a sledgehammer and crowbars, but he felt a moderated confidence in the option of the saw. All in all, his truck was loaded with a pittance after he spent the bulk of the afternoon inside.

Along the way back to the station, his resolve began to waiver when he wondered what exactly he hoped to accomplish when and if he managed to enter. The sudden rush to decision that led to all this commotion had felt as more than just a diversion. It had the contours of something important that now, on the drive over, seemed distant and less articulated. Even the flash of anger he felt in the lobby was more than a passing thought. He'd always coveted his anti-authoritarian core and raged at the months of images of police assaults; at the terrifying private force that the president had unleashed to rampage through this city. He could only watch those images from the safety of eleven time zones away, which were then faded into memory when he finally arrived here after the crisis was well over. It still sat and festered under the surface and seemed to now pull his focus when all the needs for solutions were gone.

Before he entered the building again, he took in the scene as the evening had already reddened the sky. This was pointlessness that had acquired a point only through being self-aware of how little it mattered. Only in that recognition did it make sense to proceed inside. If nothing happened and he gave up, nothing had been risked and nothing was waiting with anticipation of success. Not even himself. Nothing felt betrayed as he noticed a badge that peaked from under a pile of laundry which had hoped to cross the parking lot before it fell to the pavement and left behind what appeared to be an access ID that he might be able to use to get inside the door. Feeling considerable relief as he dumped the first tranche of tools on the ground and walked inside to find that the ID did in fact open the door; he was free to roam inside without the need for violence.

Once inside, he was in unfamiliar territory and was unsure what he'd find. There were the normal corridors of an office marked by placards and maps on the walls. He found conference rooms and desks before he understood that he was actually searching for the armory, but this was not clarified by the diagrams for how to escape the building. This information, he assumed, might be best discovered in the leadership offices which invariably were on the floors above, but it was quick for him to change his mind after the second flight up and head back down to the basement levels where he also expected to find a holding cell along with the ready rooms that might also include an armory. The assumption was accurate and he found a locker room adjacent to a room full of heavy closets that smelled like oiled metal. With that box checked, he wondered where to find a key. Surely the metro police would create a log for all weapons removed from these closets, so he only had to find what looked like a supervisor's desk and hope to find either more laundry or a set of keys. This was not as obvious as expected, since none of the nearby rooms had the feel of a quartermaster's office, so he began testing keys that he removed from where he found them in the parking lot. None fit the cabinets so he tested them on the lockers and found the match, to his surprise. Inside were personal items of no use, except that he found a reference to the owner's seating assignment upstairs, on the second floor. It was there that he found the right offices and took a grand set of keys that had fallen to the floor. Inside the cabinets, he found what he'd expected to find and more. His lack of imagination carried no further than the weaponry at the disposal of modern militarized police and he had forgotten the tactical gear they used as well. He found body armor and helmets along with other items of use. Imagining they might be useful should he want to venture into the underground tunnels, he stuffed a complete set into a bag he found.

Still with an excess of keys to which he hadn't sufficiently explored their matches, he loaded the bag of gear into his truck and pondered what to do next. One key stood out for its large size and odd functionaries. This, he guessed, went to a cell somewhere in the building. It was an ancient key that appeared quite worn and he was afraid it might be just an antique kept as a memento that long outlasted its purpose. If this was not the case, then it was likely that it was the key to an original cell for the building and most likely located in the basement. He reentered and made his way back down with more confidence than before, until he found the shallow cell tucked at the back of a larger room, the purpose for which he did not know. The bench in the rear was soiled and the paint chipped from the carvings that had been etched into it by countless detainees who spent awful hours awaiting one thing or another. There some waited, even now. These were the uniforms of ordinary people rather than detainees who had already processed through the portal into this interior world. Mindlessly, he checked the lock and it matched the key as he'd expected. His spine sharpened when it realized he had walked into the cell and deliberately shut the door with the key still inside. When he decided to sit down, his mind wandered over those who sat next to him. Both detained without control. The odd freedom of their confinement connected them. He suddenly became aware that the key in his reach was all that separated him from dehydration and eventual death. That if he made the simplest of acts to toss the key across the room, that would effect his death by suicide. Or he might fumble it while he unlocked the door so that it bounced out of reach. He recalled the fear of dying with no one to check on him when he sat behind his iron cage, customary for houses in that part of the world, during the early days of the pandemic when he was never sure if he contracted the virus on his bimonthly outings to resupply his food and water. He was again behind bars with no one coming and only fear to hold him in place. He sat there paralyzed for hours until his urge to urinate shook him alive again and he was able to turn the key and let himself out again. He shut the door to leave the others to their freedom undisturbed.

It was quite late in the evening when he reached the last of the secure doors and, before he left, he decided to drop the ID card and keys at the ledge under the ballistic glass where he sat earlier in the day. He had no need for those unless he returned to the station. Unsure of when that need might arise, he

drove off back towards home but made a detour to visit
the White House again. He pulled up to the East gate
and sat there with the headlights illuminating the
empty guardhouse and barriers before he stepped down
and approached the forbidden access point. He surveyed the grounds beyond and looked up at the security
cameras that covered the area. There would be, no
doubt, a swarm on him if anyone were left to be interested. He cautioned a few additional steps closer and
stopped. "Do you even see me? I'm here, where the
fuck are you?" He called out at the cameras but received nothing in reply. He tilted his head back and
looked up at the clear sky but saw no stars because
the city lights still drowned them out. He did, however, see several satellites carrying on as they must.
Without attempting a full insurrection that a breach
of the gate signified, he left for home and was
greeted by a dozen dogs who had begun hanging around
in greater numbers when the aroma of all the food he
brought back had feathered out onto the wind.

III
Lines

The food stocks in the freezers kept him well fed for
weeks. But for the boredom in redundancy, he would
have gained weight as he remained idle at home immersed in other worlds without his regular walks that
his pack sought. They had now grown to what seemed
near enough to the full collection of dogs he'd released. Despite this, his hunger grew interested in a
diversity that it had enjoyed for years prior. He was
in need of produce, but knew no such thing existed
now, so he contented himself with frozen vegetables.
For this he left for a more regular grocery nearby.
The sort that carried only the most popular of lines
pushed by the very consolidated food producers that
crafted uniformity across the states where there once
had been novelty. These facilities littered the metro
area and he habitually avoided them for their simulta-
neous overpricing and poor quality, and he had his go-
to items that he particularly enjoyed price matching
to voice his disdain for these stores. Scant packages
of lemongrass, for example, always sold at nearly five
times the price of the bundles sold at his favored
pan-Asian grocers. Such was the annoyance of privilege he felt permitted to hold. In the present grocery, he felt none of this entitlement as it was sub-
sumed beneath layers of disgust once he was well covered by the stale noxious air that failed to retain
even a hint of the usual aroma of floor cleaner that
used to give ones senses the impression of walking
into a food hospital. He'd already dispensed with the
tiresome routine of the main light switch to help him
as he shopped and instead opted for a headlamp and
lantern for his cart. As he made his way in, his lips
strummed a suspenseful rhythm as he visualized himself
an astronaut scavenger headed through the bowels of an
empty ship adrift deep in space. This was inspired by

a recent re-watch of one series, though he made a point not to include the possibility of a cannibal anarcho-syndicalists. He allowed each step to sound ominous and startling as he walked up and down the canned food aisles with an open pack of cookies that made him sputter crumbs as he continued his tune. This was a dalliance that differed from other outings. It was not quite an acclamation to the situation but rather a bored and cavalier fatalism of passing through a store with understanding that he owned all things everywhere. That this only happened at the expense of all people was neither his choice nor design, so he could not feel the pang of guilt at this particular moment. Nor did it occur through any conceivable action that he took, which further alienated any sense of culpability.

Perhaps this drop of guard allowed him to stand deep in an aisle in front of the refrigerated beer options. He'd stood like this countless times in countless states of mind that all washed away and were memories beached somewhere like polished driftwood. What struck him now was not the gravity of the moment, but that it came on so mindlessly and failed to even stop him from his concentration on the sweetness of the cookies, even as he eyed the bottle labels and imagined the cool coarseness locked inside. But his hands were impish and unready to cross over from being spectators to participants, so they sat there awkwardly with a bag into which they reached to pull out the cookies one by one until there were no more and the moment came when a new action was needed. They chose to wipe the crumbs on a pair of trousers already greasy from dozens of similar recent decisions so that it was not clear if anything was cleaned off in this moment or whether new grease was rubbed back in. Neither the hand nor the cloth ever learned which cleaned the other.

One moment bled into the next and he didn't notice when he shifted his definition of "should" from one of engagement with what had been haram to selection from among the bottles. If this first return to that world would indeed take place, would it be on the back of an IPA, a stout or a cider? In the past, such decisions turned on the discrete numbers towards the bottom of the label that indicated the power of the liquid inside. Would that he return to this banal criteria, else overindulge in imagination that roused the desperately forgotten flavors. His eyes recognized two labels that had been favored in these memories, each with two options. He selected the IPA, but not an American over-hopped recipe that might sicken him in its power. The prized bottle was a modest and balanced recipe with respectable numbers. And with its selection, all will to continue anything but contemplate the new companion felt overdrawn and he left the store still under the trance of his suspenseful song, if for no reason than to force levity into what he knew was a milestone act.

But the act did not end inside, next to the refrigerators. It continued along with each step. In the past, when he'd decided to end his habit but hadn't yet managed to effectuate that decision, he treated these moments as final once he grabbed the bottle, once he entered the store, once he deviated from his course in order to reach a particular store carefully selected from his roster so that his face would not seem as repetitive as it in fact was. When those moments were gone, there was no choice but to press further, even if all desire itself was gone. Now, he felt the added weight which was anything but forgettable. It tugged on him, and its shift within the cart or its gentle clank of watery glass were at the forefront of his mind as he made his way to the car outside. It dragged the car as it drove through the streets. The fronts of homes felt to him like a sinister audience to replace the faces of strangers in stores where he felt sure that everyone knew his purchase was an act of depravity by a desperate mind rather than the mundane activity of a typical adult. He drove with laser focus on the road ahead, hoping that even the trees would not see that he had a twenty-two ounce bottle of beer lurking somewhere in the car.

Inside the house, he was little better off with a mind that leapt too fast for hands to catch up as he fumbled for a glass and even lost momentary control of his bladder due to crisscrossing decisions that could not triage two urgent priorities, which left him executing them both so poorly. Once all the setup was readied, he stopped. This too was a return to the past where the frenzy of preparations ended and time slowed to accommodate the calmness of the new phase. He regained composure and left the kitchen for the toilet to finally behave like a human, but when he finished, the flash of anticipation struck a note through his prostate and up his bowels. The shoulds that had been so fluid in definition oozed inwardly and he decided to stall further by installing the bottle into the freezer to reclaim the chill lost during the transit home. He knew this trick. The delay was a fiction because it suggested an option to change course that only set a countdown for reengagement before the cold exploded the bottle as it froze. When placed properly in the refrigerator, the chill would be too slow to allow for such a quick promise and the whole matter could be forgotten indefinitely. He knowingly fooled himself and pretended not to notice. No more than thirty minutes were needed. After five minutes he remembered to let the glass join the bottle so that it too could chill. In the interim, he did what he always did and relished in the final moments of sanity by acts of atonement. After closing the freezer door he surveyed the home now not so tidy and felt that such an occasion demanded more neatness. So, he cleaned the main level of the house and let it reclaim its heroic flavorlessness. Before he returned to the freezer, he confronted the choice between a comfortable seat or one more formal at the table, or even to stand enthralled. He took the bottle and glass from their shelves and sat on a stool in the kitchen to begin.

The sharpness of the opening was a pleasant sound. The ring of the glass lip on the bottle when the cap depressurized presented the echo of celebrations at crowded restaurants as such noise could have no match for the chirp from the bartenders. There was the quick escape of thick aromatic carbon dioxide that stung his nostrils. He let the bottle stand examined and pirouette to reveal the fullness of its labels. It spun and spun as he read bits of information and notice the texture of its paper that showed bites from when it was rolled around along the distribution chain. The glass tilted toward it to lift it up as it emptied some, but not all of its contents into a frothy and smoky chamber. The dance ended and the glass proudly displayed its copper contents that boiled from slender lines deep within. He could do no more. He'd overdone attention to details that he became captive to observation. He watched too closely ever since he accidentally found himself in the aisle to stare at its collection. It seemed that his hands now managed to regain control and sat in protest on the counter surface, occasionally prodding the glass and bottle to stir emotion but not enough to make cause for teetering over the edge. Eventually, the absurdity was overwhelming and he stood up to stretch his legs. This turned into a realization that he should eat something to get the taste of stale cookie from out his mouth, so he poured a barely expired glass of orange juice and ate a sandwich on stale bread. As he did this, he watched the glass and bottle ensemble still on the counter untouched as if he flipped through a magazine while he finished his meal over the sink. He watched it again from the couch were he spent several hours immersed in a cartoon world of plumbers and pipes. As they sat unattended, their pull diminished and he nearly forgot about them when he stood back up to find a mid-game snack of energy bars and water.

By the time the house was well darkened and the beer had worn through its afternoon chill, he sat down at the counter again and the smell of stale sugars hit. Unlike the fresh blow from the bottle before, this was the echo of waking up sweaty in the middle of the night with a heart thumping under the onslaught of a chemical cascade when its inhibitor was removed. These stale sugars could transcend rooms and hover in the blackness of night. He'd known the journey to follow them as an ant to ingest more so that the intense shakiness could abate. He'd disappear for days into such cycles and exit as a fractured and frail animal. The long absence of such a powerful reminder made way for the clarity of its starkness. There was no joy in recalling the distorted hallucinations and irregular heartbeats that pushed the thick sweat out from behind ears. It was as if the first moments after the bottle opened were the naivete of youth now changed to recognize the brutality of life. There was nothing here in this space for him, not out of morals but of primal truths.

It still waited for him in the morning. More stale. More of the sourness of yeast awakened. After reliving his moments of discomfort, he switched off the lights and went upstairs to bed as if nothing more were to be done. In the morning, it was obvious that he still needed to take the most logical step and pour out the bizarre experiment. He knew just how the flavor would have changed overnight and how thick it would be in his throat. Coolness no longer would have muted the sweetness of the malts, which would be in full display at room temperature. This would have been unappealing even at the best of times, and he now looked at the glass as one does to rebuff the sexual advances of an utterly repugnant stranger. Nothing to do but grimace and escape then reflect back on how close one was to disaster.

With the bottle and glass emptied and rinsed out, he turned to what to do with the remaining hours so that a repeat might not come and flirt with a different outcome entirely. During the beginning of the end, he managed to collect himself and become dedicated to health and exercise. For up to two weeks, he'd achieve great success in exploring new areas on foot or by bicycle. And felt proud for it. These were run walks along farm roads and canals where he'd pass shanty settlements on the margins of fields. Outside observers almost certainly mistook him for someone admirable in his commitment and regularity, but would

have certainly not cared to have learned he was desperately reaching away from the pulls of alcohol that
captured them both. Now, fully out from that shadow
for many years, it seemed an appropriately nostalgic
thing for him to venture out into the American farmland to observe its own subtle strains of poverty.
This could not be accomplished from a short distance
run in Georgetown and definitely not one within the
range of his constitution.

Starting off in a car would be a disrespect to the
original intent so he decided to ride his bike. Such
a ride meant an impressive soundtrack would be needed
and he had two potential avenues for this. He loaded
a decent playlist and packed an excess of water into a
backpack. His was not a distance bike but it never
mattered to him and he was never one who complained
about the design of equipment too much, preferring to
instead to adapt his goals to the limitations of what
equipment he had. An initial stop to a bike store at
the Key bridge was a nearly missed opportunity to grab
some safety equipment like a spare tube and emergency
pump. Many years before, he'd lashed a multitude of
provisions onto an unmaintained road bike and rode it
seventy-five miles to the Oregon coast and spent a
frozen night on the beach. His tank of water fell off
repeatedly and his tent chafed the inside of his
thighs because he could not afford panniers and lashed
it to the frame. Even then, he was unable to miss out
on the pleasure of impulse. Along the way, he noticed
a dangerously low rear tire that caused a panic within
his zero knowledge of the road. He now had no interest in a similar panic, even if he knew that he might
take any car or enter any shop at any time should the
need or desire arise. With a daypack and backup plan,
he made his way back out to Leesburg on the George
Washington Parkway for its pleasant tree cover all the
way out past Great Falls. It was long as fuck but it
offered him at least five hours of a sequestered mind,
at the end of which he could simply drive home in the
way he couldn't all those years before. He gave himself the goal of paying another visit to Robert and
his colleagues Alejandro and Safi, whose personalities

had somehow managed to linger over the weeks, likely due to the imprints they made early on. They were, however, very far away and there were hundreds of points of failure along the way that could derail his arrival, least of which could be a change of mind. The earliest he could expect to meet them would be at least the mid afternoon after four hours of hills and introspection.

It was indeed grueling and full of muted drama. Despite the beauty of the road he chose, it was far more difficult that what he felt was necessary for the day. True, the trees did protect him from sunstroke and the occasional pockets of misty coolness were impressively welcome, but this stopped once he left the byway to enter Route 7 with the sun in full August effect. By the time he reached Robert's register, his daypack was emptied of substance and his legs barely worked after nearly six hours of pedaling. He brought to Robert several sports drink bottles and frozen breakfast sandwiches before he sat on the counter to eat them next to the large belted trousers that he placed folded on the ledge below the cigarette cabinet. He found that the weeks had worn through the novelty of the initial shock and he no longer felt like the vapor of another person was anything but ordinary. Perhaps fatigue had tilted the scales too far towards indifference, but he found none of what he expected to find when he set out that morning. Robert was neither a grateful nor hostile host and he felt silly at obsessing over some stranger at a gas station in Virginia. But the fatigue also locked him in place to indulge the moment of rest to the fullest and let the flood of electrolytes percolate to where they needed to be.

With his body partially revived, he dropped from the counter and nearly tumbled as if his legs were foreign objects that could not understand him. Wobbly and raw with a backache and refilled water, he proceeded down the highway to Leesburg a short distance away. Route 7 brought him directly into downtown but bifurcated first at a well known pie store and bakery, which called to him as he approached its modest exterior.

He and his family occasionally visited here over their
two years in the area, so this was a proper landmark
that beckoned to him. From the windows it appeared
that some items remained in the display boxes; the
last of the treats made by skilled hands. He hesitated to break the antique glass, but managed to con-
vince the door open somehow. Most of what was on offer was stale yet still held the mark of the intended
flavor, but with texture so utterly different and
failed to take him back to the moments with his family. From the pie shop, it was a downhill ride
through downtown, as the name might suggest. His legs
welcomed the rest and protested when he made a move to
lean back away from the saddle, so he descended more
slowly than desired so that by the time he reached it,
his mind was already in a blur and his body completely
distraught at the notion of remaining crouched across
his handlebars. He stopped and dismounted just below
the rise of a new hill. The fluidity of his fatigue
carried him away down through market street into one
of the many historic homes districts. These were
clearly either homes for wealthy new arrivals or middle class holdovers who never realized their windfall
in property values. One home in particular drew his
attention as a thing of American beauty which stood
out from among the others. Childhood dreams of castles and knights inspired in him a love of rock homes
and the sight of one never lets him forget the urge to
climb inside with his bow drawn. The steadily dimming
sky and his equally dimming body guided him up the
walk to find a way inside. He made a circuit around
the ground floor and came back to the front where he
sat in the conveniently placed rocking chair that
might be more for decoration than use, and closed his
eyes to listen to the ambient sounds. A distant dog
was more surprising than it should have been, but it
was the pelt of gnat wings that ultimately roused him
from the chair.

His laziness let him simply kick in the back door because it looked flimsy and old. Inside the home was a
dedicated madness to civil war iconography that
started from the laundry room in the form of framed

crochet of domestic scenes of women and children doting on their soldiers. Then came the numbered prints
of battle scenes and very tasteful pen and watercolor
portraits of various youths in uniform. The bathroom
where he washed his face had reproduced lithographs of
camp life with confused and reluctant faces of long-
dead men in standard issue rags. These were not the
choice reproductions with clean subjects, these were
raw images with ghosting from anyone who shifted or
passed in the background unaware that they would be
studied more than a hundred sixty years later when all
of their descendants and causes were gone. The
kitchen alone seemed unbothered by the theme and had
the feel of a boilerplate magazine design from 1974
with little to no update, except for appliances grudg-
ingly replaced some time in the early 2000s. The
pantry was a den of cans with the highest sodium levels possible for human consumption. The theme renewed
in the living room, which still boasted a CRT but with
at least a digital antenna. In between the church
paraphernalia and family photos were cedar shadow
boxes full of small trinkets salvaged from nearby battle sites. He detected the faded cigarette smoke deep
in the carpet not reinforced several decades but not
yet overpowered by the acridity of countless pots of
onion, celery and meats boiled in the next room. The
library was clearly the focal point from which all
else emanated. Incandescent lights brought an ancient
feel to the walls of knotty pine and built-in shelving
that held books from floor to ceiling on one wall.
His eyes scanned their spines and received confirmation that all were titles on military history as all
the cookbooks had been placed on the shelves he saw
outside the bathroom door near the kitchen. One title
in particular jumped out and connected to a memory of
his own father's shelves, so he gently removed it and
sat in the reading chair to rest with a bit of the familiar.

Almost immediately his leg began to cramp and he mas-
saged it as he stretched. The trip had taken more
time and more energy than he estimated and he had not
prepared enough potassium to help his muscles. This

mistake was minor but uncomfortable. Unable to rest for the moment, he stood up to continue examining the far side of the room with the racks of antique rifles on display. His father was also of the generation that kept firearms out for display without worry that children would misuse them. Now that no children existed, this practice offered a convenience for him to simply reach out and pick each up in turn and replace it on its cradle. On the other wall behind the desk, he saw a cabinet with a key in the lock so he wandered over to see what more treasures he'd find. He was greeted by a small stadium of spirits cheering him for pulling back the curtain. The light inside was many lumens brighter than the light from the combined effect of the incandescent reading lamp across the room and the musty overhead lamp. This was a bulb meant to titillate. Too exhausted to fight, he sat down at the desk and turned his back as he opened the drawers, where he found a secretary's pullout for a typewriter on one side and a complex of organized manila files in the other. But the power of that bulb created a shadow of his body in the chair as he did this. The countdown was set and he felt it until the moment where his anger welled up and he swiveled around to reach for the first bottle in the row nearest him to raise it wholesale to swill as much as was needed to end the exhausting dance.

This was never an action he felt the urge to do in the past and never attempted because he always knew the sting of ethanol would be too intense. He'd managed at times to talk about this or that being smooth and without burn, but this always was a comparison in his mind, never an absolute. He had friends capable of accomplishing this act, able to draw in quantities measured in half pints and always ended the night as bodies without volition. As the spirit gurgled inside the bottle, thin streams escaped the corner of his mouth and somehow made their way upwards to wet his eyes and exit even from there despite the tightness of his lids to hold everything in place and let him believe the moment was not real until not even all the tension could deny the intensity of the pain and he pulled back with a choke that spit the well-preserved liquid laterally to the cabinet and forcefully up his nose. His breath reclaimed was full of vapor as he felt the first wave of warmth deep inside him as though he consumed irradiated dye that left him able to vividly witness every twist from his nostrils to his stomach and lungs. His mind recalled zen and focused on the nuance of every gesture of his hand as he covered the bottle and slowly returned it to the cabinet, still unsure whether he would move on to a second effort or be done. That focus failed as the distraction of the roiling boil inside him grew and he recognized the looming crisis for what it was.

His go-to solution to end the electricity on the edges of his tongue was always to shut his eyes and squeeze his ear lobes as he swallowed through the experience, reminding himself that giddy pleasure was on the other side. Just hold on and the rewards would follow. In the years since this was last attempted he redefined his reward system and now this internal instruction was convoluted, unable to send a clear message. He continued harder. Rubbed harder. Told harder. He breathed through it by forcing air in and out, but it held nothing. Time reversed and the eruption from the bottle was discarded at an equally great force that coated everything as he instinctively clasped a hand to his mouth, in what can only be understood as the last ditch effort to seal the dye inside. The moment passed when the aftershocks had ended. He was left bathed in filth, shamed to himself and in physical pain. The promise of reward was a fiction, and he was dumbfounded there in the American castle.

Still stunned and immobile in his chair after the wrench of fluid, he stared absently at the wall of rifles and the suffocating history all around him. It spoke of trauma measured in centuries that consolidated into him now seated in an overstuffed leather office chair sour with sick and exhausted more by the past few days than the past weeks of confused solitude. There was nothing left in him to feel betrayal. There was nothing in him to entertain fantasies of loading these ancient weapons to send him along as vapor to join the rest of civilization. All he could muster was a vacant stupor that eventually faded as well and allowed him to stand up and wind his way back to the ghost faces in the bathroom to wash. As he did so, the thought of facing new violence locked in picture frames as he searched the house for car keys was uninteresting, nor did he want to stay the night here or find a neighbor's home where the knotty pine library could still be felt from the walls. Despite the depth of his fatigue, he decided the simplest decision would be to leave on his bike and destroy anything left under the crushing slowness of a dejected journey home in the black night. The act of mounting the saddle was tricky, given the shakiness of his arms and misunderstanding legs, but the natural feel of the machine let him ride on without too much trouble. Next was the question of where to go. He preferred the feel and quietude of trees but, given how dark the night was, he wondered whether heading back through the well lit highway would be smarter.

As he rode, he spotted a sign for the W&OD trail and recognized it as a long and wonderful route back to Arlington through a mostly park experience. Not leaving it to chance, he checked his location by GPS, but it took some time to orient what he saw on the small screen to what he saw now in the darkness. He was soon on his way to one of the trail heads a few blocks away and glad that he installed a lamp as one of the precautions before he left in the morning. The closeness of the road as it cut through wooded areas meant that far more branches and other debris fell directly into the cycling path compared with what he saw for most of the day on the car roads. His pace was slower and more studied than earlier, but also more interesting and less tiring.

The trail resurfaced in neighborhoods along the way, and it was as he approached one that he heard the muffled bark of dogs at play in the street ahead. Dogs at night are always a bad thing, but he didn't know how to avoid them as there were no off ramps except for the cross street itself, and he hoped to pass them unnoticed, so he sped up and kept a watchful eye around him. He hit the clearing and met the sharp image of four dogs, with two of them locked together panting. The others roused when they heard the steady hum of his chain and took off to meet him as he ducked back into the tree cover on the other side, but they kept running, and he slowed down to match the incline of the trail. This was once a regular event that he enjoyed. In the past, he slowed down to let dogs come near him, so he could swerve and kick at their faces. On occasion, he'd land a satisfying blow, but tonight was not one of those. Tonight, his foot found open air as the dog ducked away, slowing it down enough to give up the chase. With a bit of mixed relief and disappointment, he turned back to the road and the approaching bridge at the top of the hill. The coast down on the other side was freedom as the adrenaline let him keep the pace he'd attempted as he passed through the intersection. It was a long slope that had slight bend which was crowded by a thick cover of older growth with vigilant roots that rejected the asphalt surface. His aching hands had failed to catch the bump of his handlebar as he rolled over one. He flew over the front end and landed as a disoriented heap on the trail but only suffered a very minor scrape on his left elbow and knee. He was annoyed at the slight sting but remounted and continued his ride until he left the dark quarries and began to see the backsides of town homes again as he passed into Ashburn. He eventually passed an inviting row of well-lit and large homes that convinced him to stop and clean himself of blood and vomit that had now dried into the fabric of his clothes. His now fully empty stomach was also recovered from its eruption and wanted to begin processing nutrients again, so he slowed and visually took in the landscape just beyond a thin wall of trees that had at its base a thick matting of undergrowth that carpeted a canal through which an entrance was not readily clear. He walked on a bit and eventually came to an inlet to a school from which he managed to reach the neighborhood. The front sides looked less inviting as the back, with its expansive lawns below sun decks. Choosing the right home to break was less easy since they all looked like cookie cutter new builds where the trees had not yet outgrown their sapling supports. But these were the homes of wealth. Each was dotted with a family trims from luxury car lines. He couldn't decide between the Maserati or the Porsche and Audi. He assumed the former was for an asshole and the latter for a family, which hopefully would have a better stocked freezer. As he made his way to the Audi, he made a mental note to come back for the Maserati when it was time to leave.

As he walked up the drive to park his bike he noticed a sign for a home security system on the porch and assumes this would be a problem if it is armed. Thankfully, the backdoor to the deck was still unlocked in order to let party goers move about. He saw wine glasses and clothes, giving it the atmosphere of an orgy that had simply moved inside as it heated up. The dining table was draped in patriotic decorations, but the food laid out had long since spoiled. There were more clothes and glasses inside, apparently because the orgy was larger and more frisky than at first blush. Some plates and glasses had fallen for lack of support and were now filth on the carpet in the den. Too tired to care, he went straight upstairs to where he assumed would be the simplest place to find a first aid kit to wash the grit from his scrapes. The master bathroom had a wonderfully clean and large tub with water jets and a basket of bath bombs. As it filled, he brushed his teeth with the cleanest of the brushes he found and dabbed his wounds with alcohol pads before easing into the hot water and watched as a bath bomb sizzled into nothing. Everything melted. Even the sting on his arm, leg, and throat all disappeared in the envelope of pleasure. He washed away all the slime and replaced the salt on his skin with the salt of the bath before letting himself linger and soak.

The clean of his skin repelled the thought of returning to his destroyed clothes, so he walked into the bedroom wrapped in a towel, unable to discard the need for modesty in such a well-lit room. He knew this closet held secrets but could not spend the time on investigation since the bath water had awakened his hunger. He decided to purge his hours in the heat with air conditioning below even the already present low. For this experience, sweatpants, and socks were the thing of the day. The hallway back down was wide and fed several bedrooms into which he peaked but saw no children's clothing besides what was obviously tossed as living laundry in acts of disregard. The children must have been out for a sleepover tactfully scheduled the party to be outside their sight.

This emboldened him as he could walk freely without the mired sanctity that being so near where a child died demands. The den beyond had an expensive sound system that was on but no longer playing. One of the components was a turntable, so he checked the shelves nearby and found an Iron Maiden LP, so he played side two once he figured out the vacuum tube receiver and raised the volume as much as he thought the equipment could handle. He left the room as the rhythm guitar began its onslaught.

He was in the kitchen as the story line took shape for him to start with the freezer where he found several steaks that he took out to defrost in warm water first before checking for whatever else could satisfy his hunger. It was the impact of the spirit from the other house that made him feel marked by decay and disaster so that when he saw the wine fridge tucked safely under a counter he was ready. Not in the grocery nor his Georgetown retreat was he prepared for the slip into hellfire as he was now in his hidden journey outside the city, only to be betrayed by his juvenile efforts that abutted his middle-aged body. It was now that he was absorbed in fatigued anger and comforted by being surrounded by death that he opened that small door in full awareness of his intentions. He embellished every decision. Read each label and guessed its qualities. He'd fought the war and the retreat to death was all that remained for him. Finalists for agents of this destruction were the placed on the counter and all three were opened to decant as he returned to prepare the potatoes while the water slowly began to boil at which time it would receive them. Three crystal glasses on the counter also waited. The stood erect and regal. He filled each and watched the syrupy legs of the wines tumble downwards as he tested each visually first, then began to taste. There was none of the earlier nausea or the caution from the day before. They tasted like decay and disregard unwelcome for many years now finding itself the respected centerpiece again.

He began to cook in earnest, but not in haste. He was many levels of starved but felt no urgency to overcome the now nonexistent barriers. He waited for the meal before he truly began, though his lips were already blued from the tastings. He ate the first steak without breathing and then finished one glass all as a single motion. The second steak was more challenging and the potatoes were ignored, but the second glass went quickly as well. There was no need to hold on or to wish away the nausea for this journey, his muscles had known what was needed of them. But his soundtrack ended ages before and a bit of the euphoria had seeped out of the room, which was now a sad dinner in the kitchen as the remnants of an abandoned party surrounded him. Leaving the third glass, he went to the den to review the LP collection. He replaced Iron Maiden with Funkadelic and sat down on an empty ottoman surrounded by speakers. The swimming distortions from the music led him to notice the swimming distortions from the wine that his movements in the kitchen muted. He closed his eyes and shut out everything that happened over the past month and a half behind a wall of echoing harmonica and hums. He knew this album well but never heard it in vinyl, nor through a sound system powerful enough to shake his skin, nor would he have dared to try. He shook now.

He momentarily surfaced from the trance back to the empty room with the immediate impression of a crowded room that cleared out in a panic and one observer stays behind in the safe knowledge of the hoax danger. He reached down into a frump of summer dress and a broach. The light material was a wise choice for the heat of the early July night, but she must have been cold in the overdone air conditioner. Next to her were a pair of faded tangerine shorts and a blue polo shirt with the collar turned up and a visor on top; he immediately recognized the country club golf uniform. He knew without further investigation that he'd find no socks in the leather boat shoes, but he was curious to check his bias against the driver's license. Indeed, it was a Preston. He must be holding Ashley or Brittany. He tossed the broach and the license to the center of the room to check on the others. He found rings and watches, hoop earrings, and most surprising of all was the discrete Bluetooth controlled personal massager inside some laundry. He arranged all these items on the floor and sat back on the ottoman after flipping the music to side B. He sat as a voyeur over his trophies, a bit disturbed at the slight joy it brought. He imagined if this were the feelings of a serial killer who returned to his decomposed victims to wash and brush their hair. If only for the reason that he contributed nothing to their deaths, he managed to keep it light.

"I didn't find your keys, do you live next door? I really want to steal your car but don't want to have to find them," he asked Preston.

It had been a bit odd to him that so many people would be inside to a party but no cars would be lined up outside, so the only way he could rationalize it was that this was a neighborhood party. He found few keys in all the pockets and so few purses to examine. With all the trophies there on the floor, he made up little stories in his mind to map out how this little corner of Virginia interacted. To be sure, there was an even number of piles between the den and the porch, split evenly between men and women. He found only a tasteful amount of discarded alcohol bottles when he was in the kitchen, so he doubted anyone was particularly drunk, and he found no other contraband sequestered in private pockets. This party was as cookie cutter as the architecture. They had nothing left to offer him for the moment, and he stood up to explore the rest of the downstairs after a record swap to an old recording of Liszt's nocturnes, printed in the age before cassettes.

Calmer and inspired, he returned to the kitchen to look in the pantry for other snacks and on the way decided to finish the third glass that had decanted well and would be at its fullest. He walked on clouded ground. His mind was dull in its enjoyment of the house. The air was cool, and he shivered a bit inside his borrowed outfit, slightly large. For some odd operation of habit, he'd put his dishes into the sink but then considered this. How long would he stay here? This home was very comfortable and the rooms much wider than the cramped and aged ones nearer Washington. He knew Ashburn from the occasional visit, with its open streets and gardens, but other than that there was no awareness in his mind on what activities might busy him. He might use this as a way station to bike around the northern Virginia countryside, as the trek across Arlington was mundane at the best of times and the trek through Maryland was worse. There was plenty of wine, but what else was in the house?

Feeling drunk and engaged, he left the kitchen to the other side where the garage should be. It was down a dark hall where he passed an office into which he decided duck in for a moment. With the lights on, the contrast to the previous office was stark. Here was a modern office still established for remote work, with a standing desk and several monitors. As fitting that motif, there was a row machine and other exercise equipment that were well-used and not just idle accouterments of future discounting during the pandemic. The bookshelf was sparse and contained the sorts of titles you collect from airport bookstores. He saw three piles of men's clothes under and around the desk, which skewed the otherwise choreographed balance outside and his curiosity brought him in for a closer look that discovered that these men had gathered to do some lines away from the watchful eye of the others. Tempted but also quite smartly wary of mystery white powders, he rummaged through the trousers and found a Maserati key fob, which he pocketed and left the trio to their party without participating himself. The garage door opened to a workshop and storage room unused by cars. There were the archetypal kayaks mounted on the far wall, but what interested him most was the wood shop and a heavy safe that he could only estimate was the household gun closet. The crafts person was finalizing a child's firetruck play center, which was cartoonish and very skilled. He wondered if he made an effort at completion, would he fuck it up entirely? Probably.

So he focused on the safe. This was not the irresponsible key-in-lock sort that he found in the other house and with which he himself had been raised. This was a serious deterrent, so much that there was no risk in the community space of the garage. It actually would likely have damaged the interior of the home just to attempt to bring it in. He had to find a way to open it. A closer inspection showed that there was a keyhole, and he thought back to his time selecting clothing upstairs and found a small set of keys hanging on the wall. He rushed back inside, with a pause to change the music to something more violent on his way to the closet upstairs. There, tucked slightly behind the racks, high above the floor away from an enterprising child, he found a loop of oddly shaped stubby keys. He grabbed them and went back down to the garage, quipping to the powder crew that they should come with him to see something fun. His promise delivered. Inside was a disturbing collection of handguns and assault rifles that no civilian needed and no state should be allowed to use. His hands stirred to reciprocate in the knowledge that guns like to be shot and bullets like to be thrown. Having grown up in Texas, he was no puritan on guns. He could shoot a spoon from two hundred meters using a scoped .30-06, could shoot the center of an "O" on the lettering of a baseball cap with a black powder musket. Drunk, he got the rise that he failed to get when he opened the armory back in the Washington. Perhaps it was the air quality in Virginia that spoke of an armed citizenry. Designs had changed significantly since he last paid attention to them some time before the Columbine shooting, which seemed to have led to a Streisand effect that cultivated a fetishism among suburbanites ready to playact revolution fed by the weapons industry. This collection was just that. They were heavy, and he was clumsy, but he managed to cart a suitable number of rifles and handguns out to the porch and returned to grab as much ammo as he thought necessary. At first, he simply fired rounds into the treeline behind, where he had ridden past a short while before, but this got boring as bullets need an observer to complete their destruction. This need separates them from fireworks, which are satisfied with erupting for the sake of eruption. He looked around and saw little from the platform above the lawn, so he went to the front of the house to get a different vantage. He saw streetlights on a timer, partly lit homes and many cars parked in driveways. He tested them all and was satisfied with his drunken ability to aim and enjoyed the sound of alarms he triggered.

He didn't grab the ear protection slung over the workbench in the garage, so the ringing in his ears became uncomfortable, and he decided that he'd sent enough bullets out into the world for the night. But not until after he made a quick survey of the neighborhood. He turned to the Maserati that had intrigued him earlier and tested the fob he found, which as it turned out caused the lights on another machine down the street behind him to flash. This was, unfortunately, one of those that enjoyed his attention a few minutes before and the flashing was the signal that its alarm was no longer necessary. He'd have to find another fob in the morning or whenever he decided to leave. There was nothing left to do other than go back inside and finish up. To his disappointment, he could not hear the music of the new LP he put on and was mildly tempted to shoot the system out of spite. He didn't. Mostly because he didn't want it to explode in his

face, but this was paraphrased in his mind as just being a pointless waste. Back in the kitchen, he examined the bottles and strained to recall which of them
had the most agreeable flavor. They all had their
merits. They all helped propel him into the evening
despite the intensity of his fatigue. What more was
left? He decided to test a different bottle for his
fourth glass and chose a sauvignon blanc before siting
down, moving Emily and Julia aside, so he could put up
his feet. The room was empty and singing. It made
his eyes droop as the contents of the glass lowered
until he gave up the effort to finish it and put it on
the side table next to Julia's phone then turned out
the lights. Without realizing it, he had begun to
turn off all the lights in the house. He went to the
front porch and collected all the weapons he left
there and brought them inside before closing the door.
He shut everything down as one does when one is done
for the day.

Upstairs again, but this time for a stay. His feet
scraped the carpet a bit as he walked into the bedroom
and scanned the bed. From the looks of it, a team of
cleaners had been in the day of the party to help make
sure everything was tidy and no embarrassment would
slip out. They were unaware that the cleaned for him.
It was only appropriate that he take full advantage
and clean off the bit of slime that had accumulated on
his face and skin from the wine and cooking. When his
light shower was over, he pulled back the blankets and
eased into the cool and ever deepening crevasse. The
dutiful American owners had a selection of remotes on
standby to control the TV across the room. Their al-
gorithm was standard and pushed many of the shows he'd
already watched, but sleep is best with a binge of re-
runs, so he didn't mind. By the second episode, the
chatter of the characters set themselves in contrast
to the empty muteness of the house, filled with images
of personas downstairs in their resting piles as it
was. He wondered whether serial killers heard their
victims as he thought he did now. He had horrors of
bodies reconstituting from their clothes, angry at his
disturbance. This compounded to the neighborhood, he

imagined so many forces at their ready for him should he just first close his eyes. He stood up again to quietly walk down and collect the weapons at the front door and come back to sleep some sense of comfort. He locked the door behind him and moved the drawers with the TV across it as a barricade. The TV now on the floor, its images felt too comical to stay on for the night. He shut it down as the final act before his mind drifted toward the wall of ringing he heard and could not escape.

IV
Desperate Structure

All fun ends as it must. It crashes back to earth and leaves one to awaken in the wreckage. He did as he must. He explored the taboos set for himself and was experienced in the damage that waits for morning. His eyes opened in the blistering dullness of the cur-tained room that sent a shock of pain across his fore-head that he somehow felt deep from within the bounds of his sleep and surfaced from there alongside the creeping escalation of its reality. The headache gave way to the thickness of his tongue dragged across gravel and baked in the sun, or the coated and rough throat that had been dissolved by stomach acid and ethanol that twice passed through. He recalled that these could be resolved with water, but the headache would remain for as long as it must. His muscles ached from the hours on the road. The symphony of discomfort paralyzed him as he lay locked in bed even staying his breath in order to keep all thoughts away. The result was that his mind was an empty receptacle for the observation of pain; an exercise in mindful meditation where the very spacial distance of the room disappeared and he felt suspended in an open vacuum. He knew this place well. He spent years within it, fighting to escape. His final round had left him weeping and begging for an end that, when it finally came, lingered as malfunction in his inner ear that made him fall down unable to understand the nature of gravity for days. This gave way to months of muted impressions of the world until it finally faded and reality returned. The years before were marred by false starts and relapses, always hidden away from others who might see the depth of his addiction but likely already knew. In fact, the decision to stop had been made some four or more years ahead of the final round, even as the disease had escalated and carried on.

In the years since the fight was won, he removed the ramparts under the belief that they were unnecessary, as confirmed by deliberate exposure to the smells and open options of alcohol freely available. The most severe of tests had taken place two days before when he watched the glass of beer on the counter and felt the power of repulsion. No longer can time be measured in years since those days. What had been a mark of time since the last is now a return to the small increments of the early seconds ticked by a stopwatch. The one thought that penetrated the meditation was a recognition of how dreadfully slow time manifests. In quick retort to this was the expected return of rationalization that marred the early moments of hangover. If, after so many years, he had a single episode of relapse, he should not persecute himself but rather focus on the length of time of his successes. It is impossible to distinguish a pattern of behavior from a sample set of one evening. The futility of overgeneralization is unfair and unempirical. He surveyed the frustrations of the day before and characterized them as moments of water boiling around him and that led him to the predetermined explosion under the pressure. But this, he recognized, was unproductive. This was by no means a circumstance into which he was pushed. No, the better thought was the agency that he still had over the coming days to insure against a repeat. This allowed him to discard regret and accept the condition of his body, refocus on his discomfort and his posture within the void, only to restart the entire thought train anew every few minutes with always the same inspiration of fright and same comforting conclusion. Over and over. The repetition was a horror only in that he was notionally aware that it was ongoing and that he was powerless to end its flow. But eventually this gave way to an off-ramp in the form of a momentary connection to his wife, who had been with him during the throes of his prior battle. It was to she that he whimpered and meekly begged for more alcohol as a way to end the shivers and the pain. How would he begin to describe to her the night before and all the moments leading up to it? This was obvious.

To her, he never lied. His description would be a careful detailing that only left out the details that he himself forgot or inadvertently skipped over. It would start from the end and work backwards until they would try to understand the beginning together. He needed her soft patience and empathy again now. She would tell him that the beginning would be found in his own rigid punishment of himself, in the swiftness of his inward reproach. Hearing her reasoned words without hearing her voice left him more empty and alone. His eyes creaked open and allowed him to gaze into the room and confirm just this. He was alone as he had been for weeks, and he knew there would be no return for him. Not even the salvation of learning he was in an extended hallucination, which would be less horrific than this new reality because at least he could still have her somewhere to guide him on occasion. He reached deeper and tried to pull up words he crafted himself in preparation for his son, to be handed down some time years in the future when the child ascended to the family attributes of compulsions that devoured souls and destroyed homes. Not all attached to substance. Some attached to other behaviors. In his mind over the years, he worked on ways to express his open mindedness to his son for whatever form his compulsions took. How he would speak with patience and acceptance as best he could, even if he internally raged. He now strained to redirect those words knowing they would never be needed as intended.

Would that he had the patience to remind himself that he was free to make mistakes, even mistakes made with eyes wide open. This patience was so damaged from repetition already. So battle-scarred and vacant. So skeptical that a mistake would soon make way for a pattern as it had so often in the past. Patience was open and let him drift to the beginning, before the patterns and excuses. When he was the age he thought his son would be when patience was needed, when his own father had already disappeared from a failed

heart.   He recalled the leftover wine from a wedding
at the house that he was free to take to his room to
finish while listening to music in the dark.   That
solitude was his escape as he never then, nor now,
gained energy from others.   But through alcohol he
managed to create a facade that he carried, and it allowed him to use a voice that was not his own as his
own had no sound whatsoever.   It gave him access, in
those early days.   But as those days waned and the
grinding moments of life continued, the solitude
resurfaced and the access was unwanted.   The voice it
gave lost direction, but the needs of survival demanded more, so he split in two, with the freedom of
solitude on one hand and the fearful chaste soldier on
the other.

Patience listened as he recounted the shock of leaving
home abruptly with no option to return and no mementos
to take.   It listened to a youth unable to escape the
collapse of his foundation and the crippling effect of
no roots, though the complaints bordered on childish.
It listened to stories about having no direction and
no life skills, all of which needed to be determined
on the fly.   It clicked its tongue and nodded with active listening skills at the recount of credit cards
to pay rent and overtime with a flu that turned into
bronchitis that turned into an extremely expensive
visit to the emergency room, and back to work the next
day.   It smiled with encouragement at the slow arc
narrative that led to stability and the deep scars of
life learned.   It did this knowing that in the background stood demons that never relented on their terror.   It waited for the story to be told and offered
little beyond the simple act of standing in place to
let the words flow.

With the usual exercise complete, his muscles twitched
back to life as he guided himself to the bathroom to
test the day.   The sudden coolness of the room and the
tiles startled him a bit, but he then eased into them
and leaned over the counter to stare blankly at the
mirror and see all the haggard lines of age puffed by
the inflated hangover skin.   Cold water and a bit of

toothpaste were a good idea, and he revived more, but the sickness was still acute. His regular remedy had always begun with a boil in the bath to let the sweat ooze from his pores and wash out the toxins from the night. And so he bathed for the third time in twelve hours. This, like the first, was desperate medicine, and he soaked as long as he could stand. His headache was distracted by the sting of hot water as he watched the surface of the bath ripple only from his breath coming from out his nose. Completely still.

His muscles again twitched back to life and he could stand no more of the heat and stillness. The climb from the tub knocked his brain into his skull and he groaned under the pressure before staggering back to the bedroom still dripping hot water and sweat. The calmness returned under a pillow as the anterior of his naked body dried in the cold air-conditioned room, while the rest grew sticky in the sheets that absorbed the water as he lay. Under there, within a padded universe, he was able to go back to the void until the pounding lights in his eyes lessened and then ceased. On cue, his agitated body signaled discontent with the sticky sheets and the cold air and the suffocation of the pillow. This was to be expected from as the de-pressed brain chemistry cascaded back into place with exuberant overcompensation. But not welcoming a re-vived headache, he merely pulled back the pillow and let the cool air come through first. Now dry and cold, he needed to find new clothes that were better suited to the day besides his soiled sweats from be-fore. He checked the hangers and first found hers, which were nearly his size and his mind laughed a bit visualizing the experiment. But this was fleeting and uninteresting, so he instead found more comfortable trousers and a shirt, though still slightly too large so that he again felt like an overweight middle schooler with baggy clothes. Feet dragged again, and his eyes strained at the brightness beyond the bed-rooms as he entered the hallway. He stole furtive glances at the children's doors and straightened his back a bit as he passed them. There would be no need to show them the decay that would no longer await them in adulthood.

It was on full display scattered across the den. His trophies from the neighborhood, the children's parents and their friends, were laid about where he examined and discarded them. He wondered if his new persona would be a sociopath and how would this impact his memories of the past. But not all was his. The filth from the party scattered some of the items around, and he merely tossed them back where they had originally fallen. His fourth glass remained there next to Julia's phone above her shoes that were next to Emily's. In the fullness of the daylight he could see that he had not touched their delicates, nor did he bother to try and unlock their phones. Along the way to the kitchen, he saw the piles of rotting food that he managed to ignore before and arrived at his own modest contribution. The new dishes in the sink and the four bottles on the counter. To his surprise, he saw just how little from each that he poured out with his unpracticed hand. None had reached down to the quarter mark of a full glass, and of that which he poured from the last bottle, most was still in with the women. He long would go through the exercise that counted his drinks to the lowest denominator. Here, barely three glasses of wine would be around fifteen ounces at thirteen percent alcohol, fewer than two and a half shots. This surprised him given the vigor of his hangover. His surprise intersected with his cyclical reasoning from upstairs and brought up the memory from when he first began his journey and would be drunk on very few drinks while his friends would spend the night catching up. In most cases they ran out of money and took care of him on the way home.

Clearly, the years of abstinence had healed his liver and brought him full circle back to the beginning. The strength of this hangover must be due to the dehydration of the long day on the bike and an operation of too much too fast for the wine sugars. Surely the next round could be better planned and far more comfortable. This last thought terrified him. The whole of his endurance was predicated on the suffering that he would feel should he return to the bottle. Now, with the discovery on the counter, all that logic inverted and he would need to rebuild it to avoid disaster, if disaster was even anything to avoid. This was not something he thought about. In sickness, he could manage the issue alone but now that this was gone he was unsure if he could keep away the demons. He foresaw a future where the binges continued with no social pressure to resurface from his bender and dry out. There would be no limitations of money or the secrecy needed to find a new store to frequent. This would be the raw power of addiction free to erect its tower.

Unable to process this for the moment, he focused on a search for ibuprofen to damper the headache and go outside. Walking past the den with this new information brought on new aversion that he knew would wash away only with difficulty. He opened the door to find the sun ripe, but with a bit of watercolor feel as it brightened perfectly white clouds in the blue sky. He began a suburban neighborhood walk and began to feel better. The sun and the air were good medicine, but he felt annoyed as he circumnavigated bits of shatterproof glass that had exploded from his entertainment in the night. These were the new cars of wealth, and it was more than a bit of waste that he punctured them in what would surely be the initial domino in their rapid decay. By the fifth shattered car he no longer cared and was able to pretend he walked through a normal suburb on a normal late morning while everyone was out at work or inside their houses instead of on the streets. This freed him mind to wander and think about what his next steps should be. His original plan was to return to Georgetown this morning as he never expected to be away for the night. But now, he managed to become enmeshed in this neighborhood and became comfortable in this large house that differed in size from anything available in the city. But what would he do here, and how would that be any different from what he would do anywhere, including his home neighborhood to where he only recently became attached? For starters, he would have to clean the house to eradicate the rot of the parties or, alternatively, find a new home to invade and run the risk of finding new tragedies inside. This suburban neighborhood would have been infested with children, and he didn't feel ready to find their remains.

As a natural course of the walk, he had made the rounds back to the house and took a look at the Maserati in the driveway next door. His base assumption was that this was not a family home and presumably would be sterilized of children, but maybe not. At some point he would want that car, which would involve rummaging through the house to find keys, potentially while experiencing the blare of the security system, and still might find that his assumption was wrong. Those doors might hide a mountain of toys and misery for him. These risks were sundry but seemed incredible as he stood there to make his decision. In his driveway were the two other cars, attached to a home where the risks were known and already encountered. These were not shit cars, but were luxury in their own right. He had long thought that an Audi would be on menu, but opted to hold his crypto savings for cost of living instead. Now, here was one waiting for him as if in his own drive.

Back inside for the course of least resistance and to look for food again. The thought of smelling the smoke of a pan or the delays of more steaks to defrost before he could eat was not appealing. Nor did he crave the stale potatoes on their plate, but he felt ready to cook bacon if any were still alive. He found a questionable pack that was still unopened in the refrigerator and realized that he should eat more than strips of grease, though these would certainly scratch an itch. He found frozen berries and other fruits for a smoothie that could be mixed with some yogurt. The pantry had several boxes of protein bars that he stashed for later. As he prepared everything, the sight of four recently opened bottles on the counter agitated his concentration. One by one, he emptied them into the sink with the water on to wash the decanting cloud of aroma. Now safe in the room, the food went down more smoothly. He felt energized and rebounded enough to move on to whatever came next. It seemed preferable to return to his tidy house in Georgetown than to clean the disaster in this house, even if it was larger and nestled in a more inviting area. He thought about what he should strip from the house before he left, and his mind gravitated to the garage where he left a host of weaponry not used in his rampage outside. There was a lot to take. He worried about stuffing so many heavy items in the bare rear of the Audi, so he found several durable bags in which to stuff them for the ride back. As he did so, he imagined himself as a quiet gun runner preparing for a delivery, but the bags ended the fantasy under the strain effort. He thought about the woodworking station and decided that he didn't have the patience to learn carpentry at this point, so he looked about for other things in the garage. He considered the kayaks. These would give him access to a new highway on which to travel about, but they would also leave him horribly vulnerable to accident without any hope of rescue. He left them along with the climbing gear. The garage was complete and closed up. On the way inside he looked in on the boys and settled on the sane decision to leave them to their powder behind closed doors, though he did check around for more keys and more safes in this office. Finding none and unable to access the computer for other information, he went back to the kitchen and passed up the wine fridges too, knowing that this decision would be waiting for him literally everywhere. But the sound system was a treasure not worth ignoring. He carelessly ripped the plugs out from the machines and carefully pulled them off those off their support to load into the cushioned backseat. He slipped all the LPs into several file boxes from the office and put those on the floor below. Speakers joined the weapons in the back. The last to go was his bike, loaded onto the conveniently attached rack. He stood back and examined his thievery and felt the need to load more, but didn't know what to take. Valuables and money seemed unimportant now, so he failed to see why they would be worth the bother. This house had some artwork, but he now had

access to priceless works at the Smithsonians, should
he want them. Besides, none seemed attractive enough
to haul around and ultimately hang. The exertion had
left him winded and recalled the pounding behind his
eyes and made the bright of the sun now something that
pestered him as he worked. Once all the car was
loaded, he was ready to escape it for the coolness inside, where he finished the last of his icy smoothie
and rinsed the blender, just in case he returned. As
expected, the bedroom drew him in, and he went back to
the now dry sheets after stripping down to nothing.
This too fit a previous pattern, where he'd rinse his
hangover in a hustle of productivity and collapse
again feeling accomplished and ready to sleep in a way
that his nickelodeon of drunken flashes prevented.

Some hours passed and his second attempt at the day
had better promise. He felt far more human and re-
dressed before going downstairs. For one reason or
another, coffee sounded right. He'd seen a stove top
espresso maker earlier and waited as it finished its
percolation. He actually had not had much coffee in
the past month, since the need for productivity had
also disappeared. Now, with the residual caffeine in
his body long gone, this cup shocked his system awake
and he was ready to drive home.

As far as cars went, he was pleased with this acquisition. He still needed the extra time to assimilate,
but after weeks of experimentation, he had grown accustomed to this process. The wide roads and lack of
traffic certainly facilitated his learning, but they
were unfamiliar enough for him to need to use his GPS.
As he input the route, he casually wondered how people
drove around without this tool. He was disappointed
by the fact that the car only had a quarter tank of
gas left and, since he had no baseline for how long
this would last, he decided to stop at a gas station
that he passed on the way out. In the end, he didn't
mind much since he planned to hang onto this car for a
bit, so would eventually need to refill anyway. But
still, to have to do so when it felt so new was an
early annoyance. This routine of gas stations had

gone unchanged since the event. He still stopped and input his card to unlock the nozzle before he could fill the tank. He made one effort to bypass this at the counter inside, but he didn't have the correct employee codes to access the system. So here he was, still paying for expensive gas when he was able to steal everything else with impunity. This seemed normal to him, but he occasionally wondered what he would do when his money eventually ran out, no longer topped up with new paychecks. He told himself that he should look into cash deposits at the ATM using all the free money around, so he could pay for gas.

All traces of hangover were gone as he drove back on Route 7 where he had cycled the previous day. He spotted milestones here and there from his journey and marveled at how he managed to accomplish all that in a single day. Even the short drive to Sterling seemed impossibly far on bicycle. He knew this was the true cause of his aches today and new they would peak tomorrow. From the car he is able to see more than he could before, since his eyes were not fixated on the passing asphalt below. He could see random dogs in the neighborhoods and parking lots. He had been quite lucky to have only encountered one group as they were busy with other doings, rather than these hungry and skinny ones he saw now. They roamed in a manner he hadn't seen since the cities of East Asia, where dogs were not kept behind fences but left to roam the streets at night. That this was real in Virginia showed to him how much the system had broken in this ultimate of urban taboos. It belied the outward appearance that was unchanged but for small details here and there.

In the roughly six weeks without humanity, he had focused on himself and others, but almost nothing was given to his own family loss. He kept them in mind as if he was on a trip away, but not that they were permanently out of his life. Not until this morning, however. But that too was a moment of selfish pity. The years of work among community and individual trauma came to the surface, and he was made to confront the fact that his resistance to thinking of them sprung from his experience of trauma. He grieved by avoiding grief, but here it was wrapping its coldness around him to pull him into destruction. His trauma was unique, as no one had experienced the sudden and complete disappearance of civilization. That event of disappearance itself was violence on his right to grieve for a loss confirmed by certainty, which allowed him to push it out of mind and carry on in a twisted image of normality. Somewhere along the line over the last six weeks, he'd accepted the loss of everyone else. Each of his destructive acts brought him closer to that acceptance, but he held out a flame of chance that since he was exempt, so were his wife and son, despite all proof to the contrary. He would now have to recognize that chance was nil so long as he remained alone and found no one else, whether they reappeared or were exempt from the traumatic event itself.

As he drove and sorted this through, he threaded the connection between his personal loss and the loss of all humanity, who were as now fungible individuals undistinguished in their suffering or swift departure without as such. His was the only individualized suffering as the seemingly only individual exempt from that departure; the one to remain behind and absorb the shock of observation. All of them were the same. He could do no more for one or the other, and it felt immaterial now that he grieve only for his family, or that he grieve for everyone but his family. The unfathomable numbers needed to understand the scale of loss were staggeringly impossible to comprehend. A civilization of eight billion disappeared, but for one. He recalled the saying that large losses were mere statistics in contrast to the tragedy of small losses. This callousness rang in his mind as he pressed himself to feel them all. He couldn't. There was no way to imagine the billions of faces, let alone the moments of their day and the rings that formed their community. When he walked through his neighborhoods in the early days of July, he struggled even to visualize what was missing in the homes and on the streets, even if he could capture it by simply saying "people." That small number alone could not be articulated in his mind. These were outside his immediate comprehension. He began to worry that further effort to imagine this scale would end him as one who stares over a precipice and feels the overwhelming desire to leap. He was the last who remained behind to suffer without an observer to remark on his behalf. He recalled how easily such suffering was forced to endure alone. How suffering that was outside a sphere of community would become invisible unless it was documented in a book, a song, a picture or any art that would leave an observer with nothing left to say than that it reflected raw power. Even then, the underlying suffering that was everywhere would remain in isolation wanting only an observer. What he needed was to compartmentalize his slice of trauma into grief sized bites that he could process through.

The question of what exactly that would look like remained. Now on his own, he would continue to encounter the piles of remains of humanity everywhere he went, especially as he navigated the city and entered homes. Even in the bizarre chaos of the previous night, he felt comfort in exploring homes to learn about the household. The process of reassembling their images as they lived their final moments came as close to actual resurrection in these sparse days as he could imagine. Finding them at parties or in bed helped keep him alive in a snapshot of modern civilization in which he already saw the signs of decay. How this would accelerate was still yet to be seen. Even the home frozen in 1974 helped him know the distance he traveled in his own life up to the moment time disappeared. There was no doubt that this would continue as he entered new homes and found new lives no longer living. Somehow, it felt less like an invasion than it did a continuation. If he rummaged through an intimates drawer and found secret machines designed for pleasure or discovered a group of friends quietly killing themselves with mystery powder, wouldn't this just pull back the veil of invisibility from their loss? By learning their true details, he'd give them credentials and preserve them for whatever purpose he might construct. But the strike of guilt was real. In these moments of discovery, he was any-thing but reverential or prone to memorializing those gone. His actions were buffoonery made spiritual. What was lacking was right intention that could easily become the norm the next time he invaded a home. This felt like a more manageable bite of the whole of eight billion lost. In each new memorial he made, he could expect it to be a collective icon that carried the weight of observation to the whole of humanity.

Passing along through Tyson's, his mood had improved by the miles traveled in his mind. These had con-nected him now to those he lost by failure to maintain communication as part of this collective whole he would try to honor. None of those living losses mat-tered as he no longer needed to agonize over forget-ting to reach out. After he left his childhood home, he changed locations on average every six months for the last twenty-odd years. Sometimes a move was se-vere, and he lost all contact, especially for those who lived in villages or on the edge of war. Even as it no longer mattered, the residual guilt of forgotten people who mattered so much at certain times was im-possible to discard completely. He wondered how some camp had changed when the military next door decimated the government and exacted punishment on children in forest villages. He knew them and then he didn't. Or the friends with newborns for whom he always postponed congratulations. They were gone, nonetheless. Weren't they? He based the entirety of his assumption on the fact that he saw no one in the Washington area for approximately six weeks and this was bolstered by a lack of updated material online, which allowed him to stretch his assumption globally. He also assumed that since the power grid was still active around him, that it must still be active everywhere. It struck him how utterly ethnocentric this cluster of assump-tions really were. That there were worlds of possi-bility where millions if not billions of people lived out their days much like he, but without electricity and thus without Internet. Or, that he was only looking at his corner of the anglophone Internet and missed a vast community of people already reconnecting in this apocalypse. Still, he only had access to the information available, all of which indicated that he was alone. No hopeful dickering on the efficacy of data would help him in the here and now.

His moment by moment progress so far had been haphazard and unstructured survival that, if sustained, would lead to a descent into frustration. While he started out systematically with checking in on lines of communication and the information sources available, it was the rudderless drift that characterized his more recent days. He had been a follower to his curiosity as it led him from place to place, to test the boundaries that no longer seemed in place. He felt much like an idiot teenager again. What he wished he'd done was maintain the system and structure of those early days, particularly in terms of his home invasions, which were brazen and silly. Each time he entered, he was surprised by his surprise at what he found and how he went about finding it. Of course there would be piles of laundry that once held a person. Of course those piles would have belonged to the full spectrum of age groups and many of them would be children. Of course most of the doors would be locked, and he would either need to break in or figure out a softer way. What he needed was a new system for this that would help him efficiently understand who lived in the homes while also lingering long enough to strip them of useful items. He certainly could not crash a night in different homes drunkenly pondering parties and wake up with hypersensitivity. This would have to begin with the doors and maintain the politeness of small talk before moving on to the business of collection.

This didn't answer the question of what would be his purpose. He estimated that he could find most food from the groceries that had stock to supply millions of the metro area residents, so it certainly could sustain him for years to come. So why enter homes at all? How many homes? If he wanted to memorialize humanity, how would he do this exactly. As he drove, his mind drifted to the backseat and to the trophies still scattered on the floor in a large home in Ashburn. He quite enjoyed this feeling, even if tinged with a might of guilt. True, he could get these from stores as well, but there was a difference between a display shelf and an in-home demonstration to pique one's interest. So this would be his goal. Enter for the fun stuff, but stay for the memorial. He gamed out what a memorial would have looked like last night. A gathering of neighbors shooting the shit without their children. If he only searched the household, then he'd miss the reality of the final moments for almost a dozen people. He'd have to take them as they were; take the powder and the massager along with the wedding rings and photos. This was they. This was a good plan. For them. It did little for him in his own grief. Sure, he would relent bits of the pressure as he continued through this, but it still left him alone and living through a vicarious community of strange ghosts. And these ghosts would be laden with items that, as he continued, would accumulate quickly. Just a single house, or two if you count the first of the night, led him to haul away a new car, a stereo, and an arsenal. This did not account for the trophies he left behind but now planned to save in the future. He decided that the accumulation could be dealt with at another time, when his patience was not stretched as it was as he drove. His was a small corner of the city and there was unlimited space for him to use as storage until then.

He pulled up into Arlington having left these thoughts behind. In the calm, he tried to imagine a return home at that moment knowing he would continue to rehash these same thoughts endlessly until he took substantial steps towards actualizing them in order to shut his mind off from the plans. He passed any number of homes where he could begin, especially knowing that he had space in the car for more. But he was tired of strangers and wanted more connection. He knew very few people in this city, but he did know one quite well.

He turned a corner, headed to a long-time friends apartment a few miles away in Falls Church. Jack was one of the first few numbers he tried to reach that first night, knowing that his friend was awake either at work or home. He and Jack knew one another from law school and maintained the sort of intermittent communication that men prefer. Jack was the one who convinced him to move to the area, partly because he had just gone through a divorce and struggled to re-build his life in the ashes. He made the move, mostly because all the humanitarian organizations had offices in the city, but also so he could help Jack out of crisis. The tightness of Arlington and the clusters of homes around the metro stations intensified, and he wondered if it was a mistake to leave Ashburn and the openness of the yet-undeveloped suburb. Jack lived in a small apartment near the metro, since he spent nearly all his time at his office downtown. Jack al-ways said that there was no point to a larger place since he was never really there. He pulled up to the block of some forty units which had assigned parking, all of which were now taken.

Even in the apocalypse, he could not find a spot, so he left the Audi in the middle of the road outside Jack's shared entry, which was heavy in design but had a large glass panel. Not interested in fucking around with a better way, and contrary to his diligent theo-ries about methodology, he decided the best way in would be to simply shoot the glass out and reach in to unlatch it from the inside. Mindful of ricochet, he went across the street with a scoped hunting rifle and punctured the glass in four places without seeing it fall away. A closer inspection showed that he could simply bash in the safety glass and push it the rest of the way. Once inside, he felt a bit disappointed by the glass and broken tiles in the vestibule and told himself to do better next time, but never mind. He rounded the stairs that he often took to reach the second floor apartment with a vague understanding that he might not be able to get inside. Jack usually for-got to lock his door and the chance of this was about 50/50. Whenever Jack was out of town for extended pe-

riods, he would stop by to water plants and occasionally worked from their. To do this, he had his own
spare key, but that was back on his keychain that he
didn't need when he left the day before.

Unfortunately, the door was locked. Still rattled by
so quickly ignoring his own new rule about sensitivity
to the structures of homes, but mostly due to disinterest in a bullet that might come back to him, he decided against shooting out the lock. One useful as-
pect of city density is that there is rarely a fire
station too far away. He recalled that there was one
across the street, where he would certainly find a
breaching ram or other tools. Once there, these were
not difficult to find as everything had already been
organized for quick retrieval in the event of an emergency, such as the need to break into an apartment after humanity disappeared. It was ungodly heavy for a
small instrument. He dragged it back upstairs and
groaned with the strain of aching muscles. Without
the training to ram a door, he accomplished it with
inefficiency. He assumed without reason that the best
place would, of course, be the center of the door.
This caused the ram to bounce back at him as the
door's wobble absorbed the shock. Not wanting to try
this again, he aimed for the door handle and lock, but
missed and caught the handle itself, which nearly sent
him to the floor as he fought to regain control of the
ram. More experienced now, he managed several soft
but firm lands just above the handle, thus allowing
the door to give way a bit more each time. By the
last attempt, he was able to drop the ram and shove
with his shoulder to pop inside.

He knew this place well. He and his family stayed
here their first month back from overseas, not wanting
to spend on an absurdly priced BnB rental. Not much
rearrangement had happened since then, so everything
was in the right place. He looked with new eyes at
what had been placed on the shelves and understood
them in the new context of empathy for suffering. He
saw the photo of Jack and his son, whom he was only
able to see every other week. Before, this felt en-

dearing and joyful that he still had family, but now seemed like a tragic waste of human effort to invest so deeply in the petty fights and terror that humans wielded on those they had formerly loved so much. That divorce was protracted and the custody fight had been ongoing. The smiles from this photo predated all that. The one down below did not. That one showed grim and photo-ready smiles at an event onto which so much pressure was placed to have a good time while time was available. Eyes showed the difference.

He found Jack in the bedroom, between the bathroom and the bed. He must have locked the door for the night and finished his shower. There was no TV in the room. Jack was a vicious reader and spent as much time as he could, applied to the task. But looking around, there were no open books, just a laptop with a dead battery on top of a file with its contents spilled out. This was the late Friday night work of a desperate profes-sional who held onto the structure of the week and had the reputation as a high value acquisition at his firm. Jack was wealthy, but his wealth was split be-tween households, and he saved what he could to make even more available to his son. From under the file, the corner of a small leather book peaked. This did not look like part of the ensemble, so he reached for it, tossing the irrelevant papers aside as he did. This was a private journal, with a pen to mark where his friend had last been writing. He opened to that page and made out the strings of words but could not make out the individual letters sufficiently to read any of the meaning that Jack wanted to preserve that night. He flipped through and saw that he could not read any of Jack's scribbling hand, but he did see the various sketches that showed enough. These were the drawings of harsh living.

He had been gathering items he found and now had more in his hand that seemed necessary to carry, so he placed them into arrangements on the counter. The photos, the journal, the many trinkets from travels like refrigerator magnets and wall decorations. All this piled up onto the counter and began threatening to spill off to the floor as he darted around the apartment grabbing more along the way. They soon did spill to the floor and decided to form a pile in the hallway outside. In a way, he felt like he was moving on Jack's behalf, but moving from a hotel or dormitory where one leaves behind all the furniture and dishes. Soon enough, it was out of control, and he decided he would need containers to keep everything from spilling as he made his way to the car. The second bedroom was a home office that was a throwback to the pandemic. Jack had long since returned to the office full time as his home was his prison. Since then, it became a receptacle for boxes of client files he took home to review over weekends. There were dozens stacked on wire shelves and were perfect to hold the items in the hallway with their inbuilt handles. But what to do with the files themselves, which represented the narrative of important issues to some people who also vanished and needed to be remembered? This was too much for him. A line needed to be drawn.

He brought the empty boxes out to the hallway and examined the piles he made. Good god there was a lot. It seemed like everything was important, so he needed to use more discretion else he'd come away with the entire house. He couldn't. Everything was needed. Not two months before, he would have called all this junk to be discarded. Not now. Now were the only remnants of a close friend's personal world and this visit was his effort at saying goodbye. He had no willpower to return or even think about what was left behind, so this visit needed to be the last. And now that so much importance was at play, he had begun to remove his friend entirely from the house and take him home, rather than remember him more carefully. As he looked, it began to dawn on him that so much of what he brought out was in fact an item of shared memory between them. These were as many mementos of his own family as they were of Jack. This plastic cup that Jack brought back from a visit to Hershey park on his custodial week was actually the cup that his own son loved to use when they stayed at the apartment. These items here were from a trip they all shared where Jack played the eternal third wheel. Nearly everything on some level had a dual meaning that had led him to pick it up and only then begin the process to consider it. In this way, it was as if he was not remembering Jack at all. Jack's friendship and identity had become consumed by his own life that drove what he considered defining. Once this idea took root, he felt there was nothing at all of his friend loaded into the boxes, as if his very memory had been wiped even from his own home that itself was nothing more than a station where he slept. Wouldn't it be better to go to Jack's office or his ex-wife's home and invade their son's room to find what that child felt were the most important memories with his father? He felt there was little point to him even being there to sort through the mess at all. He would not find his friend. But is that what he even wanted? Was he really in search of someone gone or the indicators of what they shared, even as it diluted Jack's essence? Jack was gone and had no memory. The only meaning in that memory acted through his observation in the here and now, in the celebration of when and where their lives commingled. This needed to have a nexus that he himself felt vital, not what Jack's absent opinions might hypothetically say. Loss is memory. And these are the personal possession of those who survive and not in the acts or items that are poor replacements. There could be no dishonor in diluting his friend since only his own memory was left.

This was a bit of liberation and helped to end the selection crisis. He would be free to keep the stupid plastic cup that was an invaluable item that represented the continuity of friendship and family. There were others. He went back inside to the bedroom to continue his search. He already checked the side table and found unimportant sundries, so he went over to the sundries drawer and found a small leather satchel that he expected held a manicure set or similar hardware. Almost ready to toss it aside, he stopped because of the way it was worn from regular use. It might have been old, perhaps a family artifact from other generations. It was a needle and tourniquet set. The set remembered to bring a friend. The small packet of mystery white powder brought up fears of accidentally inhaled fentanyl or touching the residue only to wake up in a stupor. It was as if electrified and his hands failed to let go from a live current.

Memory has many rooms. Some rooms are old but never discovered. Had he known this fact about Jack? He pulled a slip of paper under the needle and unfolded it. Jack had written times and doses and the last was a time with no dose adjacent. He knew the time calculation of an addict who learned to pace the process to remain outwardly functional. He saw through the schedule and felt the dual pressures on its author. He knew that addiction at this level bled through into every interaction and thought for Jack. Every moment away from his schedule was a moment unfulfilled. Even time with his son would be timed against the tightness of this schedule. This, of all things he found, were the most Jack. Any effort to ignore this would cross over from loving shared memory to violent revision. This must go into the Jack box alone with nothing else unless it was ready to stand and bear the weight of this responsibility. Everything in the hall would need to be sorted again against this benchmark by which Jack could be isolated from the world. As he continued his search through this new lens, he found several items of the highest caliber to put aside. He went more slowly than before, when he treated Jack's home as wastefully as he had a stranger's. These were three very long days full of emotion. In them, he managed to pull away from himself and then reenter. The house was now slightly barren and the piles from the hall found their way into boxes that found their way into the car downstairs. Most of them. He could not take everything back home in one trip, but he decided to go home and return with the delivery truck so that he could finish loading, then begin his systematic memorial there with Jack's neighbors. When he returned that night, he continued for as late as he could before going to sleep in Jack's bed.

It took him a week of intensive effort to make his way through all the other units in the small complex. Without the diversion of emotion, his work went more quickly than before. He already knew to focus on the hidden world inside a home, then use that to understand the world on display. This gave him insight into the fears that lurked and needed so much outward curation to mask. All of that he took was loaded into boxes or bags that now filled the delivery truck to its fullest. He was unused to such a weighty vehicle. Not since his youth, when he rented moving trucks had he loaded a large diesel to feel it rock and threaten to tip as he drove. Without traffic, though, he simply drove slowly through the streets and bashed only few trees that were celebrating the loss of pruning sheers. He arrived home, of sorts, as his pack had thinned out from boredom, even though he left food everywhere for them to eat. He parked the truck back where it had rested before, not daring to unload the full compartment. As he unloaded the Audi, though, he felt a pull in the back of his mind that told him he was not finished at Jack's. This kept pulling as he installed the stereo to became more articulated as the music came through. He needed to destroy the building or else he would always feel the need to return and piece together more of the puzzles he found over there. He needed to effect its disappearance and let the partial memories continue as incomplete representatives of the homes, or else they could never actually become memories, just fragments of a living whole. He returned. With gasoline.

With a bit of dusting in each unit and a combustible line of fuel from each to the hallways and down the stairwells, he cleared the paths to make a rapid exit should something go wrong too early. His head swam in the fumes of this planned immolation that was not an act of clumsy destruction. When he lit the pool at the ground floor, the flame spread across the surface of the hallway up to the floors above. He cleared out to the other side of the street where he decided there would be no better place to watch the cremation than from a chair in front of the pump truck at the ready inside the station. It took longer than he thought to see the black of smoke as it took root on mattresses and furniture inside. Up to that moment, he somehow felt that he could rapidly intervene and stop the waste, but he knew this moment was gone as soon as the flame from the small lighter found a new home then expanded far through to the interior. This was an odd sensation to realize the smallness of the transition from a curious act to become an irresistible force. Soon, the flames appeared, then he could hear the structural damage inside as new fuel was found deep in crevices of the building. No one was inside. He was sure.

The show was on and beginning to lose its original thrill. The confirmation of his work now complete, he began to move on to think where he should go next. Under his system, he aimed to reach across the city and further if permitted. Would he hold the same end for each? What would be lost and irretrievable that should not be so? In this city, so many of the homes were rich in history even if they lacked a brass placard to brag about it. These should not be destroyed, he accepted, but he struggled to demarcate the line for acceptable arson. The question turned on how to define history, especially whose history mattered. A rough thought exercise came up with dozens of lines to be drawn, most with competing conclusions. The colonial homes were clear, as were those from before World War II. What about the then-cookie cutter boxes of the great migration and the post-war era of prosperity, in all their banality? Should he keep the post-civil rights public housing blocks that emerged from blight, or even those still remaining behind? All those built behind the generations of shameful redlines? History is history, except when it's not. He looked at a new build down the street. The metro area was full of these new row houses that, while quite comfortable inside, lacked what he felt was longevity. He could muster no nostalgia for them, just as maybe he would not for new homes in any era. But there now would be no social fabric to enmesh their images and create a history. They may burn.

The row houses were cleared out in a few days. They had various people living within them, where some were owners who began the process of making their marks on the new palate, while others were renters with their hodgepodge of storage containers of a life lived that never takes root. They all expired in flames as he moved on to look for a new community. He repeated this every few days, sometimes a bit longer for the more dense communities. In keeping with his respect for history, he made efforts to vary the type of home and possible profile of the occupants, using cars in the area as a proxy indicator for socio-economic levels, since he felt this would control for hidden gentrified communities that otherwise appeared blighted. He planned to follow along grocery and discount retail stores, with a preference for food deserts if he wanted to target a poor community. Over the course of a bit more than a week, he had managed to clear several blocks but had given up on the catharsis of leaving smoldering remains behind. Occasionally. For the most part, though, he left homes intact and loaded their treasures into his trucks.

His targeting worked, and he managed to learn about a large range of people over the weeks, particularly in the dense areas of Northern Virginia where you can find sherpa level diplomats living next to school teachers and lawyers. But working people and the heads of missions clustered elsewhere. He took pains to reach them all and kept to the same system of approach for each home he entered: disable the door locks, check the drawers and shelves furthest from the front, then sweep the common areas and leave. It was a system designed to gloss the surface but seep into the obvious cracks when they appear. Over time, he was rarely surprised by anything in the homes as he began to see alignment in accordance with economic commonalities. Inside homes of immigrants and citizens alike, he found more of a relationship based on what he already presumed from the stand-in indicators he devised. Racial differences fell away too, except when there was over-representation outside. The homes he visited let him peak into this world in rapid succession and with the disinterested eye of an investigator seeking out just a minimum threshold of identity so that he could move on to the next. On occasion, he would be emotionally moved, but this lessened with more homes he visited. He knew that wealth was uncommon, even in the DMV, so he skewed more towards areas where he felt he'd find less. But he still checked in on the expensive communities of Bethesda and Langley. These took more time to sweep, and he felt they slowed him down, but he found more to take from these homes and load separately from the boxes of people in his trucks. He felt guilty as he would look with disgust at the conditions of some homes in poor communities and relief in the homes of the wealthy areas, but he knew this was a normal condition. The quality of life in the nice homes of America were of the highest standard available to any human in any point of history. Even if they lacked the lacing of luxury, they still had the undertone of quality and comfort unseen elsewhere in the city. By contrast, homes in a state of poverty were categorically behind. In absolute terms, they were still far ahead of poverty he saw elsewhere in the world, and even outpaced the wealth found in history. But he knew this language. It was the gloss that marked the age since he was born. This was the rising tides lifts all boats fiction, flooding be damned. It was the language that let poverty fester and watched people suffer the grinding weight to celebrate the achievements of so few who could have done none of it alone. Poverty anywhere was rife with the opportunity costs that burden exacts just to maintain some stability. He recalled a memory where he joined one grandmother when she went out to other people's land to collect scraps of corn ears that fell during the harvest. They spent the day wringing the kernels out by hand into a sack that could be sold for little more than the cost of a few food staples. It took all day. She was eighty years old. He saw this again in homes he entered with piles of coupons cut out and readied for the next grocery run. He saw the small portions of food and packs of household goods that were priced high per unit, but to purchase in bulk would have meant eroding more of salary. Poverty everywhere demands careful planning and hard work that is absent with money.

No, absolute poverty was always the lie that assimilated into modern civilization. Absolute poverty and the policy of basic needs made invisible the injustice of coupon saving and bottle recycling. This was swallowed in the rush to compete for the attention of capital and celebrate notions of zero-sum conflict. It had failed miserably, but history is never history. He knew before he took this journey that relative inequality was the right and just indicator of social health. He saw firsthand the social order unravel into violence when these levels reached a critical tipping point, which always meant this would be met with propaganda and violence from vested interests that had captured the state policymaking processes. He saw it on January 6, too. This misguided and anti-democratic mass of discontent was no different from others he saw. It was a release of pressures built up over a generation and exported across the planet as it was welcomed by corrupt ethnonationalism everywhere who squandered the era of social protection. Of course there would be a populist movement metastasizing around abhorrence. There could be no other way to capture the diffused anger of homes that could no longer even afford the luxury of politics. A simple entry into some homes was stifling. He could feel the exhaustion in apartments with multiple staff cards and uniforms tossed near empty milk bottles and half-eaten dinners. The rows of medication on cluttered tables beside TV chairs. Absolute terms were meaningless inside. Only tired anger was home. Still, it was not absolute misery. This was not the poverty of cholera and child wasting. That it was not picturesque misery meant it could be swept aside as a problem of self achievement, which is the worst violence the system had on hand to disseminate. In more than a few homes, he saw collections notices for breathtakingly overpriced emergency room visits or for student loans that had capitalized interest well into the triple digits. And these were not always the homes of the poor. He found service of process papers for credit cards and car loans in homes that were outwardly very expensive. In one of these homes, he found a half drunk bottle near loaded a handgun that fell to the floor in a basement bathroom. Those who in the generation before would have seemed ordinary and were now called wealthy also felt the crush of the system. He found this in some manner in nearly every home and learned to ferret out the unique household flavor. Would it be the long working hours away from small children where one care-taker had to drop from the workforce in order to avoid the college tuition level costs needed for daycare or to educated children under five? Perhaps in a neigh-bor it would be the car accident and medical bills while waiting for the insurance claim to pay out. He saw lots of students raising children alone and busi-nesses that were failing. He looked for this. But in the homes of wealth, all this was usually hidden so as to not disrupt the outward image. In many of these homes, he found more debt and more fear than else-where. Invariably, this was masked by overcompensa-tion that likely led to a further slide into debt. The hard work of pretending seemed similar to the hard work of poverty, but this was only superficial when you think about the relative inequalities involved. Then you lost patience for its cowardice.

When the distress was large enough, it became a resi-dent with its own identity and its own social status within the hierarchy. If it was severe enough, the signs of trauma and toxic stress were everywhere in the house. Even the small pile of a child's pajamas in a corner behind the sofa with an adult's pile too close by were an incomplete image until you saw the empty bottles on the counter. He found children sleeping in beds with meth pipes in the next room. He found soiled hospital beds upstairs and piles of ciga-rettes in soda cans on the front porch. He found them as they lived in anticipation of the weekend ahead.

Not all was grim, of course. The homes of the mundane were aplenty. Homes of clutter did not always hide demons, and he found many homes that spoke of safety if low in their standard. Homes of wealth did not always front an image. He had to learn to quiet his bias as he made his house selection and allow himself to absorb what lay inside. There was little pattern that he could grasp from the outside, or even immediately after he entered, as every home was a unique exposure to surprise. One pattern that did emerge, across all houses, was the clear need to fight for more resources in what could only make sense as a belief in the zero-sum conflict outside each door. Few homes gave the feel of a settled state. There were always projects finalizing or starting or in preparation. Boxes and stacks always stood by to find a new location. There was always a hustle in every home, but not just the hustle of people. These were the movements of resources at the ready, waiting for more. America's motion and materialism was never a secret, but now as all this motion ceased, and he saw it in context from inside the homes; it depressed him. He saw the endlessly marshaled resources evolve from the clamor of survival to the greed of excess with no endgame. No limitations, whether ephemeral or structural. It just moved and he saw no point. The only operation it effected was in its violence on those stuck beneath the threshold of greed, held there by the power of those privileged enough to enjoy greed. And in the zero-sum rigmarole, this greed captured the exclusive right to greed and defended its monopoly with little difference between what he saw in the worst countries of the world.

As this exercise progressed through the weeks, he changed from resentment at the houses of wealth. He had to. His house was one in a neighborhood of affluence far above many of the mansions he visited. His wealth was a windfall, and he was compelled to empathize with those homes that clearly were not acquired under the privilege of generational wealth. He forced himself to strip bare the boundaries of class and focus on the system itself that exploited the obviousness of class distinctions. It was an agonizing evolution from the early grift of the Chicago school, with its capture of the American judicial system that learned to stand back from facts in an intellectually dishonest frame that courts were ill-equipped to adjudicate technical facts, even as all evidence clearly showed the need for judicial oversight. This unleashed the consolidation and supra-nationalization of the drivers of inequality that, once so large, could never be controlled again by any political system. Of course this would lead to humiliation and suffering. Immense loss must only be a statistic under this consolidation where flesh competed with legal fictions for the right to political integrity and dignified life. Whatever the cause for the end of civilization, he could not lament the loss of such a system.

For four weeks he invaded and burned homes. He was angry, he was sad, and he was inspired all alongside the piles of laundry he found inside and their personal secrets. He had gone through over a hundred different homes, but he did not destroy all of them. Somewhere in the mix, he had lost the drive to destroy and saved it for his uncontrollable moments of impulse. This had not come often. When it did, he would save it for the end of the day so that he could sit and watch before driving his loaded truck home. Altogether, the system worked. He had no relapse and felt no temptation in the stew of temptations he found. His mind was preoccupied. His mornings were average. Depending on when he arrived home, he would unload the treasure that night, so he could roll out at whatever time he felt ready. Generally this was around 09:00, give or take. At the start of the fifth week, he walked out to the street and stopped for a bit to view the line of trucks that had accumulated down the street from him, blocking that egress. Aside from the first, which he had on hand from his trip to the warehouse, he had gone to a moving truck rental depot. These were much longer than the delivery truck and carried far more, but were also more difficult to drive through the narrow streets. But each was completely full except for the last two, which were in line for this week.

Over the past four weeks, he covered areas from Gaithersburg to College Hill, down to Mount Vernon.

He was exhausted. His body ached from the constant moving and the daily impact of surprises in their many forms that pulled him from his efforts at emotional detachment. The night before had been an especially challenging drive back from Springfield due to heavy rain that caused some floods along the way after an already difficult afternoon. It only made sense to him that he stay in for the day and let himself take a rest, rather than push to the brink of burnout. He had done so much over the weeks and loaded five full sized trucks and the one delivery truck, each with a load that touched the ceiling and barely allowed for him to close the door, which was always the mark for when to swap to a new one. He was still rattled from the day before where the house had been full of rotting pets that were trapped inside with no food. The people there had brought in their four dogs and what he estimated were three cats, which combined with the unknown number of birds in the two cages. The sight was grotesque. There was feces in every room and most of the animals had been eaten by those who stayed behind to starve more slowly. But they all went, and the house was a well sealed nightmare that was infested with ants, roaches, and rats. The smell hit him as he walked up to the door, but he had already encountered this from other houses and decided to enter anyway. Once in, he recoiled but, according to a rule he set for himself, he pushed his way in to complete a job once the door was open. He wretched several times before gaining composure. Though he finished quickly, the stink stayed with him the rest of the day. Such was not atypical. He encountered cannibalized pets in many houses before. The worst was a home where a small toy dog had managed to hide from its larger dog friends, until they starved. Somehow it managed to survive them and then survive on them until he arrived. By then, it was frail and dehydrated from constant diarrhea caused by eating rotten meat. He fed it and nursed it, but it didn't survive his pack. They tore it apart after a few days.

But hospitals were the worst experience so far. Up to when he began process of entering homes, he had not thought about the need to check hospitals. Before then, he focused on confirmation that he was alone and this was achieved by simply roaming the streets. There was no reason to go to these facilities. Curiosity brought him. He felt that the long-term patients living at Sibley should benefit from his system of memorializing. Hospitals are eerie at the best of times, but he now wandered through an empty one that had begun its night shift and had partly shuttered. He found the signs of staff and patients milling about and something in him signaled the urge to check the morgue. Perhaps a vestigial fear of zombie apocalypse that he managed to push out if his mind. Once down there, he reluctantly opened a cabinet and saw a woman on the drawer. He did not check others. He panicked and ran to the first exit and scrambled around outside, unsure where his truck was parked. He drove home, which was not so far away, and locked himself in the bedroom with his arsenal and emergency rations of protein bars for the next three days before he calmed down enough to leave again. His curiosity was satiated and he did not return.

Looking at the trucks now, he tried to imagine how many people he captured and stored in their compartments. There were five and a half full trucks, but he found that he could not come up with a number. He tried to recall how many houses, assuming that each house averaged three people, but he had forgotten this as well. At any rate, he could see that there were six trucks that completely walled off an entire intersection at one end of his street. This made him fee more crowded in than normal in the tight Georgetown neighborhood. This would continue to annoy him, so he felt that a more sustainable solution be found. Given his location and the contents of the trucks, it made sense for him to take them to one of the large open spaces around the city. Since these were intended as memorials to those lost during various crises, he felt that it would also be appropriate to take them to Arlington cemetery. By the time he showed up with the first truck, he still hadn't formed a better plan than the vagueness of taking the trucks inside. In addition to this, the gates had been locked for the night, and he was obliged to ram them open before he could enter. The question of where to go was now at the fore. He thought that leaving the trucks at the reception building was off-tone as would be a burial in the lots, which would be too much work as well. The thought was that cemetery itself was massive, so six trucks could be parked almost anywhere inside. But it felt wrong to simply abandon them parked, given the gravitas of their contents. He thought back to his original intent before he began it all, and he had a mind to create some kind of new memorial to the fallen. He lacked the creativity or skills for this, but still thought it right. Maybe some of those in the boxes were veterans, but who cared now? With everyone gone all at once, those lost rose to the level of a national tragedy, if you thought of all humanity in terms of national interest.

He decided to drive up to Robert E. Lee's house overlooking the eternal flame. The house had been a garrison of Union soldiers and Arlington was itself a personal punishment to Lee for insurrection. Housing some of the memories of the last generation of Americans made sense given this history. These were the last of the Union that ended his insurrection after the staggering loss of life for the time. In these trucks were the descendants of enslaved people commingled with the American aristocracy on equal status, some of whom may in turn have been descendants of the secession and insurgency. Either way, it made sense, and he drove up the hill and began the long process of unloading into the museum. It took a few days to park, unload and return with new cargo. It was, in fact, backbreaking work unlike the process of loading them initially, since this involved short spurts pocketed with slow interludes of home inspection. Unloading the trucks was a series of all-out sprints to stash something in a random space inside the museum and repeat. He had focused on the ground floor in the hope that he would not need the additional space upstairs, but this ran out fast and he was soon rushing up and down the stairs all day. When he finished the last load, he closed the doors and walked through the courtyard of the enslavement kitchens around to the old headstones behind them before coming back to the hill that overlooks the Eternal Flame, where the Potomac valley spread out below. From that position, the federal zones across the river were prominent. He was, again, at a fork where he had felt accomplished yet directionless and nostalgic. He went over the numbers again, as this time he tallied the loads according to what he recalled of the households. Each of the trucks held around thirty households, making an approximate total of one hundred-eighty. If he averaged three to four people for each, he had memorialized fewer than eight hundred people of the eight billion who perished. This meant, he had exhausted himself emotionally and physically for a month to touch 0.00001% of humanity; a population that only represented a particularly unique corner of one nationality. He felt that such an impact was so small that it hardly merited any sense of accomplishment at all. He'd done nothing whatsoever, not even grieved the loss of his own family as a composite through those he did. He saw it for the waste that it was. His mind fixated on the numbers that he met. The depth of stories he'd uncovered were truly rich and telling, but even if this was a waste in terms of the objective to mourn, it was successful in making the scale of loss that much more tactile in his mind. Numbers as great as eight billion or as small as 0.00001% were meaningless to the human mind. But extrapolating from the amount of physical effort it took to reach that fraction allowed him to at least understand the order of magnitude involved to multiply the effort across all communities and homes, in whatever form they took. He leaned on his experience with household surveys where the quality of data was only useful to be indicative rather than representative. This helped a bit as he made his way down the hill using stairs that would lead him to the front gate. Tired of trucks and the sound of diesel, he decided to abandon the final truck and walk back across the bridge to Georgetown not far away. His body felt light without the weight of boxes and bags, and it was no longer hot in the middle of the day.

On his way to the tidy home, he first passed his own family home that he still had avoided ever since he left. It had actually come upon him by surprise. It was still early, and he was not yet smitten with sleep, so he convinced himself to go inside. The rush of memories hit him on the back of familiar smells that had lingered inside but were washed clean from his nose over the weeks. Of course, there was must. The house had been alive when he shut it, so the layer of aged grime in hidden places had built up a stronger presence than before, but all the familiarities remained. Cushions still smelled like the mix of a woman's lotion and perfume. He saw bits of food that dropped from his son's plate as he watched a movie and played in the den. He knew that this would not be a slash and burn visit. He had no stomach to confirm finality on his loss as he was so quick to exact for others. This was unhealable rawness. No system could help him here. Unable to grasp any guidance from inside himself, he mindlessly opened the coat closet near the front door and sat down to look at the collection of shoes at the bottom. More than any single items in the home, these felt the most full of memories. Every scuff of his son's shoe was a moment when he was vibrantly alive. The wearing of the sole reminded him exactly how his son walked, and he could still see his gait. The order and disorder showed him what mindset his wife was in as she rotated her shoes and those least used at that time were the most ordered in the closet. This scratch of bare floor covered over told him everything. He shut the door and left it to timelessness, then went to the other rooms to pick and choose what mementos were valuable enough to take but not important enough to keep in place. Everything made him pause. Those bits of food were important. The dirty dishes and the leftovers in the freezer were important. As he passed through the house, he realized he had inverted his process and left in place everything that spoke about his life the loudest and took that which murmured the image he and his wife constructed for the outside world. That was okay. He knew the representation behind these and did not need to disturb the secrecy of the home. He managed to cull a box of photos, important items that had already been put into storage, and other things before sealing up his museum to walk the rest of the way to the tidy house down the street, which was now free from the clutter of trucks. It was already decided that he would not continue his home invasion memorializing bullshit anymore and the invasion of his own home reinforced this. He felt accomplished in what he wanted, which was to begin the process of honest grieving.

Once he reached inside, he placed his box on the counter and looked about at the piles of treasure he collected from his month of work. This home was now an untidy home in the process of accumulation and readiness, much like what he found in others. However, there was no such thing as zero-sum anymore. America had achieved the full index of absolute equality and everything everywhere was for his taking, if and when he so decided. For the moment, he decided to sit down in a world of cartoons and bridge the gap to his world with one of the cannabis sodas he brought home from a dispensary.

V

Frayed Knot

He spent the rest of September in a state of retirement, splitting time between his untidy home in
Georgetown and his party home in Ashburn, which he
cleared of refuse and laundry during his generalized
home invasion. He went through the whole neighborhood
and found all the children had a sleepover down the
street. He cleared the collection of wine as well,
though more due to the fact that it annoyed him than
as any prophylactic to a relapse that had not come.
He visited the Maserati home and discovered it was
just the modest bachelor pad of a program manager for
a cloud storage monopoly whose Dalit family had yet to
join him from Bangalore, not the home of a country
club prick he assumed it would be. Most of his time
in either house centered around video games and
cannabis edibles. He began to go through the library
of retro games with great difficulty, with the help of
cheat codes in many cases but mainly played sandbox
games where he would be able to delve deep into side
quests and ignore the main storyline. These were the
closest he came to human interactions and his mind had
begun to unravel as he began to identify with them, so
he weaned off this for a time.

With no shortage of museums or public spaces where the
achievements of humanity were on full display, including the darkness with the numerous cemeteries for the
enslaved, he made his rounds. He went through the national gallery and carted in sofas so that he could
sit and absorb an exhibit in and out of naps. But he
was not yet free to breach the protective glass to
handle any of the displays, out of reverence for
preservation standards, though he did help himself to
climb into Discovery's cockpit and mill about in her
fuselage. The rest of the time took advantage of Ash-

burn's proximity to the farmland of rural Virginia that was perfect for cycling tours. Having learned his lesson from before, he carried a rod that was long enough to bash the head of any approaching dogs, which were abundant. He was able to dip deep into Virginia and would sleep in homes as it suited him.

Towards the end of the month, he took the scenic drive out to Harper's Ferry and nearly destroyed the Audi in the process of avoiding all the fallen debris. This was always a trip his family wanted to take but never scheduled as it involved a substantial drive from the city but only a moderate drive from the party house. Several severe late summer storms had left the road a disaster full of downed branches and undisturbed mud flows, making what should have only been a forty-minute drive into three hours. On arrival, not much had changed in a hundred-fifty years, and he had the odd experience of walking through a ghost town that had been a renovated ghost town ready for tourists. He did all those things, but he did try to spend one night in the officer's quarters and felt it too sur-real. For the rest of the week, he had set up a camp in the ruins of the episcopal church below the ceme-tery, since it struck a nostalgic vibe with its rock walls and overgrown grass. But really he had grown tired of invading homes and preferred the ease of camping. The spookiness of the cemetery was bespoke the first night, but he somehow managed to feel con-nected rather than scared. In fact, the only discom-fort was that the nights were now cold and he had un-derprepared, so he could stand only a few nights be-fore leaving.

He drove straight through to Georgetown without stop-ping over in Ashburn, and he arrived towards the evening. He pulled up and spent the usual amount of time with his pack, but dragged some new food out from a storage container he brought in for the purpose. The number of individual dogs fluctuated every time he came and went, when the gravitational effect of new food was not present. When he assumed he would be gone for a while, he would leave enough food out, but dogs generally are bad at conservation and would burn through it quite fast. Some of the more enterprising of the pack would disband to seek out new food sources, but they usually came back again after a few days when he returned. What was more surprising to him this time was that the lights in the house would not turn on. He had noticed some hint of this as he drove, because some of the usual lights about the city appeared off, but he barely noticed and was then unsure if he noticed it correctly. Now the confirmation was unmistakable as he could find nothing with power inside. He went room by room to toggled switches for lights and electronics with equal disappointment. His boilerplate solution was to check the breaker, once he could find it. Nothing. By then, it was dusk. In the past, there had been residual lights on in homes that he could have used as a spot check, but he had shut all these off some while back to give his neighborhood that less lonely feel. He had to manually go inside these homes to check them as well. He walked several blocks checking a few homes here and there. Still nothing. An impulse of panic rose up, so he drove to what he assumed was far enough away to be on a different part of the power grid, to see if there had been a short in his neighborhood alone. He checked dozens of homes before heading back to sleep in the dark.

In the morning, he checked homes in Maryland and drove back out to Ashburn. All the homes in Washington lacked power. Once he crossed the bridge, he saw a return of the normal to which he'd already adjusted. But it made him realize that the legacy system that was keeping the power stations were beginning to fail, and he had better learn how to keep them running. He went back to his Ashburn house since he was never fond of Maryland and never set up any satellite homes there, even if it might still have power. This only made sense. He was quite comfortable in his new modest mansion and had set up a large projection screen and a carousel of gaming consoles to play. This was his preferred site for disappearing into other worlds and had tailored the house for the purpose. He had also found a large lap pool and gym not far away, with the requisite dry and steam saunas. This home was an island spa but farther from the dense storehouses of provisions, so he usually wouldn't spend all his time there. From this home full of comfort and distraction, he applied himself to the task of learning the basics of electrical engineering and the power grids of modern cities. The difference between coal and natural gas made sense enough, and he felt satisfied in assuming Washington had run out of fuel before the one in Leesburg. The distractions overtook him, though, and he procrastinated on further learning in favor of play. But the vagueness of problem seemed solvable enough when he considered the strength of the solar battery he had been using from time to time. This was enough to provide substantial power to a variety of appliances. When he invaded homes, he did not want to use kitchens he encountered as these were oftentimes taint by funk and filth, so he developed a practice of carting around a portable kitchenette powered by this battery. He knew that they were enough to meet most of his needs and were relatively easy to recharge. With enough, he needn't worry about the eventual end of the power grid. What he would need, would be a battery of batteries at the ready for rapid swapping out and recharge. He had not collected this many before, so he went to the local branch of the warehouse store to take the whole stock and take them in his garage. He didn't feel the pressure to begin setting up this array or have more than a few charged up, so he put the issue out of his mind for another few days.

At some point he realized how lucky he had been, not that he alone was excluded from the evaporation, but that he was able to adjust to the loss while enjoying the sameness of living standards. It had been nearly three months with continued power. Everything he read online suggested that the grid would fail within a relatively short amount of time after this lost the constant monitor by technicians. As best he could figure, it was that this moment happened when the power load was low due to the number of businesses that were closed and homes that had already wound down for the night. He was lucky, but this certainly could not continue. When he was apt to do so, he did his best to understand the verbiage of watts and electricity, but he could not, so he shifted his research away from understanding why and how electricity does what it does to how to tweak a power plant to capture all that in such a way that he stayed plugged in indefinitely. If there was such information contained in his research, he was unable to understand it. He had to dig into forum threads and blog posts that seemed to come close to the problem set he faced, but never quite reached it so the solutions and discussion topics drifted away as soon as they approached him. His technical specialty was categorically removed from this one. He spoke the language of social structures and collective behaviors, all of which is conditioned on irrational unpredictability. Not like the science of shepherding electricity. He was still stuck on the superficial problem of stemming demand from all the empty buildings.

The trails behind his house crisscrossed suburbs and industrial parks. In either direction, he would pass by the assemblage power substation transformers. There were several within a few minute's ride, and he decided that these would be worth a brief site visit to at least get a visual understanding of what equipment with which he might need to interact. They were all the same from the outside. Bare earth and gray metal spirals laced with wires that hummed a song that attested to the unholy strength within. They were marked to excess with warnings about the certainty of death should one misstep inside. He knew the fence itself would not kill, so he cut through and walked inside. The risk seemed minor in light of the need. Should he make a mistake, he would be dead before he understood what he had done. He told himself that he needed to find a solution to the power crisis as this had implications for the freezers where he collected most of his food, but as he cut the fence he could only think about his projection setup and how inconvenient it would be to constantly switch out batteries to power it. Once inside and with extreme slowness, he managed to understand how to take it offline. He tested this in a different one that he expected was not connected to his home or any of the yet unemptied groceries he planned to visit soon. It worked. For the next few days, he drove around the areas surrounding Leesburg to shut down the substations he saw. He focused on the ones closest to the industrial parks and other centers like Dulles Airport. He was busy and had successfully pulled dozens of them offline.

When he went back home, his projector would not turn on. His new project had backfired and created new load conditions to which no technician was on duty to respond. He had done the needful in terms of reducing demand to conserve electricity, but he failed to understand how the system would have needed to adapt to this change. He had fucked up and worsened himself for it. This was an obvious outcome that amplified his frustration for how avoidable it would have been with a simple test elsewhere. He felt the rise of his demon that thrilled on self-immolation and failure. Stuck between two unpleasant homes, he saw no appeal to seek out a third that might require weeks of effort only to be back in the same situation of a surprise blackout. Frustration led to commitment as he installed a battery array for his projector and kitchen. The batteries did not service the central climate system of the house. This would have required something more. Nor did it solve the impending food shortage he would face without the unlimited freezer capacity of the legacy civilization. He had already begun the shift over to dry goods for their portability, with the occasional addition of frozen meats and fruits. This could be replaced by hunting the many deer and seasonal fruit that littered the entire region. But it was the steadily decreasing temperature at night that shook him out of his delirium.

While the mid-Atlantic zone was known for its mild winters, blizzards come. The last winter in particular was warm and without snowfall, but he knew this was the high-water mark. Without the cars and industrial scale emissions that eight billion people wanted, the human contribution to climate change would begin to dissipate over time and global average temperatures should begin to fall back to mean. This long arc meant nothing for the short spate until the next winter and there was no method by which he could predict its degree. What he could predict was the need to face it without central heating if he could not bring the power back online. He'd faced winters without heating before. One area in particular was bitterly cold and prone to nightly power outages that left his space heater quite useless. It was a miserable experience full of frozen hands afraid to be washed after handling raw meat and jumping rope in the dark to generate body heat. He knew he could survive in theory, but he would do so on his own to suffer the discomforts without an audience or companion in his misery.

Since it was most likely that the Leesburg station was still running and all he had to do was figure out how to toggle the machinery to adapt to the new load demand, he was inspired to test the remainder of his patience by finishing the experiment. He pulled up to the sprawling complex that overwhelmed him and suggested that he give up at the gates. From his walk around inside the perimeter, he could hear the din of stored electricity all around him but didn't know where to begin within the complex of buildings and large equipment, some of which was familiar from his time at the substations. He found the buildings that sounded more mechanical than electrical and went inside. He chose well. This was a building that housed turbines and generators, which appeared still operational and loud as best as he could tell given the sound and the green lights on the surrounding panels. He left for one of the more quiet buildings, which he thought would be the control centers away from the machinery. Inside were walls of displays that looked like a maze of lines converging and expanding from colored blocks. Nearly everything flashed red, though some green peaked through. He sat at the terminal under it and began to tinker with entries. It was no use. His effort devolved into entropy, and he could not manage to backtrack from the sequence of steps he did to undo the ever-increasing complexity of the lines of effort. He was utterly out of his depth, so he gave up after several hours.

If for no other reason than to satisfy his obsession, he decided to drive back to Washington and see what he could do or fail to do in that power plant. There felt like no point in trying, and he knew he would be faced with another wall of unintelligible screens and buttons that effected magic just beyond his reach. He couldn't stay away. If he gave up, the cancer of thought would fight him. Like the Leesburg facility, this one also revealed its hidden power as he approached. There was the same hum of machinery and the static of latent energy inside. It was a more compact facility that felt like an artifact already as it was winding down its function. Its proximity to the legislative offices made it feel like a part of the infrastructure of government that set it apart from the facility in Leesburg. But the distinctions eroded when he began to enter doors and viewed the interior working of another world beyond his comprehension. He spent less time there. Made fewer attempts to switch red blips to green. Sat longer in despondency to watch his winter discomfort accelerate before him. This led him through a thought dream of warmer weather elsewhere, but this dwindled as he moved on to more immediate needs.

His years with unpredictable electricity had prepared him to resign himself without predictability again. He spent months at a time shifting his activities to the daylight hours, sleeping and rising with the ancient clock. He knew for how many days food could be cooked and left at room temperature without the risk of serious food poisoning. All of this was manageable in the extreme. In the other bucket of memories was the hours spent under the rattle of large diesel generators for every home and office, souring the air with the smell of fresh pollution. These were large and covered in grime from routine use. They became household objects tucked into corners or set off at the edge of lawns, behind huge walled in courtyards. Over time, the noise faded and became the ambient sounds of his day that almost felt like a presence. He recognized that the obsession to preserve the electric infrastructure was wastefulness in action. He wouldn't need a city on powered standby just to satiate his whims. He could achieve this in pockmarked fashion even without modifying his urges. His winter would be solitary. What did worry him was the implications for the nuclear plants that would soon fail across the globe without technicians to keep their reactions in check. He accepted this truth because he had no hope of squirreling away enough knowledge in time to effect any solution.

But water is different. There was always water nearby wherever he was. Maybe it was a hand pump well or a rainwater collection barrel where he could take a daily bath, boil or add some iodine, or at least clean the shit off his hands and ass. Usually it was a storage tank that drew from the city during the hours of electricity. Never had he lived with extreme water scarcity. He almost always could turn on a tap and it would magically come out for his use. Without power, he knew the treatment plants would stop circulating clean water. Clean water would stop pumping underground for him to open a tap and draw a bath. Even the idea of a bathtub full of wasted water would become a criminal act. The lack of power meant he could no longer simply open a tap and receive the flow of clean water in any home. The same was true for Georgetown as it was for Ashburn. There was no point in visiting the plant out there to confirm the same problem. He knew that the issue was less about water for cooking or bathing as it was for the toilet. He had relied on ones that received only sparse flushes in the past. The pungent smell travels far and seeps into all areas of a home. This would destroy the last of his grip of a sense of civility and would mark his decay in the truest sense. No home he could choose would then ever be a home of sterile comfort. This was by far a bigger worry that he couldn't solve.

He recalled seeing a treatment plant not far from his home in Georgetown. It was located adjacent to Sibley hospital. The degree of worry had overshadowed his fear of the cadavers, and he managed to muster the initiative for a visit to the complex that boasted a reservoir. It had been ages since he fled the hospital, and he now felt that, after months of freedom from attack, he might as well ignore that irrational imprint from childhood. Still, he eyed the doors of the hospital, now fully darkened without even the glow from their emergency lighting. It had the feel of the deepness you see between boulders where you know there rests a den of snakes. Any invasion would become an end. The car continued past and stopped him along the road far to the other side, where he could approach on foot and with greater caution.

He arrived and saw the treatment and collection pools scattered in their sequential layout that he had a vague memory of when working with other teams that focused on water. Everything would be able to continue under the power of UV and chemicals, but all was dependent on the continued flow of electricity from the main grid. Yes, there were backup generators for the emergency pumps, but these we locked behind digital access panels for which he lacked the codes. This was expected. As was the silence from the pumps or the stillness of the swirling arms in the pools. He followed his nose to the path of least odor to find the end of the processing stages, where he found the storage tanks. A brief examination showed that the delicate chlorine vapor had not dissipated, meaning the water was safe to drink. He climbed to the height of a storage tower and confirmed the same. He did this less to see if it was clean as he did to inspect how to open it, as these towers were strategically placed across the country to signal that water had been cleaned and treated by people who knew what they were doing. He looked in on the disinfection tank next and was unsure what it should look like in order to decide if he needed to do anything at all. They looked cleaner than the sludge in the solid waste separation pools or the aerator tanks, but he felt they somehow were not fully in line with the standard progression. It seemed that, while the water in the storage tanks had passed the treatment process before the technicians evaporated, the liquid in the decontamination pools backslid without their attention. This meant that he would only have the water currently stored, even if he somehow figured out how to activate the pumps. He went over and took another look at the generators. They appeared to have an RFID sensor, so he could theoretically access the generators and restart the pumps long enough to push the process along. Over time, there would be less solid waste to clean, so the technical needs of the process would be lessened as well.

The trouble with this new plan was that he would have to find the badge with the right credentials to access the pad. With the night crew the only ones on hand, this might prove more difficult and involve a complete sweep of all the buildings. He had brought with him the tools he used for so many homes, but this required another long walk under the shadow of the hospital. He ran, but the weight of everything was far too much to do this on the way back. Once inside the administration building, he looked for the security office just in case this would have the required privileges and returned to the generator. Not even a beep to indicate a denied card. The panel was dead. With the power off for as long as it was, the emergency feed to maintain the RFID sensor had gone dark. He was now another step removed from his solution. In a moment of unthinking, he pounded the panel with his palm which inspired another and then a search for something heavy to crush the pad so that he could never search for a solution to access it again. Breathing hard and satisfied, he turned around and scanned the parking lot. There was not much to see from the tightness made by the complex of buildings. One of them had hidden the fleet of maintenance vehicles and, among them, several five thousand gallon tanker trucks that were marked potable. These must have been part of a disaster response staging ground, which was perfectly suited to his current needs. Two of the trucks were

already full, and two others were on standby.   He
drove these up to an outflow valve near the main storage tank and managed to hook them up to be filled.
Unsure about whether they were cleaned and ready to be
filled at the time they were idled, he found some
chemical tablets in a cabinet where they were parked
and dropped in what he assumed was enough.

He now had a gap solution that should carry him for a
few months. These trucks were already equipped with
faucets designed for end users in mind, rather than
industrial equipment. The problem would be in trans-
ferring them into the house for use, or changing his
behavior to simply come outside whenever he wanted to
use it. This, though, seemed asinine, so he decided
that he would need smaller storage tanks in the houses
as he had in apartments before. He re-cluttered
Georgetown with trucks one by one. Unlike his delivery trucks, these were to be permanent fixtures that
buttressed the home instead of being safely sequestered down the street. They crowded him and destroyed the aesthetic he attempted when he removed all
the cars from the neighborhood. Now, it was as if he
only did this to make way for this project. Nevertheless, it was comfort to know that a sustainable solution was at hand, even if unsightly.

The solution was initially quite fine for him. He had
collected new garbage cans and used them for the bathroom and kitchen, just as he did for so many years.
The tanks had small nozzles where he could attach a
hose that was small enough to route through the house
to refill these on a drip. The main complaint was the
lack of heated water, which was tolerable and often-
times irrelevant in the tropics but quite unpleasant
in his late September climate. He also grouched about
the number of stairs in the narrow and tall home that
matched all the narrow tallness for the rest of the
area. This was mainly a problem of water pressure to
force the flow up to the third floor, so he began to
use only the basement bathroom, which lacked a tub.
These were minor but important. When he had wanted a
bath, he would have to boil large pots and carry them

upstairs one at a time. He recalled doing this one
morning when the heat went out in an eastern Oregon
winter, but it seemed as ridiculous then as now. The
irritation was with him as he swapped the now empty
first truck for the second after about three weeks.
He looked at the line of trucks as he returned the
newly full first truck to the back of the queue. He
decided that he'd grown tired of the confined living
in the city and the shotgun row houses. He switched
off the drip, shut the house tight and dropped a month
of food for the pack before driving the trucks out to
Ashburn. Given the sparsity of the population out
there but spread over a larger distance, he discovered
that more water trucks had been stored at the main
plant than in Washington. Due to this stroke of luck,
he was able to fill six trucks and park them out of
sight.

Now mid-October, the nights were definitely cold even
as the days were still warm. As is wont, there was an
early cold front that hit and the temperature dipped
well below average and threatened an early freeze. He
had holed up in the bedroom with a propane heater running from the bathroom making everything fairly comfortable. Without an unannoying source of power for
his video game fetish he took to reading more books.
About the time of the cold front, he was reading The
Subterraneans and the image of draining a car radiator
during a freeze lingered in his mind. It took some
time to understand why this was a practice in the
1950s, but he eventually realized that the lack of an-
tifreeze would have caused the metal to burst. Although he was confident that his water trucks would
have been specially designed with insulation, he still
went out to check the manual to confirm what level of
risk he should expect. It was not good news. The
trucks would need to be drained in order to prevent
damage, so his comfortable solution was now dialed
back in its unsustainability.

He had, by that point, lived a month under the assumption that he could ride out the winter in peace at his
Ashburn home, using the cold water dripping to the

cozy downstairs guest bathroom where he had installed an outdoor propane grill in the separate shower to boil the water for his bath and enjoy a sort of makeshift steam room while he waited. This was tolerable. But it was transient. It was a warm weather vacation that couldn't last. Every stage of the last months since the evaporation was like settling down in bed only to remember one more urgent thing undone after the lights are off. What he needed was a winter plan to discard the feeling of surprise, so he made a checklist of specific categories of needs that were indispensable yet fully predictable. Of course, he would need water, and he already had a solution, but all hat was needed was to winterize the details. Food was much easier. He had long since shifted to the basics that had a much longer shelf life and could be easily stored for months of living. And whenever he was in the mood, he had taken to hunting deer. He decided to salt and smoke the meat so he could have that on hand as well. Cooking was also fairly simple, as the gas stoves had yet to give out, but he was using portable propane stoves more and more just in case. Shelter was abundant and all homes were already built to withstand the climate, though they assumed the use of heaters. For this, he could use either propane heaters or the fireplaces that all homes in Georgetown had. Mobility, however, was a challenge. He knew from headlines the severity of blizzard conditions in the area, which would turn the busiest of interstates into a snowdrift. This would be the biggest risk on which all the other categories depended, and it was by far the least predictable.

In order to safely survive the winter, he would need to keep all his store of food and water nearby so that he could reach it when and if the roads were deep under the snow. The water trucks would especially need an insulated place that would also be large enough for him to have a fleet on standby with capacity for several months in case he could not take any out to refill. He also realized that he would need to factor in the needs of his pack, which could not be expected to continue roaming the streets. They would have similar needs for a stockpile of food and water offered up in a warm place that was out of the bitter cold.

He came to the reluctant conclusion that Ashburn was inadequate when all these needs were reassembled. The portrait he saw was one predicted by the survivalists and their bunkers. They had all prepared for this moment and disappeared along with everyone else, leaving their preparations to him should he ever find them. The very detail that had made him settle in Ashburn had now become its liability. The distance between storage options for the trucks and the size of the roads to reach them would amplify the mobility risks. True, he could maintain a snow plow, but he would still need to drive the five thousand gallon trucks on those plowed icy roads then find a way back to retrieve the plow. And he could not keep the truck at the house, since the garage was too small and still insufficient at insulating against a deep freeze. And where would the dogs stay? No, he would have to find a solution in the density of Georgetown.

He waited another week until the cold front passed and the temperature rose back up, before he bothered to begin the process of migrating all of his treasures and supplies out from the party house and over to the tidy house in Georgetown. He found that he'd accumulated a substantial amount of items, but left behind what was heavily dependent on electricity. The large sound system had given way to the efficiency of portable speakers and a tablet loaded up with music. He now had a new library of books from people's homes and new furniture from the warehouses the found. All this was in addition to the palates of food, drinks and vitamins that had become his habit. Moving this required machinery and more trucks. Trucks in addition to water trucks and plowing trucks. He had moved dozens of large vehicles into his neighborhood. Whereas he hated the sight of all the congestion, he felt no particular urgency about relocating them to a permanent location. With it still October, he knew that he had many weeks where this staging ground would be safe enough. His pack, though, was very nonplussed by the commotion.

Once everything was fully consolidated, he fell back into his habit of cycling around aimlessly in the city and marvel at how small downtown actually was. Half of his mind visualized the streets full of activity again, even under the desolation of the pandemic. But he really saw emptiness except for the tattered and filthy clothes left behind in camps and at the entrances of the metro stations. He recalled all the importance that happened above them and down the streets in row after row of important cubicles. On his way back home, he would route through the streets where his preparations rested, to survey and verify the thoroughness of his plan. He had combined the water trucks from Ashburn with those from the District and now had ten on rotation, giving him an estimated two hundred days of water if liberally used, but far more if he decided to conserve. He could spend the next six months without worry. But this wasn't enough, he worried about ruptures and other damage that would erode his supply. This led him to question whether he needed the full two hundred fifty gallons per day to be clean potable water at all. This was the last of the supply treated by skilled minds, and it should be treated more respectfully. He certainly used to bathe in brackish water that convinced him to take worm medication every few months. It would also make no sense to waste the clean water on his laundry or washing pots that would be sterilized by heat. There were corners to be cut to make his plan more efficient. He found a depot for the city construction vehicles that had about a dozen more water trucks for non-potable water. The insides of the tanks were not quite clean but not quite filthy. He hesitated to use them but still proceeded with driving them down to the tidal basin to pump water from the river into them, as an emergency.

To kill time, he decided to visit an outdoors store to see what was cutting edge for survivalists. It had been decades since he seriously attempted a backwoods excursion for an extended period, mostly because these were the holidays of privilege, and he could neither afford the equipment nor the time away from earning. Later, he simply redirected this to venturing deep into the parts of human civilization where survival skills would be needed, but the availability of equipment was scant. As such, entering these stores had become an exercise in detachment. But now was not such an experience. He freely pulled from the shelves anything that he felt might be of value should all other preparations falter and he was left to fight the worst of the winter as some North Country prospector. The most intriguing were the filter straws promising the ability to safely drink any water. One could carry this and presumably the additional filters it would need and dip it into even cesspools and come away with the needs of life with danger removed. The truck outside was soon full of enough supplies to set up a base camp and a backup base camp. He also took a few GPS trackers, thinking that the power supply for the internet and the cell towers would probably soon give out, and he might need these at some point. This all found its way back to the neighborhood parking lot and was set aside for some as yet identified plan.

He continued his gathering of batteries and generators almost every time he saw them as though he was inclined to do product testing in the course of his survivalist experiment. He now had an array of diesel and propane generators along with dozens of tanks to feed into them, but also solar cells that ranged from the small and portable to the very heavy. These were scattered across trucks due to his accumulation on different trips. He had no idea how many he had grabbed, nor a more technical estimate of how many he would even need. It made sense to at least begin the process of isolating these from the rest of the supplies to see. After segregating them along the street by category and rough wattage, he saw a collection that took up half a block and stacked waist high. Clearly he had more power generation capacity than he did remaining items that needed power. It only made sense to plan out how to increase demand. This was a

titillating thought that game him some excitement for
the harshness of winter. Everything went into a new
truck and barely fit. If he was to resurrect his projection theater, he needed to solve the inconvenience
of having to constantly swap out the batteries every
few hours. He could just change to the generators,
but the rambling noise would definitely interfere with
the immersion needed to reclaim his sanity. The solution would be larger batteries or a larger array. He
had seen these installed in remote villages and knew
they could be relatively simple to operate. But they
also exploded if not installed correctly. There
should already be setups that he could find in the
city. He wished he had paid closer attention to this
sort of equipment in the homes he invaded, but he had
different blinders on at that time. As far back as
last month, he was comfortable in his blindness at the
coming expansion of decay. It would be possible to
seek out homes that had solar panels and move in. His
sketchy memory told him that there were plenty of options in nearly all the areas of the region, so he
surely could find one of adequate comfort. As appealing as this sounded, he felt averse to sweeping
through a new home to empty it of echoes. He might,
but he didn't want to do so. Short of that, he already had a solution that he built up through mindless
inertia. The collection of small propane and diesel
generators might be good enough for the medium term of
this coming winter. These units were very powerful
even if they were small. They were portable and were
designed for plug and play end users like him. He was
using propane heaters after long ago overcoming the
horror of a live flame so intimately in the home.
This meant that he had a store of tanks on the ready
and could drive around stocking up without the need
for breaking into stores along the way. Then he imagined the piles of propane canisters littering the
area. He would probably run through one canister per
day of usage, so would likely be inundated very
quickly. He could just use diesel and suffer the ex-
haust in exchange for the ease of refill. If he made
that leap then he should go the full length and requi-
sition an industrial-sized unit and be done with it.

But then there would be the mess of fuel storage and the smell of fresh gasoline everywhere. In reality, he knew he would end up cobbling together some mashup of all these options and would need to figure out the storage issue. Like propane canisters, he found that it was quite easy to find diesel tankers hiding around the city. He long since began tapping these to refill his vehicles when the power first cut and he could no longer access the gas pumps using his card. He was able to find a variety of grades, but diesel was the most abundant. He found them idled at gas stations prepared to unload in the morning or in trucks at construction sites and factories. Finding them was not the problem. Unlike small consumer gas pumps, the large hoses attached to these trucks unleashed a massive volume of liquid and fumes. Each time he tried to tap into them and refill his fleet, his unpracticed arms and leg would be doused in diesel fuel. He tried several techniques but still came away the same. His only solution was to dress in a hazmat suit that he took from a fire station nearby, whenever he was required to perform the unpleasantries. This worked, but the suit was still covered in gasoline, making it an unbelievable fire hazard that needed to be stored where it could burn in peace should the need arise. So he allowed himself to begin the consolidation of these diesel trucks.

He drove two tankers into the neighborhood and parked them far from the house before he went back out to collect the third that he left at its original site. This was to be the final step in his preparation before he turned to the winterization of his home. He had cleared more streets surrounding his home than before to make way for all the trucks. He pulled past several dozen on his way in with this final truck. As he left it behind to make way back to the house, he surveyed the long lines that extended deep into the side streets but so far lacked the organization needed for rapid distribution when the time came. He had simply parked them as he moved from checklist to checklist, not always clustered according to need. That process would now begin, and he thought out what would make the most sense. Food and water together near the house, for now. Solar panels charging in the open space out front. And so on. He still hadn't decided how to handle the water trucks, so he had brought in several two hundred gallon bins to store in the basement, which should be enough for a week, and he could always melt the snow as he dug himself out if he were barricaded for longer. This would let him store the main trucks somewhere else where they could be on standby until he could get to them. Not ideal, though. As he tested arrangements and rearrangements, he could not settle on how to best balance efficiency with his enjoyment of the neighborhood. It always looked as if there was a block party being set up that all the workers abandoned.

He had kept himself from this fight for as long as he could. The tightness of Georgetown had driven him out to his Ashburn home until that proved unworkable for the winter. The preparations he felt were necessary now exacerbated that original aversion. It was now no use. He could not store what he needed to store in his home or even the neighboring homes. He had installed dog doors on several houses to turn them over to his pack, but this was the extent of what he could move indoors. Everything needed to be in the trucks outside because it was all just too bulky. It wasn't just the clutter at his doorstep. It enveloped him and the entire community in a wall of axles that pressed against trees. There were nearly three dozen of them elongated at the curbs, and he became overwhelmed at the sight of the transformation he exacted on this historic community. All this compounded with the recognition that everything would need to be relocated ahead of January when the risks of blizzard were highest, and the amount of space needed was beyond anything he anticipated. There were fewer than two and a half months before this zero hour, but that itself was just a shorthand expression of risk and the true ascent of that risk curve had already ticked up. At any moment, there could be a freeze. Or not.

He had only crossed the first stage of the process, which was the collection. This was relatively mindless work akin to shopping. Now was the diligence of planning out sustainable storage and rationing schedules. This was the stressful hard work that oftentimes took longer. Never in his life had he confronted a full stockpile of modern comfort to be used over the course of months, yet here it was on display demanding closer attention as it fanned out and invaded his space. He would need to interact with everything again to find it a new place before consumption needs reached it. There could be no more postponement. The exhaustion of the months converged on these lanes. It might become easier in future years, but for now that offered little comfort. He might expend the effort to reach stability with his surroundings and then find that he himself would evaporate at the moment when its comforts would vest. Perhaps this might never come, and he would always find new cliffs over which the smallest of nudges would send him. The purposelessness of his survival was never so apparent. To what end did he remain behind to witness the departure of all others. It would be impossibly absurd that the remainder of his life was situated as such only to forestall time and lead to his evaporation some distance in the future. The breadth of this distance was uncertain and troubling, yet he could do little but focus on the immediacy of the rules defined by his vibrating biology.

He was aware of the continuity of the present project and the library of actions he had taken in his life, including the resource consolidation in his family. All was the act of survival with baselines scaling as time progressed, but the fabric of the relationships involved, there was complacency. That fabric adorned survival and kept some abstract existence in himself alive. Now naked survival was an uninteresting circle. Without that fabric, there were no valued purposes left, not even those imposed from the outside and pursued as a begrudging thrill. He had only his internal mechanisms to guide him. He missed people. Even the misery and exploitation that evaporated alongside them those months ago were as real as a razor. He missed the minute tragedies of a congested city brought on by inane sleights that should be forgotten but lingered and traveled with you from place to place until absorbed. It was purpose itself defined as projected emotion, which mattered little if it stagnated or flourished. Without it, one lives life as a bird staring into a mirror always hoping to peck just to the left of the reflection's beak. In the early days, he had watched his phone late into the night typing messages to customer service chatbots and even began answering the spam calls to feel the surprise. But this was a dead end from which he never receded. The time vault had captured him then offered no social feedback through which he could define his moments. In this echo chamber within which he spent his time, the critical pieces of his humanity were gone. Humans always were a triangulating animal. Nothing but the dynamism of social encounters had the power to shape an understanding of one's self. He now only had self and nature, but not even the nature from which his biology derived. This was the nature of physics overlayed by the decayed features of civilization now slipping away from him bit by bit. This was all well-know philosophical syrup before the evaporation. It could be argued and nuanced then, but now it was crisis. He knew the intractability of humanity and society; they were synonyms of sort. He lacked one so would he not also lack the other? He crossed from human to endangered species in an instant of confusion. He went from consortium to solitude without understanding what questions to ask to understand what happened. That moment ended all possibility of murder, inequality, and conspiracies. It ended politics inasmuch as it ended states.

He thought about opening some of the trucks to break the cycle and pull him back to the site of his survival that had already shifted to feel like the site of his destruction. Every item represented the lack of civilization and the disappearance of his own humanity. It was wet with meaning. There was no reprieve. All of his planning began with a recognition that there was nothing left besides him. Humanity had gone. Full stop. It existed nowhere, and he had to make the decision over how to wash his hands with re-claimed water. The madness was clear. These trucks felt more like the placements of another person. There were markings left behind by their former own-ers; the scuffs of work done in haste. He could not tell which were his and which predated him, so none of it felt connected. These had all been produced by skilled hands navigating machinery long before he touched them. He owned none of it because ownership itself had evaporated. The wall of houses reformed into faded shelters with yellowed trees standing out-side. It meant nothing more than a wall of granite might. Impressive for an instant before one moves on to marvel at the next thing. He was in a new nature learning its rules through contrast to the old. This wall was no different from walls anywhere now and he felt nauseous.

A late afternoon wind dropped some yellow leaves into the carpet along the pavement. Its symbolism was without significance; October was rife with wind and leaves. It was the source of his building panic that drove him to the accumulation of trucks in the first place. Now that he watched it from a moment of vague-ness there was no meaning here either. Winter would come as it always does. He would adapt no matter the preparations, as he always does. All this frantic ac-tion was thought-boredom.

He felt no desire to go home even as he walked in that direction. In a contradiction of emotions, he slowed his walk to calm his escalating anxiety. This was his habit. Never did he spin up into a frantic mania whenever the anxiety arrived. Instead, he would slow himself and devolve into emotionless observation. The simpleness of the angle of a leaf caught on a minus-cule abrasion of the concrete as it spun in place be-fore flipping over to continue its promenade. Squir-rels darting below the carpet of leaves to find nuts to squirrel away someplace. "Do not hit yourself." He walked on and felt superficially calmer because he rounded a different street to prolong his arrival, which usually worked. There was no need to hurry. He owned it all. Everything was his house and his lawn. He could ruin it all and still leave the world unchanged behind him. But eventually this would wear off and he would resume. Perhaps betrayed by a bladder slowly filling or a chill on the wind. Whatever the cause this time, he finally began the routine walk home. Rounding the corner after so much meaningless crisis had dissipated left him unguarded. He looked at the litter trailing into his home that made it look like an HVAC cleanup in progress with all the hoses and centered on a single door.

He'd been careless with the sundries, so he felt a tidy-up was in order. He grabbed the packaging and the bags to be carted away on some other trip, then pulled the hoses into more tightly parallel paths. The lawn looked superficially improved but the underlying clutter remained. The thought of so many hours for so much meaningless comfort was too much. He collapsed inwardly, feeling the heave of gravity falling into a matrix of colors that took on the shape of trees and homes and sky that each felt like a bleeding extension of the next. Not much was left to do other than to sit down in place and fold himself downward until he could touch his core as he made himself as small as possible. He needed to recede away and let the clenching hands pull everything in. Deeper. The silent blinding scream welled up again from nowhere headed nowhere. It deafened his mind, forcing him to secrete fluid designed to signal to others that he was suffering but no one was listening, not least himself. Some hands pulled tighter past clothing, reached past skin and grabbed clumps of loosened flesh on the inside of his elbows to rip from off his bones. Again and again. They scratched at his neck and felt soothed by the cold sting of nerves too muted by the scream to know pain.

Apparently his movements had dislodged members of his pack from their sleep, but he still could not hear them. He noticed one or two standing halfway out from their doors across the street while he was cleaning, but paid no attention. When he came up for air, he caught glimpses of them scratching at their ribs and yawning off their naps. A few were playfully growling around one who stood fully erect with a wagging tail in anticipation of an attack. This angered him more and sent him back down into himself. Predictably, a nose appeared and pushed into his hair and sniffed at the fresh blood on his neck. He breathed, and the darkness receded again. He didn't bother wiping his eyes. There was no point.

More dogs came to ask for food. "You motherfuckers." He was still angry and laughed through it knowing that none of it mattered.

Accept

VI
Insomniac Planning

The crack in the shell had irreversibly expanded and he eventually stood up from the ground where several dogs had migrated over then ran off again. They had not perceived the breakdown. He was another animal with its own hidden survival processes and they accepted him for it, but it was irrelevant in their pursuit of squirrels and one another. Less an uplift, the distraction they provided was enough to mark time for him while he waited to stand up and piddle around on the main level of the house for an hour or more before moving on back to his hallow upstairs.

There were no echos in this dark space, only unanchored memories. Some of which had been ignored while others meticulously dissected. Acceptance of the evaporation had come misleadingly quickly. He felt little reason to puzzle through the why's which were enormous, but he had grown more focused on the final days of his quiet family life that had reached crescendo with a romantic evening quietly captured. These were days where he and his wife could return to a life of two, even if for a few hours. Neither felt shunned when these days were unavailable; they were the adornments for routine domestic life that should be rare, lest they lose significance. It was to prelude a weekend of carnivals and hustle that would be punctuated by the firework shows. Many of them. This was their second year stateside, and he had been enjoying a revival of his patriotic indoctrination so that it could be passed on to his son. He enjoyed pointing out the colonial flags to explain why there were only thirteen stars and his son enjoyed the carnival atmosphere that permeated through everything in the city.

The scene of all this colored flourish melted in memory as he loaded more significance through the evaporation and the emptiness of his house. The confusion of being alone on his bed was overshadowed by the panicked disbelief when he turned on the light of his son's room, unsure why he saw pajamas in bed with no body. Sleeves were stretched out to the same side and the shirt was tipping up to the edge of a small indentation in the pillow. It was warm. There was a small dollop of saliva on its slope. He had suspended that moment to examine its details when in the fullness of the experience he had ravaged the bed in case he might find a body down deep in the sheets. He could suspend all the moments to relive them repeatedly and the sadness wore on him as it never ceased. He was low on ideas to occupy his days to distract him from all this. He looked back what he had done and it felt like wheels on fire. With the rows of trucks outside, this motion had run its course, and he knew the next phase was supposed to begin. It had a timer that was already pressing him to count days forward rather than back. On both ends were zeros between which he drifted in a tunnel. The middle was where indecision ruled, where there was comfort in the averting himself from the point of origin that burned with frost and then also to the destination's brightness, where beyond which something invisible existed. There was no purpose in the middle, as far as he could find. It was a way station where he sat to be overcome by events. And detachment was his tested means for killing time when no progress was achievable other than to watch for the incremental changes in circumstances mount to noticeable shifts. This was his late night abstraction that tumbled in his mind and became a tiresome exercise that only made to him more clear the need for change. It signified a privileged mind unwilling to depart from the comfort of civilization where the very idea of emotional intelligence was a commodity. The tunnel itself was nothing more than the corridor of survival. There was no need to dress it up further. The endpoints were markers to fade and become replaced by others. When the cycle breaks, it means his survival exercise was at a close. Until that time, there was only the biological drive to defend himself against every danger, especially from complacency at his death. Everything else was nonsense that he carried forward from modern conversations. He'd made the effort and set the stage for his survival. The brightness of the winter deadline was just foresight and urgency. Once it passed, what came next was obvious: more survival. Winter would dissipate and the weather would warm, then heat up, then cool again. The city would remain. Most of the food would not. Over time, he would discard the shell of civilization and cobble together a practice that would sustain him until it didn't. He was one of the billions who had revised survival strategies during the pandemic. He had been living in a country with only one ventilator for forty million people shuttling through crowded wet markets. He spent time watching solitary street vendors calling up to eighth floor apartments to sell food that would be put into buckets dropped from the balcony. This place still existed, even if empty of people again.

They were all out there, the same as ever. Many had long ago begun the descent into decay, so what would a bit more matter? With food and shelter settled, all else for survival would be sex and entertainment. Travel was always a stand-in for both. Even before he launched in the life of an expatriate, he was an itinerant around the nation. What lay beyond the light must be what always laid beyond it, from the start. There were infinite roaming possibilities just beyond the winter, even those that negated the existence of winter light itself. From either side, he could see landscapes of the southwest where earth and sky competed to swallow the other. Winter was an abstract there; it rarely became a presence because the competition was fierce. It was the anti-city, that which stood in contrast to this neighborhood that never felt natural like home. He was an animal nurtured in the hugeness of the southwest, where winters were mild and manageable. Why hadn't his preparations simply factored in migration as his adaptation strategy from the start? It was his oldest tool, and he now felt like his window to change course was now closed. Even a drive to Harper's ferry had tripled in duration, so a journey to the sunshine would be at least two weeks. He was exhausted at the thought of this new project. And yet, even as he gave up he recalled that he had long become a cosmopolitan and viewed the entirety of the planet as ripe for travel. Back then, successful movement was conditioned on finance and politics, but now it was rooted in the means of transport. With the end of money and states, he was free to be anywhere. This thought competed with the real end of air travel. As with the pandemic, he would be unable to fly in accordance with his intentions. His humiliation with the technicalities of the electrical grid taught him not to bother learning how to operate aerial machinery of any size. This left cars, but it reduced the aperture of destinations to the contiguous land of the Americas. Nor had he ever explored the operation of boats other than small manual ones that lived in calm waters. He was immediately aware of the number of yachts and fishing boats that must certainly be a few miles away in the piers along the mouth of the Potomac. Surely these could be learned and used to take him anywhere.

Inspired with the energy of a possible future, he allowed himself to embellish the nostalgia of travel, and he mentally returned to cities and villages he knew before. The planet was his to review with its catalog of memories locked in landscapes and places he'd reached. He could return to homes that were as offline and quiet as this city had now become, where he had enjoyed them for exactly this feature. He could conduct follow-up investigations on the households where he worked so hard to intend to reach and could never be sure if this happened. He had often-times tried to do just this through satellite images and street level navigation online, but these towns were too remote, and the images were too grainy to give satisfaction. The primal poison of hope began to infect him with allowance to doubt his own significance as a sole survivor and imagine that there might be others alive ready to be reached. The significance of his exemption necessitated the discomforting questions over what exactly had taken place to cause everyone to evaporate. Logic told him that this could not have happened over time or else there would have been signs alarm online until silenced in turn by the final wave. And what of those who might be exempt? Would there be a second event to claim them? Everything returned to understanding the event cause, which was as opaque as tools of the created used to understand the operations of a creator; it was as boring and unimportant to him as questioning god. It was more accessible to him to believe in his own capacity to seek them out or at least roam around as a palliative to his continued existence. These were practical and real for one engaged in survival, not the abstract playthings reserved for those who enjoyed the comfort of civilization. There was time for this. He had set the motions for a winter in Washington and hadn't the patience to construct an offramp. He hadn't even the energy to invest into planning this. What he needed was to suspend himself and gamble that he could rebuild himself from that point.

As the insomnia deepened, the frustration moved in. The hopeful optimism changed to a caution in wondering if other exemptees were as incompetent as he was thinking. It was possible that they might be of any age or mental awareness, so why would he relegate them to the backstreets of the globe? It might be equally true that some of them would be capable of travel, if not flight. Could it be as simple as that? There were universes of potential where the evaporation was orchestrated and those behind it might arrive in the city, as it was formerly a power center of world politics. There might be fragments of the United States government still here as targets for those orchestrators. This felt implausible, but his mind was in its insomniac throws. It did, however, feel more likely that if no arrival happened immediately following the evaporation, then it would not come until later. This meant that the threat, if any, would increase over time rather than the opposite. In that way, it could be managed through planning, so it could be forgotten.

He would not need to change course for this line of thought before the winter arrived either.

Nor did he still carry the childhood fears of mutants or zombies lurking beneath his feet in the hollows of the metro tubes. He had been all over the city by this point and found no signs of lazy science fiction to haunt him. He'd come this far and exposed himself to the strained personal analysis of character development and felt there was nothing waiting to surprise him in the long arc of his story. These fears had just been with him from before and reinforced through movies so often that he cared for little time to fret. If they were to exist, then they too would be something for which to plan and perhaps confront as the light of winter beckoned.

The real threat were his competitors in the city. He had maintained the numbers in his pack in order to keep them hospitable and to help him feel secure when he slept. But these were not the only dogs nearby. His pack would occasionally find newcomers, some welcome and others not. In his home visits and cycling trips, he routinely found dogs and family pets, most already dead. He had continued to carry his sidearm as well as a short katana he found in one home that had proven very effective on some random encounters. But he knew that there were also black bears in the parks that had learned to cross into neighborhoods and eat the sweet food trapped in homes. Sightings were rare, but they happened more regularly. The worst of all was the population of rats that had exploded inside homes and threatened him with disease and infestation as they spread. He had looked for cats on his outings, but had difficulty with them. They stayed nearby, but rarely went inside his home.

It was now 03:00. He sat up in the dark and inhaled evaporated cannabis as his mind turned more methodical to hone the contours of his winter plans. Of basic needs, he didn't think there was much more ground to cover. He'd managed to pull together everything he could imagine would be needed to make it through the harshest of weather without the need to expose himself to it. All that was lacking was a reliable place to set up and unpack. He knew the checklist; it had taken on its own personality with each the categories serving as moods. He talked to it and listened when it coaxed him on. But it was silent on identifying a new home.

The one obvious feature would be that it had to be some large facility to accommodate everything and keep it all both organized and accessible. This implied something massive, but it would also have to be comfortable and not simply a warehouse, though he did contemplate simply parking a motor home in one if need be, but then he would essentially live in a parking lot for four to five months, which made little sense. Still, the size question was troublesome given the amount of items he planned to have on hand. Perhaps a shopping mall or even a condo could be made to work. The problem with these is that he would also need to keep his pack safe, all of whom would shit and piss in any space he found. The size meant that there would have to be enough distance between their worlds so that he would not be swimming in defecation by the end of the winter. He might just periodically burn it, but this would mean that he'd have to shovel it to be relocated during a time when bathing would be least comfortable. He could not simply leave the doors open and let them come and go as they pleased, since this would also risk letting in other animals. He trusted them to keep out other dogs, bears and raccoons, but not rats and mice that would head directly to his own feed palates. Even if he managed to get several cats into the space, none would be so active around forty bored dogs.

The least of his consideration, but still on his mind, was the possibility that he would need a place to defend from other people who may still arrive. This was something of the irrational but he kept it, whether out of fear or desire was unknowable. He knew that in the depth of winter darkness, his mind would unfold, and he would seek out the smallest of spaces inside wherever he chose so that he could feel safe. If he fortified his new home from the start, then this space would be able to grow instead of pushing him into a narrow closet.

He took his time about looking, but he did become serious about his survey efforts towards the end of the month during his routine cycles through downtown. The buildings were large and imposing so none of them drew him in. Something about the office motif that had become an entrapment in his adulthood was not the sort of home he wanted under the circumstances, even if they otherwise matched many of his criteria.

He wondered whether he had been presumptuous about Virginia's failings when he originally removed it from contention during the consolidation. The whole driver of the decision was to protect the water trucks during a freeze and to be near food stores. He'd solved the latter by raiding them at the outset, carefully calculating how much of each staple he felt he might need and then doubling it. He did this for all the food and even identified metal containers where he would put his emergency store when he identified the right home. As for the water, he felt more at ease with the idea of plastic water bins and even had an army of two thousand gallon bins ready, which could be brought inside most places with some effort. This led him back over the bridge to check Arlington and further. Everything there seemed just as problematic as downtown and offered no real alternative. It would then come down to aesthetics alone.

Universities ranked high in the competition as there were so many in the area to represent the quality of open space centered around a variety of buildings that were all designed to be accessible from one another even in heavy snow. These would offer him the distraction of classrooms and laboratories for him to study many of the skills he felt would be important after the winter. He felt like to do this right, he should focus on the schools with history and gravitas. Choosing a university was always more about reputation than quality of offerings anyhow. He started in his Georgetown neighborhood, which he never before learned to appreciate for its pretentious mimicry of the old world. This still annoyed him even without anyone to whom he could complain. Howard was by contrast far more American and appealing, but what he found was that it captured what is most uncomfortable about a vacant campus, which was the haunting effect of a disappeared student body. The hollowness also whispered too many echoes and hid too many ghosts. In addition to this, the openness of all the campuses undermined his aim to have someplace he could fortify. These buildings were built to inspire through their windows and common areas, not to be locked down behind ramparts of paranoia, so he envisioned a winter hiding in a cave.

Malls, on the other hand, could be locked down and were little more than open space. There were several options, and he felt it would be more in line with intent if he focused on those malls that were dead or dying. There were many options in Maryland and Virginia. Most of these, though, had parking that was either outside or open carparks, both of which would be bitterly cold for him to access. He also discovered that the openness of the interiors was misleading as there was never any livable space. He would either have to find a way to drive in an RV or feel as though he was living in a city alley the whole winter. Sure, he could be in one of the stores, but these felt totally open and not secure. They did inspire him for wintertime projects to pass the time, and he began collecting playthings to keep him occupied, particularly the ever-tempting boxes of legos that he recalled his son would stare at but never quite saved enough to buy. He cleaned out these stores in the four malls he visited until he had a full truckload parked behind his diesel tankers.

He drove and cycled throughout the region hoping to find something that appealed to him enough to feel like it could be home for a winter shut in. He knew that once this expedition finished, his mind would take him back to a pandemic era survival setting, and he would sequester himself inside wherever he chose and likely not emerge. He braced himself for exile and his shopping had the feel of selecting his last meal from a city wide menu. Every adjective was explored and allowed to flower into an image of the future. He recalled from the lockdowns exactly how he behaved when caged and knew what was important. He knew his risks. He recalled the feeling of urgency to rush back into his sanctum every time he was out of the house, even wearing a mask as he cycled through empty streets that baked under the intense equatorial sun. This time would be different, since he was able to pull every thread for planning. But after ten days of looking, he realized that he would need to regroup and focus on the commercial spaces he passed up early on. His discrimination had eliminated so many sites that he knew would work but just didn't achieve the perfection that the expense of effort he'd made to date warranted.

He even went so far as to stress test his water bins, to see how viable they would be as an alternative. The first problem was clear. Each one was enormous and extremely heavy. In order to install one empty would require a small truck or forklift, and neither the machine nor the bin would fit through any opening but the largest that were designed to situate atop loading docks. The next issue was that these particular bins were designed to be buried, meaning they would have the support of the surrounding soil to maintain integrity when filled with water. Sitting on the floor, they sagged and threatened to collapse under the weight of two thousand gallons. This, though, was solvable with a selection of belt ties. Knowing that these would not be a part of his living space, he tested some water pumps to fill smaller bins that he could carry through the reasonably sized doors designed for people. This had potential, but it increased the number of stages to get daily water. In all likelihood, he would not choose a place where he would need to drain the water trucks to replace them

with these bins, which probably would themselves
freeze if stationed near large loading bays.

He was getting tired of himself and his indecision.
True, he had narrowed the field and learned important
facts along the way, but the horizon was approaching;
the timer had never stopped its descent. It was now
the middle of November and quite cold at night, though
no freeze had occurred yet. He was ready to be done
with this process that began back in September and
should never have taken this long. Everything was up
to him, but he especially knew that his lingering
grief and depression slowed him, and he was eager to
give them space to breathe again without the stifling
urgency of life. As his movements increased, his
longing turned to images of a hammock in the dark
where he could rest for days on end without light to
tell him what time had deigned to do without him. He
could float and sleep knowing nothing waited to be
done and no one was calling on him. There would be
his days of decay and mourning that never were. When
his family first moved back and went through a similar
process to shop for new living conditions, they were
confronted by the same hard choices he now faced. For
years, they lived in cramped town homes and apartments
that offered very little in terms of expansion. They
were overwhelmed by the size of the options in the
United States, even condos. Not for a long time had
they entertained bedroom sizes like the ones they saw
in every home they inspected. In the end, it came
down to intangibles and they selected the Georgetown
home. But it was close. They had nearly chosen the
luxury condos that swallowed one in a maze of corridors and sitting areas. They found one that had a
spiral staircase and had been decorated in a gaudy
modern facsimile of gilded age gaudiness. Others had
pools and large open spaces that opened to yawning
balconies. He found now that they offered the parking
areas and huge lobbies for storing the bins, but in an
over exuberance of comfort were primarily accessible
by elevator serving as front doors. Of course they
had stairwells for the help, but these were tight pas-

sages unfit for routine use. The real focus had always been the keypad locked elevator.

Being Washington D.C., the prominence of the huge and historic federal buildings were centerpiece, and he needed to articulate some rationale to either include them or not. By and large, the huge marble or brick buildings were miserable inside. He knew this already. These were the drab centers of functional bureaucratic offices that updated only on the tightest of budgets that were stretched out as far as the Byzantine federal procurement processes could never afford. The real reason he passed them up was that he held the lingering moral standard that these should remain unmolested, lest there be a return to the days of Washington's power. But the private offices of which he was so familiar, including his own, had relished in the excess of federal funds that flowed in to release the pressure on the federal agencies and their budget restrictions. His short time in the city taught him how the privatized federal duties opened thousands of rent seeking offices to exploit the federal workforce restrictions and cost saving legislation, making the federal agencies spend more under obscure budget lines that satisfied the cynical values of those holding the purse. These offices were lush. He previewed penthouses and rooftop gardens. Massive kitchens with wooden sideboard or clean modern trims that bled into internal balconies that faced down deep tunnels below. All of them had gyms and large mezzanine levels. The parking reached five levels into the earth where the cold but not the freeze would reach and hundreds of dogs could play in the dark without their shit manifesting as a minefield to navigate. Once he had been able to tick off all the other options before returning here, he felt more inclined to accept the habitability of them as a whole, but he settled on one just outside the line of structures that abutted the federal mall.

The first and busiest work was to clear the few cars that had remained parked in the office for late work or overnight abandonment. He assumed these were primarily the night staff and company cars that had no home of their own. This was satisfying and allowed him to play with a new machine that he had barely figured out, which was a heavy tow truck from a company that was vigilant in the city and boasted a fleet of fifteen enforcers. He recklessly hooked up each of the vehicles and pulled them out into the street where he scattered them around to maintain the impression that his area was unpopulated. In an act of overzealous paranoia, he made sure to pull each into a semblance of legal parking, which was itself exceedingly difficult to find. He circled blocks in search of reasonable places and often had to make elaborate three point turns to align the vehicles with the correct flow of traffic in order to fit them into their spaces.

Once clear, he had his moment of release when he inserted the first of his trucks. He had decided on arranging the water trucks and equipment near the stairwell, saving the food trucks for the furthest recesses of the lowest level, under the assumptions that rats would find more trouble to reach them as they would have to pass through the gauntlet of dogs exposed in the wide driveway leading down. He did his best to presort his food according to month instead of according to item, so that he would not have to expend the energy while he was in the throes of depression he knew would come. He had six trucks for each of the months he predicted and three large emergency trucks, but none of these fit through the low ceiling after the first level, so he had to drive them down on palates, but the sight of so much food resting so near the ground worried him. He went back out to his favored warehouse store to dismantle some of their industrial shelves to install in the garage. He wrapped some pigeon spikes around the legs of these and hoped for the best. With the garage stocked, he brought in palate after palate of construction supplies to seal it off and to build a small shelter for himself on the food level.

Inside, he installed his water bins along a series of pump hoses that he calculated to reach any level inside through the internal atrium. He fashioned a hoist from which he could bring up the smaller bins and scatter them around to be filled later. It was time to turn to the interior of the offices and begin the process of erasing the people inside. He did so carelessly, though he felt this process was much easier in the era of laptops and hot desks than it would have been in the past where workers nested behind heavy CRTs and paper files. He initially thought about tossing the desks and chairs into the elevator shafts, but reconsidered when he couldn't figure out how to close them even if he managed to get them open. The last thing he wanted was open shafts in the dark. Most of these were dismantled and shoved into unused sections of the office to be forgotten, as would be done in normal times.

For his living area, he had decided on what appeared to be a law firm with its pampered offices and large kitchen. He risked wasting the water to shampoo the carpets, but then also brought in a truck of rolled up wool rugs that normally would have cost several thousand dollars apiece. Some of these were laid out over the unpadded commercial carpeting. The idea of bringing in the furniture he had intended was impossible unless he wanted to carry each piece up the dozen flights of stairs to his new home. Instead, he put all these on the mezzanine that he also carpeted, giving it the feel of the reading room for a comic book villain. For the upstairs, he hoisted assemble-at-home furniture that was far easier to transport. The lobby was to be used as a staging ground for all his equipment and entertainment pieces that he didn't yet know where to place.

The small solar cells for the motion floodlights that he installed throughout the car park were up and running. He used almost a half a mile of extra wiring that ran through thousands of feet of garden hoses to have light reach almost all corners down to the lowest level. He ran extensions for the cells that came with his batteries and installed those outside while the batteries themselves were scattered about on all the floors from the rooftop down to the food storage. This took days of hoisting, drilling and fighting the strain on his arms that he held above his head for hours. But when it was done, he had electricity everywhere he wanted and he had depots of rechargeable LED lamps and flashlights everywhere his floodlights missed.

Then he took a rest and decided to walk around the federal mall. The MLK memorial was not far, so he went there first to sit by the tidal basin. On the way, he noticed a pair of dogs who noticed him. These were unfamiliar. The more he walked, he felt like the group was growing but couldn't be sure as they kept darting back and forth behind a hill. But it was clear after a while that there was indeed a small pack that had taken an unhealthy interest in him as he walked, so he moved on from the area in the hope that they would stay behind. No luck. They followed. He was being hunted. He moved quickly without running across the large street and made his way to the small poet rotunda of the District of Colombia's World War I memorial so that he could climb its high platform. It was a swift action to jump up and kick aside some laundry and a bottle as he reached for the binoculars he took to carrying in his courier bag. From this slightly elevated post he could see the entire area across to where MLK watched. He felt ashamed for letting down his guard on this walk. Perhaps the exercise had made it too burdensome, but he felt annoyed that he was in this situation where he could easily expire before acting out the pantomime he planned for himself over the winter.

He could see clearly through the leafless trees that around eleven scrawny but large dogs had paused on the other side of the road and were sniffing the air and ground. They knew where he was, but a quick gut check told him the wind was blowing off from the water and into his face. He felt safer that way, and it might even open a window for him to escape, or at least put more distance between them. He would have to circle the long way around to reach his new home again, but there were plenty of avenues to take on foot. It made sense to him that he should act quickly and make a run while they still looked distracted. The next best place would be to reach the World War II memorial behind him, where he could jump into the water if he needed the advantage, even if they chose to pursue. He began to back away from the ledge without making a sound and was turning to run when he heard the slow sound of nailed feet on the steps at the other side.

This pack had once been pets. They knew humans and were unafraid. But this one had relearned its hunting strategies that had been dormant for millennia. It had circled downwind behind him, not that he could smell anyway, and was ready to make its overture with the others waiting for the signal not far away. It was growling at him until it gnashed. He already had his blade out and was able to perform a slice across its haunches and then a solid chop into its skull, leaving it a bloody mess on the marble before he ran down the stairs as he planned. The others had heard the signal but hesitated for an instant at the sharp yelps that went silent. But they were not far behind. He did reach a clearing before he heard them close in, and he managed to unload a clip that landed a few times as it scattered the mass. He reloaded and finished his run to the Pacific Arch and climbed into a space on the wall between the pillars. He surveyed again and saw three severely injured dogs on the gravel and a few from the pack watching on. He climbed down and approached, causing them to run away. With the danger over he was able to take a good look at his hip and leg where the leader had torn his flimsy cotton trousers. The damage to the clothes was existential, but he could only find minor scratches that seemed more from a pressure abrasion of the cloth than a scrape of the teeth. Still, he had a minor panicked reminder about rabies, but more due to the thought of a revisit to the hospital and the hours needed to locate the battery of shots.

He now had four carcasses that were essentially fresh meat that could be put to good use. It was long since he crossed the taboo of dog meat since it was first offered to him so many years before. Repeatedly. He had carried on the general rule of thumb where you only eat dogs that are assholes, which these certainly were. He went back to his new home and collected a pickup truck that he stored, loaded a grill and a butchery set into the back then drove over to clean up the carcasses. His plan was ingenious. For weeks, he had tried to bring his pack across town to their winter home, but they always gave up following him after a mile. He decided that the best way would be to starve them and entice them with food that was only on offer with him. He managed to get a few to join him, but the majority would not. He now had a new plan: cannibalism.

Those at the house had already grown accustomed to his arrival and departure in a mix of vehicles. There was nothing particularly familiar about this truck except that it was yet another rattle of a diesel engine that only signified his movements. Some came to him excitedly while others were more languid, but all of them eventually pulled themselves away from their doings to greet him there in the middle of the street, sniffing the odd aroma from the back of the truck as he dropped the bed open. This was obviously a familiar yet new smell for them. Those who came first, quickly backed away in shocked understanding, leaving the way open for others to have their moment in turn. His plan was to let the blood saturate the air, so they would build up to it in their own time. He stood aside and watched as some of them began to be more than curious at the smell of open organs so near at hand. A few hopped up with their front legs to get a fuller look, but jumped down again with tails wagging and the foreplay began. This was his cue. He went over and dipped his gloves into one of the openings to draw out some blood that he began wiping here and there on faces and necks. It worked. The smell was no longer foreign. It had been absorbed into the pack and become one with them. Whatever its significance a few

moments before, it was now the sting of iron in their
nostrils that inspired them to frolic and fight. He
hopped back up into the bed and shut the gate to prevent any stage rush while he performed. The first
step was to light the grill and get it ready for the
long process of blanketing the street with what each
of these former pets had known from the brutality of
watching humans cook food that they would never enjoy.
He butchered the assholes roughly. It started before
he walked back to reach the truck, when he cut the
throats of the two that were still alive after he shot
them. The shooting was self-preservation, but the
killing was empathy. He talked them through it and
told them to take a rest. Now, they were nothing but
meat that they left behind and which he didn't bother
to skin. He cooked to sterilize, and he kept the heat
low so the smells unraveled. As larger parts cooked
on the outside, he cut them open to let the heat meet
the insides. Each of these animals he was about to
feed had already received a rabies vaccine; he made
sure of that long before. But still, cannibalism was
a sure fire way to transmit other diseases, so he did
his best to make sure they were safe. When he was
done with each section, he tossed it into the bed until it was ready to distribute. He tested some of the
pieces himself. He never cared for dog meat, which
was fatty and pungent, but then again he never cared
for lamb for the same reason. This was no better than
others he tried, but he was sure it would be a hit.
He dropped samples out to get the fluids working before attempting the three-mile drive.

It was a slow crawl. Rather than let them follow him
slowly as he had tried in the past, he raced ahead and
stopped to wait for everyone to approach, letting them
feel reestablished over and over again every few hundred meters. He had to herd more than three dozen
dogs down Pennsylvania Avenue and across the lawn. It
worked better than before, but it was frustratingly
inefficient, but once they found themselves outside
their home bubble somewhere after Foggy Bottom, he
discovered that they were more ready to chase after
him. He waited until he could see that stragglers had

caught up before tossing out huge chunks of meat for them to gain more satisfaction. When they passed near the site of the attack, he watched as a few took notice of the familiar smell and had begun marking everything in sight. This was a good sign because this was essentially their new neighborhood, and he contemplated letting them roam a bit to capture the rest of the pack that attacked him. Eventually they all arrived at the new building intact to meet the few who had joined him in earlier attempts. Rather than stop and close the doors straight away, he drove down to the second level where all of their food and beds were waiting. He had created an entire dog village with forty small shelters for a kennel and hundreds of toys for them to play with. He had reluctantly gathered some of their dried shit and spread it around along a far corner away from the ramp he would use to reach the lower levels in the hope that they would continue filling it. There was a feast waiting for them in their village. They were finally pets again.

In the end he did not let the packs merge, but he did make a few attempts at catching some from outside, though only managed to catch five. Once done, he pulled down the gate and rodent-proofed the seal with an additional wall at the base. They were all inside by the time December hit. Before all this, though, he had built up a series of similar rodent walls to the food level and a dog fence at top of the ramp down. In the space between the walls were traps to hopefully catch any of the most intrepid of rodents who made it down that far past the dozens of dogs. He parked a camper van and assembled a yurt that was covered in Persian carpet and held his shelves of cannabis products. He had already sealed off the back doors and other external access points from the main building with concrete and bricks, but he left the front accessible, though he set up rodent screens for when they were not in use. He parked all the empty trucks and transport across the street in the open garage just in case he would use them. He was all set with his new life. Everything had been considered in accordance with his adaptation limitations. Nothing was left.

He avoided sleeping in the building until everything was final. He wanted the feeling to wash over him at once instead of easing into it while all the preparations were still ongoing. Now that he was mostly sealed in, he chose to sleep in his evil lair on the expansive mezzanine. That first morning was cold, and the light was gray as it came in from the ten stories of windows that towered over his tent. He languished inside his bedding with the pleasantness of a warm body punctuated by a cold nose. When he did stand up, it was to a quietly huge room where he was utterly alone surrounded by glass and metal. He imagined himself within an intergalactic ship where he woke up too early and the rest of the passengers were still locked away for another lifetime. This was, of course, only half true. After he got his pot of tea brewing, he went down to the garage to check on his dogs. When he opened the door, the sound of a dog park echoed up from below. The main level was still dark, but he saw the glow from the ramp at the other end and knew that the lights were working. There was nothing for him to do. He had nearly automated everything for at least the next week or so. He had nowhere to be outside as all preparations were done. He had only time to drift about.

Still unable to break the line, he felt a push to do something more. What was left? Perhaps he needed another round of closure before he could manage this new freedom. The only path for that would be to return to Georgetown to let the calm emptiness burn itself into his memory, framed as a visit to clean up anything that he might have forgotten, like checking under the bed and behind chairs before a hotel room is abandoned.

Since he had the time, but didn't want a second encounter with dogs, he decided to ride his bike across town in the frosty morning. The eerie sensation of a commute to work came over him. The last time he was out this early on a winter morning was when he had just begun his new job and was sent off with warmth and love by his family. Now, he was making the same trek in the opposite direction, both in terms of course and other dimensions. He felt lightened, like taking in a sigh. As he got closer to the neighborhood houses looked more familiar, but with the distance of a refreshed sleep, he began to appreciate their character again. He reached his house and saw the remnants of the clutter that had broken him a few weeks before. The inside was an echo of itself with new whisperings of personality cultivated over the flurry of the previous months. He allowed himself to laugh at the memory of his first moments inside as he hurried through the houses rescuing trapped animals. He shuttered the house to keep out the vermin and wind. It was not time to go back to his glass and metal ship. There was no danger now. No blizzard would hit that day and he was free to walk about. As he passed his original house, he felt no compulsion to enter. He had already said goodbye but was not yet ready for nostalgia. He walked the entire way back to his new building just as the edible was spreading its wings. It had felt like a perfect day, considering the trauma he experienced. Everything had rapidly felt normal that day where all his lives converged.

VII
Fortress Home

Up in his lawyer's nest on the eleventh floor he could see partly out to the waterfront, so he set up a telescope to launch him far away from the small office he decided would be for sleeping and installed the compressed mattress he dragged up the stairs because the packing box was too bulky for his hoist. He let it expand while he set to work assembling the TV console he would use while there. Overall, the office had quite a good selection of sofas and other furniture when he arrived, so he didn't need to do more than arrange what he held back from the piled storage room. He cleaned up the kitchen and the foulness that was left behind. He didn't plan to do much cooking here and, being so far from his main water bins, he mainly stored water bottles and other drinks in the fridge that he managed to connect to a solar cell. All that was left was to ready his exercise corner with a row machine and his collection of vaporizers so that he could enjoy both while looking out the window. It was a good space indeed.

His first night in the nest was comfortable. He heaved two enormous lungs full of evaporated cannabis and rowed for an hour listening to music. He was floating in the dark as he rowed in time with the swish from the water canister. It brought him to nowhere and he didn't mind. He fell asleep after bathing with a towel dipped in boiled water. All was serene as he drifted someplace new where he felt only the painful yearning to eat fresh fruits. It pressed him between pillows of color that were both indistinct and representative of the things that were missing. It was an uncomfortable plane in an otherwise comfortable room.

He had grown more skilled in his use of solar cells. Still not confident with large panels, he used the small ones dedicated to the various lights and batteries to peak form. He had installed them along the balcony outside and extended their wires to where the overheating batteries would be most useful to warm the rooms. It was perfect balance, and it allowed him to resume his regular gaming that he had not been able to do with any satisfaction since the power had first cut in Ashburn. Thankful of the laws that govern solid state memory, all his game data was available despite the preindustrial interlude. With even less demand on his attention, he embellished his side quests. One of his favorites was to join the mage guild and spend his time honing alchemy skills with new ingredients to capture beasts within soul crystals. He spent days retreating from the struggles of reality by traveling around the map to stockpile loot at an abandoned house. The endeavor was strange and never ending, which accounted for its appeal. The screen he used was far smaller than and different from his projection theater, as it was only eighty-five inches and curved. Still, the omnipresent film of danger one feels when totally alone prevented him from using headphones as he fell into this abyss. It began as mental flashes of what one does before sleep that comes after fatigue had been disregarded for too many hours. The slippage between dreams and what one had been actually doing creates the strangeness of wakeful dream unannounced. But then it carried over to the fullness of consciousness. He would listen to master mages train him with task to seek another individual somewhere. It carried over as the quietly muttered responses he wished the game menu would allow him to make. It became parallel conversations in his mind that emerged unnoticed. He began to feel obliged to them as he did more than puzzle through the problems they presented, or guilty when he switched games and new worlds as if he violated their trust. Could these scripted characters evolve as such and offer him real companionship? He felt unhopeful.

As December intensified, it was more difficult to keep his solar array operating at more than a trickle, so he was forced to scale back his gameplay and these conversations faded as he switched to a handheld console with far less interactivity, but which allowed him to move about more in the building, meaning he was able to spend more time exploring new personas in the various corners of his ship. When he was a child, his games were costumed scenarios that he played by himself and, since they were solitary, he lacked the reference with other children that would have told him these games had to be outgrown already. He eventually left them behind out of social obligation, even over-calibrating by shunning Halloween. These echoes crept out form the cracks formed by the conversations he had with the game characters. When they faded, the itch remained, and he was soon imagining himself in the halls of a darkened palace at the edge of time, where he was the time master who kept an army of demons in the dungeon below. Soon enough, he had assembled a costume of sorts replete with a staff and a one-handed broadsword he picked up somewhere. He would light his way in the pitch blackness with a dim red LED and exaggerate the sound of his staff as he walked. Thomp-a. Thomp-a. He would make his way down to the lowest levels of the garage to collect food items or to sleep in the cold blackness of what he called his Yurt of Dismay, where he lit incense to watch the glow from his pillows and smell the aroma in the absolutely motionless air.

After several weeks inside, he noticed that there was a break in the weather and the sun was out in the sort of crisp yellow of a day well below freezing. His character had been modified and was nearly perfected by this point. He was now post-apocalyptic chic with his kevlar tactical suit that he took from the police armory, accentuated by not just the broadsword but the katana and 9 mm on a thigh holster. But it was still too cold for even this, so he also put on a heavy wool dress coat that was left in a closet and the fedora that went with it. He was ready to go outside to look around, pretending that his ship had landed, and he was exploring the remains of a disappeared civilization. Inclined to add the drama of danger, he returned to the tidal basin to investigate whether the pack that he met was still active. He saw no sign and left for the Lincoln Memorial where he narrated his approach, stopping to duck behind leafless trees along the way when he spotted the advance of an indigenous military unit cloaked in tunics as they marched through thick bushes. He bivouacked and made it past them safely. But he pretty soon had to urinate and it started to rain, so he walked back to his ship as himself, squinting under the low sun before it ducked behind a cloud.

He disarmed as he boiled his tea pot and wondered about the Korean War. It was the training ground for Cold War miscalculations that set the stage for Vietnam and the entrenchment of corrupt military dictatorships across Southeast Asia. The Viet Minh were trained in Korea before they were liberation fighters at home when the old world bravado of De Gaulle refused to relinquish his colony and the Americans maintained their misunderstood East Asian history. So much misery stemmed from the ghosts chasing those soldiers.

He took his tea down to watch his dogs play. They had reverted to their domesticated life with settled homes in their village. The ones who followed him across town with ease had the first mover advantage of claiming all the homes so that, when the rest arrived, the pack dynamic irreversibly changed and set their history on a new path with the once mid-level members now in charge; a status that was reinforced through his continued attention and favor. They had taken to sleeping near the door from where he accessed their garage, even though it was colder than down below, so he moved their homes and food up. They were the isolated elite suffering their place of uncomfortable privilege. He drank his tea and decided to take all five of them outside with him. He gave them gear too. They each had their own clip on blanket and rubber boots, but he had gone a step further and fashioned some thick face guards that also wrapped around their necks to protect them should they ever fight anything while out in the open. With everyone safe in tactical attire, they all left the confines of the ship through the main door upstairs. They ran, they played, the chased down an emaciated member of the other pack and ended its winter famine. He watched with disinterest as he continued towards the lawn below the Washington Monument. So like it for a city of history, this important hill was marked with placards and ancient photographs to teach visitors how far it had come through the years. He could still make out under the cracked lamination the forest behind him and the meadows around, during the early construction of the obelisk. It was hard to imagine this city park when it was an overgrown bit of land, even as it bore the marks of the untrimmed wilderness of grass that had gone dormant for the winter. It would soon return to that state and alternate between baking under the sun and freezing under winter.

He could plow it and grow all the vegetables he craved. Why stop there? He could be a husband again and bring in as many sheep or goat that he could find still alive in the farms outside the city. He had seen them graze outside their pens when he rode through the rural roads at a time when the world was still green. Sheep were resilient. They would not freeze, but they might starve or meet with hungry friends. There would be no point to finding them now. This would be work and winter was not for working. His pack made slow progress to find him. He realized that he gave them the taste of dog meat and they were no longer satisfied with simple murder over territory. They had to consume their victims too and come to him with faces full of blood. They might just be dangerous enough some day.

It had been a long time since he walked up to the cliff face outside the museum for indigenous Americans, which looked less like a natural feature and more like a building now that the water feature had stopped flowing and the pool was coated in a thick layer of brown leaves. But inside was still a quiet place of reflection as he watched the rainbow move about the wall of the sunlit cone that is the main room. The exhibits upstairs had always been the haunting echoes of disappeared people and their caricatured living descendants. The sounds of their already distant languages were offline, but he had heard them many times before. They reminded him of when he listened to old grandfathers speaking indigenous languages in the highlands of Southeast Asia and always sounded like the faint smell of wood smoke. He made the rounds and went back outside to see that the ducks below the Capitol still played and ate slime.

The sight of his bloodied pack made him want to hunt himself and eat one of the playful ducks that looked extremely delicious. They were the long descendants of trusting tourist attractions and did not fly away when he got close. He could begin the process to deconstruct this trust, or he could respect it. The latter seemed more in line with the austere day. He decreed that this would be a preserve for any water foul using it, so long as there was still water. But it did anchor him to the thoughts of animals and instinct as he continued his walk at the center of his panting group of dogs. They headed in the direction of the Natural History museum to look at the state of nature locked in glass displays. As they entered and saw the threatening tusks of the African elephant at the door, his pack declined to go further, so he wandered around alone to thrill at the bones and stuffed animals inside. When he reached the hominid exhibit, it was too real. Tens of thousands of years of evolution reached a cliff a few months ago. It would need to restart on a cousin's side, again in the jungles of Africa, before it could ever reclaim the modern era tens of millennia from that day. There would be no accelerated skip from the laboratory chimpanzees that science fictionists mused. Those had all starved to death in their habitats that had been meticulously designed to prevent their intelligence from finding a bypass. He sat down and watched the bronze dioramas

for a long time. He could do nothing more than dream
pointless dreams.

Back upstairs in his nest with fully recharged batteries, he resumed his games without as much unhealthy
fantasy. Instead of an adult suffering a mental
health crisis in the midst of obsession, he was more
like a child wasting his hours. He played for the
sport of playing and would cheer himself when he over-
came a technical challenge. But there was no care-
taker available to set before him the comforts of a
home. He was obligated to take breaks to tally his
needs. Foremost was water. Again. Still. He tried
to conserve when he was in his nest, but he still
found that he would use up the supply in his bins for
flushing toilets and heated bucket showers. To refill
these, he had to pump water up from the lobby with
narrow hoses, so the pumps could force the water up
those many stories. He tried using small propane
pumps from upstairs, but they performed poorly, so he
used the large and more powerful ones downstairs,
where he would have to walk down to start the process
and run back up to monitor the progress as he moved
the hose from bin to bin, then rush back downstairs to
cut the motor before the bins overfilled; even though
the bathroom drains where he stored them still worked
as designed, there was no point in wasting water. It
was agonizingly exhausting and needed to be repeated
every few days despite his best conservation efforts.
Food was more straightforward as it could be hoisted
up much more infrequently. He had even taken his lesson from lockdown and preloaded the hoist platform as
a stopgap that bought him an extra few days of food
without needing to go back downstairs. He did his
best to consolidate the food and water trips, but the
urgency of the pumps somehow prevented him from spending the time to load up the food and send it upstairs.

On many occasions, he would forget one thing or another and have to double back, whether he was headed
up or down. And god forbid if he wanted something
from the depths of the garage. For this, he used the
stairwell down to the dog's level, but would only ac-

cess the remaining levels down through the ramps. Generally, though, he tried to maintain a consistent practice for the pack to understand and would exit at the loading dock level the take a cart the rest of the way. He did all this elaborate movement in order to keep the stairwells sealed at the basement, for his own peace of mind; he had walled off the interior staircase at the dog level and the doors below that, so he had his secure basement with only one entrance at the ramp.

The main tanks in the lobby were large and rarely needed a refill. But he chose to refill regularly so as to keep the pump hoses submerged while he was up-stairs. It happened once that the nozzle moved, and he didn't realize until he reached the nest to dis-cover that no water was pumping because the hose curled above the water level. Angered, he ran back down to inspect. It wasn't until the second descent that he simply moved on to a new bin to start the process over. Filling these were easy. He needed only to change the hoses and route down one level to the loading dock and insert the other end into a truck. With the pumps next to the tanks, he had more breathing room in terms of time.

All of this was manageable strain, even as it made his body ache with effort, but it was the coldness of han-dling water in the unheated winter that he disliked most. It made him remember early winter mornings where he would go outside before school with a hammer to break the thick layer of ice that formed over the horse trough and would prevent them from drinking. The chipping ice stung his hands. These tanks too froze slightly and stung as the weather became colder and the cost of play in his nest ceased to be out-weighed by the fantasy enclave he made there.

A few weeks of growing frustration and near tumbles down the concrete stairs left him with deep questions over whether it would be worth it to continue at all. He had prepared an enormous space for himself inside this ship. There were other yet undiscovered fantasies that he could face from the comfort of not-up-stairs. It was becoming far too cold to enjoy the outside, but he had brought with him years of hours of treasure from homes and stores. His mind turned to the palate of lego that he had on the second level of the garage. These had always been the sinew that connected he and his son through its trans-generational power, and they called to him.

He retrieved several of the boxes that were reissues of editions that were released before he was old enough to play with them, but that his older siblings had. He had bragged to his son about how old the design was and listened as his son complained about how old the design was. The hook had failed, and he had never unboxed them until he brought them up to the mezzanine and laid the satchels of bricks beneath an outdoor heater. Once complete, they felt isolated from their surroundings. They needed the touch of his son's influence to find themselves in a city, with cars and people with whom to mark themselves in contrast. He built them essential services and food trucks that reached across the floor but able to pass over roads and bridges to ancient castles at the city center. He had unpacked and built more than twenty sets in a matter of days all cobbled together in a sort of eclectic theme that did his son proud. But then he inserted himself into the process. He looked at this lonely city and felt it was too unreal. Any city would sprawl into the periurban before it faded. No city would be dense and abruptly end. Not even an urban growth boundary would be effective in halting a city's bleed into the countryside. He started with a cluster of little boxes and added in their main street businesses. He connected them to the city with wide roads spotted with gas stations and ninja mansions. And these roads needed mass transit to link the bedroom communities to the city. As mayor and city planner, he brought them a metro system that served to connect one community to another by extension through the tourism district of the city. By the end of the month, his construction covered the entire length of the mezzanine and he found it difficult to move about,

but he was pleased in having had so many conversations
with his son again, even if he only played with
echoes.

One morning was particularly dark, and the sky looked
heavy. He sat in his chair and sipped coffee waiting
for the snow to begin, but nothing happened until the
afternoon when the clouds could not hold back any
longer. Although the windows were tall, he could see
little of the storm from inside the mezzanine, even if
he walked close. The best view would come from the
rooftop terrace where he originally prepared a reception room for such a day. Dressed in layers of wool
and fleece, he put on some ski overalls and his Snoopy
slippers to go upstairs. It was worth it. The sky
was huge again, and he could see the dark gray dots
floating down to disappear and reappear back in the
sky to fall down again. His eyes tracked them. Not a
child of snow, this process always fascinated him.
Now dressed in boots and a parka, he laid down in the
shallow padding of snow in the garden and let the
flakes fall onto his beard and freeze his forehead.
They blinded him, and he blinked them away in the muffled silence where it might be possible to hear a
quiet shuffle of icy flakes falling into place. He
sat up and walked to the ledge where he could see the
dome of the Capitol a few blocks away. He knew this
sight. It was a favored shot for movies and stock
footage. The blackness highlighting the dome,
slightly hidden behind the sheets that floated down.
He had stopped tracking the progress of days but was
distantly aware that this was the first week of January; another anniversary of the last attempt to overthrow the United States and install a backward-looking
government by force. That day was not blanketed in
snow, so the resemblance was not prescient.

The snow continued and began accumulating in the terrace, so he went inside to set up the heater and sit
in his chair and continue watching. The room was
frigid from the lack of insulation and the heaters
struggled to warm it up because these were smaller
propane units designed for small rooms. He doubled up

some sleeping bags and curled up near the window where he could still see part of the dome. The icy air combined with the soothing and tight warmth of the chair gave him the sensation of being locked in a hibernation chamber where all he needed to do was succumb. The light from under the clouds gave off no indication of time, nor was there the subtle glow from a living city to reflect down as pink pillows. The silence was similarly absolute except the occasional rustle from when he shifted inside the chamber. He was soon deep in a dreamless sleep.

As in most cases, his bladder pulled him back, and he woke to the orange and blue glare from the heaters against the complete blackness of the windows. He'd slept until nightfall, but he had no reference point from which to estimate how long he slept. It could have been half an hour or most of the day and evening. He only knew that the heaters failed to fight back the cold and the room felt like it had matured into a crystal. There was no possibility that he would attempt the long journey back downstairs, so he got up to empty the sack of water inside him that sapped him of his ability to keep his temperature up. He came back to the room and shut off all the heaters before crawling into his tent, but sleep did not return so easily. He laid there with sweating feet and tried to think about how long he could stand it on the roof. He had at least a week of supplies stored, but felt his was an ambitious target and revised it down to two days at most if these temperatures continued.

The morning was bright and colder. There was now eighteen or more inches of snow within the balcony, which created a bluish band at the bottom of the windowed wall. He thought about his life which had been one of privilege where he never enjoyed the responsibility to shovel a pathway in the snow. He had cleared it off windshields and banisters, but these isolated events never had staying power in his mind. Almost too conveniently, he had brought a snow shovel up to the roof when he was setting up the habitat there. It made sense. If there was ever to be snow while he sequestered in this building, he would only encounter it up on the terrace. His prediction was right. And he was curious about the utility of snow as water, so he kept an empty bin available should the opportunity present itself. This was a scientific preparation. He never questioned the process of water in and water out that went on in the clouds, but this was an investigation on the flavor of water that trapped the air above the city. He had lived off rain water before, but only out in rural jungles, never in the city. Would it taste like smog? He set to work filling the bin as he carved a line for himself to reach the edge of the outer wall.

The stove was busy melting the snow for a pot of morning tea as he leaned over the wall to look at the fondant on the street below. It was perfect. In his youth, he imagined it was like the undisturbed layer on a new jar of peanut butter that would reveal all but the lightest of touches. There was nothing below, so he shoveled himself to the other wall where he staged his telescope that could see out across to Virginia through a narrow slice between buildings along the waterfront. He knew he would find none in his unscientific survey, so this ended when the water inside began to boil.

There was nothing to do in either the habitat or on the terrace except sit and absorb some sun while it was out after the sky had bled out all it could from its clouds overnight. He made a cradle of polished snow to lay in and he let himself nap there until a shadow appeared in front of the light, signaling that the snow would return. It had apparently formed a thick resupply just beyond where he could see from the roof and moved closer without his notice. It dropped snow more ferociously than the previous day and brought with it a companion wind. But it was still bright across the water, where the early afternoon sun still reached. While vision reduced for him, he decided to test his telescope again to see what more nothing he could find and was startled to have found a northern cardinal dancing around on a branch within

Arlington cemetery. It amazed him that they could be in two separate worlds at the moment and that he could visit it in this way. He thought of the boxes that he left just a bit further up the hill and all the headstones that should be covered in wreaths at this time of year. Eventually, the clouds reached that far as well and the sheets of snow prevented him from watching more.

With nothing more to do outside as the wind increased, he went back to his habitat and his chair where he had closed the heaters into a tighter circle about himself and again dozed. He was later startled by the faint smell of melted plastic and this turned to panic when he realized that part of his sleeping back had smoldered because it was too close to the open propane flame. Of course, he felt the heat through the layers when he set everything up, but he did not translate this to a markedly higher temperature on the outside surface. He jumped out and immediately froze due to exposure. Fed up, he shut everything down and began walking through the dark.

The suddenness of the scare was not easy to shake. It made him distracted and unready for the concentration needed to lace his boots to keep his feet warm and steady as he found each step to reach his warmer tent on the mezzanine fifteen flights down. He went slowly, but still winded quickly as the adrenaline was coursing inside and he was dizzy from his spins around the handrail. The idea of maintaining this all the way down was an impossibility by the time he passed the door that would lead him to his nest, so he ended the misery and gave up. But he quickly discovered that the temperature inside there had dropped severely as well. He had assumed that the roof habitat was so cold mostly due to the fact that it was entirely made of windows, but even the insulated interior of his nest was no match for the blizzard. Back in the stairwell he went. It was an awful and deflated trip down to the mezzanine no less joyous when he discovered the same conditions there. When he selected this building as his ship, he was drawn to the size of the windows that it boasted. He had no interest in spending the winter in a cave, so the idea of a well lit ecosystem was very appealing. Now he saw that this feature was its wintertime weakness. He had long noticed the drop in temperature, but figured this would flatten out soon if not already. Perhaps it had with this storm, but only at a level beyond his tolerance. Everything he touched to try and warm himself up necessitated moments of intense cold. Removing his gloves to fill the water kettle meant grasping icy metal and breaking ice when reaching into water bins. Using still numb fingers to light heaters and stoves, and finding that the flames were not bringing back the feeling. He had prepared for this moment too, in case it happened. The bathroom had been retrofitted to become a steam room where he could boil water in large pots and warm the small space with several propane heaters. This worked well on cold mornings, and he would sit in the heat for hours, until he felt dehydrated from sweat. But the process took a very long time before it was effective, and he was disturbingly cold now. From time to time, he would warm up in a tub that he installed outside his yurt. He had tried many ways to bring the tub into at least the mezzanine, but he cracked the first one he tried to maneuver through the front doors because it was too cumbersome. He replaced it and drove that one down to the bottom of the garage and dumped it there. It heated quickly and the temperature at that level was always stable, so he knew it would not suffer the fluctuation from the past few days. It was a fulsome antique freestanding tub that could be filled from a tankless water heater and had a drainpipe fitted to send the water down a drain at the far side of the basement. It was within a spa that he designed for himself and enclosed in a large tent made from handwoven wool carpets. In a bit of exuberance, he had furnished it the same as the yurt, with heavy dark-stained furniture stocked with essential oils and salts. It was by far the most convenient and comfortable space in the entire building. When he reached it, he felt at ease in the still temperate basement level and was able to shed several layers of his clothes even before he was ready to ease into the water.

On the way down, he had stopped to check in on his pack. He had left them alone, for the most part, having taken the lazy approach of dumping huge quantities of food every week or so, which never seemed to be fully consumed before it got replenished. This way none became territorial over food. After several months indoors with this routine, they began to fatten up and would always congeal around him in a crowd of welcoming. They played and ate and some had puppies. But they were not his pets. They were his co-survivors and responsibilities ran in both directions. He never stayed long with them. He was a passerby. With everybody now so close together, there was even less to do because he had more time on hand that wasn't spent running up and down the stairs. Without sunlight to help him, he lost track of day and night so would eat and sleep at any time it made sense. He filled his moments with sodas and edibles at all hours and he rarely touched the ground as a result. He drifted around as fog, soaking in his spa or pretending to play various stringed instruments while he laid on his hammock in total blackness. But he was warm.

VIII
The Halls of Government

The winter following the evaporation event was one of
those that shuts the city down every few years. Had
anyone needed to travel anywhere, they would have been
stranded on roads for hours hoping to reach their destinations that were but a short drive away. With no
roads to dig out or late arrivals over whom to fret,
the city was simply at peace. He saw none of this and
it mattered little. Once reaching his spa at the bottom of his cave after the first of the storms, he
never left except to feed his pack. It was now late
February, nearly March. He had spent weeks at a time
in the absolute blackness when he turned off the motion sensors to his floodlights. On some days, he
even barely used a lamp or candles. Within a short
time, he totally lost sense of time and only moved according to his biological needs, which had slowed con-
siderably even as it responded to the electrodes he
fixed to his skin to prevent atrophy. Other times, he
had a light clock to give him some sensation of morning to push him into a modest routine that would break
up his days of hibernation. All this gave him over to
a life that required little to no additional effort.
This was a willful prison. He could have easily attempted to ride out the winter in other part of Virginia or Maryland where the power had not cut, but he
chose to accept the certainty of this sanitarium for
the gamble of transient comfort that may or may not
have ended in the depth of the cold, which almost certainly would have placed him in a life-threatening existence along with any of the pets that were struggling to survive on the surface now.

But his time was occupied, much like a child on school
vacation. He had supervised his preparations from the
mind of a parent to provide for the helpless boredom

of a child that he expected was waiting. These were spread out all over the ship in such a way as to let him wander about and rediscover them on a whim. In the large space of the lowest level, he brought cases of shaving mirrors and pen lasers. For days, he carefully arranged and rearranged an evermore complex thread of red until they covered every meter of the space from top to bottom. All the pens had a single point of origin and were held in place with clamps so that their first destination was all the same. From there, they began their dance of diversion as they passed through prisms and reflected off other mirrors. He couldn't see them, but he traced his progress with a clothing steamer, until the day he was finished and filled the basement with steam from boiling pots. The experience was truly incredible. On the floor, he set out an army of domino laying cars and raced them from on end to the next before they turned about. Each time he reached the bottom of his containers, he would tip the genesis block to begin the age of motion that was its destiny. Then came the cleanup shovels, so he could start all over again. In a more bizarre mindset, he committed to a long riding coat that he saw in spaghetti western. As he toured the region collecting supplies, he never found a coat that matched his image. He thought it should be an oilcloth one that could be nearly as impenetrable as his kevlar, but more practical to wear when the weather heated up again. He eventually found a bolt of very heavy dark brown canvas in a craft store that would work. His first two attempts were travesties that wasted layers from the material, but his third attempt was acceptable.

For all of December, he was diligent about collecting his waste and dumping it through an access panel leading a large construction bin that he parked just outside the loading dock. Larger debris, like propane tanks and some packaging, was stashed inside to take out later. Every couple of weeks, the packaging from new toys and food piled high, and he would open the loading dock to dump in the bin that way. Over time, he was less diligent about this, especially when he

was in the levels overlooking the mezzanine. But once
he receded to the darkness, this practice was easy to
disregard. He was focused on his hobbies or unfocused
in his fog. But never the slob, he tossed everything
on a trailer that he always meant to drive up but
never made it. And since his diet consisted mainly of
dried goods and cans, there was very little noxious
fermentation in the air. By the end of February,
though, he had loaded his trailer and let it overflow
to the ground despite his regular attempts to keep
things stacked into a tower that he eventually could
not reach. This was untenable, and he began the
process of driving through the dog village up all the
ramps expecting severe cold that did not hit, not even
when he opened the panel to begin dropping his refuse
outside. From this small window, he could still see
snow on the ledges of shaded windows across the
street, but the air was not needles of frost anymore.
This was the first indication that the worst of the
winter might have passed, which he took under advise-
ment as he returned to the warm security of his spa.

By far the most eagerly awaited hobby was his collection of psilocybe mushrooms that he had been cultivat-
ing in the stairwell to keep them safe from contamina-
tion. He had over forty small jars that sat in several repurposed balcony greenhouses spread across the
lower levels to compartmentalize the grows, in case
any one was infected. That he could only access them
from the dog level meant that he would not overly fuss
and damage the delicate jars as the mycelium cakes
performed their magic. Each of these were originally
fed by small bags of precooked rice that came from the
grocery stores. He had long felt these products were
travesties as fresh rice was itself so available and
simple to make. But they found a new purpose with
their easy to sterilize packaging. Setting these up
had been one of his first efforts after he sealed himself into the ship. He had many failures but eventually managed to get it right shortly before he permanently moved down to the basement. Now, the masses of
tubes were building, a signal that his long wait would
be over in short order. Already he was able to pull

off the first of them, but had not yet built up the confidence to start consumption. He had always tripped alone when he was younger, but this was decades before and never attempted under the trauma of being the sole survivor of his species.

He found the genesis stash in the tidy home in Georgetown. When he first saw it, he felt a strike of disbelief that such a personality-free home would be hiding such items, as if the household was a curated deceit to give freedom to the occupants in their most private of areas. It gave them a sympathetic character full of fear and desperation. Still, the stash was small and not more than two grams. He did not want to waste it on single a low-dose trip, so he chose instead to see if any of the spores could be extracted from the caps to be inoculated into a grow. He had researched a process shortly before the internet disappeared and had hoped to have made the attempt sustainable, but he met with so much failure. The spores failed to take on one of the two jars and the other spoiled from poor sterilization. He was disappointed by the waste, but soon realized that mushrooms were relatively easy to find within Washington, since consumption had been decriminalized and tracing psilocin was impracticable by the urine tests used by most employers. In fact, it was everywhere. He tried many techniques and wasted most of what he found. By the time the power grid failed, he had put aside his efforts to make his winter preparations, but made a special point to do an industrial scale attempt to grow what remained. He tried this new rice-based technique and found that it worked well. He now had hundreds of nubs growing within his jars for his first round of fruit to harvest. He felt the electricity of anticipation as his body understood that his mind was finally prepared to enter this phase.

He recalled from research that he needed to catch the caps before they dropped their veils to unleash the spores. He felt skeptical that this would destroy future yields, so he decided to run an experiment and let some fully mature inside a sterilized aquarium.

He was ready to start harvesting others as they reached what he assumed was the ideal time. By mid-month, he was pulling out the first of the mushrooms and then found that he was barely able to keep pace with them as they matured unevenly. All of these were headed into a few food dehydrators. He almost had more mushroom than dehydrator space, so he jammed them in. He was overwhelmed by the volume of drugs he grew through a process that was sharpened and published under prohibition laws to make it more efficient and available. This went on for a while and he was eventually left with all the now empty jars of mycelium, which allowed him to test his process for transforming them into a new crop. By the end, he had run out of dehydrator space and had to begin rotating them. It made him thins back to a moment between university and law school where he bought an ounce of mushrooms. He struggled to consume them then and only managed a few trips before he turned to dealing. He managed to grind them down and fill tea bags for a flight out to visit a mushroom-starved city. He now saw that he had five or more ounces with another three rounds incoming, but he had no customers.

In order to trip, he needed a proper space and trust in his surroundings. This was where his meticulous laser show and debris cleanup had factored in. He cleaned the mountain of dogshit on every level above his head to be burned in a metal drum outside the loading door. He sprayed the floors down and cleaned himself. Before he was ready, he set out speakers and phones with long randomized playlists of songs, sounds and other distortions all over the lower levels and the interior stairwell. The last thing he did before he was ready, was to begin simmering large pots that would slowly fill the level with steam and gave life to his web of lasers.

He had no scale. This seemed an irrelevant oversight when he rounded up supplies. He would eyeball his doses in a reckless approach. He selected what he figured was four grams, but was actually a bit more. He ground them down to eat in small spoonfuls washed down with ginger tea liberally sweetened with honey. Little by little, they all reached his interior and began to stew as he laid back on the floor of his yurt to wait and listen to echoing songs. He ate nothing beforehand. He had fasted and was already feeling weak with hunger when the subtle spurt of nausea arrived. He breathed through it. And another came. He became pure observation and pressed through wave after wave of knots until they slowly unwound and then stopped altogether. He never felt nausea in the past, but knew it might be possible, especially since he didn't know the potency of his grow. For this he had a small bucket on hand but hoped it would stay dry. His body began to cooperate and his stomach settled down with more tea as he felt the odd hissing presence of small stoves scattered about outside his yurt setting to work on their volumes of water. But there was more out there. He heard water dripping that he never heard before but always suspected was there. The concrete sounded cold too when it reflected the songs from off the corners and pillars. More was out there. In here, the rounded walls felt more expansive, more distant. And then it came back. He understood the sensations when he watched his eyes blink slowly, no longer in unison. They felt like bubbles of pressure and light. But there was more in here too. The Persian carpets flowed, popped and reset with each blink and his blue veins shined against the flushed red of his skin. So many things these hands touched. But there was more out there. He heard it. Someone was talking and it was not the speakers. He heard it and stood up unsteadily on the rippling ground to find his way through the tent to the fog outside where streaks of red lines blinked as he passed through; disrupting portions of their chains caused a maze of lines to lose contact for an instant before returning. The web caught him, and he tried synesthetic dances to get free. As he fell into them, he disappeared and came back near the ramp and the sound of mosquitoes from the speakers. He swatted at nothing but reflex and felt cold when his attention turned to the chattering party beyond the gate at the top of the ramp. There was more up there. He heard the voices more clearly as he walked up and saw so many eager and worried eyes staring at him. He felt as though he walked into a room that was in mid-party, where half the room stopped to welcome him and the rest continued their conversation. He joined them inside.

So many faces. They spoke to him, asking if he was alright. They knew him and intuited his suffering, but this was something else. He swaggered and waved his body slowly rolling his head on a pivot as he watched them each with his fingers outstretched to tickle their heads as they surrounded him. This one came from a room where it had knocked the door shut and bloodied its claws trying to call out for the laundry outside that never came to its rescue. Another was running around the yard unable to make its way out. He saved each one of them from certain death. He fed each of them and kept them safe from the winter. Nowhere else on the planet were animals as privileged as in that garage. He could find his way in this afterworld only because he could access most everything the civilization had to offer. But they had been ripped from where their survival was theirs to own and brought to live beside humans in comfort. He alone was able to keep this ancient cooperation and he was unsure if he had the energy. He pitied them in their joy at receiving his affection as he squatted in the middle and felt each of their thoughts pierce his.

The wave subsided and he stretched his arms wide, and spun in a swirl of freedom up to the next levels following the sound of a creek and a multicolored ambient light that billowed from phase to phase; from reds to the violets beyond and back. He turned to face this station and walked up the next ramp backwards as he still watched the colors mix with soothing bedtime noises. But he had planned the heavy whites of strobe lights and mechanical music to meet him as he walked to his trucks, which caused him to immediately tense into a curled fury. This level was dedicated to raw reminder. It infected him, eyes open or shut. Nothing changed and little was left to do besides stand dumbfounded and cry because no questions were any longer important. He washed in the light without impression until he was an ooze that reached some doors he generally recalled. He was inside a large gray craft that was parked and waiting for his delicate touch to send it off someplace new. It was a dead habitat with containers full of gelatinous fluid and silent air tanks. He was afraid that he would fall up to the ceiling if he left the safety of the walls, but he saw a civilization inside it, living unaware of their larger home. He was a giant and could crush them as they drove around, but only if they noticed that he had this power. He did not. He was a guest with them and only wanted to see them live, to watch anything continue on as if nothing happened. They drove cars and trains from homes to towers near the center. Something echoed inside him to compel his fingers to dust the bumpy surfaces of all the structures that seemed so soft and familiar.

He had sat in the middle of the city and watched life continue until his head returned to its dream of his muscles and bones. He knew that he was safe and could look up to the ceiling without being sucked into it. He now looked up and recreated the rooms above where he had spent such an impossibly short time that seemed ages before. The psilocin had begun to detach from his serotonin receptors enough to allow him to blink clearly and walk more intentionally back downstairs through his trip in reverse order until he passed laughing through the blinking red web into his yurt where it all began. He always chose to keep his trips pure until the end, where he could catch the unwind and send himself swirling ever faster with cannabis. The vapor bashed his head and careened him back to the deepest distortions where he could feel the abrasions of the rugged walls with his tongue, wiping across them from right to left as he tumbled into the ground under the floor where he felt drain pipes and rivers in the bedrock.

The violence of the swirls could not last. They were soon flattened and made restful again with music and the darkness of lamps that he switched off. There was no more outside and little left inside. The music still punctured his eyes with pillows and fractals that drew him deep into flowing colors of exhaustion. He eventually stood up and went out to draw a bath. Along the way, he was attacked by the laughing red dots before he shut them down and switched off the fires that were burning dry metal as water filled a porcelain pot a few dozen meters away. He shut off the mosquitoes that had transformed into silent crickets before he finally slipped into warm fluid. He soaked in the dark water laced with lavender and calmly scrubbed away the film left on his skin by the trip. Nothing passed through his mind except the flash of images that mixed with earlier memories, making new connections to heal his trauma. He dried off and returned to his yurt to curl up in his blankets and piece it all back together.

In the post-trip insomnia he reached back to his discovery from the garbage slot. Winter was nearly over and he would be free again to go back to the surface in comfort and watch the world wake up from the cold sleep. Just beyond today would be the cherry blossoms and the big sun made for fat fruits. All the decay would disappear and life would return. He was early. He had mobilized an existence inside a cave for months while overwhelmed by fear and change. He was early now to set in motion the comforts of life that humans always knew. He felt the power of control return to him as he hid deep in the tight blankets at the bottom of a multipurpose business tower in downtown Washington. It was the power of balance that he had mastered over the last seven months; the control over want and need so they could be met with reason and flourish. He was an insomniac king deep underground waiting for the time when he might feel interested to reclaim his dominion.

He eventually slept. When he woke up, he was still inside the cloud but ready to come out of hibernation. It had been two long months that glossed past him. He survived. His pack survived and even grew. He kept

everyone alive and safe during the worst of the winter, and it was time to shake it off. As he lay in
the early moments after waking up, his sunrise alarm
clock began to glow, telling him that it was soon to
be 09:00. He had no idea what time he slept, but his
body told him that it was not long before. No matter.
Time was time and it was time. On went the floodlights showing him the full landscape of disarray on
the level, but he was leaving this home soon and may
never return. He made a halting attempt at a morning
routine with breakfast and tea before pulling his tactical outfit out from where he had hung it by the food
shelves. It was still cold, so he kept the long wool
coat instead of testing his oilcloth. He packed a
day's worth of food and water into his courier bag and
went up the ramp. Not knowing what he would find, he
chose to keep all his dogs inside the safety of the
ship as he went out into the bright street that still
had snow and ice in the shade. Everything was normal,
except none of the snow had ever seen a disturbance.
He walked the tidal basin and found no sign of animal
life other than birds flitting around in the bare
branches. He made his way up to where he was attacked
by the feral pack and saw no signs, except the deep
red stain that seeped into the marble. He came up to
the mouth of a metro station that felt to him like the
entry to a dungeon full of special treasure, but he
knew to be filled with damp grime. He decided to
look, more to break a psychological barrier than to
discover anything of use. He carefully walked down
the intensely long and icy escalator steps with his 9
mm drawn and flashlight leading the way. He felt no
interest in being ambushed by any animals that spent
the winter actually struggling to survive. He almost
slipped several times on the way down but managed to
reach the base without breaking anything. Once beyond
the entry where wind could carry debris, the station
was as he remembered it to be when it was a busy chasm
full of tourist and the pressure from passing trains.
He made it down to the platform. The smell was unchanged except for a new sightly burnt odor that was
stronger as he went deeper. On the platform he could
see that there had been a fire not far inside one of

the tunnels. He questioned whether the rails would still be dangerous, so he kept his distance from the power on the outside edge. There, a short distance in was the wreckage of a train that must have derailed or collided with a train in front. As he stood, he caught sight of small mounds of rats walking around in the darkness, no doubt interested in the new smells he brought with him. There was nothing there for him, so he left, listening to the followers work hard to chase him down from behind.

The ascent on the escalators was far easier, mostly because he had both hands free to use the handrails, except the exertion was more than he had done for a while, and he paused at the top to let the mushroom head rush pass. As he stood there, he looked at the Smithsonian castle and tried to decide where he should walk next. Without any particular desire, he settled on his habitual visit to the duck pond at the top of the lawn. Along the way, he passed the sculpture garden across from the Hirshhorn and decided to take the time and go down, something he never did in the past. He was still unmoved by the pieces as he had not been when he passed them before. They were beautiful and grand, especially under the partial snow, but he never felt inspired as with the exhibits inside.

He climbed back to the sidewalk to face the wall of construction outside the space museum, which he had aggravated over with his son. They complained together that the construction was taking too long and affecting one of their favorite museums. Now, the incomplete work would remain permanently, and he viewed it somewhat with renewed interest to imagine what improvements they were completing inside. The Smithsonian had always been interesting with their architecture and this promised to be something impressive. He looked at the preview mural outside and tried to picture the differences. His curiosity turned back to nostalgia, and he wanted to reclaim moments inside where he and his son gaped at technology. The backside was still and evermore the entrance, so he made his way around. He never noticed before but now looked at the Department of Education across the street and he scowled in the memory of all the mismanaged student loans, with scandals and exploitation to create an entire debtor generation while everyone was astonished to learn that college education was increasingly eschewed. All those fake debts were now wiped clean despite the best efforts of so many rent seekers. But that was not this day. He returned focus to the space museum and walked up to its glass doors uninterested in a break in. He was unprepared for destruction in the afterglow of his trip. This might come later, but today was a day of observation, and he instead pressed his face to the glass and strained to look inside. He caught minor details and filled those in with memories of awe at the promise of space travel, memories when he would tell his son that he would live a life that would host unimaginable discoveries offworld. Neither would ever come.

As he headed further towards the ducks, he detoured again to look at the once immaculate botanical gardens that were now both overgrown and dying without the constant upkeep. It was not just the winter that ravaged the grounds, the lack of water and weeding gave the wilderness a savage and destroyed feel that he could only lament that he had not intervened earlier in some way. A look through the windows showed him the same condition as he saw in the outside garden. Ever the planner he wondered whether he had found the next project, the next expense of time that would be an urgent obsession. He could recreate the sensation of living inside his mezzanine surrounded by glass and metal, but fill the space with the softness of life renewed. He would discard the fragility that was the most widely appealing attractions at the garden. There would be no need to maintain anything that would demand so much from him yet offer so little utility. Instead, his garden home would be a habitat of function and would be the opposite of the darkness he fell into for the winter. How much effort would it take to remake the greenhouse? He could assume that everything still alive inside after the harsh temperatures and starvation of the past months would be hardy enough to survive alongside him with minimal attention. Surely he could run it through his process in a matter of weeks, leaving months of enjoyment before the summer heat might push him elsewhere. But then would be months again of enjoyment. His interest waned when he imagined a second winter underground, and he began to distance himself from the dream entirely.

By the time he walked away from the garden, it was 13:00 and he began to feel the press of hunger that a day of fasting had created. The sun was full and had given the lawn its warm appeal even in the winter, so he doubled back to absorb the vitamins and scenery. There at the top of the lawn was a wide expanse that drew in thousands of tourists and residents to bake in the sun or wander about chasing overpriced food trucks. He was among them on many occasions. This was nearly the time to fly kites on the hill under the obelisk where the wind grabbed best. He'd come through here in many forms of himself all thinking the same thoughts of indistinct destinations towards which he had to walk. His family slowed his movements and allowed him to draw in the colors of intense green against the dull gray band of the horizon before it gave way to the powder blue sky above. He remembered them. The grass was yellowed and shaggy, not yet green. The lines of trees were bare and did little to hide the wall of drab buildings lining the north edge of the lawn. He finally chose a place to sit after he quieted his legs that ached to continue the walk to nowhere. It was warm under his wool that he bunched into a pillow as he watched clouds pass overhead. He ate his usual lunch of jerky and shortbread with a large thermos of mint tea to dissolve it all as he let the time wash past.

There was a destination to be reached. Somewhere in the city would be a place he would reach and decide that enough walking had been had for the day. He would explore with no purpose until he discovered a capstone that would stand out in his memory to claim the day as a journey to that moment. Something still drew him back to the duck pond that was overlooked by the Capitol, the same structure he watched from the roof during the first snow. They had always stood together, and he stood up after wiping the grease and crumbs from his chest before he stuffed the packaging back in his bag. The duck pond was not far from where he sat. As he moved toward it, he strained his now sensitive ears to catch signs of ducks at play, but could not. Nor could he hear them as he approached. When he stood on the steps leading over to the edge, he saw a cesspool that was half as full compared to normal. There were no ducks to eat the slime or furtive bits of food dropped by tourists. It was now just a barren fountain enclosed by stone. There was no echo of his son laughing at the birds or dashing between places along the edge where he could insert himself into the small bird dramas. There was nothing whatsoever that reminded him of the past. Perhaps it could return in the warmer months, but now it only spoke of death and quietude. This could be no destination to mark the day. Not when there was still so much warmth from the sun and glow from his mind. It felt as if he had wandered into a funnel and circled the central eye as he was pulled down to the gravitational center of the mall. At this distance, the Capitol looked smaller and you could clearly see the stairs that surrounded it. When you looked at it from a distance, from the other end of the mall, it looked like a geographic feature rather than an apparatus of civil government. From out there, it always had the haziness of moist air that made it shimmer or fade, depending on what the sun chose to provide that day. He circled the eye once more, but now watched the deep channel that pulled him in as he did so. He made his way around the pond along his abandoned garden, neither of which had been capable of commanding his day, though he took his time as always. There would be no rush to seek out meaning. No amount of force was worth a deviation from his meandering discovery of details. Even as he approached, he looked about for a new diversion; something to take him away from the obviousness of this path.

He had stayed away from visiting the Capitol so far. His last time inside was before the outrageous escalation of security in the era of the war on terror. By the time those inconveniences had become normalized, he avoided it because of the crowds of tourists. After the evaporation, he felt too uncertain about his right to enter any of the government houses. Now he was committed to a visit and wondered what exactly he sought. He was no tourist. He had no need for photos to prove his presence or listen to guides deal out historic facts. Standing at the base of the stairs, he heard the sounds of a screaming mass. The day turned a cold gray, and he saw the barricades shake as they pushed up against them with few capitol police pushing back. They flirted and wobbled until they grew bored and wanted more thrill of the illegal. He found the place where he thought she was thrown back to have her head crushed on the steps before they poured behind the barriers and up to the Capitol. He had watched these in the dark of night on the other side of the planet, confused and angry. The images had the power to make cowards inside the chambers look like heroes, if for only for an instant before they settled back to a legacy of cowardice. A month later, he watched it again in his neighborhood where the military used the Overton shift that happened here at the Capitol to justify their own coup and order soldiers to shoot children in the head if they resisted. All of this had quieted, but it had marred him too deeply. All of their power would evaporate some short years later and all that they would leave behind was embarrassed anger.

He didn't walk up these stairs. They had been tainted. His entry to this building would not be an insurgency of force, and he could not let himself model his feet along their path. He could not use their doors to gain access. He would be reverent and walk the outside calmly, occupying the wide gulf between tourist and invader. This day would be his final memorial to the loss that happened. His final home invasion where he would aim to dissect the institution that occupied this building and make a verdict

on how to proceed once it was complete. He walked in
this manner. As he rounded the corner to the front,
he inspected the Article III house across the street
and felt the disgust that was the companion to the
anger he left back at the base of the steps. The cult
that had congealed inside there was little more than a
theatrical rubber stamp. He could not waste his time
with this distraction, so he continued on to the front
side of the Capitol. He climbed the central staircase
to reach the main doors and found that they were still
open, ready to receive staffers even at such a late
hour on a Friday. In a continuation of his deference
to distinction, he walked through the dormant metal
detectors and stepped over the uniforms scattered
about on the floor. He reached down to one and removed the keys in case these would be needed for
locked doors deeper inside. He stood a moment with
them in his glow before he walked into the rotunda.

The history hit him harder than he anticipated. He
took the care to inspect the paintings and busts. He
laid on the floor and watched the inside of the dome
while he listened for echoes. None spoke to him in
the empty building. He found the stairs up to the
gallery and above, checking each artifact along the
way. He walked each of the hallways and passed by offices that had piles to hold the doors open. He saw
more in offices and more still outside elevators. The
July 4th weekend was one that emptied the city of anyone privileged enough to have vacation rights. The
staffers and ordinary workers continued on in their
absence. They were still there, never free to leave
the building, and he saw them for this. He lost count
of how many he found, but he did not lose track of his
surprised disappointment. It was a depressing sight
that he brought into the chambers, which were locked.
He was already at the upper level when he opened a
door into a small and antique chamber, far too small
for what he recalled as the seat of government. His
light passed over tables below that were set out in
the style of schoolhouse desks for students to focus
on a vaudeville podium. He knew little of the history
but felt its age. It was in the central building and

must have been part of the original structure. Something happened here. He checked outside to find a placard and saw that this was the old host for the Senate, the chamber of state power. It was small, and the country clearly outgrew it long ago. He made his way down to the floor and wandered back inside to touch the wood grain of the desks and imagine what debates had happened here. They were too removed from him to feel critical, too antique to feel grounded in the controversies of civilization's final hours. He absorbed and observed as he moved about inside.

He was a short walk down the corridor from the modern Senate, where he could fill his outrage again. She must have died here. What would one possibly expect from an attempt to pry into the seat of any government when it was in session? In the nations that they envied, all of them would have been gunned down in the street long before they even reached the stairs outside; before they managed to constitute themselves online to rally the numbers to even reach the city. She died and they were surprised idiots. He used his key and unlocked his door. His light did not reach far inside the large chamber. He knew what it looked like from a lifetime of television. It was where presidential transitions happened and nearly unhappened through a cynical and inverted logic of democracy. The electoral college was indeed flawed and reinforced power asymmetries, but it was not a boon demanding overthrow by a small cohort. Each desk he passed was a testament against the idea of a one-person-one-vote democracy. Each was a dilution that put the people in competition with the state; it was a power share to flatten the peaks and valleys of populism that felt like a process frustrated for both in their inability to fully capture the whole. Each desk collapsed into one. He was the sole voter in a sole state where he was alone to qualify as his own representative in this chamber. He owned the building both as a structure and an institution. This was his house inasmuch as all capitals were now his. He could elect himself in an uncontested election with a unanimous vote. His voter set of one was inelastic authoritarian power.

He walked the rows fingering the desks and chairs until he navigated his way to the front and turned back
to see the emptiness of the room that was not uncommon
even in the days of legislation. He pulled out a
chair in the front row and sat down in the silence.
What would he introduce if he had the floor? How
would he debate it and would that even matter? He
surveyed the texture of the chair under him and the
legroom in front. This had been a routine seat for
someone, as were they all. He had little understanding of the table at the front, below the dais. He had
images of the house side with its podium and large
structure where leadership sat, but knew less about
this chamber. He knew that everything was arranged
towards the Vice President at top of the dais. He
made his way up and stumbled on the carpeted stairs as
he climbed to claim power.

He examined the table where only one woman in history
had ever sat as incumbent. He imagined that he took
her power through rightful succession after ascending
from the representatives' floor. He swiveled in his
chair with nothing in particular to do, until he noticed that one of the doors along the back wall was
propped open with a wheeled cart from the night cleaners. He looked at the floor and saw her pile on top
of thick-soled comfort shoes. The shine wore off, and
he felt foolish to playact government. He had shaken
the surprise he felt on the hallways and cloistered
himself in the fantasy of the chamber. The reminder
of simple struggle brought him back and the thrill of
power melted away again. He angled out of the chair
and picked her up from the floor, folding her uniform
to be placed on the nearest desk before he left the
chamber behind. Back in the hallway, he looked across
to the other chamber. The space in between was dark
but interspersed with light reflections from small
windows. He reached the House and explored in much
the same way but left the leadership seats unmolested.

He left through the back door. On the balcony, he
walked through a mob as it made its way up from the
grounds below. He saw their parodied flags waving

above their tactical gear and selfies. It was a mess from this perspective. They flooded up and waited for someone to push them through to their next stage. What exactly had they envisioned as they stood there? There were some embedded cells with a clear objective, but most were human shields to provide cover. But even shields can be culpable for their defenses, even if they lacked knowledge of their directives. Mob was the instruction. Chaos and diversion was their function. So what might they have thought would come next once they reached the balcony? It could only progress to the end, to her pointless death curated to distract. They had mobbed through the well-worn public spaces of the mall from the Ellipse across the lawn. The grass was designed as a staging ground for soldiers but put to better use by the polis. For decades, it was a destination to fill. It had not functioned well as an avenue for travel, particularly for mass movement from the Article II zone. They were clearly herded that day.

His day was still clear, and he had not invested many hours within the building behind him. Just to the right was the traditional road that linked the White House and the Capitol; Pennsylvania Avenue was designed to quickly mobilize troops and supplies between the two nerve centers. Its sidewalks were enormous and the lanes wide enough for tanks. It was an avenue designed for spectators and civic disruption. And the city was a city of civic disruption to garner public attention. He had joined the occupy protests when they encamped at McPherson Square and knew well how settled the practice of street marching was here. A march on the mall would never achieve the disruption that the mob wanted from the Senate that day. No targeted demonstration would be satisfied with a message hidden away behind the pedestrian paths on the lawn. It had to be a mobilization of forces to make any sense. Looking at it from the tactical perch of the balcony, he understood all this clearly. That was historical fact overcome by events. There was nothing special about the realization, no lessons to learn or apply anymore. These were mere statistical events for

him to file away under the general heading of knowledge. Everyone who transgressed that day was gone and
would never pass through the arc of reflection to con-
tribute to national healing. No one who benefited
from false victimhood would be held to account. It
was all just a waste.

His mind turned from January 6 and replaced it with
the intended images for the balcony of that month and
the inauguration. The transfer of power was as settled a practice as the promenade of the new leader
down Pennsylvania Avenue to the White House just beyond the clump of trees, which were barely visible at
the far end of the road. Thousands would spend the
day in front of him, reaching far across the lawn with
no hope of any actual sight of the ceremony but were
there instead to say that there they had been, just in
case history followed. He squinted to see exactly how
they would look, estimating how far they would reach,
even as this itself was a fraught exercise of
gaslighting. He laughed to himself. So much of politics was absurdity mired in gravitas, but this particular detail had brought so much lighthearted enjoyment
to so many. Yet it came on as a sad reflection that
so little consensus was available, no wonder there
were invading forces who marched through the same
grounds a few years later. Reality was so malleable
from the start that it could only end with violent
pantomime.

He was done on the balcony. The day had not found a
destination and he ached for it to continue. What he
needed was his own exuberance to exhibit a right of
ownership, and there was little better choice than to
follow the historic course from the steps down to the
avenue, where he could rest the day at the center of
power, not the center of authority he just toured.
There was a difference that he needed to explore and
this could no longer be trapped in abstraction, he
would need to feel the pressing smells of the rooms
for himself in order to give the difference over to
its true form. From the street level, there was nothing particularly interesting to see. This was a mun-

dane city road full of history as everywhere else. Nothing stood out now that it had been emptied of people. It was gray and cold. The stoplights stopped and there were no cars parked on either side. As he walked, he felt no connection to the scenes of streamers and parade. He saw the backside of the National Gallery, where he enjoyed his time, but then there were the hotels that spotted the roadside to cash in on the spectacle that happened every four years. These would be overfilled and overpriced to match the demand from entrenched wealth that knew how much they could afford the rooms against the gains they would pull in from presidents of both parties. Faces rarely changed from these balconies. Nor would they need to do so. Each successive administration lined them up and paid them out as diligently as any machine. He couldn't help himself but to waive to them with a knowing smile. They would crumble and never return to their balconies. No president would be a concessionaire for their short-sighted interests that submerged the country. He also waved and blew kisses to the families of tourists on the street who braved the cold weather and the tight restaurant reservations to watch a single man pass them by. He passed the city Mayor at the end of the road before meeting the trees.

By the time he had reached the old post office, though, he waved less and his blood cooled in the calm of the final leg of the walk. He had passed this way months before and feinted at the idea of walking in. There was a difference between authority and power. He could inject himself inside the institution of authority but the moral risk of taking power was categorically different. When he nearly reached the gate, where he stopped before, he had yet to resolve the hesitation he felt. It came up fast. He'd walked the length of history and came up empty. Its approach was a fact that failed to stall, and Alexander Hamilton gave him no advice as he passed under his gaze. He arrived and stood in the same location as before looking up at cameras that he now was certain were offline and no one was watching him from a screen on the other side. It was safe, he knew this, but was it right?

His feet moved before he resolved this question. They brought him incrementally closer, first to check the guardhouse with only laundry, then to see the barricades and test their weight. They were defensive in response, offering him no option to exact any effect. He tried to turn around and look back at the capitol. His feet deceived him and moved inside the perimeter of power instead. There was no change. No crash of the earth or snipers at the ready. He had casually walked through the gate as he had casually walked through the capitol earlier in the day. A regular sequence of banal body movements was all it took for him to enter both. He had never done a tour before, so had never looked onto the South Lawn absent the black lines of the fencing along the walkway. He watched as Nixon crossed it in humiliation to board Marine One a pariah. It was small and open, as it should be. He turned to the facade and made his way towards it as unimpeded as his entry.

The uniforms he saw in the house of power differed from the house of authority. These were the pleats of military. They were in windswept and damp piles along the outside, still standing watch over the doors to eye him as he rounded to the North side. With so much security in place, he was not surprised to find the doors open. This was a home designed to push its perimeter out to the streets and monitor all movement that managed to reach inside. There would be no point to lock a door so watched. Nor was there security once inside the door, and he found himself in the entrance hall, a conman without an audience. He had no idea where he was or how to navigate the ornate rooms of the darkened main level, so he made his way inside following intuition. This led him to the right of the entry, knowing this would take him to the West Wing that television told him was the proper set of offices. He wound his way through the lavish rooms of the entrance level before realizing he needed to go down to the ground floor to access the walkway, but this was easier in theory than practice. By the time he managed to find it, he began to see more and more piles that told him he must be heading down the right hallway, if for no other reason than that it was well-worn. Then, the piles stopped as he pushed deeper into the narrow passages. He had heard that these were the office spaces around the Oval Office that were notoriously small. He was lost in the maze. After half a dozen turns he noticed an open office door at the far corner. He had tried most doors all along his path, primarily finding closets and meeting rooms with nothing inside as everyone seemed to have had a patriotic break for the weekend. This one appeared large but darker than the others, so he assumed it was another meeting room. He nudged the door open a bit and saw the familiar rounded walls of the Oval Office darkened with heavy curtains. He felt the return of apprehension at the discovery. He waited, but his legs did not proceed. Instead, they kept him in place. He was allowed to shine his light inside and scan the floor for the familiar piles that did not seem to be there. Why would this office be open when all others were shut for the night? Something felt odd to him, and he felt the unsettled question linger without shape.

Satisfied with the sights but not the conclusion, he turned back to continue with his maze, only to realize that he was already that the start. He had chosen poorly from the first and made the full run through the halls before reaching the Oval Office that was right there. He headed back to the main building and wanted to understand what was in the East Wing, as this was never taught to him. He reached the first of the security lines along the way and understood that this must be where the public entered. When he encountered more locked doors that prevented him from investigating further, he knew this wing would be a frustrating journey through business hours that froze in time. He returned to the main building and went back upstairs. He followed the stairs all the way up until he found a wall of piles that told him he was getting close to the Presidential residence and that he had been home that night. At the top, there was a long, decorated hallway with rooms that were both open and closed. One in particular was heavily guarded by

laundry. When he tried the handle, he found that the
door was locked and if the day were to have any destination, it would be found by first inspecting the contents of this room. He first looked through the uniforms that were on the floor outside the door, but
none of the keys would fit. This room must have been
locked from the inside and contained higher levels
than would be allowed from the guards. He debated
about shoving it in, since it was unreinforced wood,
but this would be the last option. He wandered
through the other rooms to find a pile with more authority. He checked half a dozen key sets and none
would open the door, so he gently pressed his shoulder
and gave it a shove.

He was in. He learned that he was not in a room but
another hallway that was shorter than the others and
had only four doors leading off it. It had the
bizarre feel of a one-bedroom apartment which normal
people rented, with everything so congested into your
face. One door was wide open, and he could smell long
rotten food come through. The smell was old and by
that time already dwindled into the generic mustiness
of rat urine. His light showed a dining table with
binders and papers spread out across it and around the
used flatware. This was the resting place of the last
President.

He had found his destination. There, amid the binders
and papers, was the casual wear of an elder statesman
at an evening meal slash briefing. There were maps
and tablets, along with pages of reports which were in
process of being marked up. All were either orange or
yellow, and it was his first time viewing such sensitive information. As he read, he felt the difficulty
of decisions that outwardly seemed so simple to the
public. Here was page after page of complications
that could never be discussed openly. Or could they?
What would be the result in the international space if
face was lost? He pushed aside the dishes full of
smears where rodents had eaten the mainstay. He re-
viewed the briefs and tried to read the scribbles that
were made in haste by a practiced hand. He went

through them, around the world and back home. He ate
the secrets there at the dining table. Some was confirmation bias for his work, others were contradic-
tions. So much was new. So many discrete conflicts
and disasters in places of which he'd never heard. He
read furiously and realized that he was ferreting. He
was hoping to find some hint of a crisis that would
help him understand the evaporation; understand what
made eight billion lives disappear. There was nothing. It was as thrilling as it was irrelevant.

He put the pages down and looked around. He saw the
large bag that was probably the football and contained
the means to destroy the rest of life on the planet.
But this was not even a conversation piece between the
two leaders. They had nothing to talk about. He
wanted only to understand the end of civilization
while the President wanted to only prevent the end of
the United States using outdated information. He sat
there awkwardly, unable to decide how to proceed. Ultimately, all that was left was to unburden himself
and make conversation as best he could. One of them
had to present the opening salvo and run the risk of a
misdirected effort.

"Mr. President, what the hell happened?" He started
the conversation with as much plain candor as he
could.

"Why don't you have anything in all these top secret
pages that even hint at the risk of people disappearing?" He waited a moment as if he expected a response
to come from the oxford shirt and slippers. He caught
himself and felt silly for this outburst into nothing.
"You didn't know, did you? No one here knew anything."

That was his answer. Its obvious as soon as he
mouthed it. The silence was all that could be said.
If he knew, he would not be taking a briefing over
dinner. The evaporation took the most powerful intelligence apparatus in history by complete surprise.
And he survived it. So he continued and read the

President in on the crisis, from his own perspective and with as little editorializing as he could. It was organized around discoveries and details he isolated when and where possible. The President listened and asked no questions as he wove the story of the last seven months. When he reached the end, he was empty. Rehashing the experience left him feeling vacant and spent, not unburdened as he had hoped. It was not neither a confession nor a session; it was the ramblings of a man who had seen no face for nearly a year and was desperate to seize an encounter, no matter how surreal it could be. A void had opened in the room.

"I *am* your successor, I suppose." He tried again, from another angle. "I wonder if you had prepared your private letter for me somewhere in this house."

He thought about the power he held in the pages of these binders and to which he was now entitled to hold. These were secrets that could topple governments and destroy legacies. They also had the power to save countless lives. This was the power of information that was now impotent, not because the information changed, but because there were no more listeners upon whom to act. Power needs an object. It cannot act alone. Power cannot be a consensus like authority. The two occupy separate universes that only occasionally meet when conditions become so complex that solutions need to blend. But at its core, power is inert and weak, while authority is active and without objects. It exists insofar as it exists, until it doesn't. So often these two are conflated. The mob had misjudged its authority through its belief in the power it quickly found was lacking. Had either been stronger, they would have succeeded. They failed because they lacked both. He did not fail because he had both. He had the authority of a sovereign consensus and the power to overcome the institutions. His bloodless coup was immediately authoritarian and democratic. There was no separating the two from his individual right as a citizen to the sovereignty of his own design. It was not a coup, but rather a transformation. All that was missing was for him to claim it,

but in so doing he had to be sensitive to the possibility that he was pushing out against the rights of
others, which might destroy his consensus authority
and threaten his absolute power over the planet.

As his mind wandered, awkward air returned to resonate
in the words he spoke to no one. The room had transformed as well and now felt like a stuffy, poorly lit
dining room in an ordinary home. He had owned so many
mansions and museums that not even the history of the
room felt impressive anymore now. Everything was now
complete. The only thing left to do was to collect
the binders and the heavy black bag sitting to the
side, then leave the elderly man to his meal. With
the setting changed absent all the important papers,
the table looked as small as the chairs with the bits
of clothes draped across them. He said his respectful
goodbye as he closed the door that he broke an hour
before, stepping over the guards who failed to stop
him as he did.

The bag was heavy and cut into his shoulder because
the design was not made for carting such a load in
comfort. This was an aesthetic compromise. He em-
pathized with those who carried this as a duty and
could not imagine hauling it back to his ship that was
so far away. He began to wonder why he even took it
in the first place. There was nothing of value inside
anymore, and it only served to satiate his rising
power fetish. Downstairs by now, he wondered if he
shouldn't leave it somewhere. The only reasonable
resting place would be the Oval Office just down the
hall. As he pondered this, his legs moved him closer
until he was outside the door again in the midst of
the same hesitation as before. The strap was biting
by then, so he pushed the door open slowly and walked
inside.

It was another stuffy airless room, but larger than
the one where he found the President. Much smaller,
though, than television had suggested. He stood just
inside the doorway and looked about with his flashlight. The curtains had made the room quite darker

than necessary, but a thin slice of sun still managed to cut inside to leave a narrow band of gold across the Resolute Desk over to the President's meeting chair on the other side of the room. He walked over to the curtains to draw them open and fill the room with gold. Light had arrived. It touched the walls with softness and wrapped around the furniture. He could see the room in full scale. It definitely was a room of history where every detail spoke of meaning and had received the attention of an elite corps of cleaning staff. They polished and fussed over so much that there had been a remarkably limited amount of dust that had accumulated over the months of neglect. This somehow impressed him more than the power oscillating through the chamber; they had managed to create a lasting legacy of tidiness. He put the bag on the coffee table. He was now unburdened. The bag landed with a muted thud as the metallic case inside bumped against the wooden table. He sat down in the meeting chair and watched the silhouette of the desk where the low hung winter sun peeked through behind. It only made sense to change to the other side of the room where he would not need to fight the light to see. Standing behind the chair, he now had the window at his back and the full support of the sun to proceed with assuming the seat of power. He lacked a plan. He had moved from trauma to survival and now acceptance of his authority over the planet. Seated in the fiction of power now, he could think of no particular course of action. Survival was still his greatest need, and it faced threats everywhere. This desk was the decision maker's. It was the day's destination, but it offered no guidance for him on where he should go next for another day.

It was so mute that it seemed silly. He held all the power now but lacked the means to effect it. This was the greatest dilemma of a leader: how to do what needs to be done with the limited tools available with which to do it. All the nation's tools were gone. There would be no new technological advances to beat back the ancient threats of disease that would surely meet him again. He was stuck with the aging equipment that was new when civilization ended. The timer was counting down for all his batteries, generators and packaged food. He made the decision last fall to face the discomfort head on and prepare for a winter without a power grid, rather than wait for it to fail while he was unprepared with the low temperatures. He might need to face it again. He had no power to recreate the production of this equipment in any of the factories that he now owned. He needed labor to operate the machines and run the computers. He tried and he failed. He was an office worker, with skills over describing political economies in fragile countries and all the variables he needed for this had disappeared. Politics, economy, states were all gone. He was powerless to adapt these skills to the productive industries.

The disillusionment welled up from the exhaustion of walking the city under the haze of his mushroom glow. He imagined that he had at his fingers, there on the desk, an array of buttons that he need only press to operate the nation and bring it all back online. A moment of rest brought a resurgence of hallucination as he saw line of circuitry bleed out from him into the walls and beyond. He was the central processor sending commands here at the President's desk. The vision was nearly crystallized before it faded again, and he was aware that he stared at a blank section of the wall opposite him. His heart ached for all the missing destinations for those circuits. All the offices and hubs where commands would be synthesized and meted out further to maintain the fluidity of civilization. It occurred to him that this too was the leaders' lament. The clarity of the circuitry and vision that is disrupted by the reality of the complex organisms that was civilization. This was the lack of power to "just do" that so many leaders mistook for intentioned adversaries instead of the ecosystem of power-sharing with authority. The irony was that it all had collapsed together into him but the lament remained. The centrality was intact, but the circuitry had disappeared except to the extent that it followed him. There was no more significance in this desk in this house than when he sat in his cave. He was everything now. He was the endpoint of the circuits as much as he was the central processor. This was the very definition of sentient survival, which could never be fixed to a single location if it is to continue.

With no reason to stay, he stood up from the Resolute Desk and pushed the chair back into its hovel. Before he left, he took a tour of the paintings and the busts in the office, just to capture in his mind the memories that would tell him that he had been there. He left the West Wing without passing through the maze again, now that he knew the way back to the entrance and out the same gate that he felt was his, after so much wrangling. He was done with his tour of the halls of government that he had not expected nor would have shunned had he planned. As he left, he passed the Ellipse again and stood there at the origins from where the forces had mobilized before they chased shadows. He was glad that they failed. They and those who drove them failed to understand the institutions that were under threat and would have devoured them had they succeeded. But he pitied them for their dispossessed desperation. This was real. There was a system mobilized against them, and it did need to change, but would not. They should have marched down Pennsylvania Avenue instead. He put them out of his mind as he walked back across the lawn. He walked up to the base of the obelisk and looked around at the landscape that was pink as the sun was leaving. It cast a dramatic glow on all the white buildings that opened into the mall. His mushroom mind let the wind blow into his eyes. He looked again at the ancient picture and imagined how long before the forest would return and how many sheep he could graze before they did.

IX
Gates of Langley

He reached his ship a bit after the sun set because he took his time wandering around. It was cold, and he had nothing left inside him. The thought of trekking back underground left him feeling like it would be a retreat, so he resolved to stay on the surface. The trouble was that his months of neglect had made it a chaotic disaster, no less because of the rambling mushroom fingers that dragged this way and that. There was nothing left to do but push the city away and climb into his tent fully clothed. It was the sort of tired that didn't notice a thing. Pulling up the blankets was like moving under a wave just before it crashed and swallowed while the pillow hurt from a misjudgment in distance as he landed. Nevertheless, sleep came later. He was stuck in the purgatory of unconscious wakefulness. For nearly an hour he watched his hands and cheeks vibrate from blood rushing in.

The morning was cold again, and gray. He woke up hungry, so he made some oatmeal with protein mix, which had a terrible taste that he grew to like, and some powdered eggs. He ate this standing in front of the doors trying to calculate the percentage of chance that snow would fall soon. Since it looked high, he decided to stay indoors. Aching with some lingering glow, he felt the urge to play with cartoons again, so he lumbered up the stairs with a supply of bottled water that he was too lazy to raise in the hoist but couldn't leave below in case he'd run out in his nest as it was so long that he was up there. He opened a cannabis soda and started the generator that would charge his batteries while he nested. He played and napped for hours as the storm threatened outside until it could hold back no more and dumped itself onto the city. Winter was wearing thin. He lost patience for it weeks before, and now it was just a question for time to decide when it was over. Each flake annoyed him, and he realized he was too distracted to pay attention to cartoon violence to get any enjoyment from it, so he shut everything down and left the nest.

Returning to the cave was a return to defeat after his optimistic debut walk. But once reached, it was an old friend that wrapped its arm around his shoulder and whispered jokes into his ear. He stayed there as before and checked the surface every few days for weeks. He eventually started to see the progress of time with small buds popping on the trees, some at first then nearly all so that everything had a slight lime tinge. One year ago, this would have made the news as so many people were waiting for the best estimates for peak cherry blossoms that could only be made when the buds began to appear. This was the final push that gave him license to leave the garage, but it meant a large-scale cleanup inside. He carefully disassembled his city and moved it up to an office that he cleared before but did not attribute. It would now be his construction level that he could visit later should he want to continue his life in miniature. With it gone, the mezzanine mostly returned to being a villain's lair. The space was large enough to make him wonder about transporting his yurt to the surface. He left it down below, but did unseal the loading dock so that the pack could dive out from the ramp he built over the rodent wall, which he discovered was actually best suited to hold back the snow melt from inundating the garage and flooding the lower levels. They flew out only to congregate on the street in front, unsure where they might go from there. He left them to their own process of discovery.

Spring meant that he was early enough to establish his dreamed farm on the National Mall. It had seemed idiotic at first, but fell more in line with reason after he pulled the threads of detail. He would first survey the countryside to take stock of what sheep were still alive. They no doubt could last through the cold of winter, but he was unsure if they could find food on their own. He was more skeptical about finding chickens, with all the foxes looking for them, but he was starved for fresh eggs again. Little by little, he found fluffy stragglers on a variety of land in Virginia. He had to be vigilant in spotting them from the road. When he did, he would skulk up from downwind and shoot a tranquilizer dart that he collected from local humane societies. After a week, he had a dozen head of different breeds all moved to their new home below the obelisk. As he went, he entered barns and took what hay looked least moldy to pile onto the raised floor of the World War I Memorial, thus keeping the flock sort of nearby. His pack learned to harass them but not injure, and eventually they reached a point where they could congregate together. The lawn eventually became green too, and the sheep spread out. There were now fifty of them, and he had worried about finding enough hay just as the shoots started to come up. On bright days, he could sun himself and watch the flock roam around. There was little for him to do other than keep the reflecting pool full of water pumped in from the river. As the lawn greened more, he noticed that he was losing sheep. They had not moved up to other parts of the mall, nor did he believe they were eaten. This puzzled him for days until he heard bleating from all around. He found some stuck in the metro station, confused how to get back on the platform after jumping down. Others were lost in the courtyards of huge federal agencies. They had scattered all over with what seemed like no good reason. Some of the best runners of his pack had understood the task and were eager to help him chase the mindless animals back to where their food and water was. He realized that these survivors were probably the ones from each original flock who were daring enough to explore, and thus were able to escape starvation locked in their pens. But that's what he needed now. He needed a large fenced pasture to keep them inside where they were more manageable, but it would need to be one that had high and difficult to scale fences. The guard waved them through the East Gate and into the South Lawn of the White

House. It had the advantage of being close at hand. Eventually, the last one was caught and moved to its new jail. The absurdity of the image was too much that he couldn't help but call out to the President to see if he approved. There was no answer. With the sheep sequestered, he turned back to the lawn and began to churn the soil and set about planting early vegetables. So far, in all his outings, he never found any live chickens and this was his greatest tragedy. Yes, the ducks had returned, and he considered using them to replace chicken eggs, but he had never grown to like the taste in the past. Duck meat was good, but duck eggs were potent and rubbery. No, he needed chickens.

It was a good replacement life at this point. What he lacked in humanity he made up with humanity's ancient companions. His days were filled with chores and visits to the country looking for more. It was a very old social contract with each participant falling into cooperation very rapidly, with almost no discussion. This contract was so old and universal, it had never been disrupted even in the final days. There had been millions of households like his now. If any one among them survived, they would be managing well in this afterworld. They all had their place in the triangle, each reinforcing the other while taking benefits from them. It worked. If he could track any of them down, they could bring humanity back. All the resources were self-contained and ready to be deployed, if the connections could be made. The weak pillar in the troika would become strong again. It was math. But math was a numbers game. A species would require a threshold of numbers to reach sufficient genetic diversity to maintain itself through the generations. He had dozens of dogs, many of which had been sterilized, and more sheep. Neither pool would be large enough. Those husbands he imagined out there would have captured other herds to consolidate them into superherds. His was nothing of the sort. If they were out there, he may never find them. If he found them, they may be solitary like himself. If they were female of reproductive age, and if he found her before he was defunct, they would only be a pool of two. There would be no hope of population growth beyond a third generation of wretchedly inbred cretins. No, his would be the last generation. There was no point in trying to do more. He could maintain his end of the contract for as long as possible before stepping away for the other two parties to renegotiate. He was only a visitor. He was accustomed to the bipolarity of his life now. He would be manic for weeks before a cascade of misery pulled him into a depressive winter. These hit so often and so forcefully that they lost their edge and became flat. This all became part of daily life of late, and each wave lost significance so that he could see it for what it was and carry on until it passed.

The following morning was wet, the type that would be marked by the slushing sound of tires as they cut the surface of the road and tossed drops of water behind. It was a day for a walk to let the waves move along. The cherry blossoms were still unready to pop, but the tidal basin was alive nonetheless. Daffodils already appeared in their perennial hangover that made the walk feel normal. He looked out at the water and could see the Jefferson Memorial on the other side, so he made his way over before being distracted by the boats docked on the pier and wondered how many would be safe to take out, if he were to learn. He scanned the river, which looked the same as ever. It cared little whether humanity remained to navigate its surface. Just beyond was the Pentagon. Inside that structure were the implements of overseas power. In there were the small offices that altered the course of diplomacy in Iraq and led to decades of death. And that was routine for the building. The President had no information on the evaporation at his final briefing, but inside there might be the first stirrings of early warning. It might be that the event was asymmetrical and began in stages elsewhere so that these small offices could have picked up the crisis before it hit. He could have been wrong to assume that information would have been put on the public facing websites, there may be millions of private messages desperately looking for answers, just as his in those early hours. Indeed, he posted almost nothing publicly himself. He put all this aside, knowing that the information inside would be locked behind barricades then inside inaccessible devices. The normal walk continued.

He went to check on his White House sheep, who had worked their teeth to great effect on the lawn. The contract stipulated that they should be fed well, preferably grazed and not penned. They were coming up on the end of what the lawn could provide, meaning they would either need to be let out in the daytime and chased about as they ate their way through the monuments, or he could bring more food to them. He knew there was little hay left in the easy-to-reach farms, but that he could drive further to find more. There was a large flatbed trailer he used to haul some of his winter equipment that would be perfect for a long excursion into the countryside. He had driven trailers since he was back in Texas, but this was an industrial trailer that reached back far further than he had known. When he used it last fall, he drove slowly and had multiple near misses with sharp corners and parked cars. City driving was never his skill, so he was confident that the trailer would behave better out in the wideness of the farm roads. He drove out towards Shenandoah, for the scenery as much as keeping to task. Driving empty in the slick rain was an unwise choice that became very clear as he picked up speed outside the tight city roads. The day cleared a bit as the sun intensified around noon, and he was able to begin loading some huge silage rolls from where they were still fermenting in a field. The truck creaked from strain as he pulled back onto the road. A few miles on, he slowly crept up a winding hill with what he felt was a more stable haul than what he brought. On the way back down, though, the trailer began to catch up to him and pushed the truck from behind as he tried to ease around a wet curve. It slid, pulling them all off the shoulder to topple down the embankment. The truck was tossed and rolled. His mind quickly accepted the new conditions and repeated the instruction "don't grab anything!" as he waited for it to be over. When it ended, he was on the high side, partly upside down bruised and scratched. He checked all the signs. Limbs worked. Head unbashed. No smell of diesel. The windshield was an opaque matrix and he struggled with the cumbersome weight of his door as he tried to get out, scared that the truck would roll more as he began shifting. He jumped down and collapsed with pain from where his thigh hit the bottom of the wheel. It was not broken. He was safe, though there was no one to call and no one would pass. So he continued his normal walk to look for a house.

The countryside being what it is, he walked for a few miles before reaching the next home, which was a cluster of new and treeless manufactured homes. Everyone had been home when they left, so he had a good selection of cars from which to choose. The echo of the slipping wheels nagged him the entire ride back home. He thought only of having his feet on settled ground again. He nearly stopped at his Ashburn home to rest but was not confident that it would still be a place of comfort after so many months. He pressed on back to his ship. The rain had returned somewhere as he made his way into the city and the warm dark comfort of his spa was all he wanted. It could clean his scratched skin and soften his muscles which would surely begin aching. It worked. It felt like the nothingness that he needed after too much something. After he stood up again, he could already see the bluing on his leg behind the red-hot skin, so he ate ibuprofen to front run the soreness and laid down in his yurt, thankful that he did not dismantle it in a frenzy of cleaning. It was a troubled sleep. He was healing and resting, butt the problem remained that his flock needed to be fed. They could continue to graze inside the lawn, but this was not a long term situation. Then there was the question of all the silage spilled onto that hill. It would be enough to feed them for a couple months at least. He was restless because he knew that he had already decided to return and collect it the following day. The contract

would not let him retreat into his cave any longer.
So he went. He brought the rolls back in small
batches that meant he was driving back and forth to
observe the crash, which by the end was a familiar
sight. There is always the dissonance between the experience and the hotwash after the fact. Each time he
inspected the truck, he discovered new details that
would have meant death or serious injury, if only.
Eventually, though, even this became normalized as he
stopped his investigation with the last of the rolls
under the North portico.

It was inevitable that the sheep would be set out to
graze freely on the National Mall. His vegetable garden was small enough that he could make a rough fence
around it to keep them away. He had also added greenhouses for seeding the summer crop. Altogether, it
was a modest farm on huge acreage that had been pre-
cleared for him. All this stability brought back
ideas of population. He needed more sheep to let them
become self-sustaining after he died. His project to
find new heads roaming feral in the country brought
him deeper into Virginia and Maryland. All these
roads were journeys into entropy where each outing
brought new risks. He kept his haul conservative. No
more zealous flatbeds that he could not control. This
was a dualie with a plow mounted on the front pulling
a small two-horse trailer. It was powerful but manageable. He found the cache deep down a gravel road.
They had been pastured for the summer and were free to
roam the ten acres of grass and found a way to keep
eating as the snow covered it. There were another
forty head to catch and pull back to his farm and he
didn't have enough darts for them all. The first few
were easy since he could reach into the squirming
crowd of pillows and always come up with something.
But they learned to avoid him after he wrangled five
into the trailer. He spent another hour of near
misses before he gave up and brought the five back,
but returned just before dark, so he could try to
catch more in the dark while they slept. This worked
better, and he was able to load ten more each night

until all were in the city farm that had grown to almost eighty head.

To what end, though? He had a menagerie now but hadn't really planned out what he would do with them. They had been collected under some fantasy image that the mall would be much improved with a herd of livestock roaming as it was implied by the placard under the obelisk. In the days of that picture, they would have been kept for slaughter. This was theoretically intriguing but the months of an essentially vegan diet rejected the thought of greasy lamb that would adhere to his beard and never leave him. Some purpose was needed to justify all the labor and his near death to feed them. This labor became more of a daily obligation as they returned to the practice of finding ways to get lost or stuck. Eons of domestication had stripped them of basic survival, even among these who did manage to survive on their own for most of a year. In the end, they remained stupid yet cunning. Perhaps he could begin to milk them. He had refrigeration again, so cold milk was certainly possible. He could even find yogurt cultures and preserve this ancient practice. All of this was far more appealing than using them for meat.

Along his slow route between the farms, he passed through Langley and the discrete fortification of the CIA campus. This was not new. He saw it many times, but not since he had his presidential chat and all the doors that were opened that day. When he looked at the Pentagon, he felt disappointment because he knew he could not access the information there to do his due diligence on finding answers. The CIA was not the Pentagon. He would not find answers there either, but he might find survivors. It stood to reason that if the United States had any foreknowledge of the event, any indication that such a risk existed in the world, the intelligence services would know before the military. If they knew, they prepared. It could not be taken for granted that they would have informed the President or that the technology they used would have been reliable enough to share. But it might have

worked.   There were miles of bunkers below this modest
campus with research labs, he was sure of this.   In
one of those labs might have been the technology to
protect from a still present danger.   He might be bom-
barded with dangerous radiation that will kill him
some time soon, but so far hadn't manifest.   They
might be down there waiting until it was safe.

With a trailer full of sheep sheepishly waiting for
their confinement to be over, he pulled over to think
through this new manic wave.   He found himself exiting
the truck to cross the dark road and approach the un-
approachable.   There were huge signs that warned him
to turn back.   Others warned him not to touch the
fence.   Tempted by this last one, he picked up a clump
of mud and tossed it and was startled to see it sizzle.   There was still power!   Lots of it.   His September assumption was right that the grid would fail some
time during the winter.   But this must be sourced from
something else that was still very much online.   His
heart thumped as he dared to feel a sense of hope that
he was right about the labs and bunkers,   then worried
about being right about the radiation and ongoing invisible threats.   He walked over to the guardhouse,
just as he did at the East gate, and waved awkwardly.
He didn't know what to say, if anything.   If anyone
was watching, they probably had been watching him all
winter, all the months before when he raced past the
gate.   Or they were not watching at all.   They might
be cut off from the footage, locked deep down in the
darkness like he was, listless in waiting for the
right time to emerge.   What he needed was a grandiose
message that would trigger alarms.   There was nothing
left to do that night.   The sort of message he envisioned needed some planning.   And equipment.   So he
drove the sheep back across town to their new home.
One mania at a time was all that he could manage, so
the CIA would have to wait until he settled his flock
into their pasture.

Each time he passed the gate on the way out to collect
more sheep, he paused a bit to test out his mental image against the reality of the site.   Unlike his past

encounters with secure zones, this would need to be
breached. The technical complication of high voltage
meant that he could not come into contact with the
fence in order to achieve this. Simply climbing over
it was not enough because he needed to trigger the
alarms. He could not simply ram through like he did
at the power substations; the risk was too high that
the vehicle would become a trap from which he couldn't
escape. A ram, though, was likely the only way. Setting a car on course would be a challenge since the
acceleration rate would make it difficult for him to
leap out of the cab. He could jack the drive wheels
and release it, but this was also dangerous since it
would still keep his person too close to the force of
the accelerating vehicle. He couldn't simply limit
the speed or distance since it might not penetrate the
gate, which would leave a new electrified obstacle in
the way. There would only be one shot at breach. In
his mind, the best equipment would be a low speed
bulldozer with locked steering.

Not far away was the construction site in Arlington
where he already had access to the keys for the site's
fleet. He had only used the forklift before, but recalled seeing a menu of construction vehicles on hand
and presumably still worked if he had the knowledge.
In his carelessness of his prior visit, the door had
been open for raccoons to nest for the winter. They
were displeased by his presence and hissed as he
scrambled to grab as many keys as possible without being attacked. Armed with a handful of random keys, he
set about matching them to ignitions and door locks.
He had not grabbed all the keys, but he did manage to
unlock a front loader that should be strong enough to
make the breach. From within the cab, he saw some
generally familiar mechanisms, but was not confident
with the array of levers. He practiced with driving
and maneuvering to understand its fit for purpose, but
he also played with the bucket to see if he might not
need this skill later. Of the missing keys were the
set that would open and operate the three axle truck
and flatbed that were used to deliver these vehicles
in the first place. The raccoon family was by then

very aware of his repeated attempts to approach and
were very clear that he was unwelcome. He gave up and
decided to just drive the loader across town. It
needed more diesel, which he had pilfered from the
site already, so he decided to find another construction site along the way. Driving through streets from
up top this machine was surreal. He felt the full
power at his disposal and took the time to flip over
parked cars. It was a joy to destroy with no purpose
as his West Texas blood took over. Quite enlivened,
he reached within a few blocks of the gate with a full
tank of gas and parked the loader on the front lawn of
a home that he made sure to rip open beforehand. The
walk back to the original site where he parked was
giddy.

The mania had crested and dropped to a lower plateau
full of planning details now that the breach was settled. The alarms would definitely blare when the gate
was ripped apart. Then what? If nothing happened, he
would go inside and breach the front doors. Breach
after breach until he was satisfied. The gate was
low-fi and easy, but internally he would face more
controls than he did at the precinct. He might find
laundry with access cards for most, but these would
not help if the locks were biometric. He imagined
amazing security systems that felt better placed
guarding ancient tombs where doors would close and
trap an intruder such as he. Those were asinine for a
preindustrial civilization, but not for the headquarters of a secretive intelligence organization with a
massive budget and dark funding channels. Would an
acetylene torch be enough in that situation? Maybe he
could drag around a heavy metal block that could ensure a crawlspace was available through which to exit.
This rabbit hole extended for the entire drive home
and for the rest of the afternoon. The most basic
risk at the end of it was that his efforts would be
misinterpreted. He would surely be unwelcome, but humans were not raccoons. He could reason with other
people to give assurance that he only wanted assurance
back. His grandiose message needed to be carefully

crafted so that it would be properly understood as an attempt to signal for help.

His flock was waiting for him when he drove back mired in thoughts about tomb raiding. Most of them. Many new comers had wandered off and he could hear their bleats that echoed from down a side street. They took hours to regroup in the most comical way. One was caught between two parked cars when its wool snagged. He cut the wool and coaxed it out only for it to run across the street between two more parked cars and get stuck again. Eventually they were back with the rest and he was free to go inside where he thought it was a good day to eat more mushrooms, which stalled all other activity until the following day. Somewhere in there, he decided that the risks at the CIA were jus-tifiable. At least to get his message out. The sub-sequent breaches could come later, at any time. Or never. There was no urgency for anything at all. The important thing was to elicit a response of some sort and this could be done with a protracted message that stretched on for days, if not weeks. After his day of rest, he went back out to the gate to hold up some placards to the camera that he could then leave be-hind. There were three signs that said:

1. *I come in peace...Ha ha...But really, I just want to know if anyone is still alive.*

2. *I'll be coming back a lot to try and get your attention.*

3. *Please don't kill me, just tell me to go away instead.*

He stood there in front of the camera for a long time, waving and hoping to give any observers the chance to notice him before he held each placard out in front, giving each its due before moving on to the next. He cycled through them a few times before he tied them to chairs where he believed the camera pointed. The next time he went, the chairs were in the same place and there were no signs that anyone had come out. He stood there again, waving his arms for a few minutes before he decided to walk the perimeter of the fence to take a look at the campus. It was large, but there was an excess of parking spaces given the size of the buildings. His suspicion about bunkers must have been correct. There could be no other explanation. Someone had to be down there watching him. There were many buildings and he couldn't tell which might be the best place to access those underground havens. He was also on the lookout for other gates where he might keep trying more messages. The main gate adjacent to the road still felt like the best place to breach, but he found many areas with cameras and motion sensors all throughout the fence line. As there should be. This was a proper fortress and as such needed sentinels to stand watch, but the days of automation and secrecy made it preferable to distribute cameras and various sensors that could be centrally monitored. There were likely also seismic sensors that caught every step he made. Thermal sensors could pick him out as he struggled through the trees and undergrowth. If they were there, they knew he was there too. And he made sure they knew.

Over the next few days, he returned regularly to repeat his camera show in front of each one he found. There were dozens of them. He felt ridiculous each time until the third placard, then it became tangible again. "Please don't kill me, just tell me to go away instead." Such an easy request, but what if they knew something about the invisible risks that he didn't. Might he be a real threat that indeed should be killed on sight? How could he get their attention from far? Being Virginia still locked in the throes of the 4th of July, there were firework stands everywhere. He initially thought about using them for his display, but realized that few things signal threat to a skittish security sector than explosions on their doorstep, so he put this out of his mind. But as he acclimated to the site, he felt less deterred. He cleared out one stand and set up a few blocks within the neighborhood facing the gate. After dusk, he started to light everything, doing his best to get them to launch up to the sky. After the last explosion, there was a quiet that unsettled him. But soon the insects resumed their chirps and that made it much more unsettling. He felt too exposed. This was the closest he had come to threatening any facility and might finally provoke them to come out. He began to panic at the reckless moments that could not be undone and drove away back home. He called in as many of his pack as he could and sealed the loading dock again so he could sleep down in his own bunker with dogs ready to defend him in the upper levels.

The lesson from panic taught him that he needed to be more intentional about his message of peace. That and his escape route, because he predicted a serious panic once the breach actually happened. He would move more slowly, giving ample time to understand him before he crossed over to destruction. It was time to finally move the loader to the gate. He parked it as close as he could without testing the electricity. He moved in more fireworks and showed them to the camera before placing them clearly in the open. In a recent addition, he had returned to the raccoon nest to take a bullhorn he remembered seeing on a hook next to the key cupboard. This was to be his most obnoxious attention-seeking step so far. He walked the perimeter blasting the message he wrote on the placards, over and over. He took his time. Said it everywhere. His voice hurt from so much use after so much disuse. It felt safe and released him from fear. He actually felt like someone was listening to him, maybe they wanted to reach out to him too but were trapped inside their bunkers without the ability to leave. Should he break in immediately to save them? He stuck to the plan, but told them he was coming, that one of them would be rescuing the other soon. He told them about his plans to celebrate the 4th of July early, but that it didn't matter because the world never left the 4th of July. It was always the 4th and would always be; time was a consensus. Finally back to the gate from the other side, he switched the bullhorn off and drank several bottles of water. The box of fireworks sat invitingly on the ground so he began to unpack it.

This time, though, he was not going to send them upward. His plan was to send them over the fence into the campus, in a direct assault on the headquarters of the most notorious intelligence agency that ever existed. First he let the timer of the sun tick its countdown before he would begin. This needed to be seen to be effective. There would be no point in the sounds reaching the inside ears, he needed eyes to light up and chests to feel the pop. He assumed that they would know these were not the ballistics of warfare, but merely dangerous children's toys. If they saw the colors, they would know right away that he was annoying but not a threat.

The show was slower and less frenzied than the night before. It was like a drunken display with long intervals between each one. He had only brought with him the sort that would shoot out and preferably sizzle with colors. None made it to the campus proper, being so far away, but they did clear the entry and were certainly noticeable from the buildings without the need for cameras. The night was at its midpoint when the last one was ignited and the show ended. The panic did not overcome him when the quiet returned. He was far too exhausted to feel fear that even the thought of driving home was too much. One of the homes that he invaded before was not far from where he parked the loader so he decided to go there and sleep for an early start in the morning. The home was relatively clean, as he recalled, with no dead pets or food to attract rodents. When he climbed the stairs, he noticed that the air felt sticky from being closed off for so long. It was a nice home but it had the wrong feel to be his home. He used what looked like the guest room, which had no echoes to pester him as he slept. He laid there for hours without sleep before he dragged himself up and drove back home where he was underground again shortly before first light told him the time. He slept deeply after sealing himself in as before. The budding thought that no one was coming had only just formed and was ignored during his passage into the void of dreamless sleep.

It was late when he woke up. Far later than he normally would have begun his day. He had neglected his
flock for days and felt the need to check in on them.
Several needed to be returned to the lawn as always,
but he chased them down with gratitude for the chance
at procrastination. When they were all back together,
he found an irk in thinking something was out of place
in his ship and he needed to inspect it from top to
bottom. Everything was done and there was no more diversion on which he could focus. His slow moving body
rapidly built up to the agitated destination of his
mania. It made him piddle; it made him find activities without actually starting them. Nothing was settled in his mind except the growing feeling that everything towards which he recently worked would fall
flat without even the sense of finding a significant
end. Nothing ever ended anymore. It just evaporated
in frustrated nothingness. He went up to the roof to
test whether his telescope could see out to the campus. It could not. There was no reason that it
could. He just wanted to see so he could check one
more thing before making his move. On the way down,
he stopped at his nest and checked in on his cartoon
world. This failed to hold his attention either. By
14:00 he was frustrated with himself and with the CIA.
They had let him down, not because they didn't respond
to his pre-messages, but because they failed to see
the evaporation coming so they could survive it. That
was the affront. That they didn't prepare meant there
were no answers. He'd wasted enough time. Casting
off any fear, he walked downstairs full of anger.

When he reached the gate, he stopped well away from
the zone where sparks might land. He made another
round of the perimeter with his bullhorn, but this
time his message was spite and challenge. He begged
them to come out and stop him from destroying the
fence. He warned them of the timer that he set for
them both as if he had no choice left to change
course. He was acting as a force driven by unyielding
law that only could be put to rest if they came out
and told him he was not alone. The loader came back
into view from between the trees and then he was

standing right beside it, where the ground was streaked with the black marks of charred ignition. He climbed in and backed up a few feet, not that it needed the run to pick of speed, but so he had time to jump off and run away before the sparks and danger exploded.

There was nothing left to do. He'd done everything that made sense to do and there was no more time. The wheel was locked, the bucket was lifted, and the engine was idling. He prepared a crash pad where he would land when he jumped and this was ready too. The lever moved and guided the gears into place and the loader lurched forward as he leapt off, landing squarely on the pad. He rolled away as planned and ran across the street. The loader moved slowly and then more slowly as it pressed its bucket into the tall mesh fence. The sparks began as soon as it made contact, concentrated on the suddenly grounded current. As the loader pushed through, tearing huge gashes with its teeth and power, the sparks changed to a storm of popping showers. There were shorts further down the fence line, draping yellow streams onto trees. None reached him where he stood watch, eyes absorbing the image. The loader was free and inside. It dragged one of the enormous gate doors along the asphalt with a sound that lived in the space between a grind and a scream. The frame of the gate was sagging with its support beams ripped out of the ground as the hinges broke and released their doors. The loader crept along making its hybrid sound until it careened into a culvert as the driveway curved. It continued on, with one drive wheel off the ground and the other digging into the soil, trying to push away the trees that now blocked its path.

That was all. Sagging fence and impotent loader. There were no alarms and no guns. He started to walk closer and stopped where he always stopped. He looked up at the camera and then to the wreckage of the loader still stuck comically trying to destroy. There was no chance of him entering yet. His plan was to preserve that moment for another day that was less eventful, less controversial. He looked into the camera again and waved his greeting, just as before. His placards had been knocked down with one smoldering from a small flame that he waved out as he held them up, just as before. "I come in peace," "please don't kill me," but now all he could think about was "haha" as he propped them up again on the chairs that had fallen over and drove away home.

When he reached his ship again, even fewer dogs had come home than before. They had returned to their varied schedules they followed when they were all in Georgetown. Or they never changed, just moved it indoors where their opportunities to get away were fewer and he just didn't pay attention. It was still early so he didn't seal the garage. Enough had come home to protect him and it felt like punishing the others for his own madness. He tried to follow his routine. He bathed and put on music, but turned it off so he could hear any subtle sound from above in the garage. The feeling that more was out there never left him and it now prodded him from deep. He armed himself as he got under the blankets. Like the night before, no sleep came. He drifted about in purgatory listening for the sound of dogs returning to play. He wanted to hear something more as much as he was afraid that it might actually happen. And he was afraid that it actually might not so he projected so many similarities onto otherwise innocuous sounds.

The morning came on the sound of dogs waking again and he made his way back up with his 9mm full of paranoid hope. Everything was disappointingly normal on the surface as he brewed strong tea and prepared to drive back to the gate. The plan called for him to take a new route that day. He drove the long way around the city to come up from the opposite side of the campus, where he would have to walk the perimeter back to the gate. This felt absurd to him as he followed it, but did not feel a particular reason to change midcourse. He parked and walked up to the fence to toss more mud at it as a test. There was no sizzle this time. Either the circuit was cut or it shorted. Either way, the fence was dead. There was no visible change in any of the buildings, no mass of personnel preparing any sweep of the city nor had any doors suddenly been opened. When he reached the gate, he saw everything was the same as before except that the wind had blown over two of his signs that were now a few meters away. The loader was still stuck and had managed to partly topple one of the trees before its tank emptied and the power stopped.

Today was the planned day of entry. It was the last hype he could imagine that was left, so he filled each step full of meaning even when it was a normal walk. Here marks the security line. Pass this and it would have meant federal prison. Inside a criminal, he walked up to the loader and patted it for a job well done. It would never move again. It would rust away and be untraceable in a few centuries except for some pulverized rubber. Further along was the fist of the parking lots, which he saw from outside the fence. Not so many cars were left here. Anyone here would have been working late after having parked so far away in the morning. They were still inside, whether laundry or human.

He'd already selected what he thought was the main building and walked up to it. The door opened for him as it would have any other day. Inside was the famous seal laid in tile which marked the extent to which cameras were allowed. He walked through it and moved behind the security counter where he could see screens that showed him the gate and various other locations. He kicked aside the uniform and picked up the security badge. Power was on, so the badge would give him access to many of the rooms. He tossed it down and walked back home.

Hedon

X
Sovereign Citizen

Over the course of two weeks, the CIA had become a minor event in his memory as he turned back to his small life at the center of the United States Government. There were sheep to save and herd around to new portions of the lawn where grass was lush and ached to be chewed. They were joined by a few donkeys and horses that he discovered running around. Everything was plain. It had even warmed enough that he could discard some of his heaviest layers as he went about. Beyond the CIA were the months of survival reaching back to the moment of panic in his original Georgetown home. He had not visited it since he sealed it off at the end of summer. It felt better this way, as if he sealed a wound in order to heal in a messy process of gasping for air after a plunge into deep water. There were nearly nine months of moments between those two endpoints. Nine months of learning how to tread the new water. Very soon it would be the first anniversary. A full year in this new phase of humanity that will extend until he leaves. His life expectancy was already low as an American, but how much would it be lowered as a result of all this water? Would he even be lucky to call a long life full anymore? He might have another forty years of fighting plainness before the fight is gone. The longer the fight, the more challenging it will be with the back end the most depressingly weak. He might never reach those. In nine months he already narrowly avoided violent death several times. Some from stupidity and others from luck. Something was coming for him eventually and it may be as pointless as a slip and fall. Or it could be heroic as a grapple with a wild animal that had not yet been born. It would be something.

On occasion, though, the CIA worked its way into his thoughts. He enjoyed the site of the sparks showering down and felt it was a fitting image for the agency's finality. He had foregone his right to explore. In the moment when he had the power of access to some, if not all, of its secrets, he just felt tired. On some level he knew that he could go back at any time, but this was an unimportant details much like the lie you tell a child when it is time to go home. So in these moments of recollection, he was not scheming his way into the labs of the campus to uncover extraterrestrial plots. Instead, it was more important to understand what he hoped to accomplish out there. The clarity of hindsight pointed out all the red flags that proved there would be nothing waiting for him, but why had he ignored all these and pressed on? What closure had it meant to signify? It would do little to improve his condition if he discovered survivors who wished to stay quarantined from him. He would still be alone each day, but would then be reminded that his survival was an inconvenience to his only chance for companionship. He would still live the life of an exile. The worst of the trauma had already happened. He lost his family, his friends and any chance to make new ones. No replacement would have repaired that, but it was the human way to move beyond. He lost even that biological right. There was nothing to do but live out his fantasy survival in solitude. There could be no new risks that he hadn't already faced so there was nothing more to fear.

He did have fears, though. His mushroom friends taught him that the source of everything he lost was housed under civilized time, which could be marked and aggregated. He need only let slip the silent batteries on his phones so the backup cells that preserve the clocks inside stopped moving. If he forgot to mark time and lost a day, he might skip forward and lose whole months. Winter might come as a surprise then. He might never know how many anniversaries passed. He feared losing the old consensus. Without it, he would be in the prison of natural time that is unmarked except for broad phases of seasons, or lines

on his face that grew deeper. Without the consensus
time, he would only know the exchange of day and
night. The consensus of moon phases and the generali-
ties of the equinox that required effort to study and
test a hypothesis against changes. It would be a
prison of constant monitoring and recordation. Natural time was confusing and threatened to emphasize his
loss. Behind it all would be the waves of mania that
he knew would never end. He would find new obsessions
that consumed him whole until he burned all the fuel
it had and left it for another. These would be the
chapters in his new life that told him how far he swam
in the new water when he could always collect moments
from them to relive in his decrepit future far ahead.
These alone would be the only purpose left. The accumulation of memories that might palliate his end. But
this was always the objective for him. Reaching beyond the evaporation was a mind that guided a body
from memory event to memory event, and this was unchanged now. He wondered how another mind might spend
their afterworld. They might not have reached nine
months, nor might he if he returned to the first moment again to replay the game.

He walked this sandbox with his lieutenants. The five
had maintained their rank at his side and helped him
when it was time to herd sheep or punish out of line
members of the pack. They did all this with graceful
violence so that he could keep his hands clean. They
had not lost their house training and he was more ac-
cepting of their presence inside the ship with him.
They patrolled the streets together as he resumed his
bicycle roam through the city. They scouted for signs
of feral animals, particularly dogs, but found none
that survived the winter. There were the periodically
discovered carcasses that were cold and dried in
makeshift dens where they either froze or starved or
both. Rodents flourished. They were true survivors
that carried with them the prehistoric ability to outlast a freeze. They now emerged from their hiding and
set to work that dismantled the rest of civilization
which came under their mandate. Of course there were
the wild animals that were traditionally marginalized

in the city but had begun to reclaim their territory.
Foxes could cross streets without meeting tires. They
were the most common sight behind deer, which he resumed hunting for both himself and his pack. When he
made a kill, he would announce it with a loud emergency whistle, after which the rest of the pack
learned to chase. Eventually, they learned to all
follow him from a variety of distances. There were
the occasional bear sightings, mostly clustered in the
wilderness of Rock Creek Park, so he left this to them
so there would be no dead dogs to clean up. The freedom of safety allowed him to stop wearing his thick
and increasingly uncomfortable kevlar for the more
breathable but sturdy canvas overalls on which he began sewing patches and designs that became the medals
earned for his uniform.

It was also warm enough for him to wear his prized oil
cloth coat that looked quite poorly constructed out in
the unforgiving sunlight. Still, it was a mark of
achievement, a skill that he honed and could not be
lost. It also gave him the look of a well armed psychedelic cowboy. On some days, the weather was so
warm that he pulled off his sweaters and walked
through the grass without shoes, avoiding the pellets
of sheep dung that had yet to dry. As natural time
moved, these warm moments increased, and he found himself spending more time outside to enjoy it. He told
himself that it would soon be warm enough to begin
playing in the cool water of the river. The warmth
also led him to test the boundaries of fashion by taking with him the patterns that moved inside his yurt
so that they could dance on his arms. He had always
had a secret desire to wear loud paisley, but his shyness kept him modest. Now, there would be no opinion-
ated viewers for him to question, and he found no
shortage of styles to pull from the stores.

In fact, it was just this that began to overwhelm him.
Now that he was not constrained by the urgency of winter preparation, he could browse more calmly. In the
past, shopping was always muted by the dual calculus
of cost and space, but neither were an issue anymore

and the abundance was its own complication. There was
never any need to feel that any item needed special
care as everything was disposable. This was not limited to stores. Everything was fungible in its relative category. He could take any new car, destroy it
and go take another. Houses and buildings were all
for him, so long as he could tolerate the cleanup. He
had a fleet of full sized RV's now, which he could not
have fit in the garage before. He set up his new cave
that was complete with refrigeration and solar cells.
He was using fully functional toilets again. If he
wanted to test a new model, it was his too. All property rights had collapsed into him, and he need not
register anything for this to happen. It was a natural right that occurred automatically as both sole human entitled to make the claim and surviving kin in
all probate matters, whether testate or otherwise.
All the material wealth of civilization had become a
natural resource that demanded only a claim to perfect. Everything everywhere was subject to claim. He
already discussed his transition of power with the
President and claimed office. But this was a political right. It was not the right of impunity over material that is the sole right of the sovereign institution. This was still unclaimed, even as he took
from the stores and homes with no thought. But soon
it registered that he was the fullest embodiment of
civilization's achievements; that not only did he act
with actual power but with the moral power behind the
sovereign right. It demanded a loud claim that was
broadcast out in a universal dare for competition to
retaliate and test the strength of provocation. Authority is passive consensus and power is an active
defense, but sovereignty is a categorical imperative
that neither power nor authority can destroy because
it is on an incorporeal plane. It can only be
claimed. It was his to claim for the entire planet as
its sole citizen. The act of claiming this seemed
weird. Its moral imperative was a function of truth
in the afterworld as much as it was before.
Sovereignty was always about human existence, not artificial constraints. Humans began sovereign, and
they concluded as sovereign, with history interfering

in the space between because some rules-based order
was needed while the competition was fierce. His
claim would not be to assert his sovereignty, that
would be absurd, but to mark the end of history and
the end of competition.

What his mania required was a grandiose ceremony full
of gaudy pomp appropriate for the city. He had visions of parades and streamers from the rooftops. Music in the park. Shock politics. An embellishment
that might kill him as much as it might quiet the dark
library of civilization. What he envisioned was a
continuation of the ceremonies of the past that sprung
from the Capitol steps and circulated through the
city. There might be fires and destruction. Once the
dionysian frenzy began there was no controlling its
direction. His visions lacked only the audience. He
could celebrate with the sheep and dogs, but they
would fail to participate fully as only junior members
to history. He needed a stand in for humanity that he
could imbue with personality of the crowd. He needed
laundry to join the party. They needed to be mobilized from their apathy and freed from their homes.

The stage for this began with mannequins upon which
the laundry would be hung and raised from the dead.
He wanted thousands to fill the mall, larger than any
inaugural crowd. He had the power to force participa-
tion. He ransacked every department store he could
find to drag the naked bodies from their displays so
they could be unconsenting vessels for the polis.
They were dumped into piles of limbs from full dump
trucks that beeped before dropping them carelessly;
they needed to stand with shoulders, not anything
else. He snatched sleepers from their beds and pa-
trons from their drinks. He was the regime's enforcer
that swept through the shops and homes to build out
the crowd that their leader's vision demanded. They
were foisted onto bodies to become political props in
the celebration. But reality hit vision as he got
bored with the mundane process of dressing so many
mannequins. By the time he dressed and anchored the
thousandth one in the lawn below the Capitol steps, he

was done. The fervor of vision waned at the unimpressive turnout that took more than a week to complete. No matter. The celebration was in the works and had to move forward. There might be late-comers, he wasn't sure. He brought in massive speakers that required a trailer-drawn generator, and stage lighting that he propped against boxes rather than waste his mania on constructing a scaffold that would have fallen on him for its poor quality. The lights would illuminate the Capitol in rainbow to honor the lost from every spectrum. He brought boxes out from storage at Lee's mansion so they could comprise the VIP section behind him on the stage.

The day finally came and it was at night so the colors would pop. He was nervous because the mannequins looked startlingly real in the dim glow of the stage. If he squinted, he felt like he was addressing the lost who momentarily returned to pay respect to their sole survivor. After all the lights were on and the mic was confirmed to be loud, he walked out wearing Lincoln's office suit that he pulled from a Smithsonian display. He walked slowly and with grave intention. These were to be impromptu remarks that he was at pains to avoid preparing ahead of time. He stood there awkwardly aware of how ridiculous this was but angry that he should still feel so shy. "I am all there is and there's nothing left but me," is what he told himself with the microphone drooping before he was ready to speak. But this made sense. There was nothing left to say. So he screamed it. Each syllable punched through the dark and he could hear it echo off buildings. He said it again, less forcefully but with more meaning. He sat down in the middle of the stage and watched the whole setup for another hour.

He had absorbed the scene; the crowd had cheered him. He worked hard to memorialize them and now was their chance to pay him respects. He did not wrench them from their homes, he aided them with his power of mobility that they lost through evaporation. If only they could, they would cheer him down that historic avenue to his right where he would be hurled into the seat at the helm of the world. But he didn't manage to turn on the street lights so the way was dark and at any rate he could see some sheep watching him from there just beyond the glow of the stage. The rainbow lights converged onto them on the sidewalk, with legs locked under their fluff that he momentarily thought about shearing for their comfort. But behind him was the right kind of poison and he was dressed accordingly. From there, the celebration could turn a populist shade of dark. "I am all there is and there's nothing left but me."

Laws proclaim for the corporeal features of institutions what standards of compliance should be delivered and what actions it will take when those standards fall short. This is known. The enforcement of law is the most visible feature of a sovereign. It can be manifest as rule of or by law. These parallel but different roads mark the philosophy of the sovereign. It documents institutional thoughts and intentions to remind itself far into the future what it had promised earlier. It reminds sovereigns that authority demands accountability and it speaks to forfeited power. Law is fickle. It says one thing and speaks another. Laws are not for citizens, they are for the sovereign institutions alone and citizenship is irrelevant except to articulate the shape of the sovereign personality at any given moment. When he looked at the rainbow Capitol, he felt the alienation of being the collapse of all things and held out hope to remind himself what that should mean.

When he walked in from the back door this time, he did so as the sole candidate for office walking in to take his seat somewhere inside. He was the collapse of candidates, the non-choice for the ballot. He was always unaffiliated but this was no matter. The non-choice meant there was no party contention. He was the perfected autocratic ballot. The election could not happen. A legitimate contest must have at least two participants. There was no contest so there was no need to formalize the selection, he won pro forma. He walked into the Capitol as the constituency collapsed into the representative and he did not know where to sit. He stood in the rotunda in Lincoln's suit with thin splashes of color penetrating the darkness from outside. Somewhere inside would be his rightful place. Should he walk to the People's House or the State's House? What constituency had collapsed and reconstituted within him? These questions alone were irrelevant as he was independent from history now and the rules of the old civilization were unhelpful. The institution had changed and he alone had the right to define it anew. He went in neither direction. His place was at the heart, under the concave dome above where he commanded the whole of the building as the corporeal structure of the institution. From the center, he could initiate bills that would pass without debate. There would be no vote to test their merit and they were laws unless they were institutional reminders of an intent. So with a collapse of the bicameral organization that survived for over two hundred years, the separation between the political branches too collapsed into him. He was the convergence of power and authority through the pillar of the sovereign state, standing inside the rainbow light. He was at once President and Legislator, capable of debating and deciding with singular efficiency.

He searched for words to remind himself later through law. He began timidly from the obviousness of his situation with its open field to reshape the world of policy and set a national agenda that would carry forward to the global agenda. He felt like the real threat was the post-war international character of the planet, which should have to been overhauled long ago. It would have taken political will from all sides to recognize the defects in the international order that dated back even further to the formation of modern states. The President in him argued to the Legislator in him that a two pronged approach to highlight the failings of states and a restoration of the ancient right of human mobility was policy. That this message should be carried by the President's ambassador as a demarche for all nations to take back through their UN representatives in New York. He started from the understanding that states were the original sin of modern civilization, organized as they were around common language and need to protect common resources. And this was not even a universal modern phenomena. He had seen dozens of pastoralist nations that moved around borders as they had since memory began. They were the protectorates of the ancient right to move freely around the planet until they met with competitors. He felt that the contest among peoples was the wrong from which all threats emanated. It was the forever missed opportunity for collaboration that was driven by the ease with which humans created otherness. Other people on my land. Other land that should be my land. Other people always had to become subhuman, a crime against humanity itself for its threat to the idea of commonality among the species and political compartments were the modern mechanism that effectuated this through law. Statehood created a legal entitlement to belligerency through the contest of war. The just wars with the victor's spoils enabled the proto-states to congeal along a straight line to the secret treaties of defense blocs that destroyed Europe once, opening to way for Asia's revolutions. The states refused to concede to justice and it destroyed Europe once again and opened the way for the waves of decolonization that created more states empowered within with poorly drawn lines. States led to the chauvinism of ethnic domination and the dilution of the ethnic diversity that exists everywhere. He saw this in dozens of civil wars and the political capture of the government resources by ethnic elites where minorities had been gerrymandered out of their own sovereignty back when colonial administrators handed over the keys. In so many states, he saw the national narrative violently tune out the discrete people through ethnic cleansing and genocide. It was not limited to the well known victims. It was everywhere. Statehood erected barriers behind which so much murder was tolerated in deference to state sovereignty because none would accept the risk of eroding that artifice lest it come home to demand remedy for their own murders. The post-war framework was intended to protect the impotency of internationalism from the start. It had adorned the world with utopian language to bait the naive into believing progress could be made through the system it erected. This system had to be destroyed to let the artificial distinctions between plots of land on the planet fall away. They barely served a lazy political purpose before, when contests continued, but now he felt that this should be the object of his mania as he set about to recreate the world.

The President met with his permanent representatives to the UN in New York to instruct him to negotiate a binding resolution with the other permanent representatives, which would say that no member state would enforce its territorial or political boundaries with prejudice to any human, thus ending state sovereignty once and for all. Once successful, it would usher in the era of the sovereign citizen where only the boundaries set by the planet itself would have meaning. A citizen would be free to travel to any location unrestricted so long as they were not aggressive to the survival of other humans already there, assuming any might be encountered. This era was radical only in the sense that it had been so long abandoned in the era of contest through invasion of habitat. This could not persist in this afterworld. It would be the era of radical cooperation.

He assumed his rights to act through all political institutions that collapsed into him from all the legacy organizations of statehood. He could stand in the rotunda and legislate for Myanmar as the sole beneficiary of the territory that former state had occupied. This was the case for all legacies, which were now finally on equal footing with one another. The remainder of his life will be the writing of this new history and will pass with him to the next era that may find the ruins of these civilizations and build their own from there.

Then, he was tired in his itchy wool museum piece that was too small for his frame and the suit was long since tired of playing politics. The mania had cooled as he whipped himself up in a fantasy of the international system and a utopian solution that would only work for a polis of one. It was a proper handling of the celebration, but it was now late and he had been busy for weeks assembling the event. He was still standing in the colors of the rainbow that he was pleased to learn would reflect once inside the rotunda, which he had to discover over time as his eyes adjusted to the dark. It was time to go outside and shut them down for another day. His audience was still waiting for him to emerge and set them free when he made his appearance. But he left them there in the dark without the rainbow, for the sheep to find early the next morning. His lieutenants were also waiting and smelled at his antique outfit as they stood up to join him back to his RV where he could bathe away the stink of museum and replay the scenes from the night. The inside of his new home was small but clean. He was already tired of it and wished that he had made the much longer walk back to the enormity of his yurt. Surely there could be some middle ground accommodations that he could find, which preserved the portable comfort of the RV and the durable discomfort of all the homes and buildings, where he could have on hand all that he needed so long as he could tolerate the subtle hacks. The RV could be moved anywhere and freed him from the confines of the city but he had to plan ahead or be prepared to forage. He wanted luxury again.

Lincoln's suit was duly returned to the museum and he felt annoyed that he indulged his mania this far, when he could have easily procured a replica from any number of theaters or themed shops. It was done and he returned it. The itch of confinement returned to him as he left the museum, but it was now expanded from the RV to the whole of the mall, then from the mall to the whole of the metro area where he had not left since long before the evaporation. His family had planned vacations, but these had always been moderate and not far from the city. They had traveled too much the years before, had been too separated by lockdowns and closed borders. When the reached this last destination, there was more than enough to explore. Back then, the parks and museums were too new to feel boring. Everything was still amazing. They had driven out to Norfolk earlier in the summer before they were gone, to play on the beach. He was never drawn to the ocean because his silent fear of open water made it less interesting, but now this memory crept up and called him to leave. There was a planet out there for him just as before.

It all came down to transport. The planet was waiting just as the moon was waiting or Mars and beyond were waiting. Everything was waiting for his eyes to arrive and be welcomed. He had come back to this thought often over the past nine months and always hit upon this blockage that would need to be removed before his claim could be given full rights. There were so many land vehicles everywhere that he knew these to be the most dependable option for long travel. He would never need to worry about a breakdown that would strand him along the way because he could simply take another, which was rarely far away. Even in the deepest wildernesses, he could convoy in or take a motorcycle for emergencies. Same as always, he would be stuck in the Americas.

It was time to explore as an explorer and learn how to boat so that he could reach across the oceans eventually. His first oceanic expedition would have to be Europe where he could stay close to the Northern Atlantic instead of risking the open waters to reach Africa straight away. But even navigating across the Potomac from the District to Virginia would be a learning challenge as he never made any attempt to boat in the past. He had been on ferries and water buses as part of his daily commute, but operating these vehicles would be totally new. Just beyond the tidal basin was the wharf where a large selection had been docked and remained in wait. Almost a year of neglect was obvious when he made his way along the walks to inspect them more closely. Most had obvious signs of damage to their hulls from loosened mooring from repeated storms. Most were small yachts and

fishing boats that looked fast but designed to stay
close to land and could never safely carry him the
distance the Vikings traveled.

One yacht drew him in. It was much larger than the
others and still looked unbattered from the months
that it had waited for him to arrive. Unlike the others, this was designed for comfort and short term living. From the windows, he could see what looked more
like an apartment than a fishing boat would have. The
problem was that it was locked and he could not think
of where to find the keys. Unlike cars, which were
parked outside homes and businesses, the boats were
presumably far from their owners who would keep access
means to a minimum. He didn't even know where to
look. Eventually he decided to try the wharf offices
in case there was some registration information stored
in hard copy somewhere inside. There was. He found a
clipboard with a name slotted into the dock number
where the boat was moored. But only a name and a mem-
bership number. This was a printout that someone carried with them as they make their inspections, rather
than the source of information. All that remained
hidden in the computers. Without feeling lucky, he
flipped through the stack of business cards on the table and was surprised to find a name match, with an
address in DuPont. Once there, he was able to find
the former owner's office where there were keys to
many boats that belonged to the firm with which to
pamper their clients or buy access.

The interior was as lush as he thought he could see
from the tinted windows. It was in the process of being stocked with supplies for a night of fireworks on
the river, but the decorations had not yet been set up
or the perishable food brought in. There were rooms
and cubbies for him to explore. It was far better
than the confined comfort of his RV. He could expand
in here without giving up the basic detail of a working toilet. But the control room was complicated. He
managed to start the motor without issue and the
steering was intuitive, but there were many panels and
indicators that eluded him. He studied them all until

they became less mysterious and more obvious. The other details of the boat also fell into place. He understood where the fuel should go and even how to work the desalinator. When all this was settled, he made his first attempt to cross into the river and see if he could be trusted with his life in open water. He found that the general premise was the same as a car that drove on ice. Turns and stops lagged so he needed to factor the extra movements into his navigation, but it was not beyond his reach. Satisfied with his skills for the moment, he decided it was time to begin a trip to someplace new. His Ambassador would eventually need to demarche the other UN members to burn the international order to the ground, so New York seemed like a fine destination that was just far enough away to be interesting but still within the purvey of his skill. He made the transfer from his RV to his new condo. In order to make space, he ripped out the beds so the extra rooms could be used as storage. His lieutenants had been waiting for him on the pier throughout the process. He would not let them board, nor did they ask. He planned to be gone for longer than their food might hold out, so this would be a test of their survivability. They had learned to love the taste of deer but he wondered if they could be successful hunters. At least there were the brainless sheep that could be eaten if they managed to chew passed the wall of wool.

For the day of departure he planned a sending ceremony for which he would move a few hundred members of the polis to wave him off. By that point, they were saggy from the occasional rains that had picked up and to which he left them exposed. They didn't mind, they supported him despite his abuse. His pack had joined the celebration too, mostly because he spread food all along the road to entice them to the occasion. A few sheep joined and he had no expectation that they would still be around by the time he returned. He pulled away waving to the everyone, kissing his hands in gratitude.

It was an obvious stroke of luck that the GPS system still functioned as normal. He had assumed they should be unaffected from the power loss and the degraded communication network, but this was not something he yet needed to test. He had a cache of trackers, but these were collected and stored without any real effort to learn. Now that the need was so great, he was thankful that he could maintain a course that hugged the coastline around the Maryland peninsula, passing Norfolk as he did. He stopped the first day there to refuel and look for his family's beach before moving on to stop at Ocean City then Atlantic City. These were all stops of desperation as he worried through the huge horizon to the East and tired of every wave that bounced his condo. He needed sleep to break the stress but could not pull himself away from the wheel. Mechanically, the similarities to driving were enough. It was the misleading slowness of the journey that never paused that troubled him. He pulled into marinas and immediately went to sleep without bothering to check the area for threats except when he scanned the city as he passed. He woke up in Atlantic City, and it was still light enough to unfold his bike and take a tour through the city, which was shallow and long. All streets returned him back to the beach, so he obliged with a rest in the sand. The days were already very bright, but the wind kept away the heat. He swam a bit and let the salt cake on his skin, making it feel tight. He rested for a few days like this before moving on.

The mouth of New York widened to swallow him as he approached the same course that so many had through the upper bay. It felt like he approached a live vessel that had been constructed into a unitary structure comprised of individual gray teeth. It was both impressive and off putting. He was here to do a job and leave, there was no feeling of connection to what he saw building from out of the haze. While he was on the water procrastinating, he steered over to the Statue of Liberty to get a closer look of the iconic feature that he never saw before. So many words had been put to her that he felt strained to replicate as

he idled just below. He wondered whether he should
dock and take a look around, but felt intimidated by
the size of the pier. Instead, he headed back to the
city and found a place to dock at the bottom of Man-
hattan which he felt would be less technical for him
to moor his condo in the shadows of other vessels much
larger than his. This was the financial district, the
nerve center for the army of quants in their attack on
the polis. It looked no different from other cities:
it had huge towers and shops for workers to visit during shifts. Nothing from the outward appearance indicated that this was the site of the systematic destruction of individuals through the consolidation of
wealth. This is where the excesses of bonanza paid,
as did the CEO retention bonuses when the bonanza
burst and plunged the world into misery. All of it
paid and there was nothing that could stop them. The
Chief Justice in him was unswayed by the argument that
these legal fictions were entitled to the parity of
rights into which the polis was born. The corporate
veil shielded its governors from facing their personal
involvements so how could their rights to speech and
social protections penetrate from the other side? It
was a long road with incremental stops made by a cult
in black robes, washing their hands with cold logic as
they stripped humans of rights so they could no longer
compete against fictions. The Chief Justice listened
to the cases and reversed the line of opinions that
made this course inevitable under the cult of stare
decisis. It was a landmark decision that restored humanity's place at the center of this afterworld. Artificial people would no longer be supreme.

He was quickly done with the decadence of downtown and
ready to move on to finish his work so he could leave
for somewhere else. He had previously visited the UN
as part of a delegation during one General Assembly,
but could not recall exactly where it was located. He
had arrived late at night then, very jet lagged from a
twenty-four hour flight and failed to pay attention to
the map. He knew that it was near the water and that
the city was close by when he looked out, so it seemed
that his best bet would be the East River, where he

could at least look at the Brooklyn Bridge towering above him. The bridge looked as ancient as any castle he visited when he passed under it in full appreciation of its construction. The UN was far up the river and he nearly missed it because he was ready to give up. It was indeed on the water and easy to spot for its unique design. But there was no pier nearby for him so he doubled back to where he had seen a ferry dock down the river. Once back on land, he felt the unease of solid earth as his mind wanted it to flow. This passed as he made his way on foot, thinking about how awful life in such a superstructure that was the city would be. Everything was an interior. The whole of the city was dependent on the presence of other humans to give it appeal. Without them, there was nothing. He was ready to leave as he arrived at his destination. The doors were locked and he crashed through the glass without bothering to think about an alternative. He made his way to the assembly hall and approached the dais to table drop the American proposal. The assembly was silent. No one spoke as he talked through the mechanics of a unified planet. The deliberations were short. All members had made up their minds as he spoke and all that was left was to vote. Unanimous. He congratulated himself for the hard work and left without speaking to anyone else.

With the work over, it was time for him to enjoy what minimal thrills he could find in the city without people. He had gone back to his yacht to retrieve his bike so that he could cover more ground. The trees were already leaved and appealing as he headed down 36th street to imagine the mess of traffic that must have accumulated during the day. Eventually he caught partial sight of the Empire State building and made his way over to circle it, now a fairly unimpressive structure. He headed down Broadway to Central Park via Time Square, an area he had walked several times in the past on his way to the Port Authority bus station. All through the way, he saw no dogs. There were some cats in the alleys, but the formerly ubiquitous rats were also no longer thriving without the daily garbage on the streets. They had long since cleaned these out and let their population explode only to starve and die out again in mass. The cats had apparently been waiting for this but were now in the midst of their own famine. He found that the park had lost its cover of pigeons which could no longer depend on the human snacks for survival. There were some, but nothing approaching the density that existed before. The ride was pleasant in this way as he felt no threats from the shadows. He rode through the overgrown park watching the squirrels and ducks as if very little had changed at all. There were even the stashes of clothes that he knew had once been a person sleeping but could easily have been mistaken to be their bed or rumpled clothes left behind for the day, which was always a common sight in cities. There were also the occasionally overturned bicycles with police uniforms scattered about on the ground nearby. All was normal.

The glass spikes that had been under construction the last time he was here were now finished. Inside, he was told, were wraparound condos for obscenely wealthy plutocrats to overlook the city whenever they chose to visit. They were described to him then by a local friend with a mix of envy and disgust, the sort of gallows resignation of the plebeian class. They were his now so it was time to visit his unclaimed luxury. The lobby was easy to access but the elevators that served as the main entryways were naturally dormant. Even the stairwell was a hollow version of itself with no floor access and he hadn't brought with him any breaching instruments. Stuck between annoyance and curiosity, it seemed momentarily of extreme importance that he gain access to every unit in the spike and stand in each, for what purpose he'd not decided. So powerful was this impulse that he didn't bother with thinking just how heavy it would be to haul a heavy breaching ram over, then up the hundred thirty-one stories to the penthouse. It had angered him to haul the instrument up to third floor doors in the past, so this was an odd oversight driven by mania. Until he felt it in his hands after checking the local fire station, that is. He drove it the five blocks to the spike, but there was no way to mechanize the ascent within. He lashed it with belt cables and slung these across his shoulder for the long climb. It made sense to front load the difficult part, so he hauled the ram straight to the penthouse so he could let gravity help him reach the remaining units as he became more tired from the inspections. It was not easy to break the outwardly opening heavy door, but it eventually gave out before he did. He was inside a dark and likely hidden hallway that had a drab set of service elevators. His arms already burned from the effort invested to this experiment and he badly needed to rest inside.

He was in the reception hall and found the first of two kitchens he found inside the three levels. This one looked like one for a catering chef, not for household use. In sum, the space was a fairly simple mansion without a yard, except that it was at the roof of the world. He stayed the night rather than attempt to check any other units in the building. It was essentially like camping as he had only a very limited amount of food and water with him. Staying longer was an absurdity given the logistics of transporting provisions up there. The effort could not be justified even to stay for a week, let alone longer. He could think of little to do except look out the windows and marvel at how small and insignificant the island looked at those heights, which he believed was the prime appeal for families who owned nations. When he left, the door stayed open as it was hanging off its hinges. There seemed little reason to attempt at securing it; no animals would navigate their way up that many flights. This was a place where life could not exist without the benefit of public infrastructure to which this level of wealth rarely contributed. And it was still out of reach to him even in this afterworld. It will remain the same sterile and isolated box that it was designed to be until the structure collapsed and joined the garbage and rubble of the street. It took him an hour of steps and rests to calm his dizziness before he reached the bottom. At street level, the confines of the city were more apparent than before. Everything felt as if he were buried in blankets. It was not quite smothering, rather it gave the feel that everything was just cumbersome. He biked through fungible streets still jammed with cars that would never move. Everything about the city screamed humans. It was the only character of the city so that when they were removed from it, all that remained were the walls of structures to which entry was nearly impossible. Although he had developed a fair degree of skill in breaching lobbies and apartments, he found that these were especially challenging due to the heavier grades of doors with the excess of bolts. There could be no casual invasions in this city. Every attempt was a frustrating burden on his time. It was enough. He decided to return to Washington rather than burn himself out in this city. Everything he needed that was available in New York was again available in Washington. Without the people, there was no difference between the two which could justify a prolonged stay. Before he left the penthouse, he made sure to take with him a collection of diamond jewelry and collector watches that were on the family level. He put them all on rather than carry them in his bag, so he now resembled a counterfeits seller when he walked out to the street. No matter. These were eventually stuffed into a storage room in his yacht and forgotten. Aside from these treasures, he needed little else to resupply his return journey. It was tempting to switch ships to one of the larger yachts, but the burden of finding the keys made him resigned to the smallness of his vessel. It was time to leave and he barely watched the city as it receded.

Atlantic City had far more to offer him than New York so he docked there again for a few days to rest on the way down. The days were bright as ever on the beach where he sunned himself while he reflected on his winter hiding in darkness. A few short months before, this all was unthinkable and yet it came to be. But he eventually accepted that this would not be another permanent stop and cast off back out into the open waters. He did not benefit from weather alerts anymore, nor could he read the horizon until the storm had built up around him an hour after he left. At first, the water was only choppy and he managed to steer the ship through and continue on. After another couple hours, the chop had changed to churn and he was scared. It was no hurricane, but it was a dangerous storm that threatened him with deep rolls of the surface. He fought the fight of a novice who survived by accident. He wept as he did his best to navigate the vessel because he knew he was too focused to be break down but too terrified to hold back the whimpers. It went on this way for hours as he and the storm traveled the same course. It was impossible for him to know that he could have shortened his suffering down to a half hour if only he had managed to turn about and head back the way he came. Instead, they followed one another until they stopped playing their game and the storm went East, back out to sea. He was pale and nauseous by this point. But he had accidentally managed to stay on a relatively correct course back to Washington. He docked at Ocean City since it was closest when he made the full course correction, and he there underwent the traditional prostration on dry land. His immediate thought was that he would drive the remainder of the way back, rather than risk a repeat or worse out in the water. All this was put aside while he convalesced on the beach again. By a few days later, the sting of fear had left and he was more open to finishing the journey as planned. He knew from experience that driving had also become a risky enterprise given the decay of roads. He estimated that the drive would take far longer than completing the trip on the water, along totally unknown highways. With a stern face, he unmoored three days after he arrived and made his way back into open water in desperate hope that he could escape another storm.

XI
Psychedelic Swamp

Eventually all was well. He felt a strike of relief as he approached Washington again and made his way back to the wharf where the message was already received to announce his arrival. The welcome party had assembled, but many must have been weary from the long wait that day and were laying down as he pulled up to the dock and secured his moorings. Three of his lieutenants were there with tails wagging to reveal their extreme disbelief that he returned. With the episode settled and no need to ever return to New York, it was time to recuperate in his retirement.

In the immediate days, he still had not shaken the impact of the storm. He would replay moments from those hours and realize again how close he was to drowning. These memories connected to memories of the overturned truck that he recently escaped and together created electricity in his mind. When all these thought cam through, he noticed that his hands had involuntarily constricted around an imagined handle and needed to be released. Then came the return of old habits on dry land and the memory of the storm blew back out to sea as it should.

He remained on the yacht instead of moving back into his RV. When the mood hit, he would take it back out into the river to explore the Chesapeake. He went up to Baltimore and back down to Norfolk, learning to fish and wasting time on the beaches. Washington was still his main port of call where stopped on the way up and down, to refuel and grab any supplies that he staged to be on hand. When the weather turned into the volatility of late spring, he found that he docked more regularly than challenge the sky from the water. Then he eventually stopped driving out again, as the need for constant refueling began to drag on him. He much preferred the cleaner life on land where he could walk or take a bicycle anytime he felt the need to travel, and in which his pack could still follow with him instead of facing the solitude of the water. Although he had long moved out from the depths of his garage, he continued to use it in moments of depression when he needed a blackout or the largesse of the internal chamber under the mezzanine above. But it was becoming intolerably filthy as he felt no impulse to clean the way he did when it was a permanent home. It had fallen into the neglect that all former addresses do after occupants make the decision to leave, but before they do their final clean that keeps their dignity intact for when the new occupants arrive. There was little inside that he actually needed except for the food that he stored in the basement. He had over prepared last fall but such a degree that there were still dozens of shelves of untouched food. He delighted in knowing that he also over prepared his rodent control since there was not a single blob of mouse that found his supply. The excess was all brought back to the surface and locked safely in shipping containers stored at a warehouse near the wharf, so that he would no longer need to make the erstwhile short trip to the garage.

He now had so many beds and homes that he no longer felt like staying in any of them. The security in knowing he could crash at many locations made him feel more like the city itself was his living room. Three weeks after he returned from his journey, he decided to take a five gram trip that led him to wandering nonstop during the hours of melting colors as if he was being marched to death by an unknown hand. He was so exhausted by the time the comedown hit, he collapsed and fell asleep in Lafayette Park surrounded by sheep. When he woke up later in the evening, confused by where exactly he was, it became clear that he needed a permanent address again. Thus resumed the already rote process of wandering around the city shopping for houses. It was so passé that he never stopped tripping as he made his inspections. They were all the same as before. Mansions were huge, condos were logistical headaches, office buildings were no better than his ship. Each one bubbled up and then popped. None called to him. This did not continue for long. It was bizarre tedium that he'd known well over the last year. Not even the cartoon panels of psilocin made it fun, nor did they shield him from the bones of animals he found and that had been stripped bare from rodents throughout the winter. Some days were unpanelled so that he could drive out to farms, but since he already stripped these of livestock, he felt no interest to bring them all back again. By this time, the weather had made nights feel quite pleasant. Most of these days ended with him finding a place to sleep outside wherever he was that day. It was safe. His pack usually stayed with him as they roamed together, and they would keep any wild animals away at night. Whenever he did this, he would simply break open a grocery, and they would all feed on what was inside before settling down with full stomachs. These mornings always carried with them a sigh of dissatisfied boredom. None of this movement had any effect on the basic condition of his life where there was simply nothing left to do. Many of these sighs came early when he was awakened by rain and had to climb under awnings or patios if he was sleeping that night in the open.

What he really missed was the contentment he felt when he slept in his yurt. Those days came after months of accomplishment and a feeling that the aperture of daily life was only temporarily narrowed; that everything would explode in a frenzy of new beginnings once the weather warmed again. But he was squandering this time on an irrelevant project that wouldn't solve his basic malcontent. It was time for a new approach. He dragged his yurt out from the depth of the garage and set it up inside the alcove of trees below the obelisk, where he would always think about kites and his son. It had the feel of a renaissance encampment with all the psychedelic adornment he added. On the night of a really solid storm, he spent his trip in an angry tirade against the lightning out on the lawn because the roof leaked on him. Everything inside had been soaked. All the wool carpets were now unmanageably heavy as he hauled them up the hill to dry in the marble surrounding the obelisk. It rained on them again before they eventually dried out leaving behind a musty unpleasantness. The rest of the yurt had been left to dry on the lawn outside the alcove and he thought how to maintain this life without a repeat of the night.

On the night of the storm, he had stayed out screaming at the sky and bathed in the rain until he saw the Lincoln Memorial explode with each sheet of lightning. The white marble was so bright that it held onto an afterglow that pulled him to it like an insect. He stood at Lincoln's feet for the remainder of the trip, with lightning showing the statue's face until shortly before morning. He watched sunrise from the steps as it built up behind the Capitol and decided that he would make the memorial his permanent home. The first priority was to clean the interior floors and remove the generations of tourists from the stone. He ran a water pump from the river just below and used powdered laundry soap, with only a hint of irony in his mind as he scrubbed. As it dried, he installed a mobile shower and toilet on the back ledge with pipes to the river. His expensive Persian rugs were replaced with other expensive Persian rugs that were laid out all through the north chamber where he set up his yurt on an elevated platform. The South chamber was for his kitchen and storage while he set up a library reading room in the center, with deck chairs and hammocks in between the columns surrounding the outside. It was a good mix of cave and easy access.

Each morning was the same as he would rise early to watch the sunset from his new living room and doze again until late. From that vantage, there seemed little change to the mall since the evaporation because the foreground was so overrun with marble that it hid the overgrown grass dotted with gray specs of grazing sheep. Very few of his pack made the long climb up the stairs, so the courtyard was theirs.

Even his lieutenants stayed below, but tended to crowd the dirt paths just beneath the columns. It was impossible not to reflect on the history in this spot. It was empty now, but on so many occasions it had filled full of people who massed so tightly that each event could not help but become a mark of history itself. The emotions this stirred were not sadness for the lost but pride and awe that they had managed to come at all. Beyond the horizon, under the sunrise, were the rain and sun-drenched mannequins that he left out following his weird moment of celebration. Shortly after it, he dismantled the soundstage and lights, which were packed in a shipping container, but the polis stayed behind because he couldn't think of a better place to store them. He did move their boxes back to Arlington in a sign of commitment to his earlier pledge, but their laundry was more complicated. Now, it seemed important to move them over to his new home so that he could continue to mark history.

For days, he'd sit and eat round after round of mushrooms watching the crowd cheer him on from below. Each time he reached over to the small bowl that was refilled each day, there was a loud eruption of laughs and clapping. He would hold the caps up to exaggerate the consumption as would an emperor before his subjects. After the blowout of his five gram trip, he kept himself down to two. But he ate them almost every four hours which made it so that he was on a prolonged trip that stretched into weeks, which he measured with his favored pocket watch that cost more than his Georgetown house. And there was entertainment. The soundstage had been set up before the crowd arrived and now included a line of pedals for an electric guitar that he couldn't play. Each attempt at music would descend into a shoegazing mess of wah wah and feedback. There was little left of himself inside his head anymore as he wrecked it on colonnades of simmering senses. Eventually this ran out and he simply blared out ready made classical psychedelic music that was a mess of wah wah and feedback and tried to sing along to fifty year old recordings. He and the crowd swayed and writhed together under raw emotion.

When the tracks ran out, he would expound on his internal narrative through the speakers in rambling thought trains with neither stations nor passengers.

For a little under three weeks, he was on another planet with novel laws of physics, and he was exhausted again by the constant alertness that the crisscross of brain signals required. He skidded to a halt and made it through to return and see the sunrise just where it had always been as he dragged himself to a hammock with a stack of books through which to leaf. The words had come to life as his new senses looked into the texture of the paper to watch the contour of ink as each letter became a permanent companion to its surface. Heavy literature was always his way. Poetry was not. But these new eyes found it difficult to hold onto the structure of long form writing, which caused him to dabble in reading some ancient volumes of poetry that he pulled from the Library of Congress' original stacks. These were difficult to enjoy without reading them aloud. They overtook him as he realized that his shyness had kept him from ever attempting a reading and shut off an entire wing of authors. He could not help but share this with the crowd, which had grown restless waiting for the show to resume.

The break was had and he was rested. Another powerful afternoon storm suggested he enjoy it through a four gram distortion. It was over before he started, so he walked into its wake to smell the fresh ozone. He slid under the tree lined path until he reached the Natural History museum as the distortions began. He was greeted by his old friend the elephant, dusty as he was, and asked him what the trick was to stay inside without getting lost while he chased ghosts, but there was no answer. This made sense. Just stay the course and don't be distracted. He got lost at first in the maze of bones on the first floor with only his headlamp to guide him. Upstairs was where he began to melt as he looked at the geodes that had formed billions of years before. More were forming then at the moment he stood there. He reached the hope diamond under its wall of glass and almost tried to touch it until a wave of paranoia blindsided him with the stories of how severe the misfortune would be should any owner claim it for themselves. Everywhere he went, the elephant joined him. It was there at the center of the museum, a massive presence alone in the room. No matter how wild the kaleidoscopes were, the elephant never shimmered. It existed entirely outside the trip and refused to acknowledge his presence.

This was now the start of a new phase of wandering after his period of solidifying himself at home at the head of the mall. Instead of the constant trip, he smoothed them out so that he could let each one expand in full within the museums. He had already moved in special furniture to the National Gallery before, so he spent most of his time there to watch the painted waters live again as they should. Unlike the elephant, everything here spoke to him and vied for his affection. Everything was thrilled because they were creations to be viewed. In a fit of ecstasy when he passed through the gift shop, he pulled open sets of paints and stripped down to paint himself before dancing through the gallery now a part of the exhibition. He was welcomed with eager fanfare by all, particularly from the impressions. The following day he returned still coated in color to spend a day of practice at making his own art. He particularly loved the sharpness of the pastel chalks as they ground into paper. He made attempts at drawing the gallery rooms with the masterpieces as incidental details. His favorite was the favorite of many. The atrium sketching room felt like a sanctuary. He drew the bathhouse columns and the dead garden that once flourished inside. When it came to watercolors, it was the pencil sketching that ultimately derailed his efforts as he was incapable of the patient work to prepare the paper with guides before he began dabbing the colors without frames. What remained were hollow images that said nothing about what he saw. But it was the oil paintings that trapped him most. He tried to make charcoal reproductions in his own style and then fold in the color of oils that never seemed to perform as he expected.

At first, he was playing but as the arrogance of self-delusion built, he wanted to practice, so he could paint enormous murals to document his time since the evaporation. He wanted to create a huge memory that he could stand under and watch to remember the phases through which he passed. The shock of inability scaled this back and left him with an interest in just observation of the medium without oblige to study any of the countless books available. So he drew from his very old skill of constructing realistic military dioramas with the watery oil paints in an airbrush. Mixing these oils, though, required him to cake thick coats to any surface he could find, but he kept to the canvases he found in the gift shop. These globs, applied in the distorted light of his lamps, took on abstract meanings that he believed captured his mood or the particular moment. These were colored freedom. He painted seven and felt that he was ready to tackle a realistic picture. He began work on a self-portrait while the others dried. He was so smitten with his work that he brought them back home one night, so he could watch them dry and study the flavor of his own technique. When the sunrise hit them the following morning, it was the first chance he had to appreciate their smallness. The sloppy lines and clear plagiarism of the shapes startled him and he tossed them all into a dumpster in the back, abandoning further work on his portrait without assessing whether it was as bad as the others.

Instead, he decided that he should stick to what he knew and focused on coloring models that someone else produced. The idea came to him after he discarded the paintings and walked back into his living room with Lincoln seated above. Was this not just a large model? Someone else had done the work of shaping the marble into a careful resemblance of the former president, all that would be needed was the skill to mix colors and keep it in the lines. The monument itself was nothing more than a Roman temple and those originals had painted statues inside. Knowledge of this came after the artist first carved the statue, through technology that revealed the paint embedded in the

marble.   This would be no desecration but rather a
celebration of original intent.   He took from a craft
store all that he needed to begin spraying Lincoln
with oil paint to resurrect his temple.   He began at
the top and worked his way down so that his feet would
not disturb what he already completed.   Each section
required two coats, but he was finished very quickly
and was staring at a monster by the end of the second
day.

Having found his way, he continued.   When he was
young, he was a master at painting soldiers, so he
moved from the temple down to the Vietnam memorial's
bronze scenes.   At the women's memorial, he collected
the hairbands and put them in a container, so they
would not blow away over the years, then he colorized
the women and changed to the Korean War memorial, making them more haunting than when they were simply
weathered metal.   One dawn was especially beautiful
and he ate more than normal.   He chased the sky down
to the obelisk for its ability to channel messages
into the heavens.   He traced his hands in rusty spray
paint.   Hundreds of hands outlined by fluffs of or-
ange-red covered the walls as high as he could reach
and spilled onto the pavement below.   Then came the
sheep that looked like simple stick figures amassed in
a field, with he and his pack standing watch from the
temple.   This technique was brought back to Lincoln,
but then changed to something more.   His hands and
arms were covered in thick paint and the fumes had
given him a migraine when he failed to wash it off in
time.   After this passed he switched back to brushes
and worked the floor over with large spirals and
blotches of color.   These became collages that built
on one another and, over the course of the next few
weeks, had spilled out the front and down the stairs
to preserve the fact that here he made history and let
the memorial be reborn as a psychedelic house of worship.   There were purple vines that climbed the columns and bloomed into orange flowers.   There were pink
waterfalls down the stairs that mixed into a green
meadow full of red and blue pinwheels.   The crowd
loved every twist and spin that he painted.   During

another of his breaks, he had been touring the streets on a recumbent bicycle when he passed the Supreme Court and fought down a furious flash of anger. This cult of cowards had evaded him so far as he felt it was beneath his sovereignty to bother. Even in the era of civilization this cult had struggled with its own relevancy, making it the ire of all. He came back later, bringing with him several cans of spray paint to write "judicial ethics were a fiction," in red and black lettering across the front doors. It was a pointless yet satisfying endpoint for the institution that had fleeced generations with the idea that it somehow differed from all the others. He cycled back home where the fully covered temple was visible from the far side of the reflecting pool. It was an amazingly elaborate act of rebellion that took shape as a celebration which sprang from its origins as a bored act, and it needed a companion piece.

It all started with an accident. The temple decorations were supposed to bring the statue of worship to life, but a spilled bottle of paint that wouldn't clean up drew him into the world of possibilities that paint on marble presents. Every application would remain there for centuries without expensive removal technicians to erase the defacement. He would need to be more careful about using the paint for the companion piece, which he thought should be better planned than the temple piece. The options were everywhere. Marble was the stone of history that had long been a favorite medium for building structures intended to impress. It spoke of time that would outlast any observer. It was made to separate the individual from what was believed to be the endless sting of humans that stretched backwards in time to the origins of civilization and into the future, where civilization was supposed to extend indefinitely again. It did not, but the marble still spoke. What he needed was a timeless piece that drew from the reaches of history and civilization, meaning everything American-centric felt somehow limited in purpose. All except the District of Columbia's World War I memorial for its modest rotunda and discrete inscriptions dedicated to

stateless deaths in a war of empire where he inciden-
tally also slaughtered his first wild opponent. It
was small and would not stretch the capacity of his
talents, and it was also quite close enough to his
home meaning he could while away at his work without a
long commute, which was appealing for those moments
when his arms began to melt off, and he needed to dia-
logue with the jellyfish.

The site looked proper. He had ladders and safety
lines that were anchored to the columns so that he
would not need to feel the full impact of the ground
should he fall from the roof. Hundreds of gallons of
paint were brought in and mixed on the sidewalk. The
first step in his plan was to coat the entire surface
with a thin base layer, so his details would not bleed
as much and frustrate him. The roof was the biggest
challenge. He did nearly require the safety lines
several times, but it was soon coated in gray and then
with bright red. The columns became black pillars
with red inlays with which he wanted to convey the
feeling of a spider that stood over the trees, ready
to inject the venom of war without warning. The external panels on the top and bottom were where he
tested his amateurish skills to make pictographs. The
top was reserved for the story of the modern era of
civilization that marked ages through technological
leaps which were co-opted for the improvement of mass
atrocity. He could make no pictures, so he made a
collage of shadowy images in all the colors he could
think of. He connected these with dashed lines to
create the matrix of death which used all its components efficiently. The base panel told the story of
the evaporation and his journey through background
patterns that faded into one another, from the harsh
triangles of the early days through the darkness of
the garage to the colorful fractals of the mushroom
days. The ceiling inside was a difficult effort at a
cloudy sky to make him feel that the threat of war
from the outside was invisible once he stood inside,
atop a floor that outlined his cityscape and connected
to his son's on the other side. As he worked, he
thought about the original memorial and the war it

commemorated. The first world war was the apex of state decadence and unregulated international diplomacy. It began as a fracturing of the Hapsburg empire from within and infected the rest of Europe through an ever expanding network of secret defense alliances that Germany failed to harden after Bismark was dismissed. The contracts polluted the planet and sucked in colonies and capitals alike before millions of deaths were effected. It was a reminder of how far state arrogance was willing to go to protect reputation. The shock of war created another war which then rippled for another century before the economic trends of empire regained their footing. He rediscovered this narrative several times and painted it with fury.

The whole project was completed quickly and left to dry. His work had slowly drawn a crowd of onlookers as the days passed, so that the final day was observed by a few dozen mannequins oohing as he stood up to take a bow. It was not a perfect reproduction of his sketches, but it was so close that he felt proud. The weeks of practice had sharpened his skills over that which he faced with his abstract garbage still inside the bin. With his pride redeemed, he went back to retrieve his unfinished portrait to hang it from a web of small cables inside the rotunda. There he was, trapped unfinished inside a small marble memorial that someone else had agonized over in its design, died to create a call for its creation and blanketed in finger paints after none of what came before mattered. It was not clear whether this was defacement or art therapy. His work to bring the statues to life were at least attempts to preserve their origins. The murals of his temple were decorations for a home. But this was a piece that he spent time to consider how best to alter the character of the memory. If anything, he felt the additions were extensions of the original meaning, intended to bring its relevance into a new age for new tourism. It was a retrofit as necessary as drilling through ancient walls to install wiring for electric lights. It was neither defacement nor improvement. It was necessity. The memorial itself was a representation of pointless destruction of the war that failed even to create a new order of diplomacy that could keep the lessons of death fresh in the minds of states. It was a scar from the start. Now it had his own scars merged with it to remind him that these were themselves overlays on the scars he inherited. Any war memorial should be prepared for an era of defacement as the pains of memory wind through complicated healing. They must be ready for slogans and graffiti as the memory of history is always unwritten. What was settled must be ready to be opened again to painful questions, where even the very institutional foundations of a country must be reconciled with new understandings. At any rate, the marble would outlast his paint. It would shed the colors over time and return to its original white so that any explorers who found it again might never know that a survivor existed and suffered through the pain of piecing together a life alone with so many echoes. Whatever it was, it was a capstone to his painting mania, and he stared at it in appreciation. He'd completely covered the marble except for where there were blood stains from his fight with the feral pack, which was a lake of blood for the cityscape. But he could not remove the thought of war. It was everywhere in every memorial. There was no part of the city that was not a celebration of triumph of competition in war, in which even the creation of the state was a prize.

The days were now almost hot, and he spent more time sunning himself along the river where he watched the distant columns of Lee's mansion across the water. It, too, was a celebration of mass death. Even in the afterworld, he filled it with memories of death. During all this time as he ignored both his flock and pack to trip his way through the mall, they continued with their ordinary life consuming grass and spreading into the concrete city. With his attention back, he was alarmed by how few sheep remained on the mall. There was more than enough grass, but there were too many outlets through which they could meander. This happened every time he neglected them for an extended time, and he felt ashamed to discover injuries and bodies at random. It usually took him several days to comb the streets and corral them back to the South lawn, but this was far too small a space. He knew that he needed a large fenced pasture to leave them, and it finally clicked that the cemetery would be a perfect new home for them.

The painting done, it was time to herd them all from the White House across the bridge. The cemetery had become massively overgrown and was now a field of tall grass and wildflowers that nearly buried the headstones, so they would have opulence one they arrived to mow the overgrowth. They moved as sheep do, and he managed to get them across after several hours. His thinking was that they should be brought deep inside away from any gates or memorials. After the ease of herding them through the streets, he struggled to move them beyond the first patches of grass as they went to work trimming it down. It was not worth fighting them, and he drove his cart up a bit further to set up a camp under some trees where there were no graves yet. The wind was light and made for hammock sleeping as he watched the flock spread out across the hills below. It was peaceful again as he was surrounded by the remembered dead. His plan was to wait for evening and eat five grams before the moon came out, since it was bright and full on the last few nights. He waited until after the gloaming changed to night to begin the meal. As expected, the full moon was out behind the occasional fluffy clouds with the Milky Way above them all. It was a bright night that made the small marble headstones glow dimly indigo. He stood up to go for a walk through the rows as the distortions began and read each name that he passed. They went on forever in such a mass that ceased to leave any one of them an individual character. But each had a name and a life behind the name. When possible, he did math and figured each of their ages. So many were old. So many were young. To be here, they all had seen horrors. He recited them all as he went. Name after name until he found a familiar name. It was the same as his father's and it electrified his brain as he said it; a lifetime of memories where this sequence of syllables meant the earliest person he knew were activated.

Each was a commonly found name, but together they were something more and they collapsed his legs from under him. He leaned his back against the neighbor and stared at the now blindingly bright marble headstone in front of him. It was so bright that sparks began to dance on its edges. It was still warm from the sun as he traced the chiseled lettering and the years, which he could not decipher but suggested youth. Inside the veins of the white he could see forming a mountain and skyline of his home in El Paso, where his father was buried. Where his grandfather was buried. Where his great-grandfather was buried. Further back, and he might be better placed to look around Virginia, but this long line was enough. His own son would never be buried anywhere. Within the fluid of the night he stood up and painted the rows with soft fingers on the grit of stone. The trees just beyond this section grew so impossibly large that he was only an insect beneath them. Each must have massive hands holding the ground to reach up to that height, which had itself descended and brought the moon down so close that he touched its waves of light.

XII
Drive

Sunrise came again and he was waiting. After he could
no longer move, he had spent his peak hours trapped
between branches and roots until they grew into one
another. He watched the ripples of death shift the
white pegs around to exchange greetings for the
rested. And when it was calm again, he was an animal
on the ground hiding under stars in wait for sunrise.
When its expansive pink dripped over the clouds, he
made his way down the rows again to find that soldier's grave. He walked between the dead to find a
specific place within what was a forest of details in
the morning that were unavailable in the moonlight.
It was not far away, though. The plasma was gone when
he said the name again, but the vision was very much
alive. The mountains of El Paso were still outlined
in the blue vein above the 2004 that was etched under
his name. The mountain was so out of place, but he
could not unsee it. There was no mistake that this
outline was made for this name, though none of that
had anything to do with him. He projected meaning
onto them both. He interrupted their rest for a selfish aside, but it was impossible for him to do anything else now that it was found. It couldn't be any
omen, but the result was the same. It set him on a
course to question why he stayed in this city when
there was a home not far away. He knew why he came;
jobs and schools were necessary when civilization required contribution, but all of this was gone now.
Already he planned to leave before he made the decision. He wondered how he could break his tripartite
contract to leave, since it would be impossible to
take any of them along. The distance was too much to
justify shuttling back and forth to consolidate his
new life. Their survival there or along the way was
as unassured as the means of taking them. It had

taken weeks to move the flock a few dozen miles from the countryside into the city center, and this journey would be nearly a hundred times as far. If they couldn't come, and he was determined to leave, how would they survive? When he left them alone before, it was only for a month at most and he always came back to desperation. His pack in particular struggled to find their own way in the world and would face crisis when the food ran out. His flock had their food provided everywhere in the cemetery because the groundskeepers had selected grass that would remain green nearly all throughout the winter. They would be fine. They would survive on shrubs when the snow fell and shelter in wherever they could. His pack could not. They were not hunters despite his efforts. All he could do for them would be to prime the city with food for them to find in hovels. They knew the shelter of the garage and would probably return there when the weather pushed, but they would starve eventually and there was nothing he could do for them. Survival was their own personal journey to make.

With the moral barrier reasoned away, he was free to begin the preparations. It was now late June and almost the anniversary of the evaporation, as told by his watch. There was no possibility to be in El Paso by then, so he resigned to wait for it to pass first. This left him almost two weeks to make his preparations, starting with the selection of the vehicle he would take. His RV was reclaimed from storage and cleaned out to make way for all the new additions, but he realized it would never be enough space for this type of move. He thought about a large tractor rig but dismissed this as unideal living for the weeks he expected to be on the road. Reluctantly, he settled on a large trailer that could be loaded, though the terror of when he crashed the last time he attempted to haul one was still there. The RV was far larger and should be more stable pulling a heavy haul along the way. No journey was without risks. And so he chose a twenty-foot flatbed, so he could load more and be less discriminating about what he considered necessary. It was longer than anything he attempted in the past, and he was far more worried than when he initially made the decision. But he committed. At the front of the trailer, he filled plastic garbage bins with food and sealed them with sacks of rice on top. He filled a reinforced water tank, though he hoped this would not be needed. In the middle came the stacks of plastic bins for all the personal items important enough to take but not important enough to be protected inside the cab. At the rear were drums full of diesel and a spare propane tank. It all barely fit and seemed woefully insecure even with so many belt cables over a tarp. For good measure, he fashioned huge panniers that were slung on the side of the RV cab and held his collection of rugs and the priceless yurt, none of which could be left. It was a colossal disaster fit for the apocalypse. Rather than opt for the obligatory skulls and feathers, he went with the traditional psychedelic bus with colorful airbrushing over the original boilerplate black that came factory stock. When he tried to connect the two, the coupling was awkward and the navigation was strained. Nothing about the city lent itself to such a long vehicle for such an inexperienced driver, and he struggled with reaching his temple to load up. Instead, he brought in a smaller pickup and meant to drive the trailer and RV separately outside of town to join them on the highway as he left.

When he first made the decision to leave, he knew he would never return. He and his family had relocated to the area intending that it would be permanent, so they brought with them everything from overseas. There was no need to store anything as they had done in the past. He sealed his original home in Georgetown as a mausoleum with most of the important items still inside. His decision now meant that he would need to break that seal if he ever wanted to hold onto certain items from his past. It was neither a reluctant nor excited feeling to return to the neighborhood that he had been avoiding since he left last fall. All the markings of his early days were still very visible, except now carried the signs of weather. His neighbor's gate was still open, but the sounds inside had silenced. His house had generated the same funk he knew from other homes, and he felt more like he walked into a stranger's home than one that he and his family enjoyed exactly one year prior.

He knew the first item without needing to sort through closets. In that first morning, he found his wife's wedding ring burrowed inside the sheets and he placed it reverently on the dresser. After the panic and confusion subsided, he never removed it and was now headed to take it along with her jewelry because each piece in the collection was a unique memory. He had also done something similar to his son's glasses and longtime favorite plush doll. When he sealed the house, it felt right that these should stay, but not anymore. He took other things like bottles of her perfume and photo albums they created together. All the standard nostalgia left with him when he resealed the doors after having spent half a day inside.

The real goodbye was saved for his lieutenants and the rest of his pack. They had experienced their own trauma of being abandoned before rescued and were re-traumatized each time he disappeared. This cycle had made them very attached to him despite their now semi-feral life. He had many pets over the course of his life, and had to say goodbye to so many when circumstances prevented him from staying in place. But these were different. There was no one in whose care he could leave them, nor was this move particularly necessary as in the past. The decision to stay or leave was fully his own, making the trauma they would undoubtedly face a sole matter of his discretion. Harder still was the knowledge that not all of them would survive the new trauma, so his choice for a change of scenery was akin to a death sentence. He stuck to his plan and prepared the city with food for them to discover and hopefully carry them through to another year. His plan was a modification of a feeding system for when pets would be left alone in the house. He hauled in dozens of hopper bottom storage bins for use on industrial farms and scattered them in garages clustered near Rock Creek Park where they should have their best chance at learning to hunt. To make sure they knew it was there, he moved their village from the basement to one of the garages and led them all over and let them explore. They took the cue and discovered how easy it was to automatically create a pile of food instead of systematically tearing through bags that were still on the palates he periodically carted over to them. The mechanisms were just long metal shoots with a very low grade of decline from the base of the container where the food came out. All they needed to do was eat, and it was replaced. He was not worried about wild animals because he assumed the smell would excite the dogs and encourage them to hunt down the invaders, sparking their hunter instinct that he wanted to moderate while he was still around but not anymore.

As all these preparations were underway, he would occasionally check on his sheep as they wandered over the cemetery and reclaimed the land for livestock. They had scattered, but in a sustainable way that did not suggest there would be so many unnecessary deaths among the dead. They had settled in well and were making their way across the fields with neatly trimmed lawn behind them. He did notice that they seemed to have a preference for the flowers as he could find none in the areas where they roamed, even when other sections were still in full bloom. There was little need for him to worry that they would survive. They might even flourish long enough to expand more inside the grounds. But he knew their genetic concentration would ultimately destroy them in a few generations and this could not be helped.

Everything seemed ready for his departure by the first of the month. There were still another three days before the anniversary, only after which could he leave. This was a complicated line in time with nothing for him to picture as a fitting memorial. The year was an endless slog of short term vision that left him totally unable to create something for humanity that he had not already done. So he did the only thing left, which was to be a tourist in his own city. He spent

the remaining days cycling around with cameras mounted
to his bike to document his year of solitude. He took
copious pictures in all corners that he recalled
spending more than a brief few moments. Most of these
images had more in common with a forensics team than
any tourist snapping at interesting bits of history.
The oddest details had attracted his notice. For some
reason, the heaps of rubbish featured prominently as
he felt he could recall more from seeing what he consumed and discarded than from the places where he consumed them. He saw old phases where he ate nothing
but dried figs and nuts or when he loved hemp protein
with banana bread mix. Without sanitation services,
he could return to his catalog of garbage reaching all
the way back to his days in Georgetown. All of these
were loaded onto a hard drive, and he kept the cameras, so he could keep the practice going in real
time.

The anniversary was more glum than he predicted. He
woke up without energy and slept for half the day inside his RV with the shades drawn tight. By the
evening, he discovered that he was weeping as he sat
on the toilet and clawed at his arms that were wrapping ever more tightly around his shoulders. But he
was used to this and wiped himself off as usual and
went outside for a walk. A few days later was the 4th
of July and it was time.

The route he planned was down Virginia, then across
Tennessee before ebbing down to Texarkana to make the
long push across Texas itself. It was an easy route
during an easy time of year. There would be no sudden
blizzards from the North or hurricanes from the South.
This was the temperate zone that cut across what took
the nation a hundred years to take. But it was only
halfway across; it was more than two thousand miles of
highways that had not seen a single car in a year and
would now host a slow moving RV pulling a horrid
trailer. If all went well, the RV would not need gas
more than three times along the way, but he planned to
fill every night when he stopped just to be safe. Altogether, he was facing around two weeks if he pushed

nonstop at a very slow pace. The last time he and his family made this drive when they had an excess of time spending his DeFi yields, it took five days at full speed and comfortable stops. This time, each day became more than two. Perhaps it would be more if his irritation overfilled and he stopped for a vacation in one of the empty cities waiting for him.

In those five days before, they stopped and failed to explore as they did. Everything had the feel of urgency despite so much time and money to free them. By the end of the first day, the idea of driving across town to view anything else left him feeling weak, so they spent their time walking around highway hotels full of tractor rigs and gasoline. After they crossed Tennessee to make their way to Texas, the wind was wild and shoved their car from lane to lane. It slowed them and everyone else on the road, and only when they stopped for barbecue when it was over that they learned of the series of tornadoes that had built up and were destroying Memphis a few hours behind. But they had Texas ahead of them, which almost took as long to cross as the entire prior days. Tornadoes were never a thought when they initially made the trip, nor had they created any certain image in their mind as they checked weather between bites of brisket.

Now it reassured him how flat most of the drive would be except when he crossed the Smoky Mountains to Knoxville or the much larger mountains of West Texas. He was reassured that there would only be the constant threat of road debris to consider. Unlike his ramming truck, he would not have a plow mounted at the head of the RV to push through any minor obstacles. He would have to manually drag them to the side or pass over them and risk blowouts, which he anticipated by installing heavy tires more appropriate to claw through gravel roads than for a family RV. This also meant that he needed to carry a heavy jack and prefilled spares.

As the RV and trailer accumulated more, so did his nervous anticipation. This project was as ambitious

as it was unnecessary, but there was no one available
to talk him down from the irrelevant urgency. On the
morning when he left, he drove the trailer over to unlock the garage where his pack was trapped and ignored
them when they asked for attention. Instead, he drove
out to the highway to unhitch the trailer and head
back to swap the pickup for the RV. The truck whined
the entire way, threatening to break free from the
weight of its haul, and he worried that he overloaded
the trailer. When he made the swap, the RV fared better, but it still felt sluggish. He drove the RV as
slowly as he could tolerate down along the eastern
front of the Smoky Mountains that divided East and
West Virginia. It was so slow that the day barely
crosses his usual roaming path through the Virginia
countryside to the South of Ashburn.

He'd already tested the RV's GPS mapping system and
knew that it worked. That the satellites themselves
stayed powered and online was no mystery, but he was
surprised to learn that there was no terrestrial infrastructure that failed and prevented him from triangulating. It was a mystery taken without question as
he typed in his ultimate destination after the trailer
was fully hitched, and no more procrastination was
available. But the questions began when he was in-
structed to exit almost immediately, which he did with
much skepticism. When he was told to turn on an access road then routed to a U-turn to reenter the highway at the same point where he departed originally,
the skepticism turned to rage. Not because he felt
the system was failing, but that he knew the system
was behaving normally and instead was just terrible.
Once calmed again, he simply lowered the volume on the
instructions and ignored them until he could inspect
each one for signs of the irrational. At these
speeds, he would have time to course correct if he was
wrong, but the summer storm season had left its mark
everywhere that he passed. The roads were inundated
with branches. Most were small enough to drive over
or avoid, but the deposits became dense as he hugged
the mountain more closely on the second day. He
adapted with a change to the opposite side of the me-

dian and drove through oncoming traffic. There were some fallen trees on the right side of the median that he managed to avoid this way. Most were medium-sized, but he saw a few massive older trees that should never have lost their hold on the earth. They scattered debris across the highway in front of him slowing him down as he stopped to pull them aside before passing.

His second day progress was extremely slow. The imagined eleven-day prediction ahead of him was rapidly breaking under the reality of the actual pace. There was no way to revise this so early in the trip, and the only way would be to chip away by focusing on the immediate rather than become discouraged by the totality. Each day should remain a basic arithmetic of target hours and be damned the length of progress achieved during that time. He needed to adapt. But he did wonder where he should plan to stop for longer rests than just a night pulled off to the side of the road in spooky abandoned gas stations. The laws of the afterworld still applied, where he could enter any home and find keys to a less cumbersome vehicle than his moving fortress. Any city could become a regular home now that he knew how to survive. But it would be survival and not exploration as nothing felt interesting enough to explore alone. There wasn't anyone in the next seats scanning for food or who could help think through a holiday visit anywhere. He missed his family. They had always traveled together and he felt their absence more on the drive than in the last year.

The pass through the mountains came up and there was now dense forest along the road. The wide shoulders managed to push their columns farther to the side but still could not prevent the debris from washing in. Near the end of the fourth day he came up on a large pine that had crashed to where it was especially difficult for him to back out and cross to the other side. It was a hot day so the evaporating pine oil was potent in the air. Everything about the scene made him indulge the blockage and set up camp for the night. The next morning, he set about with a chainsaw to cut up the tree, so he could move on. The sound ripped the quiet apart and he was pelted with sawdust. It cut through with ease and there was soon several drum-sized logs that he rolled with considerable effort. Everything about the scene made him burn it that night in a massive fire that almost crept off the road to destroy the forest. It would have been the final manmade forest fire the valley saw and he half wanted to see it devour the mountain as he watched, but it fizzled out, and he went to sleep with a light orange glow outside his bedroom window. It took another two days to cross to Knoxville. His estimated pace had been completely destroyed. It had been nearly a week since he first pulled out from Washington, but had only gone as far as he would have covered in a day of light driving before. Now that there was no backup to get out of trouble, no neighborhoods to visit should he need more supplies, he drove so slowly that he could almost let the RV drive itself with the occasional wheel corrections. He lost a day and a half from the bonfire, then another half day when an afternoon rain picked up and convinced him to wait out. Still, it was comfortable since he could park and expand the cab until he had a full living room and kitchen everywhere he went. From the inside, there was no change to his life except the hours he spent moving the scenery in the front window. Without much outdoor exploration, he returned to the side quests of his cartoon world.

Highway life is and always had been vacant life. Once leaving urban congestion of the East, the intercity traffic was always sparse, making his drive feel less unusual. Even when he passed small towns and rest stops, it was easy to feel like it was still full of life that had moved indoors. Cars were still parked in the lots and, since he drove in the day, buildings looked as if they were still open without lights having been turned on yet. Then there were the periodic crashes from vehicles that continued on without their drivers. On the winding roads of the mountain pass, he saw many that had launched through guardrails or into ravines. More common on the straight areas were vehicles that simply decelerated with their wheels maintaining a steady line ahead. These areas made him uneasy because they looked as if a driver had lurched to the side and stopped mere minutes beforehand to resolve some emergency that came up while they drove. Unlike the dead crashes, these vehicles appeared alive and in danger. As he drove, he was able to see more clearly the emptiness of the towns now populated by ghosts. He kept to his plan to stop each night and look for a gas station with a tanker out front, so he could keep his RV full. This let him get a closer inspection of the scene that was always the same as when he found Robert tending to his register, but he didn't bother to learn new names.

After the mountain was behind and he drove into lower elevations again, he saw more and more animals while he passed through towns. He caught sight of them as he perched on overpasses that cut above the neighborhoods below. Winter must not have been as severe here as it had been in Washington. Had he not wasted so much energy preparing his ship with food for those months, he might easily have driven out to escape the winter cold. He might not have needed to hibernate in darkness at all, nor again. But his life was always a series of bifurcation and adaptation, so this thought was as fleeting as the slow moving scenery. Then he had a chance to realize what winter had brought him with a city wiped clean of feral dogs, unlike these. They had ruled the streets for one year and his passage was an obvious deviation from their day. Every time he saw them, they saw him too. It was the primal intuition of being watched that caught him first as he moved his eyes about to understand, until he saw ear pricked up and muffled barks from behind tight jaws and flapping lips. Always the same.

He decided not to stop for fuel in these towns and kept to the more remote roadside stations that dot the highways. The eeriness was uniform across them all, even in the days when customers still moved around. There was always the backdrop of rigs that created a wall on the edge of the parking area and the regular travelers were either in a rush to move on or were in the midst of a prolonged stopover. Everything had the feel of heavy use and disregard. All of these characters were now frozen in time, and he would always pull up to find car with open doors and gas pumps still connected to them at the rear. None of the pumps worked anymore, so he needed to park in the back with the other rigs where the tankers were usually set. He'd long since figured out how to use the diesel taps and had a modified nozzle to fill his tank. This required him to monitor the flow because there was no automatic cutoff, so his attention was not on the parking lot as they stalked up to him. It wasn't until he heard a dull growl a from a few feet away that he saw the two very skinny frames approaching him from the side. The lazy fatigue of driving and the roteness of the refuel process let him forget to arm himself before stepping down from the RV. He was facing these dogs as a defenseless human and only had enough time to scramble on top of his rice sacks in the trailer and hop across to the ladder at the back of the RV before they lunged. He was stuck up there as the diesel began to flood out of his tank and fill the parking lot causing them to back away to avoid the fumes. They watched him carefully and circled around when he tried to climb down from the other side of the RV where he could jump to ground that was not covered with fresh diesel. It was impossible, they were fixed on him. His only way down and back inside the RV was to cross into the fumes and carry them inside the cab where they would never leave. He moved and they moved with him. The diesel was now filling the potholes under the RV and streamed down under the trailer. He was able to climb down the ladder again and reach the bins where he had food that might encourage them to leave enough time to dash to the door without crossing the fumes. It did not work. They sniffed but preferred blood. For a moment this pleased him to see since it gave him hope for his own pack, but he saw how skinny these two were and had no idea what their original numbers were. They might have passed through a mass starvation first and now desperation told them they could not let him go. They could come back to eat what he tossed, but he might disappear if they lost focus. He thought about what to do. Would he prefer to drive the remaining weeks with a headache caused by diesel fumes, or would he risk something else? He rummaged in a bag that he stuffed between the bins and other boxes for the rifles he loaded as an afterthought. He did this so quickly that he wasn't sure if he put them in the front or the rear of the trailer. As it turned out, he had done both. He overpacked. The dogs understood, but were still committed until he dropped the first one without igniting the cloud of fumes from the muzzle blast and the second ran away. He brought the rifle with him and climbed down, managing to avoid the pool of diesel as he walked around to the passenger door. He pulled ahead, stopped to reset the gas cap and left with the lot still flooding with diesel.

The rest of the way was easier with the highway passing through flatter terrain, but he was still reluctant to drive much faster than a crawl. Several times over the drive he was suddenly confronted with wreckage or other obstacles, and nearly collided with them even at a low speed. It was painfully dull, though, to cross the country as if passing through a residential street afraid to trigger a speed camera. But when the road had flattened and was a straight line ahead, he dared to speed up to make better time. With stops, it took two and a half days to reach Nashville from Knoxville. Any time he picked up was quickly lost again due to the hours he spent napping or playing games. In the end, it almost seemed like the driving had become the breaks rather than the other way around. He cut it up into one or two hour stretches to save himself from numbing boredom. The midsummer days were long, so he could continue late into the night or start early. Some days were entirely lost if he realized that he was too high to drive and would rather spend the afternoon sunning himself on the roof. He had no idea anymore how long the drive would take. He could theoretically waste months until winter set in, but even then he was already beyond the worst of the danger and could shelter in his RV quite easily. When he pieced it together, he pretended as if he was following behind a train of settler wagons while driving a luxury RV as he gave himself a vague target of reaching Dallas within the next two weeks.

When he drove with his family, they stopped in Memphis and were able to explore a bit. He recalled that the drive in was flat and gave off the first flavor of the South. In the end they only drove around to look for places to stop but never actually made the leap. Somewhere on the way out of Nashville, he felt that it would be right to take the time he never did before, even if alone. He pulled in and everything felt the same as when he breezed through before. While slightly familiar, it would be dangerous to explore a new city in this climate without the benefit of de-tailed maps that would tell him which streets led somewhere versus which were false leads. Cycling around was out of the question, given that he was con-stantly reminded of the time when he nearly burst into flames by the now sandy diesel paste that streaked down from the gas lid. He had overpacked a few long range drones that the metropolitan police used and sent these off to study the streets for animals. He found them scattered in small packs at random among the neighborhoods, but they did not seem like prob-lems. He could not find any megapack kingdoms that would overrun any of his high capacity magazines. They roamed through what looked like fungible America; a city that had the same character as anyplace else that he knew. Like all, it had a core that was unique. The local century-old homes of the wealthy survived to be reclaimed by law firms and medical of-fices were what preserved the last details of a city that offered something different.

He dripped with sweat as he drove his drone through the streets to notice the scarcity of something dif-ferent for the modern afterworld tourist. There was little, so he brought his drone home again and took a hot shower to wash off the heat. He spent the rest of the day in his air-conditioned RV binge-watching a show he'd seen four times since December. By evening

he was ready to eat something unique. Rather than go
out to find a new, more agile, vehicle, he drove his
lumbering rig a few blocks to the grocery he spotted
from his survey. He ached to eat new flavors again.
There wouldn't be any chance to find anything fresh or
ready-prepared that would have been the mainstay of
the city in normal times, but at least there might be
the yet unknown boxes of regional brands of something
he couldn't predict. They were there, but predictable. And most required preparation to give them
life. Aside from spices, everything had been available to him in all the groceries around Washington.
Most had even followed him overseas, to the groceries
on several continents. The lines of shelving the
world over was full of the consolidated American
brands of so few producers that consumed local flavors
as they spread out and discretely re-branded. There
was no choice in shopping. Competing labels were produced from the same entities given unique existences
through legal fortitude. Across the globe. Their
reach had crystallized here in American groceries
first before they were exported and conceded moderate
shelf space to the consolidations that were able to
survive the overregulation of Europe. He remembered
this in every store, not just those for food. The
private suprastates used the world as their production
floor. Their showrooms were everywhere, expensive everywhere. Their only competition were the fractured
side hustles of production factories in China that had
dual assembly lines, one for the suprastates and one
for themselves. World shoppers no longer chose between different product lines, they chose between iterations of the same, with fluctuations in standards
of quality driving the decision. It continued still.
Cereal was his recent passion that he would eat with
rice milk that he could boil fresh and chill. He had
already depleted the named labels from Washington
shelves and had to move on to the store brands that
were identical. Now in this new city with new
shelves, the names reappeared for him to relish the
familiar boxes as he tasted the same product, wishing
he could find the German muesli he used to eat.

By the second day, he was bored with walking through the neighborhoods peaking into homes that only confirmed his assumption that everyone lived the same as in Washington. It was not even worthwhile to search for a car that he wished he could afford. Instead, he grabbed the first keys he found after he decided to drive up and down the large streets in search of inaction. It was a dowdy sedan of a single mother, stuffed with clutter that got left behind in the urgency of childcare. The inside was sour with the backseat full of crumbs and stickers. It was alive and it took him on his tour with the windows down. Interested dogs stood on the steps of buildings he passed, wondering who the invader was but not moved to chase. Downtown was a squat passionless place without its neon, except for the red brick from gentrified warehouses. But he was surprised to turn down a street and see an ancient motel that looked like a run-down flophouse of America before they came into their own. It was where the dream had died; the place where the Reverend was killed. But it was a facade. The motel itself was cut away so that the crush of development could continue without disturbing the holy site.

Memphis eventually had nothing left to offer him without its people to ignite new discoveries. There was no music anymore. No smells of the impossible to recreate. It was a city along a river with a history. He had stood at the motel and imagined the pop that evening, followed by the shrieks of confusion at another one lost. He tried to pull up a sense of the history but could no longer mourn anew after so much mourning. Either way, the battle continued and was eventually won when the struggle collapsed into pure equality. It was time to leave. The nothing in Memphis only reminded him of what he lost, not just the people but the chance to amend the missed chances. He could not build into the memory of his family's failed exploration the sights of his exploration now, as if to merge them and imagine his family there. He tried. One restaurant they had passed was closed, but he opened it for himself and sat inside to eat a meal of cereal and chat with his family in the musty dining room. The image lived in parallel to the original; it could neither replace nor coincide.

The road was the same as always but flatter and wider. He had spent weeks on it, pushing onward ever so slowly and was now only at the halfway point. The densely populated region was behind him. Everything ahead was spaced in the hugeness of the southwest, except for Dallas and Fort Worth, which welcomed him with the hugeness of their ranches and lake that stretched far to either side of the road. Its length gave it size for the eye, which obscured its narrowness under the bridge so that drivers felt as if they crossed into the sea itself before reaching the far side a few minutes later. It looked so large and so calm that he wanted to stop and explore the homes that lined it. Water living of this sort was never a thought before. He had all these homes with private docks on a lake that would not swallow him in a storm, and they were waiting for him to come home. Even a solution to the burden of searching for keys to a boat was provided by the lake with its massive boat store just off the highway. He could shop for one like anything else and be out in the water long before evening. The wear of the road had left him unable to chase down diversions. After so much preparation and driving, he was now anxious to reach the end the same as before. And there could be no end until he reached the mountain he saw in Arlington. It was a coincidence that burned a mark. Or the mark was ready to find a coincidence for him to notice. It didn't matter. The destination was unassailable at this point.

Awe gave way to an old frustration as he approached the labyrinth of the two cities that had grown together in Texas sprawl. Passing through before was an angry series of near misses, and it was a wonder how they survived. Now that the highways were open and he could crawl through, it was the nag of the GPS that remind him of the outrageousness of the course that had him simultaneously merge then exit with the perpetual construction still in place. Twice, he stopped

and fumed from inside his bedroom before he could return to the wheel and finally leave the cities behind.

Abilene was another two days out from Dallas, and it
was time to rest at what used to be his stopping
ground before and after the long stretch of isolation
to El Paso that itself took a very long day of driving
even when the roads were clear. At his wagon pace, it
would take him a week or more. A week of being dangerously far from any towns if he needed. This was
the area for which he packed the barrel of extra
diesel that sat untouched the far edge of the trailer.
Since he already marked Abilene with the importance of
an oasis, despite another Texan twin city just to the
West, it became a destination to itself. There was
nothing particularly special about the town, other
than that it fell within the Texas-high-school-foot-
ball belt. When he passed through before, it had been
football night and no hotels were available anywhere
in town. He remembered the desperate calls around
hoping to let the car stop for the night only to hang
up more discouraged than before. Football sucked all
the oxygen from the town and left it unwelcoming to
outsiders unconnected to the game. He laughed now.
The rally around a competition of children seemed no
more nonsensical than the rally around the competition
of diplomats in New York. All of it was killing time
until the evaporation wiped the canvas clean.

Everything about the road told him he was in the Texas
of his childhood, with painfully long drives to reach
anything close to another city. Huge skies over short
rolling hills that made trees look squat and gnarled.
All of this existed everywhere along the way, but
something changed when the water normally locked in
the air evaporated away. Everything that was the same
somehow changed in the dryness. Together, it all just
said that home was close by. When he pulled into
town, it was the first time he saw it in the daylight
since high school, and he couldn't recall how it
looked to him then. Now, it looked the same as anywhere. Except for the creeping dryness. He rested in
it again. He flew his drones around and inspected the

famous football stadiums scattered about. But there
was nothing much to do that he hadn't already done.
Being there was enough to relax him, since this was
already so close to El Paso that it shaped the outer
edge of his homeland. He didn't exactly know how his
great-grandfather reached El Paso after the civil war,
but it was easy to imagine that he passed through here
while still a teenager. The sky would have at least
been the same. He chased that sky to the West outside
of Abilene as the empty land took over and were marred
by small cottage oil pumps still drawing crude from
the underground reservoirs using sustainable green solar motors. Just outside town the road joined up with
the long mound of railroad tracks that all the big
empty spaces kept near to where repair equipment could
be driven with ease. Abilene had long been the junction to send cargo up to the Union line.

Trains in the Southwest were different from on the
coasts and heartland. These were massive walls of en-
gines without regard for vehicle traffic. They would
run parallel and then disappear far out to the horizon
where their horns haunted rocky valleys. They ran on
long straight lines and stopped for hours in the night
to let one another pass. All this was hidden elsewhere. He drove alongside tracks as an odd shape
shimmered in the heat distortion of the road ahead.
Until the shimmering slowed, and the shapes were easier to distinguish from the ground. There was no mis-
taking that something immense had accumulated on the
road ahead. The shapes extended far to either side of
the road, with the largest mound just out of sight.
Even before he reached it and could see clearly, he
knew that this was a train derailment caused when the
engineers and switchmen were no longer in control.
The highway had crossed a line of tracks that crossed
each other and signals were wrong. The diesels might
have run for hundreds of miles under the settings
their engineers made for track conditions far away.
They were out there alone. They ran scared and looked
for friends who could shelter them with the comfort of
explanation. Until they met and couldn't stop in
their excitement. They embraced here at the junction

and were now sleeping in the sand they pushed up. Their bodies lay strewn all over the farmland below a gypsum plant and collided with such power that they must have exploded into the air during their fervent embrace that the highway far to the side was blocked for over a mile on to the other side. He inspected and guessed that they had been headed the same direction towards Abilene. The switch couldn't handle them both and the one coming from the North broadsided the one from the South as it passed through the town. There were five miles of wreckage from start to finish, all through the town then following the highway and crushed access roads along the way. There was no path to circumvent it. The roads here were preciously rare, and he did not want to take his rig out to explore, only to find that they were narrow straight lines leading far out to other regions of Texas. All he could think to do was find equipment in town that could cut a passage stable enough for him to drive through and leave the lovers to their privacy. He checked the plant, expecting to find vehicles that were extraordinarily powerful, more so than what would be used in routine construction. But this was a soft stone plant that was more focused on processing than mines. Still, he found a tow tractor that he used to drag apart some of the cars that had broken their couplings. And that was that.

The dryness continued to grow as the ambient water evaporated even further in the summer heat of the Permian Basin. What few trees there had been, were now almost entirely gone unless they had been specially maintained near a house to beat back the heat. Since leaving, he had lived under canopies of green. He first left to chase rain and green, but now the return of brown was comforting. In the dry air, long abandoned homes he passed were still visible; no dense growth swallowed them from sight. These structures had their own afterworld and saw no change from the lack of traffic passing them by. They foreshadowed what was to become of all cities. They were the advanced guard to the end of civilization. The empty horizon also revealed all the features inside the

fields. The richness of the ocean that flowed here
left behind thick oil reserves that were still being
pumped from above by machines installed in backyards
of families who did not own them. They lost the quietude of home through the cold calculus of the property rights of artificial people who owned the mineral
rights. And they abandoned these homes to rebuild.
Everything was open for him to see so plainly that
there was no place left for his mind to wander. When
he drove through tree lines and cities, he had to visualize what lay behind them. He looked around and
watched the small details instead of the road ahead.
Now that the horizon was so naked, he could only stare
far ahead, concentrating on the road and what came
next. There was almost no wildlife, especially in the
daytime. At night, he heard the loud cackle of coyotes that told him few dogs would still be around.
These would not be interested in him in the day, so
the danger was low if he chose to walk and explore the
falling houses with their oil pumps. Walking around
reminded him that without the cover of trees or hills,
there will be intense wind fueled by columns of heated
dry air from the surface. It rocked his RV, threatening to push it over. He even nearly lost his beloved
Yurt when the panniers caught a gust and flipped over
the roof. And then there were the wind farms that
were obvious choices in this land of wind. Huge white
flowers bloomed and looked about, some at rest while
others kept their spinning play. It made him giggle
at the irony that these would be in the redoubt of
oil, placed where land rights were secure on the surface, not hidden under ancient land grant documents
archived where no one but well paid lawyers looked.
But these were owned by the artificial people too.
These hugely expensive machines served no purpose to
natural people, who still fed from the teat of oil.
Past these and the farmland changed as the height of
the vegetation continued to shorten. It now grew in
clumps between the road and railroad tracks that still
joined with him. Feisty creosote bushes began to appear and always stood alone. They made for the background scent of desert rain, and he hoped one would
pass through, so he could stop and inhale deeply.

Sand began to take over in the space between. It spread out into flows that swallowed the road and made driving even more slow. Eventually the clumps shortened into nothing but thin wires that crawled on the sand. The farmland changed too, from the traditional boxes for ease of harvest to circles for ease of watering. Everything spoke of dehydration. He felt his skin begin to evaporate as soon as he walked outside and felt the stab of the sun when he dug out wheels that gave up trying to grab at the sand. Then, even the sand started to change. Where it was once the flat layer of an ancient sea it became the jagged sand that washed up to the beaches of small mountains, with their larger cousins far to the edge of the horizon in front. He could see it all through the waterless air that flowed violently from the constant roar of wind. The road moved with it to accommodate the new terrain. It didn't so much climb as had its shoulders disappear into small arroyos that fed watershed valleys which crept back up into flat mesas far off. He was driving through the edges of a moonscape as he approached the first of the mountains that were ripped from the earth when Pangaea fell apart. The whole of the region was a respite between the mountains leading up to Alaska and others leading deep into Mexico. The pass between these chains was his destination and there was much ground yet to cover.

Further along, the small pointed formations built up to huge mountain saddles that were too small for the highway to switchback and were instead long straight lines up and down. There was no other way through, and he stopped just before the road began its first climb, so he could be fresh when the battle began. He remembered from before the sight of dozens of tractor rigs parked along the pass. Every down slope had a runaway truck ramp that always appeared to have freshly dug tracks in the soft gravel. His anxiousness at arriving beyond this obstacle was not enough to push him into it unprepared. After rest, it was time. Going up was never his concern. The RV was designed to crisscross the country and there were always mountains in the way. He was worried that he had overloaded the cab and trailer so much and ran it so continually without maintenance that something might give out on the descent. Nevertheless, he stuck to his pace and crawled up, navigating around boulders that had fallen onto the road but never removed. It creaked and complained as when he passed through the last mountains, but there were no howls. The top of the first hill flattened and led him around the base of the mountain above. From this view, everything always inverted with the tower overhead so small that you could almost touch it with an outstretched hand, while the valley below was so far away, even if the actual distances were not so. He stopped just short of where the road swooped down again and studied it. It would be technically difficult since there were so many boulders littering the lanes. He would was stuck on the side he chose that morning, with no chance to change to the other side of the highway if an impenetrable blockage came up, which so far didn't appear. He did still see the lines of rigs that rested the same as he but never finished their run again. He also saw where others broke through the guardrails and smashed into the rocks below. All of it intimidated him. It had the same feel as the escalators down into the mouths of the metro stations, which were unnecessarily long and steep. The first few times he saw those, he felt pulled down into the cavern. This decline was less steep, but it went on for what seemed like a mile before jumping straight back up to do it all again. He was finally ready and climbed back behind the wheel to let the rig slowly ease into the fall. Its weight made its decision to roll sluggish at first, but it rapidly picked up speed without help from the gas. He kept his eyes on the road and was too afraid to let his hands off the wheel, until he glanced down and saw that he was moving at triple his intended speed and accelerating. He didn't know what to do. If he eased the brakes too much, he might not slow at all. But if he pushed them harder, he might lose control or worse; he might blow them out entirely. He realized too late that he should have used the lower gear from the start and knew that engaging it now would cause a catastrophic shake that could de-

stroy the motor. All he could do was held the wheel
as straight as possible while he pumped the breaks and
let the high speed momentum carry the rig up the next
hill where he would be able to stop and try again.

Everybody survived.

At the top of the next hill, he repeated his survey
and engaged his low gear for the descent. This pattern worked, except the engine roared a protest at its
constraints, but it eventually passed, and the mountain returned to valley desert below and he was again
driving through sand as the trailer shifted back and
forth behind. He made it through what he recalled as
being the worst of the entire drive. Everything else
was muted climbs or flat hot desert. Now outside his
window was the green line of farms and trees that
thrived on the fertile banks of the Rio Grande. A bit
further still, was the gate that changed the region
into a cage that trapped all movement in an immigration bubble. This checkpoint was only an exit, not an
entrance. He passed from the opposite side and saw
cars parked under the open air warehouse, so he decided to check by crossing the median that was now
just a dusty culvert that could easily be crossed on
foot. It looked like a routine setting. There was a
short line of rigs parked behind a car, beside which
the officer's sidearm belt held trousers that tried to
fly away. He walked over and saw three passports on
the ground too. He picked them up and saw that two
were for Americans, a toddler and father, and the second belonged to a foreign woman, probably mother. It
felt strange that Americans would present a passport
for this interior immigration point, but he let it go
and tossed their documents back inside the open window
not interested to explore anything else.

The rocky desert where the checkpoint was set gave way
again to sandy desert with mesas on one side and green
river valley on the other. By now the sun was aggressively attacking his eyes as it was reflected off the
sand and asphalt. He was just on the edge of El Paso
and could make out the mountain that he chased since

that night in Arlington when a soldier told him to leave the city. The edge crept closer, and then he was in the sprawl of its outskirts where junkyards and trailer parks housed agricultural workers. Everything out here was trucks and trailers, metal and scrap. The fields were too far away to change this character. Then came the gas stations and hotels, at first far apart, then slowly more and more clustered at intersections that were recently improved from dangerous stop signs to lights. Then came the strip malls and the office parks that were all sand when he left. Each mile he drove rolled back the eras of sprawl like layers of onion. Soon, he was near the exciting new movie theater that opened when he was in high school but was now suffocated by the age of movie streaming and COVID.

Traffic increased here. For him in Washington, the evaporation was a late evening event when the city was nearly asleep and traffic had all gone home. As he crossed Texas, the effect of an earlier departure became subtly more clear, and he saw more cars crashed than before as he drove further inside. Layer by layer. Counting backwards in years as he approached the mountain that bifurcated the city. 10s...00s...80s... 50s...30s. He was at the mass of overpasses that had always felt so far from home but was really almost at the center, a bit above homes that were built a century before. Below him was a cemetery for the early Americans, where he knew his great-grandfather was buried. He passed it on his way in the same as he passed it his whole life. There were glances in at the rows of names, questions about where the right one was situated, but never enough curiosity to stop and look inside. He stopped there, though. The cemetery was too far below the highway to enter from where he stood, so instead he looked around at the mural on the park opposite and into Mexico less than a mile away, where the equis stood over a city he never explored much before due to cartel violence. He drove on towards the mountain, towards the giant star on the end which he only knew as a celebration for December but became a permanent postcard feature after he left. As he passed, the long start of the wide chain of mountains collapsed and looked like little more than a pyramid standing in the center of the city. It gave him no indication where to go. To his right was the side of the mountain that was not home. He knew he would keep driving more to the left side. But to where exactly he never planned. He decided to roll back to the outer layer and start where he left off. His university was just at the base under the tip, on the side that sloped more gently into the valley than the other and caught the fullest strike of the sun.

It had changed as did all universities. He could no longer drive into the center easily without jumping the curb to pass over a narrow walkway that used to be a road. He made it partly through before giving up to walk the remainder of the walkway. It was still the same, though. Buildings had not changed. There was still the original ones and everything kept the architecture of Lhasa. But it changed too. Parking lots were now filled with grass. Xeroscape replaced rock walls and there was a Bhutanese shrine in the middle of a meditation garden. It was locked but easy to enter and meet the kaleidoscope inside. It spoke of a complicated rest and urged him to sleep off the weeks of travel. For two days he used the shrine as his base, but it was not a good living space, and he knew that he needed to think more sustainably. He sat inside the shrine, transported back to a life in Asia that was unreachable now. For two days he was directionless and reluctant to go off campus to peel back the next layer. It was the annoyance of walking outside to piss in the rocks on the other side of the park that motivated him to seek out better accommodations. Leaving his RV parked on campus, he took a car that belonged to some professor who was locking up for the night headed home when their laundry dropped just inside the doorway. He walked through four parking areas clicking the panic button before he found the right one. He was already on his way when he realized he could have just walked to the busy restaurants a few blocks over and shortened the whole process. Nevermind. It took him deeper to the left side to the

river valley farms.   There were farms in the valley,
but no river to speak of.   What was once a small flow
of muddy water was now a depressingly thin stream that
moved so slowly that it had a sheen of algae across
the surface.   He knew the river died several years after he left.   The water wars between Texas and New
Mexico heated up, leaving the river to evaporate in a
way station a few hours to the North.   Before he even
finished peeling the layers he saw that the core was
rotten and a moment of panic made him imagine the long
drive back to Washington.

XIII
Never Go Home Again

The professor's car was new, but it was a city car.
It had cried in pain as he drove it over the dirt covered roads of the valley where a year of flooding and
sand blows had accumulated in the early phase of natural reclamation. He needed a Texan vehicle and there
were many from which to choose. He took a truck with
a heavy bumper that was added by an owner who only
drove it to grocery shop and went back to his RV after
the disappointment of the river.

It had only been a few days since he first drove into
the desert and left the climate of his RV and the
evaporation was very much affecting him. He was
thirsty all the time and the inside of his nose began
to crack. The thirst was old, but the cracking was
new. He always had a religious affinity to carry water with him because of the desert thirst, but never
did he internalize the dehydration like what happened
now every time he breathed; the nose bleeds were still
to come. He knew the thirst was permanent and needed
a durable solution that could not involve a lazy plan
to pump in from the river as he did from the Potomac.
Even in this desert, he knew there was water everywhere beneath his feet. It was the reason that such a
city was even possible and all he needed to do was
find the taps. His lesson from the water treatment
plants in Maryland taught him that it was only a
bridge. He could not both restart the pumps and figure out how to operate the treatment process designed
to fill a city full of pipes that far exceeded his
needs. He only would now need a small well that would
draw up already clean water. These household wells
were everywhere, he knew, but could not recall which
of the houses would have them, and which among those

drew deep water that was fit to drink. This knowledge was inside him somewhere.

A memory surfaced of a high school friend smiling as he tasted a glass of water that he was told had come straight up unfiltered. It was clean and didn't have the chalky taste of calcium carbonate that city water had. This friend's house was far out in the valley, and he vaguely knew where it would be based on landmarks along the way. Most of these were now missing. The second stop sign was now a six lane traffic light and the horse stables had been removed to make way for a row of two-story homes. The bamboo grove along the canal was also gone, so the canal could be pushed underground and paved over with a bike path. He eventually found the right street, but the house and well had been replaced with another cluster of homes. He was out of ideas in the shock of such dramatic change. There were still wells in the area, but he might search a dozen older homes before he found one. He needed a supply of water immediately and did not want to wait out fruition from another round of home invasions. So he did what everyone else would have done: he went to the store. During the winter, he had partly relied on palates of bottled water instead of wasting the energy needed to turn on pumps to fill his bins, even if this was only necessary every few days. It was far easier to reach for a plastic bottle and toss it into the darkness with clanks that seemed like they never stopped. And since the world had become addicted to bottled water branding, he knew the warehouse stores would be full of them.

The whole water search weened him off the seclusion of his RV and gave him reason to explore the city with a sense of purpose. It brought him down his childhood streets, most of which had changed in the twenty years since he left, but many were the same. The entire reason for the weeks of driving to come here was for him to find home inside himself by surrounding his body with the features of what he used to define as home. It only made sense that he get started on the next phase by visiting the construction that origi-

nated it all. When he came through before on a short
visit, he passed his childhood home and already knew
that it had been remodeled extensively. Gone were the
tall pines that they planted and over which he built
an igloo during the first winter that saw an excep-
tionally rare blizzard. The facade was unrecognizable
and there was now a large fence in front. The neighboring house, an ancient rock home that was cool and
dark inside like a castle, had been demolished and
construction of something new had not yet happened.
The inside was less severe and the basic floor plan
was unchanged. The last time he was inside was when
he broke in one college night after it had been abandoned for several years. He walked through in the
dark and felt like it was a house of murder. Now, it
was worse than an echo of even that. It was now someone else's home and he was an intruder. What had
given him the most foundation of personality was the
large Texas yard where everything was possible.
Projects could be started and left without cluttering
the life inside. Huge underground complexes could be
dug and no one would be walking by to fall in. The
bamboo grove was the source of every game, and he took
this with him to jungle life where bamboo was the
source of every home. All of this was gone. The
waste of grass meant it was better to pave over to
make way for basketball decks and the horse corral was
now a field of tumbleweed. Even the barn, that he
knew as home only to black widows nesting on walls
where the white was nearly black from fly shit was
renovated to be someone's cheap home with a long and
narrow fenced driveway cut through for their access to
the main road far in front of the property. For some
reason, the empty patch of desert behind the bamboo on
the adjacent property that he turned into battlefields
and trenches was still empty. This small and secret
area only accessible from the back along the dirt embankment of the irrigation canal was all that remained
of his home to match his memory. Rather than smile at
the sight of an old friend, his first thought was to
try and understand why this alone was left unruined as
an investment parcel. Sure, access was difficult, but
that could have been easily remedied. Someone made

the decision to leave it this way as if waiting for him.

But it wasn't enough. He was no child anymore and the dirt was no different from dirt on any continent into which he put his blood. Nothing in this corner of the city connected him to anything. Except the view of the mountain, which was unchanged. He could even still see the glinting windows of familiar buildings far up the slope. It was this outline that had burned deep in his mind. He knew it in all seasons; loved it when it was hidden in fog and storm that never quite reached the valley. This was the shape of the vein the soldier showed him. The accident of rock formation and the accident of masonry and the accident of assignment to that soldier with that name showed him that this mountain was home. He could not live inside it, though he had often dreamed of the chance. Instead, it was the home of presence that only meant he needed to see it. It was not eternal, but its life far exceeded the generations of humans who lived here and eventually led to himself. All of them had this same presence with them from start to finish. Any one from among the generations could stand with him there and agree that nothing had changed. Even the genocidaires on horseback could rib him and say that, without trees, the mountain was timeless as they marched their charges through the valley.

He left his destroyed childhood with the renewed vision of the mountain fresh in mind. The shrine had affected him with the Asian mindset of honoring ancestors, so he felt the best place to start his vision quest would be where his roots here began. His great-grandfather had traveled here after the war and eked out a life that was marked in the cemetery on the other side of the mountain. He walked the rows as a child, but only in his imagination when the car passed by. Never had he seen the graves, nor did he know which of the sections were the correct one. He knew his father's, which was on the mountain slope above the valley where he grew up, and his grandfather was on the other side. But he never visited this far back, so he had to repeat his Arlington meander through the headstones reading each name. It was not a large cemetery, but it was overgrown with green tumbleweeds that stung him every time he brushed them aside to read a name. Hours passed and the early sunset caused by the mountain to the West had already begun. The right one was eventually found. Modest. Old. He died just a few years into the new century. His El Paso was wild compared to his own. It was an era of unsettled borders that still rippled down to the evaporation. There was a more than zero chance that he was an aggressive racist who happened to speak Spanish as a matter of practicality. But it was an origin. Not "the" origin, but one for him nonetheless. He stood there quietly for a while in the far side of the grounds against a high wall on two sides. When he got thirsty, he searched for a bottle in his bag and heard a startled sweep behind him that immediately preceded the well known sound of small beads shaking in chitin chambers.

Years of indoctrination told him to freeze. But he moved his eyes and saw the rattlesnake poised low under some weeds very nearby to block his only way out. Even if he tried to climb the wall with some heroic parkour attempt that would more likely than not leave him flat on his ass, he'd be too slow. He calculated the distance. This snake was not the largest he'd seen, so it must be a juvenile that was only four feet long. Just a foot shorted than how far away it coiled. He stayed frozen, hoping that the snake would move on. It stayed there to eye him as his arms began to ache from the awkwardness of his pose. It continued with neither willing to give up. What had he done, continued to do, that held the snake's attention? It should have stood down by then and continued to look for food elsewhere. The aches continued and grew. He would have to find a way out before it was too dark. The second lesson from indoctrination told him that slow movements were slightly acceptable to vipers that felt threatened. If he could ease around his great-grandfather's headstone, that would put a barrier between them and he could move away faster.

The last time he met a rattlesnake, he panic-ran because the others he was with ran. Everyone went in
different directions and no one was struck. But that
snake had three threats to watch, now there was only
him. This juvenile must have felt especially threatened and unwilling to let down its guard. The longer
this went on, he believed the more venom that would be
pumped into the sacks above its fangs. He moved. The
first thing to do was release the ache and reclaim his
arms from inside the bag and begin to turn his body
back towards the headstone. The shift in weight was
imperceptible, but the suddenness of his moving feet
tripped the spring as he made his full swivel around
the grave. He felt the pressure of the strike and
imagined a scratch on the rear of his leg. Then the
panic took over and he hopped over the tumbleweeds,
stumbled at the landing before he sprinted away
through more brush. An interlude in panic made him
understand that this probably was not the only rattlesnake around him and he stopped, knowing he would
not have been pursued. He passed the light from his
headlamp around him and heard no telltale sounds, so
he reached into the rocky sand to pull out a handful
of small stones that were gathered in the huge ant
hill to throw in front of his path before he walked
through the rest of the cemetery back to the gate.

He reached his truck and the adrenaline began to unwind. Now was the time to assess the damage, whether
he would die searching the nearest hospital for an-
tivenom that he would never be able to identify even
if it was in his hand, or did he escape? He unhooked
his overalls and dropped them along with his second
layer of shorts. He was right, there was a small red
line where one fang had reached through the layers of
cloth and dragged across his skin above the backside
of his calf. There was only a thin scratch, red from
irritation but not from venom. He saw no puncture
wound that suggested the poison already seeped through
to his bloodstream as it was pumped rapidly from the
excitement. Ultimately, he decided to clean it up
later and pulled his clothes back on, but felt a
scratch again, this time lower down on his leg. There

was nothing there, so he tried to dress again and saw as he did the small fang caught in the canvas where it broke off during the strike. He had again escaped from what would have been a painful death that would in all likelihood caused him to use his 9 mm rather than wait and see how much more painful tachycardia he could tolerate. It was all too funny now. In his four decades of life, he never had so many close encounters as in the past year. He ran them through in his head, beginning with the evaporation itself. How could he be so immune from danger yet continue to so recklessly seek it out? It was as if something needed him alive to tell the story of the afterworld, which built to something large. That something was bigger than his own story, and he was only there as a prop to put it into motion and only once the tipping point was met could he be discarded. Until then, he was invincible. This was absurd. He knew that he only survived from a combination of luck and planning. He used to wear kevlar exactly for these moments, but changed to heavy farm canvas that was cooler but still very hot in the climate changed summer sun. He wore it loose, so any bite from any animal would be misjudged and fall short. All his escapes were narrow but within his margin of error that he calculated for risk. He was, indeed, quite unimportant.

Next was to continue on with the plan for paying respects. He visited his grandfather first, though he knew very little about him since he died many decades before he was born. But his father was known. He died twenty-five years earlier and he still remembered the ceremony. There was no answer when he asked for guidance; no vision met him in either place. This would have to come from himself. Again. Survival was his personal affair. He thought about where to establish his base and decided to visit the home where his father was born and raised, where he met his grandmother on her deathbed before it all was sold. All he had to go off of was a five-year-old's hazy memory of getting out of the car to walk to the door. Then it skipped to an unintelligible elderly woman in a dim room with pinkish curtains that glowed from the bright sun outside. Then nothing. It was pointed out several times over the years, so he had a general idea of the neighborhood abutting the university. He narrowed it down to three finalists and explored each. One was a medical practice and the other two were law firms. Nothing invited him in.

Giving up on vicarious living, he thought about his own life. The life he constructed after the safety line back home was cut. His old apartment was typical for El Paso. It was neither small nor livable. The city never entered the phase of condos and mixed use communities, and renters were either students or derelicts. He only went inside out of curious nostalgia, not to set up residence. The young woman who lived there was in the former group. She appeared to be a nursing student whose gaudy decorations smothered him red, black and heavy scents. He kept reaching down the layers and decided to check his high school to find that it too was now just another school that failed to prompt any real connection. He struggled to remember where his classes had been or any particular memories from inside the hallways. Only the courtyard where he hid during the first weeks when he had no friends seemed familiar. But this was more a recognition than nostalgia. After a week in town he had no base and still felt like a visitor drifting around for something to do. Surely he had this clear in his mind when he packed the rig and drove out from Washington, but that image dissipated when he tried to apply to anything tangible.

The agitation was superimposed to his surroundings and he moved from the shrine to the scenic road that cut high up on the mountain, just below the star. He set the RV up at the narrow corner where the scenic overlook was assembled out of the base rock. From here, he thought he would use the strategic vantage to scan the entire valley on either side. With his own telescope, he watched the city for new destinations then would drive out to explore. From up there, it was even possible to see as far as the immigration checkpoint several hours away. He searched, but quickly realized how unappealing the neighborhoods were to him under the circumstances of the afterworld. There was no need to visit a home that was no different from all the others without people inside. For a time, he was interested on the county jail that differed from the small holding cell where he contemplated tossing the key, but couldn't think of a reason to visit. The best he could come up with was to look out of the windows to see from inside down to the street level, where he remembered people would stand to sign out complex messages for the detainees. But then what? It hardly seemed worth the trouble just to nod his head in understanding and leave. The homes he did enjoy were the old neighborhoods above the university, the expensive homes that he always felt resembled what he imagined Berkeley to look like until he went to Berkeley. Still, the homes were antique yet did not follow the modern craftsman style of others built in the same era, and he enjoyed walking through the steep streets. The beginning and end of the walk was always the same trek up along the road cut into the mountain, with a deep cliff on the outside edge that was protected only by a squat wall. There was no cycling here. It could be done, but it was unpleasant compared to the calm contemplation of a walk. It meant that he twice passed the elite mountain neighborhood constructed at the top of its own pillar that shot out of the slopes. These were enormous mansions with hanging gardens and stacks of levels. There would be no digging a well up there, nor would he cart water to the top in order to spend time rebuilding the gardens that were now quite dead. He had learned the worthlessness of the homes in each city where the wealthy climbed. These cities on the hill came in various forms but were always a flight from civilization in their expensive bubbles of convenience. So he always walked below, even as he knew there was no water for them either.

These walks always had wind as a companion. It was the fingers of the mountain. It was the essence of the city and filled everything. Some days were light touches and others were heavy swipes. There were no tornadoes here, the mountain prevented them. But it sometimes lifted roofs off houses anyway, so the difference was little. He was accustomed to the gusts against the RV, especially at night when the rapidly cooling sand far out in the desert met the still hot rocks of the mountain. When he woke up to the sound, he was unbothered until a time his bed heaved under the weight of the mountain touch. The RV rocked each time a new wave came, and he had visions of being knocked over or even tumbling down the cliff. He tried to reassure himself that this was unlikely, but the mountain kept him awake until he got up to pivot the RV, so it was less broadside to the wind and further away from the edge. That morning was still gusty, and he slept in to catch up on the hours lost. By the early afternoon when he looked outside again, he saw the first of the haze that came out from between pebbles throughout the city to climb up into the sky. He knew this haze. This was the haze that would build up in the air upon which the scaffolding of sand could create a superstructure that would blind the sun. This was the wind that pelted skin left exposed. Being so near the ceiling, he decided to take his truck to the top of the mountain where the radio towers were installed. From there he might see the ocean of sand from an island of clarity. He had never completed the climb. He once attempted on bicycle, but it was too steep and too tall. Trucks were prohibited, so he had to break the lock and drive through the gate, up the narrow road that was more rock than gravel. He slid as the tires fought to keep traction. Up. Switch. Back. Up. He reached the top in time to see the pillow of dust come in from the mesas, moving at lightning speed that felt like a crawl only because the distance he could see was so huge. From up there, he could see far into New Mexico, nearly to Albuquerque and over to the mountain where his RV screamed down the week before. Soon, the pillow came to him and the sun dimmed, but he was too high for it to disappear. Instead, the city washed away in a milky brown pool. Then all the dusty water settled. The wind cooled, and he no longer needed to crouch down to avoid being blown into the deep new sea. He

finally made it to the top. This was always a destination that never happened. It was always unreachable
until today and he was there. His father used to walk
this spot almost a century before. The arc of generation was so long that it didn't matter that he took
his time to climb up the same trail. There was no urgency anymore because the rocks were waiting for the
last one to climb and watch the ocean it built from
the dry desert below. He saw the mountain's twin far
off to the East. These were once flat contiguous
plates that snapped and were tipped up to create two
long valleys. The river coming down chose one as its
course and crashed into the smaller mountain cousin.
Only these features were immune from humanity. Even
the river now fell victim to manipulation and choked.
The mountains could be scarred or mined, but they
could not be destroyed. There was nothing of value
under their tops, so no industry would come to take it
away. They had survived humanity and were now safe.
Humans used the mountain for a long time. He used it
that day. With the sea covering the valley, he could
see the break in the line that was the pass through
the line of mountains.

Off on the other shore were the sandy mesas where New
Mexico took over the international border before hand-
ing it to Arizona. Long flat tops that swooped down
as their sandy sides broke free. Before the era of
the militarized border, he used to trip in those sands
chasing a wailing column of indigenous families on
their death march. From up on the mountain, he could
see the high-water mark of the river as it whipped
back and forth through the valley. When the genocidaires came, they supposedly walked into a fertile
grassland that reached their stirrups. The river was
wild and unpredictable. Rain water runs fast down the
mountain, even still. It feeds the river and floods
the valley. If the river flowed wild again, it would
build from all the rain and eventually reclaim the
valley from the city. It had tried this in the past.
The entire band of neighborhoods below where he parked
his RV had to be filled with water before it was
dammed. Homes of wealth in those days already climbed

to escape the valley, into the safety of the mountain. But they climbed too far and the mountain sometimes sent walls of water down to push them back. Humans were at the mercy of the river king in the valley and the mountain god above until they conquered the river, and it now was nothing but an evaporating memory.

The sun had returned by then and was already sloping its path below the mesas. It was time to climb back down, but the thought of sliding on the truck with so much trust that the brakes would hold was less than interesting. He decided to walk, because his legs always understood him in these moments. It was a slow process, not because he was careful but because he had climbed so high. It took two more hours from the top down to the base, which was itself was still far from his RV and the sun was setting. He decided to rest in a house at the trailhead. Inside was nondescript, but the balcony was the centerpiece that overlooked the city. The former occupants were there in lounge chairs just as the sun was setting, ready to watch the lights from below pop. Now, he was there watching the sun set to watch the lights pop from above. The crispness of the dehydrated air showed the full contours of stars, even as the haze still blanketed everything. The sun set was blood with deep indigo that faded to absolute black that was cut by the edge of the galaxy. He wondered if there had been an evaporation out there too. Was it some panocide that expanded from a single source to cover all that looked down at him? The thought bored him as he just watched the sky blink slightly. He tried to count the satellites above, now so visible, and imagined what an afterworld would look like if he could access their network again, if he could reboot all the technology that made life so comfortable. He was tired from the hike and his knees ached from the constant pounding on the downhill rocks. It was time to go back to the RV and shower it all away. He checked their pockets first to see if they still had their keys, but found them instead on the counter. The RV was no longer battered by the gusts, so he managed to sleep well.

It was time to become serious about his permanent base. His strategic perch had reminded him that no human life was fit for survival outside the reach of the river, albeit so choked. This narrowed his search to the valley, where he grew up. He squeezed the rig back through the narrowness of the mountain road with its sharply winding course. On the way up, he nearly wedged in when the trailer lagged too far behind as the whole rig passed through different curves. This was annoying on the way up but terrifying on the way down. His new perch was just over the bridge nearest his childhood home, which was centrally located for the roads that ran parallel to the river banks on both sides.

In this area, it was common to race dirt bikes through the dry riverbed because it offered a long sandy course that stretched on for miles. Part of why he walked into it was because he spotted an overturned bike a hundred meters from the bridge. If the bike could be started again, then he could use it to explore the valley from the backside and get a better feel of the properties. It was up on the embankment. It had been partly buried over the last year of sandstorms and had the early stages of severe UV damage. The burial looked like wind and that it probably had not flooded. The safety suit and helmet looked small, like what a youth would wear, so none of it fit. He thought that he would need to be careful and not test his immunity again, as he pushed it back to the RV to add more fuel. The start was sluggish but it kicked over. He drove off carefully until he was confident again and then opened it up in the riverbed heading North to the farms.

In this valley, pecan was the river's queen. She spread her dress up and down the flat fertile soil that the dam had freed from flooding. They were the only forests here. When the summer bloomed, they provided thick covers in perfectly spaced grid groves. The years had pushed them further North than he remembered, but soon they were there and all he could find. Except that they were not thick and green. The forests were now patchy, but still held onto life in the hope that another rain would be just beyond. This was less unreasonable as it sounded. The era of changed climate had steadily increased the rainfall and already thickened the carpet of creosote that climbed up the mountain. But these forests needed floods from the irrigation canals that opened for them to take deep drinks. He went to check the canals. There was none of the matted cake on the surface layer of clay that dried in the sun and would have told him that the basin had been full recently. This was the smooth erosion of rainfall that failed to fill the canals, even if the channels were open. These needed to feed from the river.

The canals felt solvable or at least a workaround could be found. The river's centrality was critical for life, but he knew that the river flowed underground too, that its flooding over the ages had left pockets of water buried in the bedrock. The river didn't feed the canals from the surface, then everything kept pointing back to reliance on a well. It was time to let the search move to another day. He'd gone far enough through the sand and wanted to return to the RV more quickly, so he went across the bridge to drive back along the street. In moments all along the way he saw the signs of recent floods that accumulated on the long periurban street that never seemed important enough to install drainage despite annual pools of water. The road would have been difficult to drive had he not had the maneuverability of the dirt bike. Water had not been found that day, but he learned something of the valley. Everywhere that had invasive life was under threat of being erased by the mountains. This thrilling new challenge started with his own need to hold back his thirst without the annoying need to constantly reach for the inadequately small plastic bottles. In Washington, he knew where to go for the water treatment plant only because it had been so easy to spot over his time before the evaporation. He drove past it regularly and knew before he needed to know that this was the site that fed his taps. There was no such fortune here, where everything was tan on brown and full of factories that could themselves be anything. Without these plants, he could not even dip into the murk and filter out the river water as he had done with pumps leading into the Potomac. The river had gone dormant in its underground course and was impossible to reach. But there were swimming pools and private lakes that flew against the water conservation ethos of the city and might still provide him with something. There were several specific neighborhoods where he remembered small lakes that fed green parks for their HOA's. When he reached them to look, though, he could see how much they had fought back against the desert. These shallow pools were now dry themselves, without the community of ducks that had thrived there. The last was a deep collection pool at the center of the horse racetrack. Far down the sides was a layer of filthy water that was thick with clumpy algae. But it was water in between the cells. What he needed was a filter that could handle the volume, which could then be shocked with chemicals to make it safe. The pump and water truck were easy to find in the municipal fleet nearby, but the filter had to be fashioned himself. He had made many charcoal filters in the past when he lived in the jungle, but those had always been inside small plastic bottles. This needed to handle the flow from wide hoses. The principle was the same, but he adapted it for a grain bin. He stuffed the mouth of the hopper with folded bath towels and poured in ground up charcoal from a woodpile that he burned. On top was the thick layer of sand that would trap the algae. It all worked the same, except the weight of the water he pumped in nearly toppled the vehicle he used to stabilize the filter that fed into a plastic pool underneath. He pumped this into two dirty water truck just like before. He dropped a low concentration pool chlorine and let it sit for a couple days. It tasted awful with the chlorine being so strong; he knew this would evaporate off. This new process would work, but the layers of lines along the edge of the pond told him it was a temporary solution at best. He bought some time, but he still needed to find a well. The search for water was ancient for the area. The original humans traveled seasonally to find it and even had a special mountain that built for them thousands of water bowls. The Queen must have a backup plan that he missed from his first visit, when he was distracted by focusing on the canals.

It was time to be systematic in the valley as he had been in Washington when he burned through so much mania to chip away at doubt that he was truly alone. He was growing tired of RV life after having huge ecosystems in which to live. He needed to explore with a plan and not let himself be distracted by jumping ahead to a new mania for a project that was not yet ready to begin. Wells should be everywhere. The older homes that were built before they fit within the incorporated municipal boundaries must be the likeliest ones, so his plan was to inspect them one by one to see if any could be the right fit for his new base. The change that overtook the valley in all places. He already saw it when he searched for his friend's home, but it was now everywhere he looked. His plan to find older homes became more complicated than he thought because finding them was no longer as easy as before. The roads he followed used to be lined with horse pastures and alfalfa sprouts. There was plowing season and games in the fallow fields that were themselves all a mark of change from the white flats where gypsum leached. But they were the change that he knew as baseline that were now covered over by a valley of subdivisions. The spread of sprawl made it difficult to find the older homes that were now pushed farther away from the city. The onion continued to grow in his absence, and it was fat with sticky layers he couldn't peel away anymore. The cancer was now benign as it would not grow any further than it already had; the valley was safe from the encroaching homes. There were wells in the orchards, as he predicted. One pumped water up to a pool that was home to a community of geese and ducks, which were all gone now. He found so many torn up bones of the domesticated fowls scattered across the banks of the dry pool. Refilling it was easy, as was restarting the aerator pump so that he now had a better source of water for his trucks

than the filth he found at the racetrack. He let the
water fill the pool and flood the orchard again. This
was no home, but it could be his forest garden.

But far away, though, he did find a home. It was the
stables where he had ridden many years before, where
the house was fully connected to the well. The stables were all filled with the heavy carcasses of
horses trapped inside the dry paddock. He saw two
that had jumped the fence looking for food, but must
have injured their legs on the metal pipes because
they did not graze far. The pump depended on the city
electricity, unlike the orchard pump that had its own
diesel generator. Since surviving on his own, he had
learned some basics of rewiring without a fire result-
ing, and soon the pump was connected to a small generator with the intention being that he would swap it
out for a solar panel. As he worked, the sour smell
of dried horse skin nagged. If this was to be his
home, he needed to clear it out, and he couldn't work
with so much rawhide, so he started with pulling the
horses far to the back of the paddock where he lit
them on fire. The smell successfully changed to
charred horse which allowed him to embellish his new
source of water by making sure it would be secure in
plastic bins should the pump give out. It was one
thing to urgently search for a well when he had nothing, but it would be another to search for one because
he failed to prepare.

Before shutting the pump down after the bins were
full, he went inside to confirm that taps were all
working. Not since the power grid failed had he seen
a home with normal plumbing. His yacht and RV both
had their own water, but these were embargoed for conservation. Now, he could simply waste as much as he
wanted without worry. It was finally time to retire
the RV after parking it outside his new home. There
was no place large enough with sufficient cover to install his yurt, but he removed it to let it air out in
the sun after so long stuffed inside the panniers.

He was only there a few days before the neighbors
bothered him. Each time he drove past, he bristled at
the sight of the new subdivision at the main road.
The walls and roofs were so close that they only mag-
nified the heat that should have been trapped in the
sand. He bristled because he had bought his home when
the flood of buyers spiked home prices so high in response to the shortages in new construction. There
had been decades of exploding subdivisions full of
cheap ready-made homes, but there was never enough
housing. Before he bought his, the family stayed in
short term rentals that were nearly double the rate of
other apartments. They had no credit having lived
overseas for so long. No apartments would take them
even if there were vacancies, which there weren't.
Housing was just another industry with a fetish for
the proven and the valley was destroyed to feed it.
This particular corner bothered him because it used to
be a large training ground for new racehorses. There
were several arenas and a small track where he used to
ride. He dug tunnels in the mountains of sawdust for
the stalls. Now it was buried under homes where families had to be locked inside to escape the oven between their homes. The neighborhood inside fit the
pattern of all new developments. The homes were trim
and neat, with no trees or gardens yet growing. But
this was the desert and most homes had uprooted their
trees after the water crisis of the 90s, to be replaced with colored rock and cactus. This neighborhood didn't even have this decor yet. There were
driveways marred by dirt islands against the dirt
brown stucco walls. Everything inside the neighborhood was heat. Cars cooked. Garages were billows of
hot air. Inside, though, was well-sealed and temperate. These were homes designed to be habitat capsules
to which you escape and stay inside so that the connection to the desert was severed and families inside
could pretend to be anywhere else in the world but.
He tried to be understanding. The need for private
space was strong, and he couldn't blame families for
their choice. But it felt hard for him to justify the
loss of so much of what made the valley unique, only
to be replaced with what was so fungible. He long

knew that the city hated apartment living. Compared
to other cities, there was nothing of the luxury
stacks. Multifamily living was temporary or at least
shameful if long term. Land was too disposable to
waste construction cost on stacking people in tall
hundred thirty story spikes. The plutocrats here
bought up neighborhoods and demolished them to rebuild
into mansions. Renters rented houses.

It was too much, and he wanted to destroy it all so
that he could reclaim the land for himself. Whatever
empathy he mustered for the families who moved in,
they were never returning and there was no need to
preserve them. He was past memorial. In order to reclaim the neighborhood, he would need to completely
destroy everything down to the foundation. He would
need to rip out the wires and pipes by digging into
the ground to extract the desert from below. It would
have to be so complete that he would not be able to
see any trace left as he passed by. Then what? He
would pass by a gaping hole where he wanted an old
arena and piles of sawdust. Would the scar be worse
than the wound? At least it would open up a bit of
extra skyline. The destruction itself would be a
challenge. In order to begin the healing process he
would need some immediate satisfaction that couldn't
wait for the long process to build a scar. It would
have to begin with symbolism. He felt the mania return again as he dreamed out the celebrated destruction. He imagined bringing in the polis to watch a
wild festival. In Washington, during the early days
of his home invasions, he used fire to cleanse the
homes he felt had no history. The wooden homes there
burned down to cinders. These stucco homes had wooden
bones, but he wasn't sure that everything else would
burn well at all. At best, it was likely that they
would smolder into a pile of rubble that would then
need to be pulverized before it could be removed.
This meant demolition vehicles were needed. He imagined himself a one-person crew that worked day after
day to deconstruct what was so recently constructed.
This would need a fleet of loaders and wrecking balls
to smash the homes apart. It would be easier to do if

they were not charred first; he would need intact wall frames that could be pulled apart but not crumble. This would take forever and failed to keep the symbolism he needed. It would just be work. Explosives could rip them apart so completely that he might bulldoze them into a mound. Instead of a scar, he could make a sculpture garden full of broken debris. In time, the desert would take it over. He could accelerate this by burning the sculpture with barrels of gasoline. This would compound the enjoyment of destruction across two phases. To what end? The question never left. Each time his violence projected onto the neighborhood or anything else that had changed in the city in a way he didn't like, he returned to the question that deflated his mania. There was no answer to explain to himself what the point of the destruction and anger could be. There was nothing inside it. These were empty projections for a city that had continued to be home for others after he abandoned it. Land had no affiliation. No time investment gave ownership to land or natural features. His roots here were just fictions that he created from a hallucination. What he destroyed with fire or explosions would not yield a return him to before he abandoned the city. It could not transport him back, even if he demolished everything new and changed the landscape to what it once was. The home he envisioned was gone long before he was aware, so that all he could do now would be to built a replica at best. He felt like he should not have come. He wished he left the hallucination alone so that it could stay a nostalgia, not a proven disappointment.

He pushed this all aside and continued to explore the valley up along the mesas where there was only sand. He passed the villages and saw another familiar riding area that hugged the river. It had the typical desert stables that were dusty and dry long before the water shut off. There were around ten carcasses inside the stalls and each had crushed their hooves in the effort to kick out the metal pipes that locked them in. A metropolis of huge black ants had been hard at work to strip them down for the past year, day after day.

They worked in small increments that went straight to the rich guts inside, but were now busy at the dry skin. The thought struck him that he could hear clucking from somewhere nearby. It was so muffled that it could have been a phantom sound welling up through environmental memory. But then he actually could hear it. Some chickens had survived the coyotes and set up somewhere near the stables. He looked for several days, but never found them. They were clever.

Evening distractions were easy. He found more sodas at a new dispensary in New Mexico and used them to help him focus on the tedious work of clearing his new home. The furniture inside was a hodgepodge that annoyed him, so he carted it all out and stuffed it in the neighborhood he planned to destroy. The taps needed time to clear out the grime that got in when there was no steady flow of water. He ran all of them for a full day until the chalky redness disappeared again. He now had a large empty ranch house that felt as if he had just moved in before the electricity service started. He scrubbed everything down, cleared the cabinets and shampooed the carpet that needed to be ripped out later anyway. It was the cleanest living he had for a long time. When it was done, he felt safe, and it was time to dip back into his dwindling sack of mushrooms. He took a long break from them in order to prepare for the journey here and never felt safe enough along the way to test his mind on the road. Now that there was another lull in his roughshod path, he drew the first hot bath he'd had since dismantling his spa and ate three grams that took him to the yard to watch the stars in front of a small bonfire.

On another exploration run with his dirt bike, he came across a nursery that was far up the farm roads. Many of the plants inside were still hanging on because of the large greenhouses where they lived. The front office also had so many seeds that he felt a revival of his farmer blood, except this was checked by the dearth of water. He was a bit confused why the greenhouses were still so moist, but he discovered that the well pumps were already rigged with solar panels and the pipes that led to the hoses leaked into pools that drained under the greenhouse walls. There must have been a timer system for the sprinklers that was no longer working, so he picked up a hose and made the rounds. This was the only place where he didn't evaporate. There had to be something that he could do with the space other than farm, but this wasn't clear. A tour of the grounds did not turn up a house, nor was the neighbor nearby enough to be convenient. He thought about setting up his yurt inside, but thought about how hot and stuffy the humid enclosures were shut this down quite quickly.

He rode all through the area, piecing together bits of memory with new details. After he passed an old church school he noticed an out-of-place gate, behind which were large sized homes, but ones didn't seem worthy of gating, so he pushed it open. It was a bizarre neighborhood that looked like it had its own traffic rules, with stop signs for extremely wide bike paths. All the garages had huge doors that he thought were designed for RVs. Not until he saw the runway and a sign for crossing airplanes did he understand that this was a community that had fully devoted itself to flight. Every house was set up for this. Every neighbor spoke the same language. This was the truest community he'd seen that locked itself behind gates. He was keen. One by one, he opened hangars and saw their hidden storage. Not all had hangars, as he assumed. Nor did all the hangars have planes inside. The purity of the community fell apart somewhat, but he was by now more focused on the equipment he found.

Everything looked complicated. In the last year, he managed to learn so many new systems, but everything operated on the two-dimensional plane of the ground. These machines operated in all three. The consoles inside were a dizzying spread of dials with digital panels added in. There was one biplane that was totally analog. A refurbished antique that he assumed could still fly since he found scads of items inside that fell during use. It was encouraging, at least to give it an effort. Like all else in the afterworld, the keys were in the house. But unlike cars, he had to dig deeper to find them. They were in a locked drawer in the office, within a special box. The plane was lighter than he thought as he edged it out of the hangar. It was bright red and ribbed, with an exposed engine up front behind the propellers. There were decals and other lettering that he didn't understand, but it looked magnificent. Not knowing what else to do once this course of action was set irreversibly in motion when he began to search the house, he climbed inside the cockpit and felt immediately small. He played dog fighter for a few minutes before he settled back to the seriousness of the moment. It took a moment to figure out how to start the engine, but it finally turned over and the propellers roared in front of him. He knew this would happen, but it startled him so much that he shut it off right away lest he accidentally lurch forward into something that would send the blades into his face. He pushed the plane back into its hangar with the keys on the seat and moved on to the next one. Inside was a familiar beast. He'd grown to appreciate the modern RVs that were categorically different from the Winnebagos of before. They were luxury vehicles at scale. The one he found was roughly the same as his, but had been customized by someone with skills, not the stock trim he drove. The inside had been decorated properly a sleekness that impressed him. But it was still a cramped living space for which he now had no need, now that he lived in a house again. He took a last smell of the interior and shut it again.

The other discovery he made there was far more of a relief than what was inside the hangars. Nearly all the homes had their own well pumps, most of which were on solar. He was now rapidly accumulating alternative water sources that meant he would no longer need to depend on storage tanks. There was magic behind the gate here. It whispered for him to stay in the homes, that were far nicer than the ratty ranch house and stables he was preparing. These were more like his

one in Ashburn: spacious and neat. Set up to entertain guests who would never come. But he was no
longer a cheap date. He had a plan that would expand
out from the ranch house into the surrounding land.
He would need those stables if he ever found any livestock alive. The house could be remade, but the land
was essentially untouched.

He could visit the neighbors, though. The gate was a
few minutes from the ranch house, and he began to stop
by every day to learn more about the plane, whether he
could master his confidence enough to master its controls. If he could do this without maiming himself in
the process, then it would open the world to him
again. He could take short hops across the country
that would have taken him a week to drive. He could
return to Washington and come back often. Eventually,
the larger planes might be accessible to him, and he
could finally cross back overseas. The more he examined and tested, the more he wanted to know. Soon, he
was sleeping at the hangar house, so he wouldn't need
to watch the sun. This new plan had to be systematic.
The risks for mistakes were too high, and he seemed to
have a tendency to court danger more often these days.
First was understanding the dials and controls. He
already had a basic knowledge of stall and lift, so a
desk study was his first approach. He read through
the manual inside the cockpit, pausing to imagine what
he would need to do at certain moments. He turned the
propellers on and off. He let the plane lurch and
stop. Everything was in moderation at first. Then
came the first of his tests. He planned to drive the
plane around the community as if it were a car. Like
any new driver, he was too serious and too cautious.
Everything felt like death. He pulled out from the
drive at a crawl and found that the same principles of
driving applied even under these new controls. It was
much like a video game, in some ways. Except that the
engine sputtered and the blades whirred in front of
him. The sound was terrifying. It was not like a
gamepad. The controls connected to real machinery
that required force to maneuver. It was cumbersome,
and he found that he overcorrected too often. There

was too much to consider inside the cockpit. He was too overwhelmed with caution because he knew there would be no rescue if he made a mistake, and that caution created mistakes that fed into ever more caution. It was a death spiral of worry. It was too much. He shut the engine down when he reached back to the drive and struggled to push the plane back into its hangar. He told himself that this was not giving up. He would not unlearn all that he studied. It was a period of rest to assimilate the knowledge so that he could come back and try again. He told himself this over and over again, even if he felt that he wouldn't follow through.

XIV
Wanton Destruction

That feeling of yet another failure burrowed under his skin where he couldn't scratch. The drive back to the ranch house was short, but rife with thoughts that all culminated in renewed frustration at the hot neighborhood. He left one failure and needed redemption by finally solving the daily annoyance. He pulled in among the houses and parked to walk around and plot out exactly what would be needed to level them all. Twenty houses wrapped tightly around the central cul-de-sac, each with only a dozen feet between roofs that were separated below by a low wall of rocks that served as a fence to reflect the sun. The homes themselves would be easy to crush, but the walls would continue on to mark where they stood. A wrecking ball would be the best way to wipe them clear in a few motions, but these were not as common in the construction sites focused on making new layers of sprawl, not removing the old ones to replace them. In fact, he had not seen any in his lazy searches so far. He would need to be more intentional to seek one out. He left the wideness of the valley to drive around the clusters of equipment yards in the tight central streets, where he thought the best chance of spotting demolition vehicles would be. These were still not easy to find. He inspected many equipment yards before he finally found one. The slow moving machine had to be driven over in a flatbed that barely fit inside the cul-de-sac.

His plan was to fell them as dominoes. The genesis house was the one nearest the road to the ranch house, since it was the one that most sparked his anger as he passed. The heavy ball crashed into the master bedroom as if it were made of cake. The next swing seemed to do little damage at all. Again and again, he swiped, but the domino fell so slowly. Down it came into a pile of rubble that filled the basin left by its rock wall. The roof was the touchpoint in the domino line that collapsed down into the next yard and pushed into the kitchen of its neighbor. Instead of aiding with removal of the next house, the weight of the roof added support that prevented him from reaching that section of the house. The ball would strike, but the loose pressure it created absorbed the impact so that very little damage was actually inflicted. Initially, he was focused on the accomplishment of destruction so that he would not feel the pang of failure anymore. But with each crash, he lost this objective and listened to the sound of the impact that split wood and glass. In the slowness of the actual destruction, he changed his attention to the movement of the machinery and the damage it caused in each blow. He measured the success of each one with how satisfying the sound was. The overall objective began to matter less than the simple pleasure of destruction as an act. The second domino did fall. It could do nothing else with the constant erosion from the wrecking ball, even if the first house gave all the support it could to save it. But it took hours, and he now looked at a neighborhood that was only ten percent satisfying. What he needed for the other ninety was destruction that was more efficient and more pronounced. The only place in the city with such efficient destruction was on Fort Bliss, where he could take the implements of war home.

He left El Paso as the war in Iraq was only starting to drain the efforts of the war in Afghanistan, which was still a quiet war. He missed the effect of a military that chased sunk cost with a massive scale up of the base. When he left, it was nothing like it was at the end, though it still had the officer's residences at the front that looked more at home in Georgetown than in El Paso. The rest of the base was unlike these row houses. They were drab tan and hot. It was a small city that had everything a city should, and it surprised him to see shopping malls and fast food, though he quickly understood why. His tour brought him through more neighborhoods of tightly packed homes that were their own layers in this enclave. Moving around, the sections changed fast, and he was soon surrounded by motor pools with huge lines of greasy equipment. Then came a neatly organized field for Blackhawks parked inside grid lines painted on the blacktop. These brought back his failure with the antique plane that he couldn't understand. Rather than explore what certainly were proven to be amazingly effective demolition machines, he kept driving. But not far from these he found his first tanks, wrapped in tan canvas under huge warehouses. Their cannons would rip the houses apart. It would be as symbolic as was possible, a scene for a movie. The suffering first two dominoes would hear the squeak of the treads crushing the road after so much silence. They would watch the tan box stop and pivot a straw towards their friends and cry out in renewed yet resigned weeping as another domino exploded.

He parked and walked into the warehouse. There was a wall of them stretching far into the enclosure. They had been used. Each one had some story of its crew. The inside flooded him with failure as he looked over the complexity of the panels. The obviousness of this took time to settle on his mind. These were the pinnacle of state power and its crew had to undergo months of training and retraining to master the controls. He could not casually walk up and drive one off. Disappointment did not last. He was accustomed to it these days. More exploration was needed to uncover the weaponry he knew was nearby. More driving and more warehouses that turned out to be wrong. Until he saw one cluster of buildings that were behind a fence and monitored from a guardhouse. A guard inside a guarded base meant something. More security meant restrictions to mitigate risks, which implied weapons. The guard waved him through and turned over her keys. The signs outside the doors were unclear because he could not read the military vocabulary. But inside was different. It was dark, and through it, he smelled the wooden crates that had the faint sting of iron and oil. He moved his lamp around as he walked in and let the door close behind. Rows and rows of stacked boxes. A quick test of their weight told him they were heavier than their size suggested. This must be the place.

The first boxes were grenades. He never held one before, but knew that each was capable of considerable destruction if used properly. He knew the basic function, pull the pin and throw, but was afraid of how simple it could be to have a mistake. Still, this was within his technical capacity to learn. Another set of boxes were long black tubes that were very heavy. He took one out and learned that these were shoulder delivered rockets, likely far better than the RPGs he knew from movies. He liked the idea of these, which did not involve him holding a bomb that he had to throw a certain distance in a certain amount of time to escape death. He took a collection of each and a pair of ear muffs out to the large parking lot across the street for some tests. The grenades worried him. Would he fuck up and lose his immunity? To mitigate, he decided to toss it towards a parked car from where he could slide around the corner of a cinder-block building. He could manage this, he thought. He piled all his testing material at the far end from where he planned to stand, pulled the pin and threw. It felt like a long wait before a tremendous pressure spread dust and wind from the corner. Next was the rocket. He looked around for a good target and saw a restaurant down the street that was around the distance the instructions told him a target should be. He aimed for a delivery truck that was parked out front and fired, with a rumble and shake in the tube, then intense heat at his back. The rocket was sent off, and he saw it hit the back of the truck and heard a crash, then the explosion. The grenade hardly seemed worth the risk, since the damage was minimal if it were scaled up to the size of a house. The van was seriously damaged, but it was not destroyed. He could not go room by room tossing grenades around and hope not to get injured in the process. That would test death too much. The rocket on the other hand was safer to use, and it was far more destructive. He saw that it had punctured the van easily, and even passed through the outer wall of the restaurant, which surprised him. It exploded when it hit the interior wall between the kitchen and dining room, caving it in. It was obviously a bunker busting weapon, not suitable for the soft wood and stucco of the residential homes. But still very invigorating to use.

What he needed was a larger explosion. Something for an airstrike like he saw in Mosul, where whole neighborhoods were nothing but broken concrete. This was an unrealistic benchmark since he could not even fly an antique, let alone do a precision bombing run. He had to keep within his capacity. The idea of a detonating a box of grenades made sense. If one grenade was powerful but lacked a punch, then fifty or so all exploding at once might be enough to take down a house. He decided to experiment on the family barracks he passed earlier in the day, which roughly matched the construction grade of the homes in the valley, even though these were constructed with brick exteriors. If the box could damage them, then they would tear open the cheaper material. The box needed a cart to pull it from the warehouse to the truck, but since he couldn't lift it into the bed, he ended up walking the distance with the cart dragging behind. Overheated and sweaty, he brought the box into one of the homes and left it in the center room, trying not to look around at the collection of children's toys or the quiet bird cage.

This was as far as he thought. He had no plan yet for how to detonate the box. It would be stupid for him to simply stand there and drop one on top before he escaped, nor did he think he could toss it inside from the stoop with enough accuracy. Then it occurred to him that the blast from one grenade might not fully detonate the others, let alone all simultaneously. This experiment might just be like lighting a string of firecrackers where the destructive force never combined, it might just be a sequence of individual explosions popping off. But that was the purpose of the test. There would be no point in making assumptions

without data. It did highlight a flaw in his thinking. He should try to detonate more than one at the
same time at least. This meant pulling multiple pins
together, from a safe distance. He checked around the
house and found some strong twine that could be used
for a draw. He duct-taped a ball of grenades together
and tied bits of string to four of the pins and then
ran the length of twine out through the front door.
To make sure the ball didn't shift, he taped it down
tightly to the inside of the box where the rest of the
grenades still sat. He carefully jostled the mashup
and there was barely any give, so he felt it wouldn't
tumble when he yanked the line. He tested the tension
on the pins and adjusted the split end that connected
all four sections to the main line to see that they
would pull smoothly and simultaneously. Everything
looked secure and ready, so he went outside to check
on his position. The twine was only a hundred feet,
but he thought this should be enough given the brick
exterior of the home. This was an estimate and he
knew it. He knew nothing about ballistics except for
the unexploded 120 mm mortar he came across in a field
once, which had washed into town in a flash flood. He
was terrified when the people he was with began tossing rocks to see who could hit it first. He made all
of them clear out after he measured the coordinates to
report it. Nothing more. The estimate also assumed
the explosion would be lateral, and neglected any debris from the blast wave as it passed through the
roof. There was no telling how much or how far this
would carry. Already the heat and planning wore him
out. He decided to just wing it and hope for the
best. He did open a neighbor's door so he could at
least pull the cord near enough to run inside.

He sat there with the cord in hand, gently tested the
tension and released it again, half wanting to destroy
everything and half afraid of the risks. He balanced
between these. Test. Release. False starts and pre-
mature running. Finally, he committed and gave a
solid yank that made the line taught then overly slack
from a loss of anchorage on the far side. He ran
through the door, all the way to the backyard. There

was no crash. He waited longer, nothing. Too long. The box should have erupted so many seconds before. A minute before. After five minutes he walked back through the house and picked up the line to reel it in. No pins. The line snapped, or rather his main knot failed to hold. He started to walk back across the street until he froze. "Don't toss rocks," he told himself as he recalled the mortar incident. Once you cross into the universe of possibly armed fuses, you don't muck about like an idiot. Instead, he went over to the truck where he had a pair of binoculars in his bag. From the neighbor's porch, he tried to look into the opposite living room that was dim in the sunlight of the afternoon. He couldn't see anything. He decided to cross to the backside of the house to try and look through the large glass door from the street on the other side. The rock wall got in his way so he had to climb onto a roof to see the box and the ugly ball that he adhered to it still there. But this was obvious. He had anchored it so that it would only have moved if it exploded, which he knew that it hadn't. What he needed to see was what happened to the pins, which were facing the other house, so he climbed down and walked back over. A bit more annoyed, he let himself approach the door, watching through the lenses as he did. When he was finally close enough to see that all four pins were nestled in their slots, he went back inside. This was too complicated a test. Grenades were too volatile for him to fuck with anymore and it was time to move on. What he needed was a huge explosion that he could exact from safety. His mind returned to the image of the mortar and he wondered if there were any in the warehouse that he could use. He knew these were also dangerous to fire, but he felt he could learn it well enough to make it reasonably safe.

Back at the warehouse, he went through the stacks again. Most were personnel weapons and munitions that would not be helpful to him. He did find boxes of .50 caliber rounds and took them outside to find a gun to load, which he discovered later in another warehouse without their mounts. But none of the six buildings

had what he recognized as mortars. These had to be on
base somewhere, he just needed to keep his search. He
left for the day, but took with him some very appealing belt-fed machine guns that he used on the homes,
to much delight. When he returned to base, he drove
deeper to look for warehouses that might be kept away
from the offices, in case they exploded. At the back,
he crossed through a gap to another section of motor
pools with huge flatbeds and warehouses. They were
curious looking buildings from the outside. He saw
other vehicles there, squat boxy transporters with
caterpillar treads. These looked too small for people
to fit inside, but he couldn't be sure that the military didn't squeeze humans into tight compartments to
make them part of the machinery. When he pulled away
the cover, the inside looked indeed as if humans were
expected to ride there, but there was no roof on the
back, just a circular opening for an item to be installed. This intrigued him, so he went inside the
warehouse to look for what might be added to the vehicle.

This was the artillery warehouse. It was full of
enormous crates and rows of cannons at rest. There
were columns of wheeled cannons that could be towed
behind a car and another cluster of huge cannons on
top of folded platforms. He found crates full of
shells that fit all and, most importantly, he found
the 120 mm mortars for which he was searching. This
warehouse could destroy any city he decided was ex-
pendable. It was all his. First, he needed to figure
out how to use them. The basic mechanisms for all
were relatively simple. Moving each piece was more
complicated, though. The mortars were comparatively
light, but light does not mean light. Each one
weighed him down, even the smaller variety. He had
known people who used to carry these through the jungle as child porters and he now had a new appreciation
for them, gone as they were. He struggled to set up
the firing plate to get the feel of the equipment. As
he did so, his mind matched the setup with the squat
vehicle outside. It must be the transporter for the
120mm mortar so soldiers wouldn't need child porters

anymore. He tried it and it fit. Thankfully the driving panels were of reasonable complexity and he decided to take it out for a test. Take both of them out for tests. The mortar had its ready-made transportation, which he fueled up and loaded with shells, but the cannons were another question. The smaller wheeled one seemed to fit the hitch for some large multipurpose vehicles outside, but the larger one didn't appear very mobile. He assumed they should be placed on the large flatbeds, but didn't see a way to lift them up to accomplish this, or to pull them back down again at the new location. He decided to focus on the smaller cannon and had it hitched up, with a few cases of 105mm shells that were beyond heavy and required a forklift, which terrified him as he maneuvered the crates in place.

Ready to go, he needed a destination and a target so that he could learn how to aim the pieces. Up the valley was where the military did its tests. The missile range replaced the older range that was just outside of town and its munitions still pollute part of the mountain. They only went so far because they needed to escape from the city to keep it safe. He needn't worry about this. His whole mission was to destroy part of the city that he wanted removed. He just needed to find a comparable neighborhood near the base to destroy first before moving back to the other side to finish his dominoes. It would have to be easy to spot from the base and far enough away, at least a mile or two. He drove around the area across the highway, just overlooking the airstrip where he thought would be the best place to set up. The VA hospital was easy to spot, but it felt wrong to destroy it this way so he chose an apartment complex nearby, three and a half miles from the setup. In the same line, he found another housing complex that was only two miles away, where he could aim the mortars. All was falling into place. He drove the squat transport over and walked back to the warehouse to drive over the cannon. Everything to that point was simple. He backed the cannon so that it mostly pointed in the right direction and then dropped it form the hitch.

Soon, both pieces were at rough ready. Now was the challenge of math. He had the coordinates for both targets and this was measured against the coordinates of each piece, so he had all the information he needed, but lacked the skill for making good use of it. The cannon had a system for automated calibration that took him a long time to figure out. The mortar was more manual and he had to guess at the settings based on the direction, distance and elevation. In reality, all the shells could land anywhere and he'd be fine with checking. None of the houses were of special importance to him without the people of the city to give them character. They were just abandoned material, sad as it was.

The cannon was ready. He had mastered the GPS aiming and felt confident that he ticked all the boxes. He loaded the 105 mm shell and closed the chamber. The firing lever was smooth and the concussion was erotic. Again. He fired off seven rounds into the apartments that he could see through his binoculars had been hit squarely. Then he wondered if he could lower the barrel and just site fire at targets closer, which would let him feel the doubly erotic sensation of the concussion followed by an explosion. There was a small shopping district of exclusively local shops just on the other side of the highway where he tested this theory. He watched the buildings crash down. Someone's livelihood. Maybe their passionate dynasty was now just target practice. He glowed with enjoyment and was now eager to experiment with the mortar. He was less confident as he dropped the first shell in and quickly moved away, like he'd seen in movies. The pop of air startled him even as he knew it would come. And then the waiting. He took off his earmuffs in time to hear the whine of the shell as it dropped and exploded on the edge of the target neighborhood. He recalibrated and tried again. Closer. Again. It was enough of a central hit, but he didn't care for the pop. It was alarming rather than erotic. It was caution, not fun.

Now came the time to inspect the damage. Would it be
enough to knock all the dominoes down or was it just
some fun explosions to pass the time? He already knew
about the destroyed business that were in his face
when they were destroyed. There was something left,
but it was nothing recognizable to those who built it.
Like Mosul, all that remained of the shops were hollow
heaps of concrete and inventory that hadn't been
looted yet. It was promising. The homes that he
mortared were less impressive. He was accurate with
his aim, but with so much empty space from the roads
and lawns, there were few homes that had actually collapsed from the explosions. The apartments complex
faced a similar problem. He was accurate, but the destruction was not widespread enough. He was an untal-
ented carpet bomber. Neither of these results were
promising. Direct aiming with the cannon was the extent of his abilities, which had the benefit of far
more satisfaction anyway. He could witness the explosions in real time when the cut into the homes. The
symbolism he desired was both external and inside him;
he fed off the explosions now. Each rupture would
lead to the next, on and on until his cup was full.

It was time to return the squat transporter and move
the cannon across town with several crates of rounds.
Should he need more, should the ruptures fail to cease
their chain of need, he could return at any time.
When they were depleted, he could graduate to more destruction by changing over to the larger ones, which
still lay in storage for whatever whim. There was the
question of where to set up, since the flatness of the
valley differed from the upward slope of the mountain
above the base. It tightened the obstacles that prevented him from making the distance he needed to stay
safe. He could still try to aim from coordinates, but
his lust for destruction meant that this was an impossibility even if he was capable of accuracy. So he
wheeled to the far edge of the ranch house, what he
hoped far enough back with a direct view to half of
the neighborhood from behind. He would start there
and decide where to move next for the others.

The first round glanced off a tree he didn't realize was partly in the way, and it bounced down the road to land unexploded in the opposite field. He recalibrated and tried again. Unlike the concrete shops, the rounds cut through the flimsy homes. He fired and watched the crash of splintered wood and the explosion from deep inside that blew out everything. The destruction was so complete that he immediately saw the second row of homes open up behind the gap. More and again. The houses were no longer dominoes, they were dandelions in the wind. The eighteen that remained were soon gone. He accomplished what his anger needed, but it was soon fueled on with an erotic need. More was needed and more was out there. It didn't matter anymore. He had another crate of rounds. More at the base. More bases. From the rear of the ranch, he saw the distinctive roof of his high school. It was an invitation. He didn't need GPS, it wouldn't matter where the shells fell. He needed the concussion and a target as an object on which to place his frenzy. All that was needed was to reposition and estimate. It was as simple as shooting cans for the thrill of the recoil. He barely paused between shots. Load and pull the level. Then some item left and arrived elsewhere. He tweaked the trajectory in between, so that the destruction would be spread out. So when he drove through later to examine, there would be more stops to make. More time to make a viewing. He emptied the crates in a few minutes. It was over and he wanted more, wished he brought the squat transport to backstop. But he had belt-fed guns. These too sent out items that occasionally streaked red as the sun was setting red behind him. Until they too were empty and there was nothing but the smell of spent powder and hot metal.

In the quiet, he still wanted more. But the more he wanted was a real object. Something he could study and destroy with care. He had erected a new mania that needed to feel accomplished before it could wither out. Aiming at his school fed something older than the evaporation and his trauma. It came from an old agitation that loved to destroy for the sake of destruction. Since he left El Paso, he learned to overlay systems to channel that destruction into something useful, but still preserved the love of destruction itself. These channels had many destinations, but those were all gone. There was no more illiberal corruption to dismantle; no more reconciliation to close chapters of war; no more artificial people to combat. Everything he hated accidentally evaporated with everything he loved. These homes and his school were poor replacements to keep the systems alive, and he fell back to old demons.

He went back inside the ranch house with ringing ears to consider the emptiness that was now forming again. It kept him awake. He had no visions for how to hold onto this last of his civilized feelings. Not even a walk through the neighborhood in the morning or his drive along the streets up on the mountain that were now pockmarked carried anything to fill the growing void; what had been growing for more than a year and which he had desperately worked to fill. One of his shells did manage to hit his school. Just a minor strike on the roof that he could see from inside the courtyard. It was a feckless effort. Crossing back to the ranch house, the next object was revealed. He fumed at the sandy riverbed that had a specific structure as the cause. The river was choked and the valley was dying. Destroying the dam would be an act of systemic improvement to repair the valley. It was built to feed civilization, which would never have grown to the size it had with so much flooding, but its destruction would be the last thread of civilized meaning anywhere on the planet.

Under normal conditions, the drive up to the dam was around two hours, but the highway was sand now. Not all of it, but so much that it would be better to plan for a solid journey through the desert rather than expect actual roads. It would be a tough journey to take everything he needed. The 105 mm cannon alone should be enough, if he pommeled the concrete face with shells over and over. He thought about the 155mm cannon, but he was forced to circle back to the challenge of loading it onto a truck, let alone all the other issues with over such large shells or aiming the monster. He also wanted to use the bunker munitions just in case the breach needed some extra help. He filled the multipurpose vehicle with fuel, weapons and ballistics. The rig was an invitation to death should anything happen along the way. All of his cargo was capable of destroying the vehicle and he packed it all in as tightly as he could. Now he would be driving it on damaged roads only to hope that nothing went wrong. And nothing did because he was prepared for the trip and the vehicle was prepared for the march through the desert. He crawled again, but this time pushed through and made it in a day, with enough time to still explore.

He would need to be close under the concrete face. Probably well within the danger zone of water pouring out after the breach began. He wished that he could have had more time to master the distance aiming before his obsession forced him there, but this was a question already in the past. Now, he stood on the road overlooking the dam to scout for the safest and most effective place to set the cannon, without the need for an awkward low angle firing from higher up where it would be safe. He needed balance. Somewhere between the floor of the canyon and the height of the alcoves above the road. There was no such place, so he moved in on the road very close to the dam that would still allow him to make quick escape to the far side as the water exploded out. Based on what he already knew of the artillery, he would need many rounds to break through the deep concrete. The base was thickest, but if he could weaken it enough then the whole structure would collapse. He could help it along by weakening it from above as well, in the expectation that everything would topple over like an embankment around a sand castle. He would weaken it all over, then focus on the base.

It only made sense to see if he could open the valves to release as much water as possible beforehand, so that the moving force of the flow beneath would help

rip the dam apart from the inside. The dam was small.
There was only one modest outflow next to the power
plant. It took time to find the mechanism to lift the
gate and more time to struggle with turning the tight
wheels so that the water began to pour out. He
thought about how this was the gate which marked the
highest volume of river he'd ever known. There was
another catchment further down, with a broader flood
outflow, but this was the feeder. A small gate at the
base of a cement wall was his river.

It was late, and he hadn't set up yet. The destruction might only take a short while, but the resurrection of the river would be something that needed hours
of daylight to fully appreciate. He had no interest
in wasting the violence under nightfall. Instead, he
set up his stations and waited for morning. When it
came, it was a sharp expansion from the mountains to
the East. He didn't sleep much. The sounds of coyotes and owls were too distracting. The glowing concrete where he tried to camp was too warm. So when
the sun finally peaked over the already bright valley,
he was well on his way back to the first cache of
bunker munitions. He had set up two stations for the
rockets. The first was directly at the base, with the
dam looming above him like a canvas. From there he
would scatter the rockets around. The other station
was high up on the canyon overlooking the scene. After the cannon effected breach, he would scramble up
the canyon wall to this station and apply some touch
ups. It was time. He stood there, recklessly close
with dangerous equipment to do a stupid act. He fired
the first rocket, and it collided at the median line
off to the left. There was a large pock that so far
didn't leak. He thought about the next one. Where to
paint on this canvas? Just to the side, a bit lower.
Then another in the same way until he had a line that
curved down like a bowl that crested at the center of
the base. There was no place left except to finish
the bowl to the other side. His canvas smiled at him
and he smiled back. It spoke to him agreeably after
he gave it eyes, but then a tear began to form on one
of them and drained down its face. Smiling and cry-

ing. The dam knew it was time to give back the river.
The two stared at one another and he felt pity.

The reasons for all his effort suddenly came into
doubt, and he wondered why he would need to destroy
the dam at all. Already the river was filling back up
from the open gate and he was sure that the river he
know as a child would return. There were no inter-
state water wars to bicker about when to open this
gate. He'd permanently ended the dispute. Now,
couldn't he calm his need to destroy with civility?
The dam was useful and he had alternatives. This
power station could provide nonstop electricity. He
wouldn't need to figure out a grid, he could just master a direct line back to his ranch house, or he could
move to a new ranch in this space of desert, with an
eternal supply of fish and water. Yet, why even
bother to stay in the valley at all? He owned the
planet. Every corner of productive land was his, so
why should he fight out his years of survival here in
the desert where so much comfort would be foregone?
He even had a home in Washington that was not an impossible distance away. He crawled here only because
he packed so much unnecessary garbage. Why had he
done that? He could make a return so much faster now
that he knew the dangers along the way. He needn't
plan for winter in a cave, he could roam at the edge
of weather, fleeing the extremes. The dam was hopeful. It could compromise and give back part of the
river and still live on. The butte behind it could
continue to give life to everything in the ecosystem
that sprung up in the decades since the desert valley
was flooded for the last time. But this was a fantasy
whose facade was already peeling away. The ecosystem
was dying. The lines that ringed the valley above the
shoreline were clear. The butte was evaporating. Ev-
eryday, a million gallons disappeared. The dam kept a
privileged ecosystem alive under the surface without a
spread to the surface, which remained dry desert.
There were no lush forests or grasslands to feed thousands of ecosystems downriver until the water joined
its family again. The butte was a waste if it wasn't
giving life to civilization. It was just trapped wa-

ter that choked the valley for no purpose. And he alone was able to cut out the obstruction. Alone in that he could do it in time to give hope to the life living below. The mountain would remove the dam in its own time, after countless generations of fish evolved in the receding waters and might be ready to explore the valley themselves. The dam was asking for him to choose natural destruction, not human destruction.

He stood there unable to make a choice. The damage was already done, the water was already in the process of eroding through and would only build. The weeping eye would soon become a fracture and the dam was destined to crumble under human destruction as it was built from human civility. All this nonsense streamed in his mind until he recalled the stories of a hospital for tuberculosis patients that was in the valley when it flooded. It should still be there. It could still be explored with the right equipment. But he hadn't the patience to learn how to fill the air tanks and explore, so he dragged the cache back into the vehicle and drove it above the canyon to be joined with second. The dam still smiled because it knew he'd made his choice and it was time.

The next stage was the most dangerous. He would be firing directly at the base over and over until the dam crumbled. He knew that he would panic when he saw the first sign of gushing water, but also that this might not be the final stroke. He prepared himself to delay as much as he could stand, firing at another point to create another gush. There would be some moment when he would need to escape. Some last chance at survival would need to be recognized so that he could run up the hill to climb into his lightened vehicle and drive to the other side of the dam where he'd be safe from the violent water. Recognizing this was his sole focus as he began firing rounds that crashed into the face. The first was a return to that erotic feeling, and he basked in the afterglow. This need not be some orgy of destruction, this was precision that he should relish. The second was more. After each one, he adjusted his aim a bit. The site where he chose was not stable and the cannon bounced slightly more than it should. The shells soon formed a cluster of pocks that grew deeper until he saw cracks that connected the dots along the base of the smile up to one side, making it look as if the dam was now smirking. A few more and the cracks began to split the face, webbing out along to reach the eyes then above to reach the walkway that crossed overhead. He pulled the cannon back from where it had bounced towards the edge of the road, where it could have dropped off into the canyon a few dozen feet below. Its metal was hot from the sun and so many rounds that passed through its rifling. It burned when he brushed it to cross over and try to pull from a different angle. Just a few more items and the face should disappear. He now aimed for the deepest cracks, then back to the now huge pock next to the gate. There were leaks everywhere. The dam was pummeled and bled from its mouth and nose. The river was rising up as the water passed through the gate found its way into adjoining cracks. Time was now marked by water. He soon ran after each of the rounds he fired. He'd ready himself to sprint after each time the lever was pulled. So many darts that slowed then reversed. He was so winded by the hill and elevation. His legs were beginning to burn from the sun exertion. But the destruction couldn't stop. Water time needed to continue. Then time came. The dam bulged until it spurted. He managed one last round and ran as fast as he could, nearly dead by the time he reached the wheel as he struggled to make his legs understand the urgency.

When he reached the top of the dam, he saw that the water had already filled the valley and was building up to just below where the cannon sat. It reached its wheels a few seconds later and enveloped it thereafter. Another minute and the barrel sent a column of steam as it cooled under the surface and disappeared. All his planning had focused on the downriver face of the dam that he never thought about the water rising in the butte as the fast flow pulled the lake towards him. Out of the suddenness of danger, he was able to drive further and park away from the shore and amble over to the top of the canyon where he could get a better view of the scene. The face was still there. He saw that the pock had collapsed with the gate and took half of the smile and nose, but left everything else. It was a tremendous breach that would almost empty the butte, but the dam was not yet gone. It needed more coaxing to pull it from its anchors. There was time for this, though. This was precision that could take breaks. He sat and watched the dark spot where the cannon was still wading. The water rose up to his station, but it was not the torrent he imagined. Had he stayed, he would certainly have been terrified and wet, but it seemed that he would have been able to swim. Rivers were always misleading in this way. A powerful suction might be lurking just below that would have dragged him through the valley dropping pieces along the way.

With his break over, he was ready to return to destruction. There were still so many rockets to fire at so many targets. He began. Each one landed with less impact than before now that he was much further away from the canvas. But they continued to inflict damage. They chipped the face and the water did the rest. By the last one, there was nothing left except for the bowl shape of the jawline and pieces of the dam's forehead.

It was noon and already extremely hot. The morning had been a six-hour journey of explosions and risk. Now it was over. In those few hours, he forever changed the valley all the way to the ocean. It would take time for that. He surveyed the change from his perch and could see that the road back to the town was now cut by the river that swelled to fill the tight twists of the canyon below where the dam once stood. He would not be able to return to El Paso from that way. He expected this, but hadn't made a plan to compensate. The town itself was disappearing too. The lower part that was the ancient accretion zone had been reclaimed as the water moved up and deeper into

the town center. He could see that all the homes and
shops that were along the banks were underwater, with
only roofs to mark their place. And the water was
rising. And with more force. The initial breach had
let the valley fill with water, but the total destruction had meant everything was caught in the fast flow.
Even at his high perch, the water threatened to touch
him. It was now only ten or so feet below him. Its
force ripped cars and trailer homes out from where
they parked. These drifted out as the canyon opened,
slowing the intensity of the water as it diffused.
The landscape would be saturate with debris from the
town that would be reclaimed by the desert. The river
would discard them and return to its narrow channel
over the coming days. For now, the butte had simply
been sucked out of the dam and was moving as if unwilling to give up its shape. The town was not totally lost. Like all desert towns, it was cut around
mountains so that half the town was unaware that the
other half had been wiped away. Under civil rule,
there would have been alarms and evacuations followed
by a mobilization of disaster teams to come in. The
town would not suffer alone. Now, the town was not
even aware of its own crisis. This was just another
empty day where nothing happened.

He tried to think about how he might get back across.
He could wait out the crisis on this side, where there
might be a chance to simply swim and take a truck,
just as normal. The butte was noticeably lower than
when he started in the morning, but there was still so
much water left to drain that he had no expectation
that waiting would be viable. It might take a week
before the force of water let the canyon begin to dry
out. It might take longer before the flow was safe
enough to cross. Everything down river from the dam
would be this way. He could not simply walk through
the desert in search of a crossing that might not be
there. He climbed down to get close to the dam again.
The fractured swirls in the canyon changed to the
smooth surface of water funneled into free fall. Just
inside the butte, he saw that the level had risen so
much that it nearly topped the dam, when before he be-

gan it was about twenty feet below. The butte surface
had been tilted. His mind pictured the mound of water
that builds up around a drain. This was a surprise
that he felt was so basic that it was a marvel to see.
Water behaved like water no matter the scale. When he
looked at the damp exposed beach on the outcropping
that faced this drain, he was no longer sure that the
butte level as a whole had gone down or if the pressure had just pulled from here to build the mound. It
could be weeks before the water would let him back to
the highway. The only way, then was to keep going
North. The backside of the butte would be less violent, less extreme. Further than that, there would
only be river that was yet unaware that it was free.
He could cross any number of bridges South of Albuquerque. He could even stay there for a visit while
the butte emptied into the valley. But he needed to
see the water as it filled the sand again. Reaching
the highway on the other side was now an urgent destination. Every hour he wasted meant he might miss
more. He got back to his vehicle, now no longer a box
of explosives. It was designed for the roadless sand,
but it was slow. He would need to drive across the
desert for hours to reach the top of the butte, then
drive hours back down the highway to catch up to the
water. He would certainly miss the continuation of
the show if he didn't find a way to speed up he
course. The only alternative would be to cross the
butte and find a truck from there. He could see several boats float adrift where they were left unanchored, so their drivers could enjoy the last of the
sunlight before they returned to the dock. He saw
some houseboats still looking for a place to camp.
But all of these were headed towards the dam. They
were being sucked up and would eventually crash
through the canyon to join the field of debris beyond
the town. Swimming out to them would be dangerous,
and there may not be gas in their tanks to fight back
against the current assuming he could reach them.
There was no choice now except keep driving his slow
monster through the sand and hope he spots another way
to cross the water further along. Except that the
terrain worsened. It had changed to deep arroyos that

went on for a long time, meaning he could no longer
drive around them. He was burning fuel fast. The
last of the extra canisters he brought was already inside the tank. His planning fell short on this point.
He failed to bring more diesel in favor of stuffing
more ballistics inside, and now he had to face this
fact as he linked up with a paved road that led away
from the shoreline, but still headed North. It
brought him up a mesa to a remote neighborhood for
houses that wanted to overlook the water but needed to
run away from the towns. There were empty side
streets that led to the mesa edge in anticipation of
some housing boom that would never take place. He
drove on and looked for driveable dirt paths back down
to the water, but found nothing. He pushed in all the
way to the end of the plateau, with the last house far
behind him. There was edge on three sides of him now.
The water was only a mile away, once down at the base
of the mesas, but there was no way to get there with
the vehicle. He already resolved to walk down and
swim across if he had to, but paused first to see what
he would find when he reached the shore. He still saw
a few boats in the water but these were now far enough
upriver they were not being sucked into the canyon.
He was a strong swimmer and could reach them. Maybe
they had enough gas to make it across, or at least
some emergency raft that he could use to paddle the
rest of the way. He scouted the valley he'd have to
cross. It was very hot now so he wouldn't need to
worry about snakes except in the rocks just below him.
Not far away he could see another dry river, which
would be the easiest path to walk to the butte. Then
he spotted something that thrilled him. Along the
beach at the mouth of the river were a cluster of
house boats that had become trapped in the large
jagged inlet. He would not need to swim, he could
find a raft in one of these.

He carefully climbed off the plateau and landed on the
face of the mesa. He went down at an angle, letting
his feet slide to quicken the descent. Then he was in
the valley. Desert crossing is fairly quick. You
walk blind from the glare of the sun hitting your

face, but the rocky ground lets you take broad steps. A bit more than a mile of this and he was in the dry river and able to move fast to the shore where the first boat had landed. The motor started, but he couldn't unbeach it to get it back in the water. Nor was there a raft, only tubes. The second and third were also beached. They pulled in and the wind had built up the soil around them. On the second one, though, he found an inflatable boat and paddle that looked flimsy for open water. He was in a hurry so he spent a half hour blowing air in. Flimsy as it was, he only needed it for a short crossing. He fought the wind-swept surface in a trance until he reached the other side where he saw a town from up on the plateau. His flimsy boat ripped apart on the rocks as he tried to get closer to the shore, dumping him into the water still trapped in the looseness of its plastic. Wet, but on time, he found a truck but not a road to the highway. He drove around dead ends and dirt roads. The highway was somewhere to the West, but it was hidden away among the rocks. He eventually made it to the main town and was able to start seeing road signs to point him the right way. Everything was back on track and the sun was still many long hours from setting.

He pulled back onto the main highway headed South to El Paso driving very fast, which would take him past the flooded town, but not the dam. He would be able to see how much destruction had taken place since he left the site a few hours before. The butte was now clearly draining. He was far enough away from the mound that it wouldn't explain the line of wet beach that he saw when he swam out after clearing himself from the plastic boat. He could see it more now as he drove closer to the mound, until the butte curved away from the highway. The town had not changed. It was still flooded along the river bank but untouched here where the highway crossed. There was no need to stop and look again. Now was the time to hurry and catch the water that had such a long head start back to El Paso. The further away from the town he got, the more normal the river began to look. There were wide flats that absorbed the initial flooding, but the small river canyons eventually took control again to keep the water fast and narrow. Further down, the catchment lake filled up. It was the last pool before the river would be free. He reached the gravel dam at the head and saw that the water was beginning to flow through the overflow channel. He wondered if this was enough. It was far larger than the gate that he opened at the dam. It let far more of the river come out. He examined the gravel and understood how easy it would be to remove, since he'd proven himself with the much stronger dam. But, he'd had hours of destruction and fight that day. There was nothing left and he decided he'd had enough. The river would take it in its own time.

XV
Abyss

Water took its time to build in the catchment before
it was truly ready to flow again. The dry concrete of
the outflow channels waited as much as he did for the
river to finally break free from the slight trickle
that it had been. Together they watched the water
level inside the lake rise up to make a new mound that
shoved through the channel. They watched the mound
grow until it bled over the gravel wall, making new
river channels down the slope. Everything converged
back into the surprised riverbed below. He left the
outflow channel to its work and drove to catch up to
the head of the mound that was racing through its old
sandy lane, then he stayed with it. As it rolled, it
met more surprised sand and then sank in to wrap itself around the rooms below. He left the smooth asphalt of the highway behind so that he could drive
alongside the mound. He would hug the banks closely
but sometimes curved away and lost sight of the water.
Everything now was governed by its movement. When it
was out of sight, he sped up, looking for the next
open break to view it. He was a father unable to join
his child as it learned some new chapter of its inde-
pendence.

He looked ahead at the sand and tried to predict how
the water would respond to the contours when it
touched them fresh. It was all the dance of gravity
and inertia over time. He could drive backwards to
see the past again, but only to see it in the largest
of obstacles like boulders and trees that had grown in
the sand. He went to see how the water looked after
the mound pulled its blanket over the sand, where the
river was yet a strong juvenile. He drove all the way
back to the outflow channel to see the fingers that
had been cut into the gravel slope of the small dam

flow down to the now deep pool that was dug from the crashing water at the base of the outflow. The pool swirled and foamed as it received the river. Brown funnels of fast water pushed through and folded many times before slowing down to reach the lower pool, which was a full waiting room where the river collected before it took the exit cut by gravity. Here he could be more than a spectator. He walked over the white powder on the ground made from leached gypsum. It crunched under his foot as he walked to the water edge and felt that it was hot from the baking sand. He walked into it up to the waist and felt it shift around him for the exit.

It was time to see the mound again. That was the edge of time, where the valley reclaimed the hope of survival. It had to start with the smallness of surprise before it could build. He jumped into the truck still soaked, with boots that made ridiculous squishing noises that he tossed into the back to evaporate in the sun. He drove. It was a long time before he reached the mound again. It seemed to have picked up speed, and he was surprised by how far it had come while he blinked. By then, it was already near Las Cruces. He did his best to follow alongside it all the way, but orchards and ranches pushed the road away from the banks. He kept his paternal dance of driving fast ahead to find a spot to watch the mound as it waved past him, only to repeat. He raced as much as it raced. They fought the sand together. He stayed a while to watch the blanket build and begin flowing into the laterals that were meant to pull water from the river and feed the irrigation canals. Not all of them were open. Many still blocked the exits and the blanket moved on, not needing to seek out a way through; it would let the mature river seep under instead. By now the sun was nearing the end of its own race, unable to watch much further. But there was still more time. The mound was ready to reach his own orchards and the light hung on to let him see its arrival before it would duck behind the mesas.

The main lateral above the orchard that he first explored on the dirt bike was open and receiving the blanket slowly. He was already there watching the thin line of the first tiny breach feed a forming pool that was no larger than his hand. More came. There were swirls and foam just like the crashing pool below the outflow. It was the same. Water never changed except that surface tension made it bulge, with powdery dust stuck to the outside as it rolled up sides then receded because inertia was not enough yet to climb. There was no need to keep chasing the bulge, they'd reached a destination together. By now the system of gates was becoming more clear to him. This lateral was open, but there was no guarantee that all the gates along the canal were as well, so he drove over to the orchard and pulled up to the gate that fed it. This gate opened with a struggle, and he began the walk that would trace the canal back to the river, so the water could exit and reach the forest of pecans that so desperately wanted to see it. Along the way, he continued the struggle with gates whose metal wheels had been locked or had been cooked shut. There were only a few that had been closed. Many were already open until he reached the outermost that was directly off the main lateral. He opened this last one and watched the water that had pooled up and was busy flowing out along the lateral excited to make the trip to roots beneath the pecan trees.

The sun had done its best to stay with him for the whole journey. From destruction to resurrection and now to salvation. It could do no more. It had left behind a red glow that let him see the water flowing into the canal, too fast for him to watch any mound at the front. The father no longer kept pace and could only cheer on from behind as his voice faded. He kept the light lamp that he found in the truck on the water surface that was a bumpy neon brown glowing against the indigo evening. All the way back to where he was. The canal soon pulled the water through more exits, then more, until he was back at a trickling mound on its way toward the last gate. Then it split. One mound moved into the indigo and the other glowed through the gate into a flat field of breathless trees. There, opportunity and gravity overwhelmed the mound and it sank. But it was now just changing direction and headed towards invisible roots, then eventually all the way through to underground caverns. Water never rested.

The flow kept moving in and blanketed the surface of the orchard around the gate. It came in rippling sheets that spread out across to saturate the ground. The roots were desperate and were at risk of overindulgence. He knew from childhood that they could handle a complete flood that would stay for days, but they were not water plants. The flood was only needed to be locked within the thick clay soil, but not to permanently surround the roots. He would have to shut the gate. The fight was won, but the reward was transient. The cycle of water that the orchard needed had only just begun and he wondered for how long he could maintain it. Along the course of the river since the catchment lake, he passed hundreds of orchards that were all the same as his. He could not open and shut gates to all of them. Most would be drinking too deeply soon, while others would demand answers as to why they were overlooked. All of them would be dead soon. They were not native to the valley. They would need to adapt to the new conditions in their personal journey of survival. He brought them their best hope, but he knew that hope itself was toxic and needed to be mastered before it killed.

With the fight of the day over he felt the wave of fatigue wash over and leave him deflated with a need to rest but still too insecure lest not enough was done. He felt that he should have felt uplifted and accomplished. Water time was moving in the valley again, why did he only feel anxious and burdened? Not knowing what else to do, he walked back along the canal, struggling with gates as he went. Free water and saved orchards. Or stolen water sent further along to give poison hope to trees that were already near death. He couldn't stop. More was out there. Each new strain thought only brought the next one. When the wheels broke free, and he heard the water moving again, he was momentarily excited before the fatigue came back to pull again. It followed everywhere along the canal. He was soon so far from the orchard, from the truck, that it made more sense to simply walk back to the ranch house along the river. He stopped opening gates as he made his way down to the bank. Once there, he was met with the face of the river he knew. There was no more desperate sand, just fast water. He knew that this would never stop. The river flowed down into the sand and was already under his feet even though he walked on the dry surface. It will spread roots all the way to the ocean. Even then, it would find new paths. Water never rested even when it seemed like it was home. Everywhere on the planet, water wore its crown and raced to find new opportunities where it could flow. It changed shape. It even evaporated. But it never left. Everything on the surface was its kingdom to explore.

The sight of the full river was a bit of a surprise. He hadn't expected this to happen so fast. He watched this water earlier in the day when it crashed through the dam. He swam in it when he paddled across the butte and again when he waded into the pool. It was a finite collection of molecules so numerous and so identical that it could only be understood as a composite the world over. He sat down on a clear patch of the bank and dropped his feet back into it, feeling water everywhere. When he was young, the canals behind him were full of crayfish that he caught with bacon tied between metal washers. How long before they come back? The toads, he knew, were hibernating and would come out soon to see what he had done, but he wasn't sure if the crayfish would ever come back. Even full of water, the canals would never again be what he knew. He sat there with his feet stinging in the black water, no longer worried that something lived beneath the surface that might bite him. Surely there was something next, but he struggled to find it. All he felt was the exhaustion of the day. The sunburn and dehydration surrounded by water. It made him vague. It was time to continue to a destination just further in the darkness. He couldn't estimate exactly where the ranch house was, but he would know it from the smell of burned horses and splintered pine. Something was waiting for him there. Something more that hadn't been discovered. It was always there to be examined, it changed form each time he thought he caught it and could rest. Whether it changed to escape or he changed it to avoid the need to stop, it was impossible to know, even if there was no distinction whatsoever. The endless repetition of days and plans driven by the mania of survival was weakening him bit by bit. Every new day began the same. Restless dreams faded into the grim stillness of wherever he slept, followed by a thrown together plan for how the day might unfold. Forever sleep was never an option. He never took the road of clearing out the pharmacies to numb reality or mute the anxiety. He lived it, even if he let it become distorted to show him new paths. But nothing changed. There was no reward except to have the chance to replay the struggle that was only there to be passed on for the next ones to survive and struggle. He knew the ending for the game that he now played alone. He played for team mania that didn't care if it had no opponent, no fans. It played because it couldn't stop. It now dragged him across the field, chasing after phantoms and echoes without giving him any moment to rest without first prodding him to continue. But even mania was fatigued and demanded a rest just when he was himself ready to continue. Water was not time. He told himself this to feed his mania of the moment. Water was just another material byproduct of time. Water was just a natural event that became a human tool of measurement. It never rests because humans never rested. It evaporates and humans evaporated. He is in the middle, walking in the night where time has no meaning and water is free from its evaporation in the butte. Or at least it can now evaporate along the course that gravity and opportunity set before it. He did nothing to change the properties of the condition at all. Would it not instead seem like evaporation was itself the destination? In the middle, he couldn't achieve this. At times, he thought he survived and this was a reward.

But at other times he felt like he was overlooked and
might never receive the reward of finding his destination. He would just continue to relive the same day.
Survival is a prison that holds all living things in
the cage of hope that there is another option just
around the corner, and it leaves only confusion when
all options are gone. Leaves everything to ask why
that last moment is so different from all the others
when a chance to fix a mistake was still possible. It
always drives the need to see what comes next, what
new opportunity to flourish is waiting if only the
next moment could be lived. Trees drink water then
drown.

It was very late when he reached the smell of burned
horse and splintered pine. He managed to arrive at
the ranch house twenty minutes later. His feet were
severely blistered so that removing his boots was slow
agony that left him unable to breathe. He looked at
his shriveled gray skin that throbbed in the open air
and wondered whether he should pour the alcohol on
them immediately or wait until the morning. Knives
blinded him with pain as the alcohol met the fresh
wounds, and he went to sleep with his socks on to protect the bandages from his kicking legs. He was back
in the purgatory of insomnia, thinking about the river
mound as it pushed down the length of Texas to the
Gulf. Thinking about the Gulf flowing into the ocean
and the whole process of weather driven by evaporation
and heat. The planet still moved. He was ready to
rest. There was no need to reach the planet anymore.
The fullness of the day happened in an isolated corner
that was enormous for him. He could stay here and it
would be the same as anywhere. The Americas would be
enough to contain hundreds of lifetimes. He could
waste his days floating with no destinations anymore,
just the bare minimum to survive with gifts that civilization left to him. He needn't bother with those
that were off limits. There was just so much that was
there for him. If he were someone else, someone with
roots, he might have already died. But he had always
been a transient human, resilient in his movements.
Whatever was off limits was unnecessary to his sur-

vival. He needn't bother with what he could not
change. His unchanged purgatory continued until he
saw the sun come back to check in on him, then he
slept.

The depression lingered for several days. He slept
inside, then outside to listen to the sound of toads
taking roll. He ate mushrooms and watched the sky until the depression washed away leaving healed feet
that were curious to travel again. He was unsure
where to go and packed the RV lightly as he headed
back towards Washington. It had been two months in El
Paso since he peeled back the onion layers of sprawl.
He now folded them back on as he past headed East to
the other side of the desert. There was no guarantee
in his mind that he was leaving yet. He drove the RV
again because he wanted the freedom to choose, then to
unchoose. It wouldn't matter. As he moved into the
zone of the red sand, he felt like the air was
crisper. The river was now flowing off to his right,
but it was too far away to see. But knowing that it
was full made the desert seem more alive and timeless.
This was projection. The river had made no impact on
the desert this far away.

Something changed. He unchose to make the long drive
back. It felt like a continuation of the draining mania that never let him rest, not another phase in his
roaming survival. He made a U-turn at the immigration
station, with the passports and line of cars still
frozen in time. As he crossed the desert he saw a
junction that was the outermost layer of the onion and
decided to head through it North, into the dry valley.
The loop was new; a beltway around the sprawling city,
crossing what used to be a sea of sand, now the edge
of the city. He came back around to the back of the
base but wanted nothing there either so he made another turn to head the opposite way. The highway was
familiar but still new. It took time to realize he
was driving towards a pile of rocks in the distance,
with a gray cloud following overhead, brushing the
sand behind him with its hair.

The rain caught up to him as he drove into the rocks that were sacred for their small bowls that collected rain. When the drops fall in the desert, they are heavy and large, but so spread out that they evaporate immediately after impact. They were just beginning to paint the rocks blood-red when he arrived. The dark circles popped, then faded from the hot surface. The steam they made left an iron smell of desert rain that joined the creosote. The hair was coming, but distance was impossible to estimate in the open valley. Not until something faded inside it could you know exactly how far away the storm was. For that moment, all he know was that it was raining now and more was out there. He had time to climb the rocks so that his fingers could feel the smooth bowls. He saw the huge wall where he knew someone who fell and died when they scrambled up it without a rope. There were still chalk deposits from the generations of other climbers who marked their courses so clearly. Eventually more arrived and the creosote began to disappear. He made his way back to the RV in time for the hair to brush it with a loud fury. He climbed back inside and watched from his windows. When it passed, it was time to expand the awning and set up outside, since this was his destination for the day. The lightning came next, chasing the static made by the hair. Bright flashes continued all afternoon and into the early sunset. From his hammock, the sound of coyotes were not far. He heard them every night as they moved into the river valley from where they were pushed by sprawl. But here, there was no sprawl and they knew nothing about the evaporation except that it happened after rain filled the bowls. So they came.

It was a good setting. The rain had cooled the desert and left a mild wind. It was the right time for mushrooms, but he held the stash without eating. He was bored and tired. The idea of distortions to prevent sleep chilled his hand until it was time to simply go sleep in his bed. The next morning was moist and he felt less bored, so it felt more right to bend spacetime. It was a two gram distortion with breakfast. As it rose, he fell back into his hammock and never

left for the entirety of the visions. His body was
worn out from the months of mania. Not even the heat
of the sun shook him from his cradle. The sun moved
in spurts of colored heat overhead as he laid with
neither eyes open nor closed able to change the shin-
ing waves until the afternoon, when the sun began to
fall from its peak. It was thirst that pulled him up
while the colors slowed to a simmer. His bottle from
the morning was already empty and he needed to walk
over to refill it, forgetting why he did so after he
replaced the cap. The rocks glowed in the bright neon
brown that hurt his eyes to look at. The sand was
more stable now so he walked over to the alley nearest
him that gave way to a maze of boulders all around
him, each with a distinct character. The bowls were
now partly full of murky water, but clean enough to
wash his face. The salt that had accumulated for days
was now trapped in his beard and dripped into his
mouth. It was much too bright. The colors burned too
severely. He wondered if the small caves hosted
friends, so he tossed in handfuls of stones to announce his approach. Nobody home. He escaped winter
in a cave and now escaped the hot sun in a cave. It
was all the same. Humans were always fragile and
needed shelter. He knew this from the wall of intolerably ancient psychedelic faces that he saw covering
the cave. Orange insect eyes watched him as they told
him about the rain and sun that never changed in the
desert. He sat there to listen as a thousand year old
voice told timeless stories with colors cracking the
rocks. He sat there smelling the hair move somewhere
nearby; near enough to darken the sky without painting
the rocks outside.

And next to these were the later images, letters
strung together to sound out names and dates of animals who sat where he was to shelter from the sun and
hear the same stories. They carved their work into
the rock, merging their names in a way not chosen by
the original artists. It was no longer a defacement
now that there was no risk of overuse for the canvas.
No new humans would come so everything was now equal
records of a life looking for a home. Deeper along

the wall, he saw more names, less ancient. Among these he saw another familiar name carved into the rock more than a century before. It was so plain, so weird, that he wondered if the glow still bent his mind to suggest more truths that were not there. But the letters were not swirling anymore. He could see them clearly. The first name was flat and without emotion, but the surname was his. His grandfather had sat here too and took the time to etch his name among the other. It was stupid graffiti. An advertisement for his business. A calling card left for anyone who might come and think to themselves that they needed to buy some residential property in El Paso before the depression. How odd it seemed to place it here. But it was graffiti with its own self-contained meaning. It was graffiti of survival. As worthless as the space could be to build a client base, it was a young man's desperate destruction of himself to build a brand that might feed his family. It was as pitiful as the psychedelic monsters that explained the violence of thunder. All of them, himself included, were delicate animals crouching in rocks whose sole power was the recognition of time.

He thought about etching an addendum to the advertisement, but saw no point. He lost track of days long ago and only had a vague notion of the months. He couldn't mark when he stopped by, nor would there be another animal to sit in the cave and contemplate their meaning. It was time to head back to the RV before the sun dipped more and the snakes would be roused from their nests. His march back around the rocks followed the formerly maintained trail which followed the traditional paths through the maze. He was alone in the company of echoes. They followed him back to his RV, whispering about the flashes of electricity outside his window. They told him nothing about where to go next.

The air was fresh, and he slept with his window open to let the creosote smell come in. The days were still hot, but he learned how cold the nights were becoming. So far from the mountain, the sand had no nighttime insulation. He shivered in his bed until he climbed into a sleeping bag. Another winter was on its way. the first anniversary of solitude had long gone and he was approaching the anniversary of his deconstruction in the garage. Then would be the anniversary of the end of nations, then the second anniversary. Where would he go and for how much longer? He tried to drive back to Washington. It failed before it began. There might be something there for him after so many anniversaries led him to nostalgia, but now there was nothing there for him. He spent the city. El Paso was changing and not yet ready for him to stay. The river was busy with the valley and no longer needed him until everything settled. It would have to flood the orchards to let them explode with growth, to test their adaptability to see what could meet the high standard of being called native. Humans selected them for to approximate this evolution, but kept them frozen in time with artificial weather. Until this was further along, he may as well roam someplace else lest he fall into the human trap of working to control the inevitable. The southwest was open to him. The desert was enormous. He could wander for a lifetime and never see it all. Surely a winter of exploration was enough. He had enough of caves. This winter could not be a hibernation driven by fear. Caves were for temporary protection now. He had the destructive force of civilization to keep him safe, so the era of hiding in caves was over.

It would be the era of freedom to roam that he dreamed of in that first fall a year before. He never destroyed borders to make this possible, they just never existed. They evaporated along with the humans who controlled them. All he faced were the borders of survival, and he had technology to expand those out far beyond anything he actually needed. More was out there. At least this anniversary could be spent as a desert human roaming under the insect gods. He could take more than this. He resurrected a river king and saved a valley. He crossed a lake and countless desert seas. He was immune from the rattlesnakes and the sun. If something found him and he died, nothing

would be lost. The survival game was never something
to be won. Time never stopped; he just lost interest.
All this manic fantasy was easy, but he would need to
place his feet in some direction to start moving.
Where might that be, he wondered. He was at the center of the continent with even the entirety of the
planet spanning full circle in all directions. He
came from Northeast. He knew West and North; South
would be more desert and then jungle. He knew jungle.
The deserts to cross before them were the plains of
death, as were those to the West before he reached the
beaches beyond. North. This would bring him to roam
directly into winter. This was now early October and
he had several months before this happened. He could
take his time. He could take his time on foot. Take
a rest from diesel and trailers. New Mexico was large
enough to be lost while still have towns enough to
survive when needed. Colorado was a wilderness that
demanded timing. He would never reach there, but
could cross to the Pacific from Utah, as he did so
many years before. The desert winter would be cold,
but he knew it would never be dark. If he stayed below Colorado, the winter would remain in the desert
and he could survive in the open where he would be
free. There was so much time for his roam to still
stay below Santa Fe. It could be a tour of the river
valley that he rescued from civility. Everywhere
along the route he passed, the valley was waking up to
the smell of water again. He could become a passenger
to see it happen. The river went directly up from
where he was all the way into Colorado, feeding civilization the entire way. He could walk through the
valley and survive. The era of the desperate search
for water was forever over for him as it was for other
life in the valley. Not all would survive the flood,
but he would. He could drink from it any time and
walk away when it was too much. Then he came back to
the end of winter, where he might go and who he might
be then. He certainly was no longer the man of panic
and grief. The loss was too large that it burned him;
the wounds were cauterized by the scale of trauma he
endured. He chose to destroy himself and rebuild into
something programmed for survival. His only enter-

tainment now was making the choice between cooperation and competition with other lives that were programmed for survival too. After a winter of competition, he knew he would return to cooperation. There were other valleys for this. Other desert rivers that choked behind dams. They were his to destroy.

There was so much time for roaming that he left right away in the morning. His blisters had healed and were now new skin under flaps of leather that would let him easily walk. He would be back in El Paso within a day if he moved normally. He left with a light pack full of water and not much else, heading straight through the desert towards the mountain off in the distance. He would eventually connect to a road again, but in the openness of the valley he needed no map. All he needed was a view of the sky with the mountain at the base. That sky swallowed him and he felt like he might fall into it if his feet were to give out. It was electric blue with blindingly white clouds. There was no haze left from the rains. These had all evaporated again. But he could see it return to the dry valley far to the North where more hair brushed the mountains just to the East of the dam, two hundred miles away. It was far away and he was still safe. The sky above was still huge. With the wind pushing away from him to the rain. It could change at any moment, but for now he knew he had time. With luck, he'd be at the edge of El Paso before the oven got started. Until then, he had nothing to do but take steps and follow the mountain. It was freedom, like he thought it would be. He took his time not from a concern over safety, but because he was done with manic destinations. He used to walk fiercely before, letting his feet levitate from the ground listening to music for miles. This was a return to those days.

By the time he reached the outermost layers, the sun was still high and the walk through the city would not be the same as that of the morning. He took a truck back to the ranch house having finished all his water. It was a new city. There were no more layers to peel away. All he saw now were etchings in the desert that were marks of survival. People passed their days busy with situations that were constructed to bring them the means of feeding their families. New families came and needed new constructions applied in globs here and there. Without the newness, the city was frozen and complete. Now, there were only two eyes that remained behind to see the full span of civilization as it existed in the final second. He saw the changes he made to it. The destruction came back as meaningless as when he did it. All it did was help him see what remained of civilization by observing what was removed. His eyes could see.

The river had been flowing for days. The butte crashed open and was already draining while he was there to see. It never stopped while he left it alone. It was hard to see from the road as he drove through the city, but when he reached the bridge near his childhood home, on his way to the ranch house, he saw how far it had come. The dry bed from a week before was gone. Water flowed over the original banks and saturated the flood zone below the berms, but he could see that it had been higher not long before he arrived. At times, this level of flooding happened overnight when flash floods swept down the mountain all at once. The berms always held, but this was the first realization that the age of real floods returned. The river and the mountain were back in control of the valley and had no debt to him. There would come a time when all the homes he knew would be washed away. He had agonized over the sprawl that took it over, and now his symbolic destruction seemed so slight. It was done. There was nothing for him the valley. Although he knew there was no danger yet, nor even serious danger in the next several decades, this was a human estimate that had no relationship with the river. A strong rain that night could signal the moment when everything he hauled from his home in Georgetown would disappear in the water. The ranch house was old, so it had seen floods, but it was not older than the dam. It had never been tested against the epic flooding that hit. If he were to leave on a months long roam that was to mean freedom, without being tethered to a particular spot, he would need to move all the memories he took with him somewhere safe.

The comedy of it was easy to see. He would be driving back to retrieve the RV that he hastily discarded that morning, so he could pack it full of all his memories again. He had been tried to escape the RV since before he climbed into the yacht, now it was still attached to him, about to become the keeper of all things he cherished. The rain he saw to the North had moved down the mountain and was dropping water as it wrapped around to cross the pass and enter the river valley. His truck was pelted with thick drops as he went through, but was soon back out in the sunshine and reached the RV with plenty of time. He brought everything with him except for the truck and reached the ranch house as the rain picked up strength from the cooling sand. He loaded it quickly, crossing through the muddy driveway as the paddock was flooding. When he crossed the bridge in the dark, he stopped to check the river and saw that he was right. The berm was holding but the water level was now quite far up compared to earlier. He drove to his shrine at the university, where he knew the RV would be safe from even the century floods.

The night was a standard night of storm that would have knocked out the power. There was wind, of course, that rocked the RV. He was asleep in the shrine, listening to it all and contemplating his freedom. In the morning he took a car back to the ranch house to pack more properly for the trip. As bad as the storm was, it had not crested the berm. The homes survived yet again. He packed lightly, but carried far too much. When he tried to fit himself into the pack, it was already thirty kilos. He would be dead in a week. Then came the tedium of deciding what to leave behind, which took a few hours. By the end, he had twenty kilos, not counting water. Instead of lots of water, he would travel along the river and use his emergency straws that had yet to be very useful since he first found them. Now, they were the

only items he felt were vital. He set out with the
plan to only walk a few hours.

The day was muggy from the rain, which made his head
swirl. At one point, his vision faded to a pinpoint
and he felt like he was in a hot dark dream until it
all came back. He knew the signs for heatstroke, so
he stopped in some shade and sipped muddy water. It
took him three days to reach the town square at Old
Mesilla. The rains had gone away, leaving the air to
evaporate and cool back down. The adobe was again hot
and cracking when he passed. He found his way into
the bookstore he loved as a child. Its walls were New
Mexico thick, so it felt cool inside as he dropped his
pack and cleared books to sleep. A bit later, he went
across to the Billy the Kid store to enjoy the cheap
swag that was inside. It was as if the town was only
asleep. It was years since he saw it last, and everything looked the same. On the other street was the
famous Mexican restaurant that was so old his father
ate there as a youth. Inside was like an old wagon
courtyard that never felt hot. They had parrots that
talked to him when he went there as a child. He
wanted to see it all but felt afraid to confront their
silent cages now. The curiosity was too much and he
went inside anyway. Everything looked the same, but
with the mustiness of aged food, which itself was part
of what was normal. The cages were clustered at the
reception podium. He saw the telltale patch of bright
colors at the bottom of one, but was confused that the
other three cages were empty. When he looked again,
all their doors were open. Even the cage full of
feathers turned out to be just that. There were no
carcasses. It was strange to see, but stranger still
was the feeling he had that something watched from a
distance. Up in the rafters were two parrots and a
conure, whose bald patches explained the feathers.

There they were. What was more shock than strange was
that he recognized one. It had to be the same parrot
with which he used have chirping conversations. It
was. He saw from the cage that she was old. She had
lived longer than he had. One of them had decided

that when no one came to feed them, it had to survive.
It knew how its cage worked and eventually managed to
match that knowledge with skills to be free. Either
the others learned too or one freed its companions, it
was impossible to know. But the feathers on the cage
floor told him that conure went through intense stress
before was free. They looked at him now, more surprised than he. They lived for more than a year by
tearing at food in the kitchen and drank drips from
faucets. They had fat sacks under their jaws from all
the high calorie human food. But they were alive. He
became emotional in a way that he hadn't in more than
a year. The story of their survival crushed him.
They were alive but needed help. The floor was thick
with shit and food was running low. He spent the
next days cleaning the restaurant and the fatty human
food was removed. He brought in huge sacks of seed
and alfalfa pellets, anything healthy they could eat.
They should be able survive on what he brought for a
year or more, but they needed water. The drippings
had turned red from rust and dropped into a sink that
was cloudy with shit and old food. His solution was
to make a new drip system out of bottled water that
fell directly onto a perch where they could catch
clean water. He made a dozen such bottles and sealed
all but one. They were smart. They were survivors
and would learn to open the others as needed. After
the work was done and his face was dry, he promised
them he would come back before the bottles ran out.
There was no taking them with him. He was unprepared.
He was still too raw and needed more until he was
ready for life again. Before leaving, he made sure to
teach them how to open a window, so they would never
again be forgotten prisoners.

Another week and he was at the dam again. The shock
of finding the birds had lingered but had not crippled
him. It was another reminder of the fight in which
all living things engaged. All of those that were
tied to civilization were still connected by the sudden loss of their means of survival, and he felt it
was his responsibility to bridge them across to the
far side where they had to fight alone. What he did

for the birds connected to what he had done to the dam. It was all cooperation with life. Destruction for the sake of preservation. He had wiped half a town away that day. When he left, the damage was still under water. Now he saw nothing but foundations where the buildings once stood. The rest of the city was completely untouched. He could enter them all and might find one survivor in a thousand, an exertion he could not survive himself. It had to be accidental and driven by his own self needs. The river was swollen, not because he wanted to save life, but because he needed to quiet his anger through destruction. All life that survived because of that was from accidental hope. It was traded for the entire ecosystem that was inside the butte, now almost completely empty. The water still poured through the face of the dam, but not much more in volume than what fed into it from the backside. The level still left a long slow moving pool that ran the length of miles into the canyon. Everything still alive from the butte clung to its existence in that pool. Where there was once abundant space for food was now a sliver over which they would compete.

The canyon below the dam had receded too. He saw the road where his second station was set, the cannon long gone. This was where the event happened, but nothing remained to show how significant it was. When he noticed the cannon jutting out from the mud just below the empty foundations, it looked so small and incapable. The foundations above it had marked where people lived, where they marshaled resources to feed their families and nothing remained to show how significant they were either. Only water. It was enough. He didn't need to linger anymore to keep this fuse of thought lit. It never rested in his mind. Everywhere was somebody's significant place that now looked so small and unimportant. He climbed over the wreckage of the dam so that he could pass through into the dry sandy bed of the butte. He would walk this valley, the original river path all the way to the top.

It took him several days. Sometimes he would stay in one place all day, sleeping in the shade provided by buried boats. From down at the new shoreline, the sky looked larger despite the high walls made by the mesas and mountains. There was no rain in this traveler's avenue. He sat in the heat of day and froze at night. When it was behind him, he moved on. Just as always.

***